Wishes of the Heart

Roberta L Greenwald

This is a work of fiction. Names, characters, places, events, and incidents are either the product of the author's imagination or are used fictitiously. Any resemblance to persons living or dead is entirely coincidental.

All rights reserved. Reprinting of this book or sale is entirely unauthorized. No part of this manuscript may be reproduced, stored in a retrieval system, or transmitted in any form or by any means – electronic, mechanical, photocopy, recording, or any other- without the prior permission of the author.

Wishes of the Heart

Copyright © 2018 Greenwald, Roberta L

All rights reserved.

ISBN: 9781791576325

Wishes of the Heart

I DEDICATE THIS BOOK TO MY MOTHER, DOROTHY, WHO HAS TAUGHT ME TO PERSEVERE AND NEVER GIVE UP ON YOUR DREAMS AND THE WISHES OF YOUR HEART.

WISHES OF THE HEART

Chapter One

It was a day of newness and life, much like what a newborn experiences taking it first gasp of breath, fresh out of its mother's womb. In the same way, Ellen felt revived and alive from her morning shower, ready to take on the world, although she was not a morning person. She had longed for spring and the warm and sunny days that it brings, after months of being stuck indoors with not much to do. The winter had been exceptionally hard with unrelenting snow storms that went on month after month. One preceded the next without so much as a break of a few days between them. Today, she was going to enjoy the outdoors to its fullest. The intermittent rain of the past three days had finally ended the night before, and only sunny skies were being forecasted for a while. In her bathrobe with her hair still towel-wrapped in a turban-style, she glanced out of her bedroom window making sure the weatherman was true to his word. Just as promised, the sky couldn't be any bluer, and there wasn't a cloud as far as the eye could see.

Ellen slipped into a pair of jeans she had worn the day before, which she had carelessly flung over one of the footboard bedposts; and thumbed through several shirts in her dresser drawer until she found a sentimental faded old T-shirt that was on its last days of usefulness. She brushed her teeth and dried her hair, before combing her shiny auburn locks into a tight ponytail high on top of her head. Pushing back the wooden doors on her bedroom closet, Ellen searched for a hooded fleece jacket that she tugged from its hanger, and slid on a pair of sneakers with the laces removed.

Anxious to be outside, she decided to postpone eating until she came back into the house later. Finally, she would have a chance to catch up on some of the outdoor things that she had wanted to do. Her annuals of geraniums, marigolds, petunias and alyssum, needed to go into some clay pots. While the perennial beds that wrapped around the side of the house needed to be pruned and cleared of their dead branches and debris. However, the day was just too beautiful not to take the time to appreciate it for a while. For just a couple of hours, the daily grind of a hectic schedule would be left behind, so that Ellen could admire the view and breathe deeply of the fresh spring air.

She walked from her two-story, whitewashed clapboard house that was much in need of painting, and stood on the side porch taking in the scene at hand. All those that knew Ellen, and the comings and goings of the farm, used this side door.

The front of the house, which was reached by a stone path, that was sadly in need of new mortar, and the rotted wooden steps leading up to the front porch, needed to be totally rebuilt. The roof on the house had been replaced last year, after the rain made its way in through the kitchen ceiling. She was keeping her fingers crossed that the furnace wouldn't go out anytime soon, even though an irritating rattling and banging would voice from it on occasion.

The barn caught her eye, being directly across from this side of the house, which lay beyond a side yard that included a well pump and a gravel parking area. It was in need of attention just as much, if not more so, than the house with its chipped and peeling paint, and broken panes of glass that were haphazardly missing or cracked over the entire structure. Ellen wondered, as she so often did, how the glass could have even broken. Maybe it was a storm, the wind, or even a bird banging into it accidentally. Whatever the cause, the windows were in need of repair. The birds, as well as the bats, had taken up residence inside of the barn, along with probably a host of other rodents that Ellen didn't want to even consider. She vowed that another season wouldn't go by without this problem being resolved. It was hard for her to walk into the barn anymore, without feeling afraid that something would swoop down or jump on her at any second.

Beyond the barn, was a vegetable garden that provided Ellen with her main source of income seven months out of the year. She would sell the produce, along with assorted baked goods that she prepared daily, at a stand that was placed at the end of her lane every spring. The garden was only in the beginning stages of being planted, and much in need of a good weeding. It was hard for her to keep steady help around the place since she couldn't afford to pay much. The monotonous and lonely work seemed to grow old quickly for the majority of the drifters who came to apply.

The side of the house was practical and yet held beauty, with its clothesline, flower gardens, and the shade trees, the biggest being an old oak that was rumored to be around long before the town even existed. Expanding the length at the border of the yard was pasture that had once held cattle. The fencing surrounding the pasture land was also showing signs of wear and tear with the same aged paint that all of the other structures possessed, as well as sporadic broken boards that were too many to be numbered.

Things were in a sorry state, and the reality of the magnitude of all the farm's problems, weighed heavily upon her mind on a day-to-day basis. Usually, she could find someone to maintain the garden, but as far as all of the repairs that were needed to fix the place up, that was another story.

No one whom she employed seemed to be willing to extend

himself to the degree necessary to fix things beyond the normal day-to-day work, probably because of what little she was willing to pay. It was a frustrating reality, but she knew it was time to place another ad in the local paper again. Ellen needed to find a farm hand, and she prayed that this time one would make it without quitting before the fall arrived. After all, it was her busiest time of the year, and dealing with someone new around the place every couple of weeks was wearing thin on her patience.

She hoped that it would be someone local this time answering the ad. Maybe they would have a conscience and not leave her high and dry, as so many others had done in the past. It usually was someone just passing through, wanting to make some quick money, as was the case of her latest charge, who had up and pulled out after only three days. They always requested room and board, which Ellen wasn't willing to provide. Even camping out in the barn wasn't an option. That was where Ellen drew the line. It was bad enough having to deal with the usual vagabond eight hours a day. No way was she willing to give up anymore of her privacy, to make what was a constant problem less complicated for some.

Later, she would call the local paper with the revised ad that she had worked on the night before. She considered changing the wording or even advertising the pay this time. Maybe she would consider paying an extra fifty a week. It wouldn't hurt her to do without, in this regard. She would rather deal with less money than the lack of her privacy. Anything was worth a try. For now, she would forget about her troubles, and try to find some joy in the day.

Ellen descended the side porch steps, making her way to the backyard. The clothesline she passed had a string of raindrops neatly hanging from the two vinyl ropes that extended its entire length. They glistened in the late morning sun, already evaporating from the unseasonably warm day. From there, she wandered to a predetermined destination, which she usually visited at least once a day. All was quiet, except for the occasional chirping of a bird. Peace and solitude were all around here. As she ventured down the well-worn path, the light rain from the night before as well as the morning dew, that still kissed the ground with softness, made the sides of her sneakers wet. May… was good for her well being… therapeutic … after a cold, harsh winter, promising life after months of bleakness. *What a special gift from God*, she thought with a warm contented smile.

Ellen spread the wool plaid tartan blanket that her brother had given to her as a wedding present, underneath the massive ancient oak, sitting down Indian fashion. She closed her eyes, taking in a deep meditating breath. Ellen thought she could smell celery, after being washed and freshly cut for a salad. *It was funny somehow,* she considered, *how smell and taste could cross over from time to time, becoming one and the same sense.* She opened her eyes again, relaxing her form, while lying on her side against the soft, furry fabric of the blanket. The bushes in the distance were beginning to bloom, as well as the wild flowers and surrounding trees. She felt almost like an intruder, that she shouldn't be observing the changing of the seasons, but she swore she could almost see the chlorophyll transforming the dead of winter into life around her. It was as if a symphony of nature was rejoicing inn the newness of life again. Turning over, and looking up into the leafy branches of the tree, Ellen fell asleep, imagining angel's wings of protection covering her.

A short time later, a slight nudge to the arm awoke her with a start, from a stranger glaring down at her. *I must be dreaming,* was her only conclusion, as she studied the face that was framed by sky and leafy greenness. The peace, that has been so much a part of her only minutes earlier, was now turned to panic, as a thundering drumming went on within her chest. Her heart beat frantically, wanting only to escape from the potential danger at hand. She was vividly aware of the reality that what was occurring was not a dream.

"*What do you want?*" she asked cautiously, sitting up in a daze. Nothing else would come out. Politeness was not a thing to be considered, as she eyed the trespasser. The man was one of well-defined, medium build, dressed in dusty blue jeans and a flannel shirt rolled up at the sleeves. His hair was sandy blonde with golden highlights, suntanned flawless skin, and sky blue eyes; as blue as the sky Ellen was looking up into. She had to admit the stranger was pleasant to look at, but that did not excuse his rude and inappropriate behavior of encroaching upon her property, and finding her in such a vulnerable state. She stood, zippering her jacket completely up to her neck, finding his stare disturbing. He smiled down at her, catching her off guard once again.

"I asked you *what you wanted,* and sir, I am not used to having strangers walk on my property unannounced."

Glen began to grin again. *She is quite the high-strung, ruffled-feathered female*, he surmised. "I didn't mean to alarm you. I am only looking for a job, and I was told there may be work here."

Ellen adjusted her stance backing away further towards the oak tree, as she took in the man's height in comparison to her own. She was a head shorter than he was, and for some reason, his close proximity disturbed her beyond the initial fear she had felt. She stood quietly, with arms crossed in front of her trying to give a twenty second appraisal of whether she should trust this man's words and actions. Kindness was in his face. She could see that. Her heart beat a little less frantically, but never the less still on its guard, with her conclusion that he probably was harmless.

"Work here? Who would have told you that?" she asked sternly. "I haven't placed an ad in the paper yet."

"Ma'am, I'm really sorry that I disturbed you. I can see that you apparently don't need the help, and my intentions were not to put you on the defensive, but I was given directions to this farm and was told that help was needed for someone to do the spring planting."

"Who told you that?" Ellen snapped, this time more adamantly.

"The man at the end of the lane, ma'am," Glen pointed, in the direction of her neighbor's farm. "He said you really needed the help."

Ellen could see she was making him feel uncomfortable, as he shifted his feet restlessly, one behind the other. She smugly felt a sense of satisfaction for unnerving him, since he had done the same to her minutes before. Her bitterness, as well as her willingness to take on any foe, be it man or beast, always overrode Ellen's common sense of fear. Learning to be brave was an acquired art, when faced with being alone after so many years of being sheltered and protected by her husband who had died only two years earlier in a fatal car crash. The farm was his dream, not hers, and now it had become a nightmare with its demanding upkeep. The cattle were gone, and only the garden remained. Why she did not sell it, was a question she could never bring herself to answer. Something kept her here. Maybe it was the memoires or just her determination to not be a quitter. She would give it through the summer. If her feelings weren't any different, maybe it would be time to start over someplace else.

"I do need help, but I don't generally go by my neighbor's suggestions as to whom I will hire," she retorted assertively. "You see, I keep to myself and I can't say anyone close by is my friend, so I figure there has to be some ulterior motive for these people wanting to help me."

"Excuse me for saying so ma'am, but you don't seem to trust your neighbors very much. Maybe they really are trying to do you a favor. The guy I talked to seemed nice enough."

That was more than Ellen wanted to hear. She wanted her morning to be tranquil, before the day's activities began. The planting needed be done, but by damn if some outspoken man sent by her nosey neighbor, was going to give his uneducated opinion about her prying neighbors, and determine her choice!

"Mr....ah...sir, I don't even know your name."

"The name ma'am is Glen."

"Well, Glen, if I do consider you for employment, I will get back to you on my on time table. You can write down your phone number where I can reach you, and stick it in my side porch screen door, thank you very much," Ellen remarked matter-of-factly, as she started walking back up the hill, turning her back on him purposely, hoping it would end the conversation.

"Ma'am?"

"Yes, Glen," Ellen responded, as she continued to walk with her shapely backside to him that he took notice of.

"I walked from town, and I don't have a piece of paper or a pen on me," he said loudly, as she continued to walk out of ear range.

"That's too bad," she said sarcastically, as she reached the house again.

He cupped his hands to his mouth, not ready to give up yet. "My phone number where I can be reached is 692-7221."

Immediately Ellen registered the number, as if it was a jolt of electricity to her brain, stopping her dead in her tracts. The number was that, one and the same, of her enemy Eric Cummings! Ellen turned to stare at Glen, as if seeing him anew for the very first time.

"Are you related to Eric Cummings?" Ellen exclaimed breathlessly, almost with disbelief at the possibility.

"Yeah, he's my brother. Do you know him?" Glen asked nonchalantly with a smile, not realizing the pressure cooker ready to explode in Ellen.

"Do I know him?" she spit out venomously. *"Do I know him?"* she laughed bitterly. "Yes, I know him. *All too well!* I'm sorry to say *Mr. Cummings,* but that does settle it for any consideration on my part of you working for me! You see, I *detest* the very site of your brother, and I live by the creed of not sticking my fingers in the fire more than once. I especially won't make that mistake a second time of trusting a Cummings. Good day, and get off my property!" Ellen declared emphatically, as she climbed the porch steps, slamming the screen door as well as the solid wooden door loudly in Glen's face, knocking over a pot of pink petunias to the painted wide-planked porch floor, crashing it in an array of pieces.

As he left the farm, Glen was dumbfounded. Not only by this

impetuous woman, but also by this new discovered knowledge of what his brother Eric could have possibly done to get a rise out of a wildcat such as she. He never cared if he encountered her again. What a hornet's nest he had walked into. She may have her creeds she lives by, but so did he. Even though Glen was a simple man, no woman would talk to him that way!

"Fingers in the fire…getting burned…bullshit!" he said aloud, as he purposely kicked a splattering of dirt and gravel up in the air with his boot, making his way out of the farm lane.

Eric would have to shed some light on the situation, that was, if Glen could make a connection with him. He had been camped out in Eric's house for two days now, and he was anxious to see his brother again. After the neighbor had left him in with an explanation for a lack of a key, he informed Glen that Eric traveled a lot on business, but usually was not gone for more than a few days. It has been five years since they had last seen each other at their father's funeral, and Glen had lost touch, never venturing out of the state of Virginia where they has been raised. The cell number his mother gave him of Eric's was no longer working, so he had no way to reach him.

Eric had told him that the door was always open if he ever wanted to come for a visit or even stay with him for a while, but he never felt the need to take him up on his offer. That was, until now…things had changed, and Glen was trying to put the past behind him. He was counting on Eric to be true to his word, and help him make that fresh break that he wanted in his life now. He looked forward to starting over, in a new town, with new opportunities and new friends; but if this day was any indication as to how his future was unfolding, he might reconsider staying in this town of Fillmore, Nebraska.

Chapter Two

Ellen stormed into the house, realizing once again that she had allowed her out-of-control temper to get the best of her. What had her therapist told her to do again, when faced with situations like this that totally made her lose her sense of well-being? *Why do I always have to feel so bitter?* She pondered.

It hadn't always been this way. Ellen had been known for being easy going, that was, until life brought about a lot of sudden changes. Now, it was hard for her to find joy in the day to day, although she was trying to work at changing. To be brave and keep persevering, while trying to run a farm that Ellen never really wanted in the first place, was a lesson in tolerance that she was not sure she could endure forever.

Ellen lay on her bed for some time just staring at the ceiling, contemplating the hand life had dealt her. The white ruffled eyelet curtains blew gently in the breeze, while her cat Cuddles slept peacefully on her overstuffed, floral-print slipper chair that had been her mother's. *What was Eric up to?* She considered in frustration. *He has a lot of nerve to send his so-called brother to the farm just to get a rise out of me!*

It made her blood boil just to think about it. *Well, this will be the last time!* She determined adamantly as her fists clenched in tight balls of frustration. If she could ignore him every time she ran into him in town, he better well give her the same courtesy, especially on her own property. As soon as Eric Cummings was back in town, he would be receiving a phone call from her. Just yesterday as the local King Mart grocery store, she recalled hearing David Bryan talking to Matt Smith, which were two of Eric's drinking buddies, about how long he would be out of town on business. Soon enough he would be back, if not already today. After all, he had a houseguest that needed a job, and by damn, it wasn't going to be on her farm!

Cuddles became impatient by the late morning lying around. He wanted his breakfast that Ellen had forgotten to feed him. Jumping up on the bed, stretching and yawning with his back arched high in the air, he gave Ellen a high-pitched meow that stirred her back to the present, away from her plans of revenge and retaliation.

"Cuddles," she cooed while scratching the top of his head. "I didn't mean to forget you baby, but Mommy has been a million miles away today. Thank you for reminding me that I need to get up and attend to you."

Picking Cuddles up and snuggling him close the whole way to the kitchen; she opened the refrigerator door and found a half-used can of cat food. She dished the remainder out into his pottery bowl with his name painted on it, over-emphasizing how yummy it looked as if she had to convince the feline that it was an acceptable breakfast. Cuddles gingerly sniffed the fare, took two small nibbles and then ran off to another room. Ellen laughed good-naturedly. At least Cuddles truly loved her, even if he was finicky!

With breakfast behind her, she decided it was time to call the local newspaper and place the ad in the paper again that she had placed one too many times in the past. She truly hoped it wouldn't take more than a day or two to find someone to help her plant the garden, because the work was more than she could physically handle on her own. It was a harsh reality, but she knew that she couldn't make it without the money that the produce stand generated. As it was, that income was barely enough to get by on. The insurance money from her husband's death did help, but the policy wasn't big enough to live on exclusively. Maybe that was where part of the bitterness came from.

Ellen's hired hand had just quit the day before yesterday. He said it had something to do with the distance it took him to get to her house, but she knew what he said was an excuse, and not the real reason. It had to be the pay. She could only afford a meager weekly set amount, and she expected a lot in return. Maybe after thinking about it, she had been too rough on him. Yes, it was the bitterness again.

With the ad in place, and the promise that it would begin tomorrow, she donned a pair of work gloves and boots, and headed off to the barn to find the bag of corn seed that should have been in the ground a week prior, but the constant rain had delayed things. At least the ground had been turned and made ready for planting, and a few other things had been put in so far. Now she would hand sow the seed until her back ached, but the job would get done before the day was over.

Chapter Three

After a walk that took a couple of hours and left his feet aching, Glen returned to Eric's with the hope that his brother would be at his house waiting. Unfortunately, the house was still quiet, just the way Glen had left it, with only the ticking of the hall grandfather clock to greet him.

When Eric had moved to Fillmore, a realtor had showed him numerous properties, including apartments and townhouses. Nothing caught his eye though until she showed him what he now owned. Although the house was fifty years old, he felt an instantaneous attraction to the remodeled and updated place, getting the same warm feelings that he felt from his childhood home.

A lady's touch was definitely lacking, and it wasn't hard to discern that a bachelor abode there. A thorough housecleaning was in order, even though Eric could easily afford to have someone come in every week to keep up with the place. Time was of a premium, and yet he still preferred cleaning it himself. He wasn't one to admit it easily, but he was known by his friends to be one to pinch pennies in areas of his life that were foolish and impractical. His mother never had a housekeeper, therefore he could do without one also, he announced firmly to his card-playing buddies on numerous occasions when they commented after one too many beers about his dusty furniture. Usually once a month, and on a weekend, was when he reluctantly broke down and brought the vacuum out of the closet.

The house had a haphazard look, since nothing really matched or flowed from room to room. The living room, kitchen, dining room, office, half bath and foyer were on the first floor; with a steep staircase leading to the second floor that contained three bedrooms and two baths. Windows were minus curtains, with only cheap plastic blinds that were left mostly closed.

The kitchen contained a simple oak table with six chairs that his friends sat around and played poker with him from time to time. The cabinets held a scanty array of easy-to-fix foods, and the refrigerator was bare, except for a jug of wine and a six-pack of beer. A couch, two chairs, and a recliner sat in the living room with fabric that seemed to hint of a mixture of several eras. The dining room was minus furniture, but held several neglected floor-size plants that had been given to Eric at Christmas from fellow employees over the years. Eric's bedroom held a queen size bed with dresser and a couple of nightstands, while the other two only had full size beds and a dresser in each. One of the original bedrooms, from when the house was built, was turned into an extra bathroom that made it nice for his buddies when they decided to crash. In contrast to the majority of his home, no expense was spared in his office. It held the most up-to-date computer equipment, which he utilized when he was home in the evenings. The walls were mostly bare, but at one point African wall art was purchased and hung by an over-zealous female who hoped to domesticate the man and transform his dwelling into a real home. With that dream, - so went the girl and her artwork.

He thought from time to time about finding one special lady that he could be committed to - maybe even settle down, get married, and have a kid or two. But that desire was not there now. He was enjoying playing the field too much, and not answering to just one person.

Eric was not one to be told what to do especially when it involved change on his part. He liked himself, maybe a little too much, and his life just the way it was.

Glen, in comparison, was totally different from his brother in a lot of ways. Where he was blonde and blue-eyed like his mother, Eric favored his father with brown eyes and wavy brown hair. Each was strikingly handsome, but in his own unique way.

Their personalities were different also. Eric was the guy everyone wanted to claim as his or her friend in high school. While Glen was the quieter one, having fewer friends, but nevertheless, good and loyal ones.

Glen and Eric unanimously shared in their athletic abilities, whereas Glen was the better football player, Eric excelled in basketball. They equally carried the high school soccer team from victory to victory, being featured in the local newspaper as a "force to be reckoned with". Each lettered in their particular sports, and each was captain of their various teams during their senior year.

Academics on the other hand, was something that came easy for Eric, but not for Glen. Eric was one of those lucky ones who hardly had to study for a test, and still made only A's on his report card. Glen, on the other hand, struggled from elementary school on, always having to be helped on a nightly basis by either his mom or dad. A tutor had to be hired during his high school years, when the subject matter went beyond his parent's level of ability to help him. Eric was just naturally self-assured and born to achieve, while Glen lost his confidence in himself as he entered those trying years of puberty.

While they were in school together, Eric was Glen's social glue – getting him into parties and helping him meet the most popular girls and guys. The parting of the ways finally occurred, when Eric, being the older brother, went off to college. Glen didn't feel comfortable after that hanging out with Eric's friends who stayed in town. He felt more secure just hanging with the jocks that were on his current sports teams. His only real focus was to keep his grades high enough to stay in sports.

Once graduation occurred, Glen decided college wasn't for him. Against his parent's wishes, he went off to work at a local hardware store. That job lasted for only a short time, and he dabbled in a few more before settling into farming.

Eric was sexually active from his early years of high school while Glen was shy and reserved and only took it as far as heavy petting. He started to date once he graduated from high school, and had his first sexual encounter at age 19. Unfortunately, Glen allowed women to manipulate him, leading to many bad decisions on his part. He would move in his girlfriends way too quickly, thinking everyone was the one he would marry. He was too nice for his own good. It didn't take long for women to recognize the signs that Glen was easy to "walk all over". He overspent his money on them, and even put up with a few cheating on him from time to time.

He wanted to change, but his self-confidence was lacking as this pattern repeated itself. He was burned one too many times, and now he was sick and tired of the old Glen, not wanting to repeat his old ways of doing things. With new determination and putting the past behind him, he would not allow any women to control him ever again! He had made that mistake more times than he cared to remember, leading to where he was today - without a job and a place to live. Change wasn't going to come by hoping for it. He knew he had to have a plan and work hard to make it a reality. With Eric's help, he was resolved that time could be now.

Chapter Four

Three more stops, and the train would be back in Fillmore. Eric was glad to be getting home, after a couple weeks of being on the road. The rank smell of cigar smoke filled the space that Eric shared with the oversized, balding gentleman, who offered him no chance of quietude during the whole returning train ride. Eric was growing weary of his endless questions and remarks; be it his line of work, where he lived, or the general state of world events. Not that his comments and answers would have been any different if another person had been sitting beside of him, but Eric needed some time just to unwind and digest the business transactions that had taken place. He wanted to savor in his success.

Eric always succeeded in winning over his clients, especially if they were females. Moreover, he prided himself in knowing he could undo the most perfect examples of the unmovable. He had fallen into his trade, just as he did with everything else so far in his life. He was the golden boy with the "Midas Touch".

After attending Harvard, which he accomplished on scholarship, he met his future boss while having a drink at a bar. Peter Winston was instantly drawn to Eric's charismatic personality. They met at a bar in Chicago while each was on their own perspective business trip. As the conversation continued as well as the Gin and Tonics, Peter talked about Eric considering living and working in Fillmore, Nebraska. He was trying to sell Eric on Fillmore's "small town charm", and the warm-hearted people living there. They discussed the differences as well as the similarities between their institutes of higher learning. Without Eric even realizing it, he was being interviewed for a top management position in Peter's company, which he exclusively owned.

By the end of the evening, Peter had offered Eric a job, fully expecting Eric to double his sales volume with his expertise in computers as well as his educational background in business. Eric had already established many professional contacts that were going to be future customers. Peter's hunch paid off. Within a short period of time, Eric landed numerous sales agreements within the widespread business community that no one else in the company had accomplished up until that point. With these successes, came raises and bonuses as well as an ego that was hard for most women to stomach, when given the chance to know Eric on a more intimate basis.

Three years later, Eric had grown in the ranks to be promoted to President of Operations of Computer World Systems. Stock, as well as other incentives, had been offered and accepted. One day he knew a partnership would be forthcoming. He would not stop until an equal partnership was signed, sealed and delivered by Peter Winston. After all, he was the brain behind the works of the operation, tripling the profits over the past three years. Three seemed to be his lucky number. Peter knew that too, but he was just holding out as long as he could before Eric wanted something more.

The train finally pulled into Fillmore at 7 pm. Eric said his polite goodbyes to his travel mate who he had been straddled with for several hours. He was already deep in thought behind a newspaper with swirling smoke drifting around his head, as Eric departed the train with his briefcase and suitcase in hand. All he wanted to do was to get home to a hot shower, throw a frozen dinner in the microwave, and review his notes for tomorrow's meeting with Peter.

Eric called Snelling Cab, which was his typical ride, and they had him at his front door within 15 minutes. "How have things been in Fillmore?" Eric asked the disinterested cab driver on the ride home, who was apparently just as tired to converse with Eric as he was with the bald man on the train.

"Same as usual. Do you live here?"

"Yeah, I live here," Eric acknowledged the obvious new driver, with an equal amount of disinterest. "You can drop me off at 159 Summit Street."

Eric began walking up to his front door, stopping half way, realizing something was amidst. Lights were on in the living room. *What could be going on?* He thought, ready to dial the police. From a distance, he studied the room that had it blinds pulled up. He saw a man enter with a drink in hand and then sit on the couch. The face looked familiar, but it was too dark to make him out clearly. He could tell he was watching TV. For some reason, Eric didn't feel uneasy about entering, as irrational as he knew that was. He unlocked the door, and Glen turned with his drink still in hand as he saw the familiar face of his brother.

Eric stopped, staring in disbelief at his brother, seeing a vision from his past. A grin crossed his face at the unexpected but welcome houseguest.

Glen, put his drink down, and got up and crossed the room and extended his hand for Eric to shake. Eric too put his things down at the very same time, and with one hand grabbed his brother's out-stretched one and with his other he pulled Glen close, giving him a brotherly slap on the back while hugging him warmly.

"Glen, how long have you been here, and how did you even get in the house?" Eric asked inquisitively.

"I've been here for a week, Eric, waiting for you to get home. I called Mom, and she gave me your address and phone number. I tried to call you, but it said the number was out of order, so neither mom nor I could reach you.

"Sorry, Glen. I just changed my number a few weeks ago…new business phone. I should have given it to mom, but I have been very busy with work. So how did you get in the place?"

Glen felt awkward explaining. "Well to be honest, you always told me I could come for a visit, so when I got here and you didn't answer, I waited on your front porch for over 2 hours hoping you would show up. Finally, I decided to go next door to your neighbor's house, and told them who I was and how far I had come. They said that you were out of town on business, and they weren't sure when you would be back. After showing them a family picture of all of us in my wallet and my driver's license, they offered me the spare key that you gave them in case of an emergency. Oh…and by the way, they told me to take it and have one made. Which I did."

Eric began to chuckle and shake his head. "Well I gotta tell you, Glen, it's real good seeing you after all this time, but that story about my neighbors has me a little concerned. It's a good thing that the whole scenario was legit, or I might not have anything left inside."

"Ah, bro, get real, what other than your TV or computer would anyone really want in here anyways? Glen remarked teasingly while looking around, as if those five years had never separated them.

Eric jumped in, grabbling Glen in a headlock. "Nobody would want you, that's for sure!"

Glen twisted his way out of the maneuver, pulling Eric's arms playfully behind his back in a restraining hold. Eric's dress buttons were being tested to their limit of popping, as the fabric pulled against each one. "I still know how to pin you, don't I, Eric?"

Eric laughed, as Glen released him "Only because I had a long day, and I am tired. I'll claim a rematch in a day or two," he added jokingly, as he took a seat on the sofa. "What brings you to town, Glen?" Eric asked with interest, while loosening and removing his black leather dress shoes, and throwing his suit jacket on the couch cushion beside of him.

"Well, to tell you the truth, Eric, I needed to get away from Virginia and start over somewhere else. I figured maybe I could hang out here for awhile until I can decide where or what I want to do."

Eric looked at his brother in surprise. "Glen, I know I always told you that you were welcome here anytime, but I got to be honest, I never thought you would take me up on the offer. What changed your mind?"

Glen sat in the ugly plaid chair with its loose frame opposite the sofa, sighing deeply before he began. "I just needed to start over… My life has gone nowhere in Virginia. You have always been the lucky one, Eric… going to college, while *Mr. Chill* here, thought he could do it without all that time and effort. However, I was wrong," he shared with downcast eyes. "It has been one dead end job after another. The women I have been involved with have totally made my situation worse. A lot of divorcees out there, thinking you are going to take on them and their kids, and then they won't help out with working. I got suckered into that situation one too many times. I got attached to the kids. That was the hard part. So, I guess I'm here with my hat in my hand, asking if I can stay with you for awhile until I can get back on my feet."

Eric felt overwhelmed with compassion for Glen. He knew he must be desperate, because he was never one to beg. Even when they were kids, Glen would never admit that Eric had something he wanted, be it possessions or even a female. He only hoped he could set Glen on the right course in this small town, where he himself had been lucky enough to stumble into opportunity.

It was Eric's turn to sigh, as he looked at his brother. "I'm sorry things haven't gone so well for you lately, Glen. Of course you can stay here for however long you would like. I must warn you though, I'm not home much, between work and travel."

"I don't need you to entertain me, Eric. I plan to get a job anyways while I'm here."

"Have you had a chance to look in the want ads?"

"Yeah, I did," Glen, replied. "But nothing has worked out so far. A couple of warehouse positions I checked into, but no one has called me back yet." Taking another sip of beer he just remembered one other job he had applied to. "Oh by the way, there was one more job I checked out. Someone needing help on their farm, but when I got out to the place, the job had already been filled."

“Sorry to hear that, but no worries…I have a lot of contacts in this town,” Eric encouraged. “I’ll ask around and see who is hiring. I should be able to help you find something soon.”

“That reminds me, I asked a farmer if he knew of anyone else needing farm help out that way, and he sent me down the road to his neighbor’s place. He said she was a widow, and he had heard that someone had just quit on her. He thought that maybe she hadn’t found a replacement yet to help her with the spring planting. What a wacko she was!” Glen exclaimed with raised brows. “Threw me off the place when she found out you were my brother.”

Eric’s eyes were filled with understanding and amusement as he began to laugh. “The name wouldn’t happen to be Ellen Harper, would it?”

“You got it!” Glen replied, curious to see what his brother would say next about the sour-as-lemons female.

“She and I have had our problems since I have lived in this town. She seems to think I am responsible for all her misfortunes. She isn’t known for having much common sense, although she isn’t bad to look at. Ellen is pretty, with her auburn hair, green eyes, and a figure that could easily compete in a beauty pageant if she was so inclined in that way. However, she isn’t. A day’s work is her primary goal, not what her hair, face and nails look like.”

“It sounds to me like you have checked out the merchandise,” Glen said with a cocky grin.

“Maybe from a far,” Eric responded coyly. “But there is more to that story. You see, Ellen was married to a guy by the name of Jack Harper. Jack worked for the same company as I do, Computer World Systems. He was there a couple of years prior to me coming on board, and we became good friends within a few months of me working there. He was a likeable guy, and we shared a lot of the same interests. We would watch football and baseball games together, play golf and have a beer or two. At times, a date and I would get together with him and Ellen, and we would go out. Over time, I really began to excel at work, but Jack unfortunately began to lose his edge. It was apparent it bothered Jack, but instead of becoming more driven to climb the ladder along with me, he became withdrawn. Our relationship changed. It was almost as if he was jealous of what he seen occurring with me. No one had ever threatened his position within CWS. This was not being done intentionally on my part. I never meant the guy any harm. After all, the guy was my friend, for gosh sakes!" he said in exasperation. "He started not showing up for work more and more frequently. It became apparent to Peter, my boss, that someone needed to step into the power seat and take over, and I became that man. I was promoted to President of Operations. Jack was never told he was demoted, but he was given different job responsibilities and a different job title. He could read between the lines."

Glen continued to listen with keen interest as Eric shifted restlessly on the sofa. "So you were actually friends with her at one time?"

"Yes…believe it or not, I was," he replied with a sigh of sadness. "Unfortunately, a horrible fatal car accident occurred. It involved Jack in his car and an on-coming tractor-trailer. They say he fell asleep behind the wheel and was killed instantly. Thank God, the insurance company deemed it an accident or Ellen wouldn't even have the money she has to live on today. Everyone in town knows she has had it hard. The insurance money won't last forever, but it's been enough for her to stay at the farm and run her produce stand from spring though fall."

Glen took another swig of his beer. "Well, that explains a lot to me. Anyone losing a spouse in a tragic car accident would feel a lot of remorse if they were in a similar situation such as that."

"You're right to a degree. She does have the right to feel grief, but to blame me for Jack's depression and death, is another story. I saw the change in him, and I guess if I could do one thing over, I would have told him to get some professional help and speak to someone about how he was feeling. However, you know the stigma about mental health, and the last thing I wanted him to think was that I was prying into his life. When I first met Jack, he and everyone else in his path thought he was immortal. He seemed to be unstoppable and could beat down any obstacle in his way. But change came in him. It is incredible how much a person can change," Eric sighed heavily still in disbelief over his friend's passing. "I went to the funeral, and I was really torn up by the whole thing. I let Ellen know before I left that day, that whatever I could do for her, she should never hesitate to call if she needed me. I didn't hear from her until a couple weeks later, and then one evening she called and asked if she could come over to my house to talk."

"What did you say?" Glen questioned inquisitively.

"I told her, of course. I said yes. I hadn't seen her in awhile, but I swear Glen…when she came to my door…she looked like a totally different person than what I had remembered." Eric looked at his brother with a sincere, far-off distant look as he replayed the painful memory. "Bitterness and shock were written all over her face. She wouldn't even sit down. She just started crying and yelling at me, telling me it was all my fault that Jack was dead. She said that they were happy and fine, until I started intruding and moving in on Jack's position at CWS. I tried to tell her that her accusations were not true, and to talk to Peter. I knew he would set her straight, but she would not hear of it. She had made up her mind. Ellen needed a scapegoat and I became it. She left my house that evening telling me she would never forgive me for Jack's death, holding me responsible for destroying any future happiness that she and Jack may have had." Eric's eyes held deep hurt as he revealed the rest. "The hardest part was when she told me that they had just made the decision to start a family. She blurted out that because of me, that dream would never happen now," Eric added grievously with his head bent.

"That's not your fault, bro. And that's a heavy load for that chick to have put on you," he exclaimed as he finished and crushed his beer can. "If she didn't get help then, I would say sh*e still* needs to see a counselor, as much as her *husband did* before he died."

Eric looked up at the caring and friendly face of his brother. He was glad he was there. It was good to have someone to talk to, especially about this. He had kept the situation to himself for far too long. "*You can't tell her anything, Glen.* That's why she is frustrated and acts the way she does. To say the least, I didn't get any sleep that night. Her words were quite a shock. I called Peter at 6 a.m. and told him it was urgent that I speak with him as soon as possible. He met me for coffee, and was as dumbfounded as I was by Ellen's irrational conclusions, but he felt there was really nothing we could do about it. Peter hoped she would come to her senses after she grieved awhile, and that consoled me temporarily," he interjected. "I really had hoped that she would have gotten some counseling by now and had put the past behind her. It sounds like your conversation with her though, proves that theory wrong."

Glen thought about Ellen from a slightly different angle now, after hearing the tale Eric had just told. One side of him thought she was a real bitch to hate his brother and jump to the wrong conclusions so quickly, and yet the other side of him felt sorry for her. Probably she was lonely as hell out there on that farm, and scared to boot without a man around to help and protect her. He guessed that her crusty exterior was just a front she had acquired for survival, so as to appear tough to those around her.

Glen was determined now to go back to the farm, and have her reconsider him for a job. He was not Eric, and if what Eric was saying were true, he would convince Ellen of his brother's innocence. Glen knew it wouldn't be easy, but he was up for the challenge.

Chapter Five

Glen headed out early to Ellen's farm again, a little tired, but determined. It was a beautiful day. The sky was a brilliant blue without a cloud in sight. He thought about the night previous. It felt like old times again, sitting up with Eric until 2 a.m. talking about all the good memories and carefree days of their youth. They both realized that they had allowed too much time to go by without seeing each other. Glen felt good knowing that Eric had extended an indefinite invite for him to stay as long as he needed at his house. Now it was time to make Ellen Harper see some reason too. He was not leaving her place this time, no matter how loudly she protested, short of the police doing it for her.

Eric didn't think it was the best idea for him to return to Ellen's, discussing it with Glen over a hurried cup of morning coffee. He even bet Glen that Ellen wouldn't give him more than 5 minutes of her time before shutting him down. Reluctantly, Eric ended up supporting Glen's decision by allowing him to borrow his car. Eric arranged a ride with one of his secretaries that was "more-than-willing" to accommodate him.

Glen slowly drove up the gravel lane, realizing there were some deep gullies that needed filled. Maybe if she hired him, he could get that problem fixed in a short time. Glen had to chuckle to himself, how he was already making plans for the place. His goal was to make her see the sensibility of taking him on as a worker. If all went as planned, he hoped she would come around full circle after they talked again today.

Ellen was going through her typical daily morning ritual of feeding Cuddles, when she heard a car coming up the lane. *Who could that be?* She thought. *Maybe it is the delivery I'm waiting on from the Farm Store.*

Peaking out from behind the yellow gingham curtains in her kitchen, she saw a man getting out of a sporty-red Mustang convertible. The car looked familiar, but she couldn't place where she had seen it before. The man looked familiar too, and then it hit her who the man was, and who's car he was driving. *It was Glen Cummings, probably back to harass me further at the prompting of his brother*, she concluded bitterly.

Ellen quickly ran and opened her kitchen door widely, not giving Glen a chance to knock. "What do you want?" she asked cruelly. "I told you to never come back here! Do you always go places where you are not wanted?" she gritted out.

Glen just stood on the porch in silence, staring at Ellen, realizing how pretty she really was even when angry. Her eyes were fiery emerald green pools of lusciousness. He couldn't help but smile at her. His actions unnerved and infuriated her even further.

"Mr. Cummings, I don't care for your attitude and I *demand* you get off of my property! And for the last time, don't ever come back here!" Ellen screamed out her warning, while trying to slam the door in Glen's face.

Glen speedily blocked her move by wedging his foot between the door and frame. "Mrs. Harper, I know how you feel about my brother, but I think you are being very unfair. I am *not* Eric, and I *can* be of help to you around here. All I want is a job. I don't see why you can't at least try me out."

"Try you out, Mr. Cummings?" she asked in disbelief. "Why would I want to *try you out,* as you say?" she challenged with a nasty lift to her voice and head.

"Because I have done farm work, and I am willing to work for a week for free. If you like the results, then you can decide if I can continue *with* pay. Oh…and by the way, if that day does come about, I would like $300.00 a week."

Ellen's was flabbergasted and surprised. She couldn't decide what stunned her more, Glen being willing to work a week for free; or him telling her what his future wage would be, instead of her telling him. Ellen reluctantly pondered his proposal for a few moments. The thought of someone helping her for a whole week during the busy season, and not expecting to get paid, was a morsel she had not anticipated Glen would dangle in front of her. *What would it really hurt to use him for all he was worth for a week for free help*? She contemplated, even if it was Eric's brother. *Maybe this can work*, she concluded on second thought. She would work him harder than he had ever been worked before, with long hours, and then give him the boot at the end of the week. *That would be great way to get back at Eric*, she resolved, smirking triumphantly to herself as she continued her daydream.

"Mrs. Harper?" Glen questioned, sensing Ellen's far-off daze.

"Oh yes…" Ellen responded, shaking her head to clear out the cobwebs. "All right, Mr. Cummings. You got a deal. One week of work without pay, and you will do whatever I say needs to be done. Is that clear?"

"Yeah, that's clear," Glen, replied hesitantly, sensing Ellen was up to something.

"The day needs to begin at 5:30 a.m. and will end at 3:30 p.m. A ten-hour workday is what it is around here. You better be able to handle that! Be sure to bring your lunch and a thermos of cold water, because I will *not* be supplying any of those creature comforts. You will be allowed 30 minutes for lunch at 11 a.m., as well as 2 - fifteen minute breaks; one in the morning and one in the afternoon," Ellen said with authority. "If you need to use the bathroom, there is an old outhouse down behind the barn, with God knows what could run out when you go in there. My first inclination was to make you use the bathroom at the gas station at the edge of town, but that would take too much time away from the work at the farm. So, Mr. Cummings, don't get any ideas that I am softening up. I am just trying to get the most work out of you in a day," she said sternly with arms crossed in front of her chest defensively.

"I think I can handle all that," Glen answered with a side-ways cocky grin that made Ellen look as if she wanted to kill him with her green dagger eyes. Glen couldn't believe her spunk. He knew what Ellen was up to now. She was hoping that he would give in to the pressure of a long hard day of labor, and quit before the week was up. That would give her the satisfaction of knowing that she could make a Cummings bend and break, just as much as she thought Eric had done to her husband Jack.

"What exactly needs to be done around here?" Glen asked as they were walking to the barn.

"A lot, Mr. Cummings, a lot," Ellen, replied with realistic frustration, as she gave him a look of despair. It took Ellen the better part of an hour to show Glen the barn and the farm equipment and the planting schedule she had set up. "As you can see, I am behind with getting the crops in the ground. The fences have missing and broken boards that need to be fixed, although there isn't any livestock to be contained in the pastures at this time."

"Why is that, Mrs. Harper?" Glen questioned.

"I'm not sure that is any of your business, but I do hope to replace them one day when I feel I have a reliable overseer of the farm," she answered curtly with a look of disdain.

They continued to tour the property, as she pointed out the broken windows and painting that needed to be done, as well as the disintegrating front walkway, that she considered to be at the bottom of her priority list for getting fixed.

Ellen's father and mother had stayed with her a month after the funeral, and her dad had tried to help her with the immediate decisions that needed to be made concerning the farm. From his suggestion, she had sold the cattle, not wanting to deal with the extra responsibility during her time of grief. They both tried to convince her to sell the place and move back home to Denver with them. After all, she had no family in the area, but Ellen was determined to make a go of it, at least for a while. It had been over two years now, and although it was extremely hard to face each new day, somehow she had found the inner strength to do so.

Ellen knew a week wouldn't even dent the amount of backlog she had around the place. She had no time to spare, with only a one-week free commitment from Glen. "Do we have an agreement then, Mr. Cummings?" Ellen asked with an edge to her voice.

Glen extended his hand to seal the deal, but Ellen kept her arms securely by her sides. Glen wasn't going to let the lady intimidate him, so he took both hands and combed them through his hair. Ellen noticed the gesture, and the color of his hair that reminded her of golden sun-kissed wheat. She didn't want to admit it to herself, but that simple act of what Glen had just done, stirred her somewhere deep inside. She just as quickly dismissed it, hating herself for being allured by this man for even just a moment.

"Yes, we have an agreement," Glen affirmed.

Ellen's fiery green, emerald eyes locked with Glen's blue ones. "Then I suggest you get started, Mr. Cummings. It is already 9 a.m. and I *expect* the already missed hours of today to be made up some time throughout the week."

Glen was taken back by her lack graciousness for his gift of charity. *It wasn't every day that someone got a week of free labor out of him*, he thought. "Don't worry about me," Mrs. Harper. "I won't cut you short on any agreed upon time," he replied sarcastically. "But I do have one complication."

"And what would that be, Mr. Cummings?" Ellen asked with mutual smugness.

"I didn't really think I was starting work today, so I didn't bring any food or water along with me. I will have to drive back into town, and pick something up."

Ellen hadn't considered that obstacle. She turned on her heel, and started walking towards the house not wanting to give him any satisfaction of getting to her. "You will find a pitcher of ice water and your lunch on the porch by the table, Mr. Cummings, but only for today," she snapped out with her back still turned. "I don't need to lose any more time by you leaving and driving back into town. As you should know, I *don't* have the daylight hours to spare." Ellen gave a quick glance in Glen's direction and then shut the door without slamming it.

No slamming door at least. That's somewhat of an improvement, Glen thought. "I knew I could make this work out," he said aloud with a satisfied grin.

Chapter Six

Glen got right to work. As he looked over the planting list that Ellen had prepared, he knew the schedule was already behind by several days as they had discussed. He decided to plant the green beans, limas, and carrots before lunch. As least the last farmhand had gotten the peas and onions in early, and they seemed to be doing well. Ellen had planted the corn yesterday, and after lunch he would tackle the potatoes, which required a little more effort than sowing seeds. His goal was to plant the seedling items by the next day, which included the tomatoes, zucchini, cabbage and peppers. Ellen had the seedling trays by the barn, and they were in need of a thorough watering, as they drooped with the lack thereof.

The day became humid and unseasonably hot by 11 a.m. Ellen didn't waste any time bringing Glen a plastic pitcher of water, filling it up and delivering it as soon as she went back to the house. She spoke not a word, as she left the pitcher, minus a glass, by the garden on what remained of a tree stump instead of on the porch as she promised.

"Thanks, Mrs. Harper," Glen yelled after her, as he wiped his brow on the handkerchief stuffed in his back jean's pocket. She didn't stop to reply as she made a speedy retreat back into her house. Glen took a long drink, downing half of the pitcher. He snickered, shaking his head in disbelief. "That lady has some serious problems."

By noon, Ellen exited the screen door to the porch, holding a tray with two ham and cheese on rye sandwiches, chips and an apple. She stopped and stared in Glen's general direction, as she watched him at a safe distance. He was still hard at work and not even aware of her presence, or at least it seemed to appear that way. Ellen placed the tray on the table, and returned to the house; slamming the door behind her in way of announcing his lunch was served. She didn't feel she needed to call out that it was his lunch hour, especially if he was ignoring her purposely. She opened the screen-door noisily several more times, hoping to gain his attention, but he didn't seem to notice or care about the racket she was making. She placed another pitcher of cold water on the metal vintage patio table, and slammed the screen door and heavy wooden door one more time in frustration from his lack of response.

Ellen sat at her kitchen table, feeling weary and irritated, not sure what to do next. "This whole situation just isn't going to work," she announced in frustration as she watched the hands of her clock move way too slowly. At 1 p.m., against her better judgment, she would tell Mr. Cummings that his lunch was rotting in the hot afternoon sun. That sounded reasonable enough, without too much concern. *It's only for today*, she kept reminding herself. Tomorrow would be different and she would not even have to come in contact with him. He would come prepared, and there would be no need to communicate again about food or water.

Ellen walked back to the garden, and Glen was still hard at work. He did not acknowledge her presence as he continued to plant the seedlings. "Mr. Cummings, I feel I must inform you that your lunch has been sitting out on my front porch for one hour now. The hot suns, as well as the ants, are going to ruin it. I will not be remaking your lunch, so if you do not eat it within 15 minutes, I will assume you do not want it and I will throw it away.

I do not need anymore problems on my hands, and ants in my home is one I do not want!"

Glen stopped and turned to stare at Ellen, shovel in hand. "All you had to do was tell me it was ready, and I would have stopped what I was doing and eaten it," he said calmly with a grin. *That is lesson number one*, he thought with smug satisfaction as he walked towards her.

She was seething, ready to explode by his sarcasm. *"I'm telling you now..."* she replied smugly with her hands on her trim hips, flashing him darts of warning from her tempestuous green eyes. She turned, not giving Glen a chance to answer her again. He watched as she mounted the steps.

"*I just can't win with her*," he concluded, knowing he was to blame for her frustration but not caring that he was. Again, the screen door slammed loudly as Ellen made her way back into the safe refuge of her house, and the wooden door was next to follow.

Glen walked away from the garden just shaking his head, propping the shovel against the barn. His back was stiff from bending over for so many hours. He raised his arms high above his head trying to get the kinks out. He had gotten so caught up in what he was doing, time had just seemed to drift by. This was always the way it was on a sunny hot day. He loved the outside, and could almost become trance-like when the weather was this perfect.

Glen felt the perspiration sticking to him, making him uncomfortable as he walked towards the house. He spotted a well pump that would give him the refreshing relief that he desired. Glen lifted the handle and began the up and down motion of getting the water flowing. His arms were bronzed and muscular, glistening with sweat as a steady stream of cold water began pouring from the pump's spout.

Ellen watched his every move from her kitchen window, hiding behind the curtain to keep herself out of plain view. Glen had removed his shirt and had laid it on the grass. He began splashing the cool water on his face, upper chest, and arms. He shivered and gave a small yell, from the initial shock of the bone-chilling cold of the water. She noticed his strong, firm muscular chest that held a soft fringe of hair that spread out over his breastbone, and that led upward from his shorts also. Ellen was totally unnerved by her desire to stare at the man, and as much as she tried to stop herself, she couldn't. He was truly a prime specimen of a physically fit, handsome male. She could not allow herself to forget what her goal for the week was, to humiliate Glen as much as Eric had humiliated Jack.

Glen picked up his shirt again, and used it as a towel, drying off his upper body and running it through his hair. He was slightly shivering, and Ellen could see goose bumps as well as his erect nipples sticking out. Her mouth hung open in fascination. The scene was suddenly making her feel hot inside, and she knew it had nothing to do with the heat of the day. She hated that her bodily desires could betray her emotions like that. There had been no one since her husband and she missed intimacy and sex. She tightly shut her eyes trying to immediately erase the memory but couldn't.

Glen quickly re-donned his shirt, buttoning the last button, as he climbed the porch steps. Seeing his lunch, made him realize how hungry he had really been. He was surprised that Ellen would offer so much. Two heels of crust and another glass of water were all he expected. *The lady was too driven by hatred to be letting her guard down so soon*, Glen concluded. He wasted no time finishing his lunch, leaving half of it still on the tray. He didn't want to become too dragged down by eating a lot, because he planned to work beyond the promised 3:30 p.m. time Ellen had asked for. The water was welcome though, which he downed half of the pitcher, taking the rest with him back to the field.

Once Glen was safely off of the porch, heading for the garden again, Ellen came back out on the porch. "Look at this," she blurted to herself, "He wasted half of what I gave him!" She gathered the tray, throwing the remainder of the lunch in the trash. She sat at her kitchen table pondering things with the same restless anxiety that she had experienced earlier. "What am I thinking of by having this man here? I don't need this aggravation," she complained, as she resumed her place in front of the kitchen window. Ellen noticed Glen was back in the garden spading out the weeds. *Why couldn't she keep from staring at him like a schoolgirl? Why didn't she want to admit that she almost hoped he would walk up to her front door to ask a question? What madness was getting to her from another Cummings man?* She pondered helplessly. Ellen pulled herself away from the curtain after a twenty-minute period, forcing herself to vacuum the house.

Glen worked until it became dark. He was surprised when he finally glanced at his phone realizing that it was nearly 8 p.m., but the goal of getting all of the seeds and seedlings in the ground had been accomplished. He was tired, but it was a good tired. Shifting his attention to the house, he noticed Ellen had turned on the lights in several rooms. It just dawned on him, how quiet things had become with her after lunch. He hadn't seen Ellen except for once, when she picked up the food tray and left her cat outside.

Glen climbed the porch steps, and tapped lightly on the door. He could smell the aroma of food that had been cooking. *Probably Ellen's dinner,* he thought. He could use some of the same, about this time. Ellen answered the door donned in her bathrobe, with a bowl of ice cream in hand. Glen was caught off guard by the picture she made, framed in the door with her pink terry cloth robe wrapped snugly around her waist. Her auburn hair was hanging loosely down in soft gentle curls. He had always seen it pulled back in a tight ponytail. This picture of a temptress was causing an unexpected tightening in his groin that Ellen Harper didn't deserve.

"What can I help you with, Mr. Cummings?" Ellen asked, with a drizzle of the sweet creamy concoction running down her chin, which she was not aware of.

Glen was at a lost for words. "Ah…I just wanted to tell you I am finished for the day, and I will be back early in the morning."

"That was what we agreed upon, Mr. Cummings," she answered curtly, not giving Glen much mind as she continued to eat her ice cream in front of him.

He responded awkwardly. "I will be going then…see you in the morning." Glen began walking off the porch when Ellen interrupted him from doing so, as he turned back around to face her.

"Mr. Cummings, it is not necessary to come to my door at 5:30 in the morning, and announce your arrival. I will be sleeping, and I will take it that you can be trusted and you will be here when you say you will be here."

Glen was too weary to argue. "You don't have to worry about me, Mrs. Harper. *I will be her on time,"* he answered with a raised eyebrow that left her shaken.

Chapter Seven

It took a lot to get Glen's temper flaring, but Ellen had done just that. He just shook his head to himself, and kept walking to the car. Glen took off, speeding down the lane much too quickly, not giving a damn what Ellen Harper and her snippy little attitude could do to his genitals. She was rude and demanding, and the one-week work deal was going to be it. *Wake her up indeed! As if he had been bothering her all day.* Glen came in the house, slamming the door behind him, rattling a picture on the foyer wall.

"What's up, bro?" Eric asked, looking up from over his laptop.

"It sure as hell isn't my dick," Glen irritably replied. "That Ellen Harper is a real bitch!" he continued, removing his work-boots in the foyer, before joining Eric in the living room. "She is rude and insulting. She made it clear to me that I wasn't to disturb her beauty sleep in the morning, and that she would just trust me to be there as early as was agree upon."

"I *warned you,"* Eric laughed.

"Yes you *did,* and I must be a fool to be putting up with her crap now. Oh, and get this… she wants me to use the rodent-filled outhouse, and if she really had her preference I would use the bathroom at the gas station at the edge of town."

Eric started to burst out laughing, flashing Glen a told-you-so look. "Sorry to be laughing bro, but this is just so typical of her.

She's really giving you a run for your money already, isn't she?"

"Well, that's what she may think, but I don't need any woman treating me this way."

"Do you think you will even make it to the end of the week?" Eric questioned with a grin on his face.

"Yeah…I'll make it…but only to prove to Ellen that she won't get the best of me. I really got a lot done in the garden today. I'll just keep my distance from her for the rest of the week."

"About the car…."

"Hey Eric, before you go on, I know I can't use it for the rest of the week. I'll just grab a cab out to the Harper place."

Eric started laughing again, grabbing Glen's shoulder with a firm squeeze. "You got to slow down, man. That woman has gotten you hyper! I was just going to tell you that I arranged to have a ride for the whole week, so you can use the car. But, I will reclaim it once you get home in the evening," he added good-naturedly.

"I can't take your car."

"Yes, you can, Glen. I insist."

"Alright…alright, you win," Glen, conceded. "You want to give up your Mustang, who am I to argue," he said with his arms in the air. "Hey, I'm sorry Eric. That woman just has me jumpy."

"That's an understatement. I'd be jumpy too," he added with a smirk, getting up and walking to the kitchen. "I need a beer. Have you eaten?"

"No, I haven't," Glen, answered, following his brother into

the kitchen.

"Well, let's go figure out if there is anything here that can be thrown together for your dinner. I've already had mine," Eric replied, throwing an arm around his brother's neck. "You know cooking isn't one of my finer points."

"Mine either, but I still seem to survive." Glen said with a chuckle, as they both looked in the refrigerator and freezer.

The mood of earlier had passed, and Glen was feeling much better for eating. Eric has made it quite clear that it was "every man for himself" when it came to meals. He had already had dinner before he had gotten home, stopping at the local Park and Dine Café with his "ride for the week". His chauffeur, and his secretary Melinda Philips, was more than willing to be his dinner companion. They had been involved in a flirtatious game for months, and Melinda offered her services without hesitation. She had always hoped that Eric would ask her out on an official date, and now she was optimistic that the possibility could become a reality. Although, it wasn't an absolute offer yet, she would take what she could get. Just to be close to Eric, as so many other females had desired in the past, seemed to now be within her reach.

The alarm blared in Glen's ear, interrupting his sleep much too abruptly. Four-thirty was way too early, especially when the hoped-for results may not even be worth his while. It had just hit him last night that the whole thing was more than ludicrous for him to be even attempting. Getting up before the crack of dawn, just to prove a point, was beginning to sound too far-fetched especially when a paycheck wasn't involved. Not one to give up so easily, he would persevere at least for another day. A quick shower, coffee, toast, and Glen was out the door. He had found a large thermos of

Eric's and had filled it up with ice water, but there was nothing substantial in the refrigerator or cabinets for a lunch. He ended up at the local convenience store and bought a sandwich and fruit.

The girl behind the register was beaming as Glen approached her. "Is there anything else I can get for you?" she giggled, finding him very attractive.

"No that should do it," Glen replied with a faint tired smile, as he threw a few singles on the counter, still feeling half asleep.

The drive out to Ellen's was beautiful. The sun was already coming up, glistening upon the dew-laden fields as Glen approached the lane. He took the tree-lined lane more slowly this time, listening to the sound of the birds chirping overhead. They spoke of a hard day's work ahead of them also, planning for the construction of their nest homes and the hope of the birth of their young. Life was so simple for those lowly creatures of God. *If only people could live their lives in the same way, instead of being bitter towards each other*, Glen thought. That was his attempt at meditation for the day. He knew the hope for that reality was far from existing with Ellen Harper.

He shut the door of the Mustang as quietly as he could, not wanting to awaken the queen from her slumber. *Why do I even care if I ruffle her feathers?* He thought as he got out of the car. Ellen was doing her best to intimidate him, and so far in every incident up to this point, she seemed to have the upper hand.

Ellen's alarm went off at 7 a.m. She reached up, patting for it with half-closed eyes, until she found it and turned it off. She had every intention of going back to sleep for awhile, but Cuddles had other plans, as he kept meowing loudly in Ellen's ear and tickling her face with his whiskers. "Cuddles, leave Mommy alone for awhile," she moaned sleepily. "I promise I will feed you and let you out soon." Cuddles wouldn't take *no* for an answer, as he started to nibble on Ellen's hair. "Cuddles!" she yelled, scaring the cat off of the bed as he dashed out of the room, running into the kitchen, meowing all the way. "Ok, I'm up and I'm coming to get you!" she growled playfully in her most ferocious voice, creeping from room to room trying to catch the little nudge. Cuddles loved the "chase and find" game, and Ellen played it with him often. He was her main source of companionship and she loved him like a child.

Ellen opened the kitchen door, and let Cuddles outside after he had his breakfast. It had totally slipped her mind that Glen was coming back, and it surprised her to see him in the garden hard at work. There was not a doubt in her mind that he had been angry the night before when he had left. She was even feeling a little guilty now, the way she had spoken to him, after he worked so hard the day before. Now she questioned whether he truly intended to stick out the week.

Glen stayed busy, trying to avoid Ellen as best he could. She noticed him eating his lunch under the oak tree. He sat against the tree with his knees drawn up and his head slightly tilted back, just relaxing. It was a scene reminiscent of times she had spent there also. She could tell he had jeans on again, but this time he was wearing a blue jean shirt with the sleeves torn out. He made an arresting site, just as he had done the day before, and she hoped for the chance to talk with him as much as she didn't want to admit it. The game of peaking at him from behind the kitchen curtains… she knew it was bordering on ridiculous. "I am acting so juvenile," she said to herself. "This just has to stop!" she vowed, as she straightened the curtain back in its place.

The seedlings were in the ground by mid-afternoon, but Glen was concerned that they wouldn't survive from the lack of water they had received. He had avoided the inevitable all day, but he knew he couldn't put it off forever. He needed to talk to Ellen. Glen approached the porch door, hesitant to knock. He knew she would have a snide comment or two, and he was too damn tired to put up with her attitude again. Glen took a long, slow breath, and knocked lightly several times. There was no response. "Now what?" he questioned to himself in aggravation, trying to figure out what to do next. "I'll just have to catch up with her tomorrow," he resigned, as he turned to leave and walk off the porch.

"Hello, Mr. Cummings. Have you seen my cat anywhere?" Ellen asked, standing with her screen door half open.

Glen turned back in surprise. "Sorry, I can't say that I have, but I have been very busy getting the seedlings in today."

"Does that mean the whole garden is planted then?" Ellen asked with interest.

"Yes, it does, except for caging the tomatoes."

"Thank you," she said humbly, having a hard time making full eye contact with him. She made her way to the porch swing and took a seat. "So what are your plans for tomorrow?" she questioned.

"Well, that's what I wanted to talk to you about," Glen began, as he climbed the steps again, leaning against the railing opposite the swing. "The barn is in desperate need of painting, and there are a lot of broken windows that need to be replaced as we discussed yesterday. If you can swing it, I would like some money to go into town tomorrow and buy paint, glass, and other supplies."

Ellen was transfixed, finding it difficult to formulate the words to answer Glen. He was so close to her, and she couldn't keep her eyes and mind off of his tight blue jeans that were at her eye level's advantage.

"Mrs. Harper? Did you hear me?" he asked, as he stared at Ellen in confusion from her lack of response. He couldn't believe his eyes. He swore he saw her staring for a moment where he would never dream her eyes would wander. The thought was almost comical to him, if it were true.

"Oh, Mr. Cummings, I'm sorry," she replied with embarrassment, hoping he had missed the obvious blunder of where she was staring. "I was thinking about Cuddles again, and where he was. I wasn't concentrating."

"I noticed," he answered in suspicious amusement. "What I wanted to know was if I could buy a few things tomorrow to work on the barn."

She cleared her throat, realizing that she was dealing with him more than she had anticipated. "I never expected anything like this, but if you are offering, I can hardly say no now, can I?" she replied with a faint smile.

Glen knew he needed to proceed slowly with this skittish kitten, and gain her confidence in him. "I am just trying to accomplish as much for you this week as possible. Whatever needs to be done around here, I will try to do if I have the time."

"Thank you, Mr. Cummings. I do appreciate *that* if you sincerely mean it," she replied with a doubtful tone as she went back to the screen door. A soft, furry body rubbed up against her bare leg. "There you are, Cuddles," she lovingly scolded, as she scooped the returning cat up in her arms. "I will see you tomorrow, Mr. Cummings," she added with a pretense of a smile, holding the feline close to her face as she retreated back into her house.

"That was interesting," Glen mentioned aloud, as he made his way to the Mustang. *"She was staring at my crotch,"* he said with a laugh. "Will wonders ever cease!"

Chapter Eight

Glen was up early again on Wednesday. Same routine as the morning before, but this time he packed his lunch instead of buying it at the convenience store. He needed to be careful how he spent his money, with being out of work for a while. Lunchmeat, cheese and a loaf of bread would go further in a week than take-out food everyday. On the way home from Ellen's, the night before, Glen had gone to the grocery store and attempted to restock the food supply in Eric's house. That was the least he could do to thank his brother for a free place to stay and the use of the Mustang.

The lack of a car was going to present a real problem after this week. Glen had cleaned out his savings account, which amounted to only $3,000, and he knew he needed to live on that amount for a while. Samantha, his last live-in girlfriend, had just up and left one day, unannounced while Glen was at work, and ran off with her kids and his car. Repeated phone calls to Samantha were left unanswered. Glen waited a week before going to the police to report the car stolen. He initially considered that something bad might have happened to Samantha and her kids, or that she just happened to take a trip, but then he recalled a past conversation that he had with her. He realized she had done this before, to one of her kid's father's. At least that guy was lucky…she may have run off and left him, but she came back with the car. Her mother hinted a few weeks later after Glen went to talk to her, that Samantha and her kids were fine, but she didn't want to have anything to do with him anymore. Glen thought about taking the information back to the police, but decided it wasn't worth it. She was out of his life. Maybe it was a blessing in disguise, and a small price to pay since it motivated him to take a serious look at his life and track down Eric.

Glen made his way back to the farm again by 5:30 a.m. He knew he had some time to kill before the hardware store would be open for business. He caged the fifty tomato plants, and then looked around in the barn until he found a paint scraper and ladder. He was busy scraping large areas of paint off of the worst of the barn's exterior walls, when Ellen walked up behind him.

"Good morning, Mr. Cummings."

Glen turned around, a little surprised at seeing Ellen up so early. And there it was again.... a smile, and one that was a little less haughty than it had been before. Her attitude seemed to be softening, and Glen was skeptical but happy to see it. The ice princess was melting, and he hadn't really done anything to bring about that end. After all, he hadn't talked to her that much, and she wanted it that way. He couldn't explain the sudden change, but it sure was a lot more pleasant to deal with.

Glen stopped what he was doing and crossed his arms in front of him, still holding onto the scraper. "Good morning to you too, Mrs. Harper."

"I was just down at the garden and noticed how nice everything looks."

"Thank you," Glen answered in surprise, suddenly taken back by her willingness to compliment him

"The rows are so straight, and the seedlings look well

supported. I am very pleased, " Ellen added with some hesitancy.

Glen smiled. "I do take pride in my work."

"I can see that, Mr. Cummings. And to be perfectly honest, I wasn't sure if you really even knew anything about gardening and farming. But I see I was wrong," Ellen confessed.

"I worked in the garden with my father from the time I was little, and did farm work back in Virginia where I am from," Glen added while he resumed the scraping.

Ellen shifted restlessly, trying to regain Glen's attention. "I have an account at Miller's Hardware, and if you would like, I could go with you this morning and introduce you to Mr. Miller. That way he will know I am giving my permission for you to bill items… to my account… in the future."

"That will be fine," Glen, said with a slight smile, as he stopped again to acknowledge Ellen. His eyes lingered just a little too long on her as she spoke. Ellen felt uncomfortable and yet strangely pleased at his gaze that mesmerized her in its hold. Glen looked at his watch and then into Ellen's eyes once more. "If it is ok with you, I would like to get going in 30 minutes."

"Ok…" she said quietly, feeling suddenly as if she couldn't breathe. *What is happening to me, and why would I even want to go into town with him?* She thought with a whirlwind of confusion. His brother was her enemy now and forever! "I'll be waiting on the front porch, whenever you are ready, Mr. Cummings," she said with a snap, remembering who she was dealing with.

"I'll only be a few minutes," Glen returned with his infectious smile that unnerved her to no end.

Glen took a quick inventory of what he thought would be needed to buy to get started on the painting and the windows, and wrote down the items. Ellen was waiting on the front porch as she promised. She had changed her clothes, and even though she didn't want to admit it, she hoped Glen would notice. At the barn, she was outfitted in shorts and a t-shirt, but now she had on a pretty sleeveless dress of white and aqua strips with white sandals to match. Her hair was partially pulled up in the front into a wispy bun, allowing the rest to hang down in soft waves.

Glen *was* taken back by how beautiful she looked. He tried to keep his eyes diverted from looking at her. Maybe it was her way of getting back at him for last night, and his remarks. He felt like a fish on a line, ready to be reeled in by this conniving woman - first the smile, and now this. She had to be up to something, but as long as she remained civil, he would relax his guard.

Glen walked over to the passenger's side of the Mustang, and opened the door for Ellen. She realized at that moment, his intention. He wanted her to ride in Eric's car with him. How could she tell Glen that she would never get into his brother's car, without sending him off into a tailspin again?

Ellen walked off the porch, but stopped half way to the car. "Mr. Cummings, I appreciate you opening the car door for me, but why don't we take my truck instead? It would hold so much more, and there are enough dents and scratches on it that I don't have to worry if something bumps around in the back. Your car, on the other hand, is much too nice to be taking the risk of something like that occurring," she offered, pointing in the direction of her pickup.

"That's fine with me, but I hope you don't get that pretty dress of your dirty," Glen answered with a grin that made her heart swoon. It was Glen's first real compliment that he had given to Ellen, and she was flattered! She wanted to kick herself, but she did love how it made her feel. Why did she have to be so weak when she had such strong convictions not wanting to be?

Glen drove the truck on Ellen's insistence, convincing him that he could use the truck for supply pickups from then on. The truck bumped down the lane making the vehicle lean when every gully was hit.

"Mrs. Harper, this lane really could use some gravel. It's not very good on the vehicle's shocks," Glen expressed with concern as he tried to steer the truck out of the path of the next upcoming rut.

Ellen shrugged nonchalantly at the mention of it. "The lane doesn't bother me in the least," she replied with indifference as she looked out the window. "As long as I can get to my house is all I care about."

Glen glanced in her direction and gave her a look of disbelief, but kept his comments to himself. The rest of the way into town an occasional word was spoken about the weather, the farm, and the lack of things to do in Fillmore. The conversation was strained but at least civil. Miller's Hardware had everything that Glen needed. It had the "cracker barrel charm" of days gone by, but with all the modern conveniences thrown in with its very own electronic cash register and computer system.

"Mrs. Harper, if it is alright with you, I thought the barn should be painted white and the trim green, as it originally was."

"Whatever you think would look best…" was her reply, as she absent-mindedly paged through a sales flyer from Miller's. Looking up, she saw the store's owner approach. "Mr. Miller, this is Glen Cummings," she said with a pleasant smile as she laid the brochure down. "He's doing some work for me out at my farm, and I thought it would be a good idea to stop in today, and let you know that I am giving him permission to bill items to my account now and in the future."

"Glad to meet you, Glen," he offered with a hardy handshake. "You by chance wouldn't be related to Eric Cummings, would you?"

"Yes… he is my brother," he hesitantly revealed, as he glanced at Ellen out of the corner of his eye, waiting for her reaction.

"Eric's a good guy. He helped me decide on a computer system for the store. It's made my life a whole lot easier."

"I'm glad you're pleased," he grinned. "I'll have to let Eric know that you feel that way."

Ellen seemed to be unfazed by the exchange between the two men. Glen truly expected fireworks at the mention of his brother's name, but Ellen remained controlled and calm turning her attention to things around the store.

Mr. Miller was quite adept at putting all new residents of Fillmore under a microscope, and Glen was no exception. He questioned him on such things as how long he had worked for Ellen, where he was staying, how long he would be in town, and if he was married. Ellen listened inquisitively, a few rows down, acting as if she were interested in canning supplies only. She honestly did want to hear Glen's answers to those questions herself. Discovering that Glen was planning to be around indefinitely, and he wasn't married, made her feel unexplainably relieved and happy for some reason. Her traitor persona was trying to show its face again! She continued to move around the store, looking over some new barbecue grill accessories that had just come in, keeping an ear perked to their conversation.

"I'll give you a hand with that paint, Glen, if you need it."

"Thanks, Mr. Miller, that would be great," Glen answered, as he bent over to pick up two more 5 gallon buckets of the paint.

Ellen could plainly see that Glen had won Mr. Miller over, and that wasn't always the easiest accomplishment for everyone. She grabbed the bag of brushes, rollers and sandpaper, while Mr. Miller got the other things.

Ellen's mood was different on the drive home. She became quiet and distant again, staring out the window continuously. Glen was growing tired of staring only at the back of her head.

"Is there something wrong, Mrs. Harper?"

"No, why do you ask?" Ellen answered abruptly, as she turned back around to face Glen in surprise.

"You are just so quiet all at once. I thought maybe I said or did something back at Miller's to upset you."

"I am fine," she answered with a faint smile. "I just have a lot on my mind today."

Glen guessed her mood stemmed from the mention of Eric. He really wanted to talk about that whole situation, but he knew in his heart it probably wasn't the best time to bring it up. For the time being, being quiet was his best option, he had decided. The last thing he wanted to do was back track. After all, they had made some progress in being civil towards one another.

Ellen wasted no time in going back into her house. "If you

need anything else, please just cover it with me before your purchase it. That is all I ask. See you later...."

"Of course I would go over things before making any purchases," he yelled in her direction as he unlatched the back tailgate.

The beginning phases of the painting went well. Glen finished the first coat on one of the walls of the barn by early afternoon, and then he sat down to a late lunch under the oak tree, needing the time to unwind. His plan was to stay until it got dark, or he would never get the barn done before the end of the week. He was relaxing, sitting with his fingers laced behind his head staring out over the pasture, when he heard the soft rustle of feet and turned to see Ellen approaching. She had changed her clothes again, and was back in her jeans and t-shirt. She carried a laundry basket filled with clothes, and was heading in the direction of the wash line. Glen got up immediately without thinking, and went to help her.

"Why don't you let me carry that for you?" he asked with out-stretched arms. "It looks heavy."

"I am used to carrying my own laundry basket down the hill every week, Mr. Cummings," she answered curtly. "But if you insist...why not."

Ellen noticed Glen's strong, muscular arms bulging from the weight of the basket, and his ever-so-tight backside, as he bent over to put it down. This guy was getting to her, and as much as she didn't want to admit it, he was turning her on. At first, she blamed it on being without a man for so long, but then she realized it was something more. Glen *was* a nice guy, and he truly was trying his best to give her an honest day's work. Maybe she had been a little too harsh in judging Glen by his sibling's ways. He acted nothing like his power-hungry brother Eric.

"It looks like the line needs tightening," Glen observed. "I can fix that for you in a couple minutes, if you would like," he said with a pleasant smile.

Even things as small and insignificant as a clothesline were causing her attraction to be deepening for him. Glen noticed what needed to be done around the place, and he was trying to make things better for her without expecting something in return.

"You are busy with the painting," Ellen said sincerely, "And I don't want to inconvenience you with something so insignificant."

"It's no bother at all…really," Glen answered, while already beginning to untie the knot that held the line. "If you could just pull the line taunt there in the middle, Ellen, I will get a tighter stretching of the line."

He called me Ellen! She thought with a leap of her heart. "Sure," she replied, acting as if she hadn't noticed his familiarity.

Glen realized his slip-up as soon as her name came out of his mouth, and he immediately waited for her reprimand, but instead she flashed him a pleasant smile. *Surprise of surprises,* he thought with a silent chuckle. The lady was so damn unpredictable!

The line was re-secured and Glen excused himself to go back to the painting. As he departed, he noticed Ellen bending down and picking up a pair of shorts and a couple of clips. She snapped the shorts a couple times in the air, trying to remove the wrinkles, before securing them to the line with the clothespins.

Glen inconspicuously watched her as he dipped the roller into the paint, and Ellen couldn't help but notice Glen when his back was to her, as he painted the barn. They both knew that they were assessing the other, when a glance wasn't diverted quick enough. Playing the game and pretending that it wasn't happening was the easiest thing to do. Certainly, neither one wanted to consider their newfound feelings and what they should do with them.

Chapter Nine

By nightfall, Glen had completed the base coat on the whole barn. It already looked a lot better than it did. He was tired, hungry, and his back ached from climbing up and down the ladder all day. He knew the smell of food would be greeting his senses, when he approached Ellen's house. Eric would have eaten already, and Glen was in no mood to "take care of himself," as Eric had so often reminded him. It would have to be canned soup and a sandwich again, which was becoming the all-too-familiar dinner fare of the evening. Glen approached the house as he rubbed the sore muscles of his lower back. Ellen was sitting on the porch swing, with Cuddles on her lap.

"Mrs. Harper, I am done for the evening."

"Mr. Cummings, is it too late for you to come in for awhile? I would like to review with you how things are coming along," she requested with a smile.

Glen hesitated to answer, mainly because his hunger pangs were getting the better of him and he really wanted to go home and put something in his stomach. "Sure…that would be fine."

"It's all right if you have plan. We can discuss things tomorrow," Ellen answered apprehensively, sensing Glen's hesitancy.

"No, that's fine… Now is as good of a time as any," he smiled with a somewhat weary expression on his face.

Ellen showed Glen the kitchen table, as Cuddles scurried in

behind her. “Could I get you something to eat or drink? I know it has been a long day.”

“To be honest, I would love something to eat and drink, since you asked,” he added, already feeling better she was offering.

“I had spaghetti tonight, and it will only take a few minutes to heat up a plate in the microwave…if that is alright?”

Glen smiled at her, a little taken back by the friendly change in her, but happy never-the-less by her invite. “That would be great! I love spaghetti, and it’s one of my favorites.”

Glen glanced around the kitchen, as Ellen was preparing his dinner. The place had a homespun quality that he liked. It made him feel comfortable, like taking off his shoes and walking around in his socks.

“Iced tea, salad and garlic bread ok?” Ellen asked, breaking into Glen’s thoughts.

“Anything is fine, but I feel guilty that you are going to so much trouble for me.”

“No trouble at all. Like I said…. I already had it ready for dinner,” Ellen mentioned, as she ladled a generous helping of sauce and meatballs over the pasta.

Glen was pleasantly surprised by Ellen’s expertise in the kitchen. Ellen was a good cook, and he hadn’t had a home-cooked meal in weeks. He ate greedily of all she offered.

“So how are things going with the work that you are doing?” Ellen inquired.

“Just fine. There isn’t too much more I can do with the garden this week, other than to keep a watch out for rodents, and to pull the occasional weed when it pops up. I rigged up several flying tin pie-pans on poles today, that I found in the barn, as a deterrent," Glen added.

Ellen had begun to clean up her kitchen, when she stopped to look at Glen. "Oh, I forgot to tell you about them. I get those out every year, and they work great at keeping the birds away."

"Yeah, we used tin pans at home in Virginia also, and they always did the job," Glen said as he took another bite of pasta. "I am concerned about groundhogs and raccoons, though. I saw a groundhog yesterday, and they can do a lot of damage to a garden. I may need to put a fence up once the vegetables become mature, if they start biting and chewing on the produce." Glen caught his mistake as soon as the words were out. God, the woman put him on edge! He didn't want the wrong words to come out of his mouth to set her off again. He thought how he had called her by her first name, and how she had let that one pass; but to be making plans for the upcoming weeks past this test week, was being presumptuous on his part, he knew.

After all, the fence wouldn't be needed for several weeks yet. He wanted *her* to make the decision if he was coming back past this week. Her fragile state of mind towards Eric could play havoc on any working relationship that Glen and she may establish. That was, if Ellen didn't sort it out on her own. The last thing Glen wanted to do was sway her decision. He wanted her to decide to keep him based on his merit alone - one of being a good worker, not afraid of long hours and hard work, without any persuasion on his part.

Ellen *did catch* Glen's slip on words, and was pleased to hear that he spoke of the future that went beyond the free week's commitment. She feared that any day he would walk up to her door and inform her he wouldn't be back after the week's end. However, now she knew Glen planned to stay.

"Can I refill your glass, Mr. Cummings?" she asked with a smile.

"That would be nice. I guess I could use a little extra," Glen replied with warmth that captured her green eyes, as he extended the glass in Ellen's direction. As Ellen refilled the glass with the amber-colored tea, Glen continued to outline his plans for the rest of the week with her. "I hope to be done painting the barn by Saturday. I plan to apply the second coat of paint to the walls tomorrow, and start the trim."

"What about the broken windows?" Ellen inquired inquisitively while sipping on her tea.

"I hope to fix them also on Friday, and continue to paint the trim. On Saturday, if all goes well, I will have the barn looking as good as new; and then I plan to work on the lane, filling in the gullies with some dirt."

"That lane really bothers you, doesn't it?" Ellen teased, while giggling and spilling iced tea down her shirt. She started dabbing at it with a dishtowel that was thrown over a chair, making the wet mark unintentionally more noticeable over her left breast. Realizing her mistake, she glanced up and saw Glen with his eyes transfixed on her. Her nipples involuntarily started to harden. Ellen retreated quickly to the sink, resuming her task of cleaning the dishes that were still soaking in the sudsy water. Now it was her turn to feel embarrassment.

"I don't know if putting dirt in those gullies will accomplish much. I've tried that before, and one good rain washes a lot of it back away," she commented with her back still turned, and her face red-hot from remembering the intimate hungry-look that Glen had just given her. How quickly his expression had changed to passion, and the thought of it almost scared her.

"What you need is several loads of gravel over that dirt fill. That will at least solve *that problem,*" Glen replied, while eyeing her back. He had to chuckle to himself, that both of them were well aware of why Ellen was trying to conceal her front as she continued the conversation without turning around. What she didn't realize though, was that the slight bending over of her backside was causing equally, if not more so, the same stirring inside of Glen. Ellen turned around again, slinging the dishtowel over the shoulder of her wet breast. Glen's astute eyes were still on her while he held an incredibly sexy grin that made his face appear even more handsome. She was caught off guard by his penetrating stare of pleasure, but she wouldn't give him the satisfaction of thinking that she cared, as she sat down again at the table.

"I'll get a price on the gravel, Mr. Cummings, but I'm not sure I want to put out the additional money right now for that."

"That's fine…but if and when you do decide you want to get into that project, I will take care of it for you," Glen answered, feeling a little guilty for not considering first if she could even afford all of his proposed improvements.

"You really have been doing a good job. I want to apologize for underestimating your abilities," Ellen confessed sincerely, catching his sky-blue eyes with her own. He was so darn handsome, and at the moment, she was having a tough time remembering his intentions for being there.

"That's ok…I knew if you would just give it some time, you

would see things differently," he added with a pleasant smile, finding the *softer her* so appealing.

"I may see things differently about you Mr. Cummings, but not your brother. I am sorry to bring that subject up again, but I want you to know that my feelings *have not and will not change,* where he is concerned! I *know* it is his car that you bring here. That is why I wouldn't ride in it when we went into town."

Glen crossed his arms and sighed, realizing she had put up her defenses again, just like a frightened animal out in the wild. "Can we talk about Eric, and what happened with… with…your hus…?"

"Absolutely, no we can't!" she stammered. "And *please* don't try to bring the subject up again," Ellen retorted with pleading and a lot of emotion in her voice.

"I'm sorry. I didn't mean to upset you," Glen said gently, as he pushed out the chair and got to his feet. I guess it's time I get going."

"Alright…yes," Ellen hastily answered, feeling a sense of hurt and yet relief at his departure. It disheartened her to think that he would try to force her hand so soon concerning Eric, and yet he apologized in the next breath. She hated to see the change in his mood, but she also realized she was responsible for that. There was a definite chemistry occurring just moment's earlier, and now the flames of desire had definitely been extinguished. Ellen knew she was the cause of the breakdown, but she would not allow this man or anyone else for that matter, convince her Eric Cummings was innocent where Jack was concerned.

"Thanks for dinner. It was very good," Glen offered with perfunctory politeness.

"You're welcome, Mr. Cummings," Ellen replied with a smile, attempting to break the barrier back down again, just as it had been moments earlier.

"Mrs. Harper, could I make one last request?" Glen asked with some hesitation.

"Sure."

"Could we call each other by our first names? It would make things a lot more comfortable for me if we were on a first name basis."

"That would be fine," Ellen answered shyly with a meek smile, knowing a new door had just been opened for her and Glen.

"Good night, Ellen," Glen said with a turn and a wave, as he made his way to Eric's car.

"Good night, Glen," Ellen replied, half in and out of the screen door with the dish towel still slung over her shoulder.

The drive home for Glen was therapeutic. The top was down on the Mustang, and the temperature was unseasonably warm for early May. The air smelled sweet and heavy from the new flower and leaf growth, covering every tree along the way. Glen felt lazy and relaxed from being fed so well, and from putting in such a hard day's work. *It was too bad that Ellen had to lose it at the end*, he thought. *She never seems to maintain a happy deposition for long. If only she could just let go of the past, maybe things would be different.* "Damn… why do I even care?" he pondered. "*I won't let myself be dragged back into another crazy relationship. Not after Samantha!"*

Eric was already in bed when Glen got home. A note was on the kitchen counter, waiting to be read.

Glen,

Long day. Went to bed early. See you in the morning, since I'll be up early also.

Eric

Glen had to smile. It was nice to be with Eric again; although, they hadn't had much time together yet. Maybe over the weekend they could catch a local ballgame or something. Glen called it a night too, and laid awake long into the night thinking of Ellen Harper. As hard as he tried to put her out of his mind, he couldn't. He kept thinking of her breast with its hardened nipple popping out from the wet, tea-stained shirt. He imagined his mouth covering it as Ellen moaned for him not to stop, as she clutched his head closer to her chest. He knew that it was insane to even allow his mind to wander there, but he couldn't stop himself.

Ellen was having her own insomnia attack. Glen was lying nude under her favorite oak tree, sleeping. He was completely exposed to her view, and she had the freedom to stare at his Adonis physique with abandon. Upon his awakening, he reached for her hand and Ellen became nude also. They made glorious love, like she had never experienced before in her life. Afterwards, she lay secure in his embrace, never desiring to move from under the protection of the tree or his arms. How foolish she felt to have such longings. *He's probably involved with someone*, she thought. *He's too good-looking and nice not to have a girlfriend, unless he is gay. No…that is doubtful,* she resolved with a restless sigh, remembering how he stared at her breast earlier. "I think that is *definitely* doubtful!"

Chapter 10

The alarm sounded it endless series of beeps, as Glen yawned and realized that he had to get up already. His head ached with the heavy sensation of not having enough sleep. He knew he couldn't give into his carnal desires again tonight, or he wouldn't be able to uphold his commitment to Ellen through the end of the week.

Eric was waiting downstairs as promised, watching the weather channel and drinking a cup of coffee. "You look baadd…" he grinned mischievously. "You stop at a bar or something last night?"

"Nope, no bar. Just had a hard time sleeping…. A lot on my mind," Glen answered while pouring himself a cup of coffee also.

"Anything I can help you with?" Eric offered, taking on a more serious tone.

"It's really no big deal."

"Well apparently it is, or it wouldn't keep you up half of the night."

"Had dinner at Ellen Harper's last night," Glen interjected, trying to change the subject.

"Oh, *really?*" Eric smirked.

"What's that suppose to mean?" Glen asked while making eye contact with his brother.

"Nothing really…. I just thought you two were at odds just a few days ago, and now it seems like a real about face in such a short time."

"It was purely business. She had already eaten, anyways. She knew she was keeping me from my dinner and it was late, so she offered me some food, and I accepted."

"So where did the business part come in?" Eric grinned, still using his sarcastic edge of a moment ago.

"You really can be an asshole at times," Glen said with a shake of his head, knowing Eric was just trying to get his goat.

"Come on bro, you know I can't resist getting you in the morning when your defenses are down. Just like the old days, remember?"

"I remember, Eric. To answer your question though, we discussed what I've done so far at the farm, and what I plan to do for the rest of the week," he replied while taking a seat at the table.

"What have you done?" Eric asked, not really taking the conversation seriously.

"Well nothing compared to your accomplishments this week, I'm sure," Glen teased, getting in his own jab. "But the garden is all planted, and I have started to paint the barn. I plan to completely finish it and replace the broken windows before the week is up. Other than that, I want to smooth out the gullies in her lane and fix the fence."

Eric looked at his brother in surprise. "Why not paint the house inside and out, and mow the lawn too. Come on Glen…why so much?"

“She needs the help.”

“You’re not getting paid for this.”

“I will be hopefully, after this week.”

“She ought to be damn grateful that her garden is in. All those other things in one week are too much. Say goodbye Saturday, and then try to find a *real job.”*

The teasing was one thing, but now Eric had hit a nerve and Glen was angry. He wasn’t happy with Eric minimizing his backbreaking labor of the week, while Eric sat behind a desk in a cushy office environment.

“Eric, when Ellen Harper asks me to stay…I’m telling her I will do so… past this week, and I will help her out for however long she needs me.”

Eric just smirked. “Hey, I’m sorry bro. I didn’t think the job meant that much to you. I actually thought you were playing the lady. You know… the family honor thing.”

“Give me a break! This kind of hard labor makes family honor a thing to be forgotten! Ellen’s not so bad, Eric. She just hasn’t gotten over her husband dying. Talking about you and your part in that whole mess is a subject that is totally off limits. She made that very clear to me last night.”

Eric shook his head in silent understanding, realizing what his brother was up against. “I’ll give you a tip, don’t even try. If Ellen Harper wants to be irrational, that’s her problem,” he said while placing his empty coffee mug in the dishwasher. “Well, I gotta get going. My secretary will be here in ten minutes. We’re taking the commuter to Omaha, and I’ll be home late. Oh, and by the way…I’m out of town next week, so you can use the car while I’m gone,” Eric rattled off matter-of-factly, while grabbing his cream linen jacket.

Glen felt relieved that he had another week of time to use Eric's car. He didn't know what he was going to do, other than take a cab out to the farm until he could afford a down payment on a car or truck, but preferably a truck or SUV. That's the image he wanted now. There would be no future threat of another female wanting to steal his nice comfortable Sedan.

The drive out to the farm was as pleasant as all the previous mornings. The weather had been kind for painting. Even a fine drizzle could ruin wet paint, but the air had been "dry-as-bones", with low humidity. Ellen's house was quiet. He knew she was till sleeping, but he wondered what she was wearing, if anything. It would be so easy to peak into her half-opened window as the breeze blew her curtains apart, and find out the answer to his question; but he knew that would be pure foolishness.

Glen walked into the barn and found the painting supplies, just as he had left them the evening before. The second coat on the barn was his goal for the day, and he knew he wouldn't stop until he accomplished that feat. The humidity wasn't making it easy on him though, slowing the job down considerably. By nine o'clock Glen had removed his white t-shirt and downed half of his thermos of water. He plugged in the boom box he brought, finding an outlet beside the barn door. He loved the oldies station and was crooning loudly to a love ballad as Ellen was leaving Cuddles out. She caught the site of his nude, muscular tanned back. He held a paintbrush and was beating out a rhythm with each stroke, while his hips swayed gently to the music. She was surprised by how well he sang. He held a tune nicely, and could have easily sung in a church choir or even a local nightclub band.

Ellen pulled on a pair of cut off blue jean shorts that were a little too short, and a tight fitting white tank top. White ankle socks and sneakers completed her attire. She pulled her hair straight back into a sleek ponytail, and dressed it up with a white scrungie. After brushing her teeth, she studied her appearance and realized makeup would be too much. She pinched her cheeks instead, giving them some color. One last appraisal and she approved of the desire effect; but not to the point of being too obvious. She wanted Glen to notice her today. As much as Ellen hated to admit it, she liked the way he had stared at her breasts the night before. Maybe today he would notice other parts of her too, she considered with womanly insight.

She prided herself for being disciplined at maintaining a good body. It would be so easy to drown her sorrows in food, just as she had done after Jack died. She learned her lesson quickly though, realizing the downfall of overeating, gaining ten pounds in a month after his death. Her clothes began to feel tight and uncomfortable, and after weighing herself one evening, she realized the full impact of the newest problem she was encountering. Shock registered as she saw the scale climb higher than it had ever been before. Ellen ruled out pregnancy, and then set out to gain control of at least this part of her life. She could not bring Jack back, but she could do something about the way she looked. She began taking walks and going to dance class at a ladies gym. The increased activity along with better eating choices, got her into a good routine of a healthier lifestyle. After a few months, the weight came off. Now she had surpassed her original expectations, not only reaching her ideal weight, but also becoming firmer and more toned than what she had been before her husband's death.

Ellen had made a pitcher of lemonade earlier, as well as some oatmeal cookies. She prepared the tray with the lemonade, cookies, and two glasses filled with ice. "Hello, Glen, I thought maybe you could use something cold to drink?" Ellen offered cheerfully, as Glen turned around. He felt somewhat awkward, since he knew Ellen had heard him singing, and she had caught him off-guard once again.

"That would be great," he answered while taking in her sultry appearance. "Just let me put this paint brush down and get this paint off my hands, and I'll be right with you," he smiled with an appraising look that showed he was pleasantly surprised by her appearance.

She noticed Glen was still bare-chested and hadn't put his shirt back on, when he came back out from the barn. Her pulse quickened at the site of him.

"Ellen, I still need to get this paint cleaner off of my hands," Glen remarked while walking to the water pump. "If it's alright with you", he grinned, "That snack would be especially nice under the oak tree."

"That's fine," Ellen replied with a slight blush, hoping Glen realized she had included a glass for herself.

Glen met Ellen under the oak tree, as she was still standing and holding the tray. He reached out, and grabbed if from her, and placed it on the ground. Not standing on ceremony, Glen sat and started pouring the lemonade over the ice. He looked up, with a glass pointing in her direction, smiling at her with a lazy grin that invited her to join him under the tree.

Those eyes again, she thought, and his golden hair, wet and slicked back, with his bronzed, muscular bare chest. He looked like something out of a woman's skin flick magazine. *Do I dare sit down?* She did, but not until she took the glass from Glen first. “I hope you don’t mind that I wanted to join you, but lemonade and cookies tastes better shared,” she said with a cute coy smile.

Glen chuckled and nodded his agreement, while drinking of the refreshing nectar. “I never thought of it that way, but I guess you got a point there. To be honest, I’m glad you decided to join me Ellen,” he confessed. “It gets kinda lonely at times, working by myself, and having no one to talk to all day.”

His revealing friendly words warmed her beyond the heat of the day. “I should send Cuddles out to visit you. He does a fine job of keeping me company,” Ellen said with a laugh.

Glen meekly studied Ellen, occasionally catching a glimpse of her as she ate her cookie. She avoided direct eye contact with him for the majority of the time, staring out over the pasture instead. He noticed her outfit. It was a different Ellen that he had seen up onto this point, but one he liked. Her legs were slim and well shaped, muscular but feminine. The shorts, as well as the snugly fitting tank top, gave her a youthful appearance. Her breasts were not overly large, but had enough of a swell to cause a seductive cleavage. Her hair, even though it was pulled back, held soft tendrils that had come lose and whispered around her neck. The look was clean and healthy, one he could get lost in. She was tense, but Glen could tell she wanted to be there with him. Things were starting to happen, with these allowances of shared food, first names and conversations.

“Did you bake the cookies, Ellen?”

“Yes, I baked them this morning, I hope you like raisins because I seem to get too many in the batter,” she said with a smile.

“They’re great, and so is the lemonade. I haven’t had

homemade lemonade since I was a kid. My mom used to make it all the time for us. I even had a lemonade stand in the front of my house, and sold it to the neighborhood kids."

Ellen giggled with his words, reminding her of a childhood memory of her own. "I used to have a lemonade stand also, but my sister seemed to always take most of the money out of the jar before I could get my hands on it."

Glen shared in the laughter. "Where did you grow up, Ellen?"

"I grew up in Denver," she replied between gulps of the sweet but tangy beverage.

"What brought you to Nebraska?" Glen asked, sincere with interest and yet continuing to pry as if he was an investigator.

Ellen shifted restlessly, not sure if she wanted to open up to him about her past yet. She took another gulp of her drink, and after a moment of hesitation, she began. "I moved here once I was married, and it's been quite a difference from growing up in a big city."

"Do you miss Denver?"

"Not really, it's been six years, but I do miss an easier lifestyle at times. My father is a dentist, and we never did any work like gardening. We had a maid and even someone planted the few flowers that were in the urns surrounding the pool and yard. I was your typical spoiled, rich city girl," she confessed.

Glen was surprised by Ellen's honesty. He knew the type, since Eric always scored with societies' finest while they were high school.

"I've grown to love the scenery here, and the peace and quiet.

I don't think I want to give that up now," Ellen responded with a sigh. She turned back to face Glen. "What was life like in Virginia?" Ellen asked shyly as she took a swallow of lemonade, recapturing Glen's brilliant blue eyes.

"I grew up in a middle class neighborhood in the suburbs. My dad worked in a boat-building factory, and my mom stayed at home and took care of the kids. Life was good for us with lots of friends. I was involved in sports in high school but unfortunately never went to college. That's something I regret. Never would listen to my parents on that issue…" he mentioned in a far-off distant way. After high school, I worked in retail for a while and on a couple farms. Virginia really is a beautiful state," he said with a pleasant smile.

"Why did you leave then?"

Glen paused, not really sure if he wanted to answer that question. He had his own set of skeletons in the closet to deal with. "I needed a change. I was involved in a relationship with a woman who really screwed me up emotionally. She even stole my car. That's why I am borrowing Eric's."

"Where is she now?" Ellen asked with keen interest, breaking off a small piece of cookie.

"Wish I knew…" he answered with a stern look, throwing a rock at the fence post making it ricochet off of it in a sideways direction. "The car wasn't new, but it was in mint condition, and it sure would be nice to have it now. Her name was Samantha Winters, and we both knew it was over between us before she pulled that stunt. That just permanently sealed our ending. Her mother assured me she was alive and well, but she didn't want to hear from me. I guess I should have the police track her down since I filed a police report, but I don't want a problem for her mother. She isn't a bad person. It's too involved to explain, but just take my word for it, that I got off easy with her getting out of my life with only the loss of my car."

Ellen sympathized with Glen's misfortune. She felt somewhat embarrassed now, realizing she wasn't the only one with problems. It just served as another reminder that she may have been too presumptuous, judging him solely on his brother's reputation. He was a really nice person, and seemed sincere enough. She took a deep breath, and plunged right in with her speech before she lost her nerve.

"Glen, I have been thinking…. I know I was harsh when we first met, and I have reconsidered some things. You may use the bathroom in my house instead of the outhouse. I'm sure the warm water in the sink would be more welcome than the cold water of the well pump."

Glen looked up in surprise, still chewing a bite of the delicious cookie. "I may take you up on that, but to be honest, the outhouse is close by and I don't mind using it. No rodents so far," he grinned. "And as far as the cold water goes, I'm used to it now. Believe it or not, I find it refreshing as hot outside as it has been. But thanks anyways," Glen replied, while rising with his hands on his thighs for balance. "It was nice talking with you," he said with a smile, "But I better get back to work or I will never get the painting finished on the barn."

"Oh… of course," Ellen answered awkwardly, knowing she had kept Glen longer than she had intended.

"Can I help you with the tray, Ellen?"

"No, that's ok. I will be fine," Ellen commented, as she was on her knees gathering the glasses and cookie-crumb filled napkins onto the tray. "If you need anything, let me know, Glen."

"Will do," he answered in a delighted daze, as he watched Ellen in her kneeling position gathering the scattered items. A little too-much skin was exposed to his view, as her shorts crept up revealing the seductive beginning of her derriere.

The phone was ringing, as Ellen sat the tray down on the kitchen counter. "Hello?"

"Hi El, it's Megan."

"I know silly that it's you. It hasn't been that long, has it?" Ellen asked her best friend, as she placed the dirty dishes in the sink.

"Long enough, and that's why I am calling. I was hoping we could get together for lunch today."

"Today?" Ellen answered hesitantly. "Well I guess that would be alright."

"If it's not a good day, just say so."

"No, it will be fine. It's just that I have someone at my house doing some work. But he knows what he needs to do, so I don't see it being a problem."

"So how about meeting me at Albright's at 12:30?"

"Sounds good to me. I'll see you soon."

Ellen hurried and changed into a silky floral print skirt and cream-colored blouse. She upswept her hair into a barrette and finished her look with silver earrings and a matching necklace.

She noticed her wedding ring laying in her jewelry box, while searching for a bracelet. She took it out, and turned it over several times in her hands, studying it under the bright nightstand lamp beside of her bed. It was one single band with the highest quality diamonds surrounding it. The ring was simple but elegant. Jack had wanted her to have it, although she had protested that a less expensive ring would suffice. However, Jack wouldn't hear of it. He always spoiled Ellen, from the beginning and throughout their marriage. She touched each diamond, rolling the ring around on her finger, with tear-filled eyes, as she recalled the love that she and Jack had stolen from them before its time should have ended. "Enough of this," was Ellen's statement of composure, as she returned the treasured possession to its shrine. Wiping her eyes, she studied her face in the mirror, and tried to hide her emotions well with carefully applied makeup. Megan had been a shoulder to cry on one too many times. She didn't want to ruin lunch today, as she had done so many times in the past.

Unfortunately, Megan's presence had always brought Jack to mind. They both had worked for Computer World Systems, although Megan never grew in the ranks past being an executive secretary, and she had no desire to do so for that matter. Ellen had met Megan at a summer picnic. She was bubbly and bright, four inches shorter than Ellen, with copper-red hair cropped in a bob below her ears, with freckles and a turned-up nose. She instantaneously latched onto Ellen, and made the decision for both of them that they would be *the best of friends until the day they died.* Ellen didn't need a lot of persuasion, being drawn to her in the same way. From the start, they were never at a loss for words and they realized they had a lot in common growing up in the same state.

Jack had always found Megan to be pleasant at work, relying

on her exclusively for help with his special projects that came up frequently. He found a tennis partner with her husband Mike, who was a soft-spoken guy who would give the shirt off his back to anyone who asked for it. Mike's only downfall was that he allowed Megan to rule the roost, but their marriage wouldn't survive if he didn't. The two couples had gotten together often, even sharing in several vacations. Neither of them had started a family, but often they would talk about how fun it would be for their children to grow up together. That bubble was also one to burst, with the passing of Jack. Megan was like a sister to Ellen, and had lent endless support and comfort since Jack's death. She knew though, that even the best of friends could grow weary from the same depressed mood all of the time. So Ellen was trying her best to make a more concentrated effort at presenting a more positive side to her friend.

Glen was still painting when Ellen approached the barn. "I'm going into town for awhile. Feel free to use the bathroom, she offered with a smile. I'll leave the house unlocked."

"All right.... thanks," is all Glen could say as he took in Ellen's appearance. She looked so sophisticated in her outfit. He had seen the casual wholesome country-look with a hint of sexiness; but this was different – working woman's attire, giving off an aura of her being on her way to work. His eyes followed her backside as she walked to the Saab. He could still remember their close proximity of only an hour earlier, and how badly he had just wanted to reach out and slide his hand the rest of the way up her shorts, and squeeze the firmness of her butt. He grew hard with the memory of it.

Megan was waiting in a booth already enjoying her iced tea.

"Sorry I'm a little late. I had to cover a few things with Glen before I left."

"Glen, huh?"

"What's that suppose to mean?"

"We are on a first name basis with the hired help?" Megan prodded teasingly.

"Yes, we are *ME…GAN*. What's the big deal?" Ellen dished, giving it back and acting unperturbed.

"Ok… It's no big deal," Megan added with a giggle. "I just haven't known you to call anyone who works for you by their first name, that's all."

The waiter approached at that moment, granting Ellen reprieve from Megan's constant teasing. "Are you ladies ready to order?" he asked with his notepad in hand ready to write.

"*Quite ready,*" Ellen responded, giving Megan a look of warning.

Megan just smiled back at her buddy with a devilish grin, resting her chin on her palm. "I'll have whatever she is having, since she always makes the most wonderful choices."

Ellen just shook her head in amusement. Megan was too damn sharp for her own good!

Lunch was salad and soup for the both of them, and they couldn't resist splitting a piece of apple pie for desert.

Wiping her mouth and reapplying her lipstick Megan asked, "So what are you having done at your place?"

"Well you know, Meg, I needed someone to put the garden in after Roy quit. So besides the work of the garden, I am having my barn repainted," Ellen answered, while spooning up the last bit of pie.

"Does this guy seem more stable than Roy was?"

"Yes, he is, and you know I hate to admit it but I feel guilty now about an agreement we came up with."

"Oh… what kind of agreement is that?" Megan asked with curiosity while stirring sugar into her coffee.

"This guy, Glen, is working a week for me for free. And he works long days, twelve to fourteen hours."

"Is he crazy? Why would he agree to something so ridiculous?"

"Because I really didn't want to hire him, and he wanted to prove his worth for a week of free work. After this week though, he wants to be paid."

"Well… now," Megan began, resting her elbows on the table, leaning forward and raising her eyebrows questionably. Is he good looking, married, have kids, divorced? What? Spill it."

"ME…GAN, can't you *ever* stop?" Ellen said with a giggle.

"Oh lighten up El, it's time you get back in the dating scene anyways."

Ellen lowered her head momentarily. She knew Megan was right, but it was still hard to realize that. She felt like she was breaking her marriage vows for even considering it. Raising her head again, she gave Megan the signature solemn look that was unfortunately so much a part of her now. "Megan, there was a reason I didn't want to hire Glen. It's because his brother is Eric Cummings."

"You're kidding, right? No way is that possible!" she exclaimed in disbelief.

"I wish I was… she answered softly. As hard as it is to believe, it is true. He is staying with Eric and needed a job. A neighbor of mine suggested he come over to my place and ask me about work, since his farmhand position had already been filled. I know it sounds far-fetched and very coincidental, but I think he is telling me the truth. I had my doubts initially, thinking that Eric was pulling a cruel joke on me, sending him out there just to harass me, but now I feel that isn't the case."

Megan sat in silence, too stunned to believe this was happening. *Maybe it is a twist of fate*, she thought to herself. "I'm sorry Ellen, I would have never imagined the possibility."

"I know you wouldn't, and it's ok…really," she reassured with a pat to Megan's hand. "Glen is nothing like Eric, and I was wrong to cast judgment on him just because of the history between his brother and myself. After all, he is an individual and should have the chance to prove himself based on his own worth. I hate to say it, but I was really mean to him when he first showed up at my house," she confessed.

"I guess so. Who wouldn't be," Megan consoled. "Eric never mentioned that he had a brother," she added with fascination over the whole situation.

"Well he does. He's from Virginia, and he is staying with Eric. Apparently, he has had some problems with an old girlfriend and she even stole his car. Eric has been letting him drive his

Mustang out to my farm. As much as I hate to admit it, I'm starting to feel sorry for him."

"You surprise me, Ellen," Megan said with a shake of her head. "I never thought I would hear you say you feel sorry for a Cummings. Why did he have come to your house for a job anyways? Surely, Eric would have forewarned him about staying away from your place."

"That was my initial thought also, until I realized that Eric had been out of town on business, and Glen claimed he knew nothing of Eric and my problems. Apparently, he just stumbled upon my place. He did farm work in Virginia," she added as she sipped her coffee.

"So are you going to keep him on after this week?"

"I think so, although I haven't told him yet. And for that matter, he may not even want to stay even if I make him that offer."

Ellen couldn't bring herself to tell Megan how she was starting to have romantic feelings towards Glen. Things were happening too quickly, and there was a slim-to-none chance that Glen felt the same way, especially after the way they had gotten off to such a bad start. She didn't want nor desire Megan's insistence on her pursuing this male. She constantly tried to pair her off with every single guy that she knew, be it friend, business acquaintance, or relative.

"Well, I guess I better get back to the office, or there won't be an office to get back to," Megan said as she stood up.

"We never seem to have enough time to visit. Why don't you come out to the farm this weekend?"

"I'll see what's up with Mike. He mentioned about driving to

Lincoln to go antique shopping Saturday, but maybe Sunday afternoon would work."

"Sounds good. Just let me know," Ellen answered with a warm smile and hug, before getting into her car. She was having a tough time giving up the "old gal", since the Saab had been a high school graduation present from her parents. "See you soon!"

"Yeah, see ya later. Oh, and by the way, say hi to Glen for me. Tell him that I'm looking forward to meeting him one day," she said with a wink and sly smile.

"Oh sure, Meg. I'll do that as soon as I get home," Ellen answered sarcastically, as she pulled away.

Chapter Eleven

Melinda Philips lay in perfect contentment and bliss as she cuddled against the sleeping man 's chest. The soft rhythmic breathing from his rising form made her happier than she had been in months. Her fantasy of fantasies had all come true today. She had been on the scene of the closing of the largest deal Computer World Systems had ever negotiated. Now she was savoring in that victory, with a personal trophy of her own, that of Eric Cummings. Never had she thought that victory could be so sweet.

The acceptance of a simple favor, of taking Eric back and forth to work, had helped to develop the flirtation that had already been building at work. Eric had been so on top-of-the world from conquering Viswell, Inc., and Melinda was there to celebrate with him, and reap the pleasant after affects of his victory.

Many months of observation and analysis of what the competition would offer went into the preparation of the proposal. Melinda was an invaluable source of help in whatever needed to be done in way of research or reports. Her efforts were now being rewarded with a raise as well as Eric's body.

Eric sealed the deal after his third meeting with the principals at Viswell. Their expectations were outrageous in some regards, but with Eric's smooth way of changing minds as well as his concession on minor points, the final contract was signed. No one in the computer business could beat CWS's reputation, thanks to Eric putting them on the top. The price, as well as the ongoing maintenance agreement after the system was installed, was always beating the competition hands down. Or if it didn't start out that way, Eric would revise the offer until the potential client was satisfied and couldn't say no.

Peter Winston had to learn to trust Eric's approach initially, because he had always been more conservative in the area of how far he would extend himself for a sale. But the risk paid off with unprecedented sales volume and profit. Eric knew Peter would celebrate with him on his return. It was Peter after all, who thought this deal would be the one to break Eric's consistent winning streak of late. It had been over a year since anyone had turned Eric down on a system. Peter had even waged a bet with him, before he left town that dinner would be on him if he could pull another one off. The owners of Viswell were tight-asses with their money, and not any amount of coercing with honey-coated words and promises would give the account to CWS. Eric would have to produce a package with a support network that was solid beyond compare.

The promise of one of CWS's technical staff advisors to be on site with Viswell, free of charge for one year accomplished the goal. Within that time, Eric hoped all the bugs would be out of the system, and the office staff at Viswell would be thoroughly trained, efficient at running things on their own. CWS would absorb the costs for this, and Viswell would never suffer in productivity loss.

Eric had broken the barrier down once again. A temporary replacement would have to be brought in to CWS for the year until the technical support time was up. Two salaries, instead of one, would have to paid. In return, the promise of Viswell's parent company coming aboard with CWS would be forthcoming. This added feather in Eric's cap would bring him closer to the promised partnership with Peter Winston.

After the deal was signed, sealed and delivered, Eric and Melinda shared an early dinner and drinks. Much touching and feeling went on under the table, which led to a quick rendezvous at the hotel across the street.

Melinda started drawing delicate circles around Eric's lips, touching him as light as a feather. Eric tried to brush the presence away with his hand, still in a state of semi-sleep. "Wake up sleepy head," she cooed seductively.

"Hmmm…" Eric replied, trying to remember where he was and with whom. "Oh, Melinda, what's the time?"

"Time to start where we left off an hour ago," Melinda teased, while propped up on one elbow on her side, continuing to stroke Eric over his chest.

"I would love to babe, but we gotta catch a flight or we won't get back to Fillmore tonight," Eric stated, while sitting up and glancing around the room for his clothes.

"Would that be so terrible?" Melinda whispered.

Eric smiled, reaching over to give her a kiss on the forehead. "You know I would love to stay awhile longer, but duty calls. Peter and I are scheduled for a meeting first thing in the morning. And I haven't stood him up yet."

Melinda wasn't going to give up that easy as she continued her massaging caresses lower and lower on his body. She accomplished her goal of wearing down his defenses. "The plane doesn't leave for 1 hour and 45 minutes yet, and we are only 10 minutes away from the airport. That leaves us 5 minutes to shower and dress, and anther twenty to relive the moment; and I won't take no for an answer," Melinda continued enticingly as she trialed kisses down his chest.

He reached out and pulled her up to his waiting mouth. Their lips met and meshed in a frenzy of tangled heat and tongues, dueling for the other one's mouth. Eric couldn't deny Melinda's advances. He was a helpless victim to her charms. She was a spirited lover, matching his own advances and every move; surprisingly, even able to show him some of her own magic. They lay wrapped in each other's embrace, with a sheen of perspiration covering both of them, after a star-shattering climatic finale.

"Are you glad I detained you a little longer?" she asked.

"Do you even need to ask?" Eric questioned with a contented smile as he grabbed Melinda's hand heading for the shower. "You said 15 minutes, and we now only have five, so we better hurry," Eric teased with a playful smack to her backside.

Chapter Twelve

Ellen could see Glen hard at work, painting the barn's trim, as she rounded the last part of the farm's lane. Glen looked up, hearing the car's engine as it pulled into the lane. He recognized the growling muffler sound; it was Ellen's Saab. *Funny*, he thought, *how the sound of a car engine could be as familiar as a person's voice.* He waved, as she shut her car door. Ellen waved back as she headed in Glen's direction.

"I haven't ever seen the barn look this good before," she said with genuine heart-felt praise.

Glen lazily gazed at her from head to toe. "I can think of other things that I haven't seen look this good in a long time. You look great in that outfit, Ellen," he replied, with a sexy grin that left Ellen's pulse racing.

Ellen's face reddened with embarrassment, taken back by Glen's boldness. "Thank you, Glen…" she answered shyly with downcast eyes.

Glen smiled again, reveling in the knowledge that he was making her squirm with discomfort. "It's amazing what a little paint will do," Glen commented, while standing back at a distance, admiring his handiwork.

Awkwardly, she shifted her feet, not knowing what to say after his outward show of frankness. Ellen still had a hard time believing he was being sincere. "I guess I better get back to the house," she said while turning to leave. "But things do look good," she added, reaffirming her compliment.

Ellen was making her way back to the clothesline to take the laundry down, when she spotted Glen taking his afternoon break beneath the oak tree again. She noticed he had given himself the daily dousing at the well pump, which she was now growing accustomed to seeing. His hair was wet and finger combed, and his shirt was off and lying in a heap beside his outstretched form. He was drinking from the spout of his thermos. It was a repeat performance of the same disturbing sensual picture that he always made whenever she saw him like that – wet, slicked back hair, and bare-chested.

Ellen longed to repeat the morning, and sit under the tree with him again, starting up the conversation where they left off earlier. But she dare not. Not one to be an aggressor, at least in the early stages of a relationship, she would keep her distance. She had only been involved seriously, for any length of time, with three men - her husband Jack, and two other guys while in high school. Jack, she met in college, and they dated most of her junior and senior years, marrying as soon as she graduated. The one guy in high school was a blind date that her best friend had set her up with. They dated for a year, and he broke up with her to "go steady" with the head cheerleader of their school. She was devastated, at least her pride was. In that particular case, a bigger set of boobs was the true cause of their breakup. The other guy, she broke up with in 6 months, because their relationship had lost its spark. He was very hurt, claiming she was the "love of his life" and hoped they would have married one day. The balance scale was even - with one guy breaking her heart, and the other guy she caused unintentional pain.

Glen took in Ellen's backside again, just as he had done the night before in the kitchen. She was removing the clothespins, folding each item before it went in the laundry basket. He realized she had changed back into the outfit of the morning. Glen wondered where Ellen had gone while she was away earlier. For some strange reason, he missed her while she was gone. He even felt pangs of envy for whoever got to spend that time with her, for even those few short hours.

Ellen bent over and lifted the heavy wicker basket up to her waist balancing the clothespin holder on top of it, as she rested it on her hip. She smiled at him, acknowledging his presence, ready to walk back up to the house again.

Glen quickly snapped to, springing to his feet, advancing in Ellen's direction. "Let me help you with that."

"That's quite alright, Glen. As I told you earlier, I do this every day," she said matter-of-factly.

Glen's hands came forward, brushing over Ellen's softly, grabbing the basket along with her. Ellen glanced down at the basket and then back up at Glen. Her emotions held a torrent of confusion as she tried to read Glen's thoughts. They were so close…shoes touching.

"I insist…" Glen answered softly, gazing deeply into Ellen's emerald green eyes, locking his sky-blue ones with hers.

She stood mesmerized, realizing she was only inches away from Glen's bare chest. She couldn't release her grasp on the basket, as much as she wanted to. The erotic force was too intense between them, pulling her deeper into its spell. Glen felt his restraint slipping as his fingers touched the tips of Ellen's. He closed his eyes and took a long deep breath while trying to regain some control, realizing his will was no longer his own. When his eyes opened again, he was surprised to discover Ellen quietly staring at him, almost like she was studying is face.

An immediate ravenous look crossed Glen's face that would not be appeased by any amount of deep breathing. Ellen's heart thundered in her chest not having the ability to tell Glen to stop. Nothing would be the same after this for either one of them.

Glen slowly bent forward, gently kissing Ellen on the lips. He just knew this would be a moment that he would cherish forever. They lingered together, touching ever so briefly, memorizing the feel of flesh on flesh.

Glen drew back in alarm, suddenly aware of the potential mistake he had just made. "Aah…Ellen... I'm so sorry about that. You just look so damn pretty, that I couldn't help myself," he grinned sheepishly.

"It's ok, Glen," Ellen replied with a gently reassuring smile. Longing was in both of their faces as they tried to regain their composure, even though they felt awkward for what they had just done. Ellen relented her hold on the basket, and stepped back from Glen. They walked side by side up to the house, not knowing what to say to the other. Cuddles was on the porch, stretched out on his back, looking quite comfortable. "Are you hot, baby?"

Yes I am, Glen thought, knowing her comments were being directed towards the cat, and not to him.

Ellen addressed Cuddles in baby talk, the way a mother speaks to her young child, while she petted the fluffy white of his stomach. Cuddles meowed weakly, squinting with half-open eyes;

not sure he liked the disruption from his nap. Ellen's soft and sensitive side was showing again, the one that Glen was attracted and drawn to.

"Do you think he will let me pet him?" Glen asked with a smile, still holding the laundry basket. "I had a couple cats in Virginia that I had to leave behind, and I guess I kinda miss them."

Ellen looked up at Glen, while she scratched Cuddles head. "He loves the attention. Pet away," she announced with a pleased smile, while rising and taking the laundry basket back from Glen. "I still have some lemonade left. Could I interest you in a glass?"

"Sounds good to me, but I had hoped to get in a few more hours work before the day was up, so maybe I should take it with me."

"It's hot. A few more minutes to rejuvenate out of the sun, while hanging out with Cuddles, won't make that much of a difference, will it Glen?" Ellen asked with a hint of the same baby tone she used on the cat.

"I guess you're right," Glen conceded, having a difficult time saying no to her.

Ellen watched from the kitchen window, as she poured lemonade over the two glasses of ice. Cuddles seemed to be immensely enjoying the attention Glen was giving him, as he scratched the top of his head and under his chin. Ellen smiled warmly remembering the kiss that was still scorching in her mind, as she returned to the porch.

Ellen handed Glen a glass of the refreshing citrus-filled beverage. "Here we go. It's the last of the pitcher."

"Thanks."

Ellen proceeded to the porch swing, stretching out the full length of it, with her knees slightly drawn up, sipping from her own glass. Glen glanced over in her direction, noticing her long shapely legs and the soft sway of the swing, as Ellen rested her head on a pillow with her eyes closed.

"You look content,"

"Hmmm. I am," she answered, while opening her eyes and looking at Glen with a smile. "I just love being out here on this swing sipping an iced tea or lemonade. It really is heaven on earth to me!"

Glen had to agree. At the moment, it did seem like heaven on earth, just being there with Ellen and Cuddles.

Glen kept busy the rest of the day, finishing the first coat of paint on the barn's trim, and setting up a water sprinkler over the garden. He hoped the rain would come in a few days since the young plants really needed it. The paintbrushes and rollers had been cleaned and set neatly in a row on a shelf in the barn, and he unplugged the boom box, placing it also in the barn along with the other supplies. Glen could smell dinner in the air again, as he was finishing up, ready to go home.

Ellen's heart skipped a beat as she heard the anticipated knock.

"Just wanted to let you know I'm done for the day," he shared with a pleasant smile, looking a little weary, but as handsome as ever.

"Alright…"

"I guess I'll see you tomorrow, Ellen," he replied ineptly, not sure what to do or say next.

"Glen…would you like to come in for awhile? I made a baked chicken with vegetables for dinner. There is plenty, and you are welcome to join me." Ellen was surprised by her forwardness. It was not in her character, but she enjoyed Glen's company, and she didn't want him to leave yet.

"I should get going. It's been a long day, and I need a hot bath and need to go to bed early."

Ellen felt hurt. Maybe the kiss didn't have the impact on Glen that it did on her. Had she misread the earlier look of passion she thought she saw in his eyes?

"Ellen, you are sweet to offer," Glen answered with a fatigued smile, lightly squeezing her hand that rested on the screen door. "I'm just more tired than hungry. Could I have a rain check some time soon?"

"Sure, Glen," Ellen responded disconcertingly, feeling her confidence suddenly shaken. She was having her doubts once again about Glen, and wasn't sure if he was being upfront with her.

Driving home, Glen reviewed the week since meeting this woman. *Ellen Harper has one heck of a multi-faceted personality* he thought. *She seems to do 180's from spitfire to gentle lamb.* He never imagined anything more than animosity existing between them, but now he was beginning to feel the growing pangs of desire.

"It has to be lust and nothing else. Women cause me nothing but pain!" Glen contemplated aloud, while clutching the steering wheel a little more firmly. "This definitely will never work out, especially with the history between Eric and Ellen. I think she's attracted to me. Certainly, she wouldn't offer me drinks, meals and say a kiss was ok if something wasn't mutually happening between us," Glen continued in frustration as he drummed on his dash.

He had seen Ellen staring at him on numerous occasions, not to say that he hadn't done his share of staring back. Ellen was one hell of a fine looking woman, at least in his eyes. Glen continued to consider the whole mess, as he pulled into the local hamburger joint. He was maneuvering through the drive-up window's obstacle course, trying hard not to scratch the paint job on Eric's car.

"They never make these things wide enough," he muttered to himself.

"May I help you, sir?"

"Double cheese burger, large fries, and a large Coke."

"Anything else?"

"Couple extra napkins would be nice." *And maybe some words of wisdom about a lady who has my mind messed up*, he thought as he pulled up to the window to receive his food.

Glen ate his food on his way back to Eric's, and took the long way home. He could smell the scent of roses in the air. This situation with Ellen he wanted to give more consideration to, and there was no sense in getting home too early. Eric had said he probably wouldn't be home before late, but just in case he was there, Glen decided to stay away awhile longer.

"Ellen, Ellen… what should I do about us?" he continued to speak aloud in frustration. "Maybe the direct approach is best.

Tell her I don't want Eric to be standing in the way of us taking our relationship to a more serious level. But maybe she won't be ready for that, and I am reading her wrong. What if she is waiting for me to say something? Damnit, this is stupid!" he said, while stuffing his wadded-up papers that had been wrapped around the fast food, away in the bag that it came in. "Tomorrow night after work, I am going to talk to her!" Glen had made up his mind. He had nothing to lose, and everything to gain. He knew Ellen wasn't Samantha, and it was time to give love a chance again.

Eric got home late, just as Glen assumed he would. It was too bad that he wasn't better at guessing the outcome of things as precisely as Eric seemed to be. Glen could hear the slamming of car doors and sensual laughter that hinted of a recent intimate encounter.

Eric complemented Melinda, as if the two were models in a magazine. Melinda was dressed in a pale green two-piece suit, with matching pearl earrings and necklace. Her hair was cropped short and neat around her face, and her long slender legs framed the business attire off perfectly. Eric was in a pinstriped tan and cream suit with a silk tie displaying a rhapsody of spring colors, and his brown Italian loafers finished off his well-groomed look.

"He held her close as he asked, "Pick me up at 7:30?"

"I'll be here," she whispered in his ear.

"You better be," Eric answered with a sultry response, planting a kiss at the hollow of her neck, making her giggle.

It was awhile before Eric walked into the house. Glen pretended to be asleep on the couch. He felt guilty eavesdropping, but he couldn't help but wish it were he and Ellen sharing a tête-à-tête on the front porch instead.

"Glen, you home?" Eric beckoned, as he entered into the darkness of the house.

"Huh?" Glen responded, trying to act the part.

"Sorry to wake you. I didn't think you'd be asleep yet," Eric said while grabbing a chair and taking his suit jacket off.

"It's been a long day."

"Tell me you aren't still hanging in there with that bitch!"

Glen sat up on the couch, rubbing his hand over his face in frustration. "Eric, seriously, stop talking about Ellen that way. She really has been pretty nice to me, once we got through the first few days."

"What's going on with you, Glen?"

"What do you mean what's going on with me?" he said defensively, sitting up.

"I mean you did this lady one hell of a favor this week. There has to be another reason why you are hanging around, unless you have became a priest or something while you were in Virginia," Eric said with a laugh.

Glen shook his head and snickered. "No, that i*sn't* the case. And since you won't let this thing die, I'll tell you what's happening. I like Ellen. I want it to be more, but I'm not sure about her feelings. Matter-of-face, I kissed her today."

"You did what?" Eric responded in disbelief.

"You heard me right. I said, I kissed her. I don't know what the big deal is. I think you did your fair share of kissing today also, big brother," Glen prodded teasingly.

Eric laughed. "How would you know that?" he said with dawning awareness, while getting back up from the chair, and then settling down again on the sofa by Glen. "Unless you were snooping on Melinda and I," Eric accused, grabbing Glen in the familiar headlock. He started laughing, allowing his brother to play the game. "Spying out the windows, when I though you were asleep. Boy, I guess you are more desperate for pussy than I realized," Eric teased.

"I wasn't asleep, but I wasn't spying out the windows either," Glen interjected defensively, throwing Eric playfully to the rug. "You two were just so damn loud that I, as well as your whole neighborhood, probably heard every word you said."

"You're just jealous. How long has it been since you'd *had pussy*, Glen?"

"I'd be careful if I were you, Eric. When your girlfriend finally meets me, she won't even remember your name."

"You think so, huh?"

"I know so!"

The wrestling went on for several minutes - the thing that brings brothers together of all ages, hand to hand contact and conquering. Breathing heavily, while lying back on the rug, propped up only by their elbows with Eric's disheveled tie now thrown over one shoulder, Glen was the first to speak.

"So her name is Melinda?"

"Yeah, Melinda Philips."

"Is that who has been taking you to work all week?"

"She has, and since you opened up and spilled your guts about Ellen, I guess I'll tell you about Melinda, although I don't usually kiss and tell," Eric confessed while pushing the hair out of his face. "She's my secretary, and I like her a lot. I have known her for a little over a year now. She's intelligent, beautiful, and makes me laugh… and for some strange reason, I look forward to seeing her everyday."

"You find that to be strange?" Glen asked looking at his brother.

"Brother, I can see it's been a long time since we were in high school. I try to stay as unattached as possible. My love is my work, and most of the time I prefer it that way. Women never seem to compare to the thrill that my career gives me, that was, up until now."

Glen continued to listen with interest.

"Melinda shares my vision, and we seem to want the same things. She knows what I want even before I say it, in and out of the office. So I guess, bro, you and I want the same thing – a more serious relationship with a lady."

"I guess so, but I think you're father along in your pursuit than I am."

Eric finished with reluctant words of wisdom. "Give it time…. I can't see it between you and Ellen, but if it's meant to be, it will be."

Melinda softly tapped on the door at 7:30 a.m. sharp. She

didn't ring the bell, since she remembered Eric saying his brother was staying with him. If Glen was still sleeping she didn't want to wake him.

"Hi," Eric greeted with a big grin and a quick kiss. "Come in. I just have to get my briefcase."

It was the first time Melinda had been invited into Eric's house. She noticed the *male* furnishings and dirty dishes still sitting on the coffee table. The overwhelming desire of straightening the room crossed her mind, along with a pleasant thought that maybe one day she would live there with Eric. It was just a far-fetched dream, but one that made her feel good inside.

"I hope I didn't wake your brother," Melinda whispered to Eric, trying to keep her voice low.

"Glen? Heavens no. He's been out of here since 5:15."

"Why so early?" Melinda inquired.

"He's working out at Ellen Harper's farm. He's helping her with the spring planting and whatever else she needs done around the place."

"That surprises me, I thought there were problems between…."

"You'd heard the rumors, I take it," Eric revealed with a smug look on his face, that spoke of nothing getting past him.

Melinda felt embarrassed. "I'm sorry, Eric. You know how the gossip flies around the office."

"Unfortunately, yes, I do; but Glen seems to be overcoming any obstacles Ellen may have had with me."

Eric set his briefcase down, reclaiming Melinda in his

arms, giving her a questioning sensual smile. "And tell me, my sweet, what is the office saying about you and I?"

Her arms came lovingly up around Eric's neck. "They tease me."

"The tease you *about what*?" Eric asked, while rubbing her back in pleasurable little circles along her spine.

"About us arriving and leaving together."

"*And?*" he asked, nibbling on her ear.

"And… us having lunch together," she answered, now feeling breathless.

"*Anything else?*" he whispered, coming up for air.

"The way we talk quietly at my desk, and about what we do beyond the closed door of your office."

"*All that, huh?*" Eric teased with an amused laugh. "Maybe we should send out an office memo detailing all that we do, especially the details of yesterday!"

"Eric!" Melinda scolded playfully. "That's all I would need circulated in that *Peyton Place*!"

Eric raised Melinda's chin to his lips, looking directly into her eyes. "You were wonderful last night," he praised in a sincere virile way.

"No more wonderful than you were," Melinda replied contently, remembering the perfection of the evening that they had just shared.

Eric was the first to regain his composure, after a series of intimate kisses that left them both weak with desire. "We better get going. Peter will be waiting on me, wanting to hear all the details of the Viswell deal."

"I can hardly wait to hear what his reaction will be."

"We did it together, Melinda," he said earnestly as he held her in his arms. "I couldn't have done everything that needed to be done without your help. Thank you," he breathed gratefully, giving her one last kiss.

"You're welcome," she answered, feeling deliriously in love, although she hadn't actually confessed those words of affection yet to Eric. There would be plenty of time for that….

Chapter Thirteen

Glen noticed the air was cooler and less humid, as he drove out to Ellen's. The sun's intensity had left him feeling drained the day previous. He hoped the coolness would last or at least some cloud cover would occur as the heat of the day set in. Giving up the Mustang was going to be tough once Eric wanted it back. He liked the way it handled, and also the feel of the wind blowing through his hair when the top was down. Today, he would work on the broken windows, the painting of the trim surrounding them, and the barn doors. He planned to work on the lane the following day, if he got the chance. There was so much he wanted to do around the place.

The lights were off in Ellen's house, as he expected them to be. The image of Ellen lying in her bad asleep in a white eyelet lace gown, with Cuddles curled up at the foot of the bed, tormented his thoughts again. He didn't know why he thought it would be white eyelet lace, but somehow the femininity of it seemed to suit her. She probably still slept to one side of the bed, out of a habit ingrained from having to share a bed with Jack for so many years. How he longed to see if it were true, and join her in that safe haven. Any actual intention of a move so bold would surely bring about the demise of his job; so he would keep his acceptable distance.

Ellen awoke to the sensation of something tickling her nose. "Cuddles, let me sleep!" she begged. As soon as she drifted back to sleep the irritant was at her again. "Cuddles stop!" Ellen sat up realizing it wasn't Cuddles, but a pesky fly that had gotten in to her room. "Sorry Cuddles, I didn't mean to snap at you that way," Ellen softly confessed as she petted his soft fur. He squinted his eyes and pulled back his ears, forgiving his mistress for the misunderstanding. He gave her one long meow as he excused himself and jumped from the bed, running from the room at a hurried pace. *Only six a.m....* she thought, staring at the alarm clock. *I wanted to stay in bed until seven, but I might as well get moving now.*

Ellen wasn't sleeping well, and last night was no exception. Glen Cummings was weighing heavily on her mind. She wondered what these romantic feelings were exactly that she was beginning to have for him. She hadn't felt this attracted to a man since Jack. She knew it wasn't wise to pursue, considering the past circumstances with Eric. "Too many complications," she announced aloud as she was making her bed. "And even if I do like him, it's doubtful he would feel the same way."

Glen hadn't seen Ellen outside all morning. *Usually by mid morning she would be out hanging up laundry or at least leaving Cuddles out by now*, he concluded, while glancing up at the house. He hoped she would be sharing a snack under the oak tree again with him. It became apparent to Glen that the oak tree was becoming *their tree*. "If she won't come to me, I guess I will have to go to her," he said in a determined manner, already heading for the house.

"Glen...what can I do for you?" Ellen asked, surprised with the knock on the door, and yet pleased to see him. She was already dressed for the day and had just finished feeding Cuddles.

"I was just wondering if I could use the bathroom."

"Why sure. To be honest, I was wondering why you haven't bothered asking me up until this point."

"I didn't want to inconvenience you."

"And you do now?" she said in a carefree jesting manner.

Glen was caught off-guard, knowing he had made an excuse just to see her, and now he felt somewhat foolish making the attempt. "Well, it's just…it's just so hot. I guess a break from the heat is really what I needed."

Ellen smiled broadly. "Why didn't you just say so?"

Glen had enough with her pretenses, and he needed the cards out on the table. "Ellen this is foolishness. We have been playing a game with each other since we met, and I can't go on without telling you how I feel. The truth is…. I came up here to see you because….damnit… I've been looking for you all morning, hoping you would come to me, and that didn't happen. So here I am. I think we need to sit down and talk."

Glen's words came out in a hurried apprehensive tumble. Ellen was shocked, and her expression changed from one of teasing to utter amazement and disbelief. She had only dreamt of Glen coming to her in this fashion, but never did she really believe that it would become a reality so soon.

"Well, aren't you going to say something?" Glen asked, concerned by her reaction.

"The living room is in there," Ellen replied, pointing in the direction, but still in a daze. "I'll be with you in a minute. I have to leave Cuddles outside."

Glen realized that as he entered the room, he had only been in the foyer and kitchen of Ellen's home. It had the feel of an interior decorator once being in its midst. The room was filled with country charm. Several overstuffed sofas and chairs were grouped in a cozy setting, with many coordinating pillows placed strategically on each piece in patterns of blues, creams and rose-colored plaids and floral prints. A fine wall covering of cream and blue stripes brought all the other busy patterns together in a calming fashion. There was a matching braided multi-colored rug over the wide-plank pine floor, with complimenting swags above each wide-silled window. A massive stone fireplace graced one of the walls. Several pictures that he assumed were of relatives and friends were on the mantel above it.

On the adjoining wall was a gilded-framed picture of a bride and groom in wedding attire. Glen moved closer to study the picture. He realized it was Ellen and Jack. She looked happy and beautiful. A glow surrounded her face, and a thrill of excitement was in her eyes. He guessed she anticipated the joy of her future – husband, home and family; but never the jolt of pain of the loss that would lie ahead, erasing all hope for a future with Jack.

Ellen noticed Glen staring at the wedding portrait, as she joined him. He looked at her awkwardly. "It's ok…" she said touching his arm to stop him from moving. They stood side by side gazing at it astutely. "That's Jack and I on our wedding day. We would have been married eight years next month."

"I'm sorry, Ellen," Glen said with sincere heartfelt sympathy in his voice, as he turned to face her. She turned and faced him also, not needing any encouragement.

"Thanks for caring, Glen. It hasn't been easy for me," she added with emotion in her voice.

"I can only imagine…" he replied, being at a loss at what else to say.

"I'm sure Eric told you all the details, hasn't he?"

"Yes… we talked."

"Sometime I will sit down and tell you the whole story, but *not* today. I don't really feel up to talking about it right now." Her voice was quivering with each word.

Glen thought for sure she was going to break down and cry, and he wasn't sure how he would handle it if it happened. "Whenever you want to talk about it, let me know. I promise I'll be there to listen," Glen answered softly as he turned to her, bringing his hands up to Ellen's upper arms, almost for a means of support for his words.

His touch was foreign to her, and she slightly jumped at the contact, looking at her wedding picture and then back at Glen feeling guilty.

"I care about you Ellen, he said with a sincere effort while holding her still. I want to have a relationship with you beyond the time I spend working on the farm. This week of getting to know you, talking under the oak tree, seeing your reaction and your praise for my work and what I am accomplishing here, is attracting me to you. Most of all, you are beautiful, Ellen." Her eyes were filled with newfound understanding. "I have a hard time concentrating whenever your approach me, or even when you are away from me anymore, for that matter."

Ellen's heart was racing wildly, as Glen grabbed her arms a little too closely to her breasts. She could feel the slight contact between the tops of his fingers and the sides of her breasts. She wanted him too, and she prayed she wasn't dreaming.

"Glen…I'm attracted to you too. I really didn't want it to be so, but it is happening, and I'm not sure what to do about my feelings," Ellen admitted, lowering her head with the confession. She felt uncomfortable talking so intimately in front of her wedding picture.

Glen was quick to respond by raising her chin, reclaiming the eye contact he wanted to have with her. "I'll tell you what we're going to do about it. We are going to thank God that we have found each other and stop denying our feelings!" Glen said boldly while lowering his mouth to Ellen's.

She melted in response with slightly parted lips. Not like the first time, when Glen took her by surprise, but ready and receptive to his advances. Glen encircles her in his arms, and her arms wrapped around his neck in kind. They felt strong and protective, and she liked that. His scent was one of hard working male, but not to the point of being offensive. She could tell he had cleaned himself at the well pump again, before he knocked on the door. She loved his cleanliness, and he never looked unkempt.

Glen's lips were magic to Ellen, full and passionate against her own, intense in their desire yet gently exploring, tempting to beckon her beyond the first shy contact. His tongue entered her mouth, memorizing the feel of her gums, teeth, inner recesses of her cheeks, and finally her own tongue. They played the lover's game, suddenly eager to please the other in mutual sexual response.

Retreating to one of the sofas, they were lost in each other's arms, not remembering or caring how they got there. Ellen's breath caught, hardly believing the exquisiteness and freedom of Glen's touch. No longer did he hold back in his emotions, as he rubbed her arms, and caressed her breasts through the cotton t-shirt that she wore. Her nipples hardened at his persistent touch, making Ellen moan with desire.

"Oh, Ellen…you are so beautiful. I just can't get enough of you," Glen beckoned, already hard with desire.

Ellen was barely able to respond, lost in ecstasy. "I never…thought…. this would happen between us…. even though I wanted it."

"It's happening, darling…. believe it now," he answered raggedly, continuing to lower his touch to the center core of her desire. The feel of his hand rubbing between her legs, even with her jeans still on, was lighting a fire in Ellen she had not felt in a very long time.

Glen began to unzip Ellen's jeans and she was too weak to resist. She responded in like fashion, wanting only to touch Glen as he was touching her; tired of fighting her pent-up desires and needing release. Her caresses began to be equally as bold, as she reached into his briefs grasping his manhood.

"Oh Ellen, that feels so good…don't stop," Glen groaned.

"Glen, please hurry, I can't wait any longer," was Ellen's throaty request as their clothes fell quickly to the floor in front of the couch.

Ellen was transfixed by the site of Glen standing totally nude in front of her, extending his hand for her to come into his embrace. He was a bronzed god, sleek and hard from his constant laborious routine, with slim hips and a well-endowed male organ.

And the site of her was totally woman – full perfect breasts, soft curving hips, and shapely legs. Her auburn hair fell in soft waves down her back, with her lips and checks slightly red with desire from being over-kissed. Glen only wanted to touch her as she happily rose to his waiting arms, walking side by side to Ellen's bedroom.

Cuddles scurried off of the bed, as Glen and Ellen fell entangled into the awaiting softness. Glen rolled on top of Ellen with one sleek move, his mouth coming down over one hard-extended nipple, sucking and nipping, while rubbing the other. Ellen in turn stroked Glen's chest, causing the same stimulating reaction in him. Their caresses became equally as confident, as they massaged back and buttocks, exploring and stimulating for the first time without fear.

"Ellen, you make me mad with desire," he breathed lovingly, as he parted her legs rubbing his swollen shaft against her.

"Oh please, Glen. I want you so badly!" Ellen begged, guiding Glen's stiffness into her opening.

"I want you too, baby," he gasped, hardly able to speak as he entered Ellen, filling her completely with every inch of his penis. For several moments, they lay entirely still. Ellen adjusting to the size of Glen's largeness, and Glen relishing in the feeling of being total sheathed in her. There was a sense of newness in it for Ellen, different from Jack, as if she was experiencing a man for the very first time.

"Are you alright?" Glena asked, sensing a lapse in their passion.

"I couldn't be better," she replied as she smiled into his eyes, moving against him, beginning the "age-old rhythm".

Their bodies moved as one, as if they were made for each other – hand in glove, machinery finely tuned. Glen plunged and retreated repeatedly as his hand massaged and caressed her intimately. Ellen was hot with desire as her longing escalated, begging to be fulfilled. When she felt she could not take any more of the torment inside of her, an explosion ignited her being in a demanding climax that made her shout out Glen's name loudly in response. Only then, did he give way to his own shattering release of finality; leaving them both breathless as they lay in each other's embrace.

Glen tenderly smoothed the hair away from Ellen's face. "You were so wonderful," he said sweetly, while planting small kisses along her cheeks and eyelids.

"Hmmm, I can never begin to tell you how wonderful you were. I only thought those things happened in romance novels."

"*You did?*" he chuckled, resting his chin between her breasts. "Well today we are making the novel," he grinned, bringing his hand back up to her breast, suddenly wanting to start where they just left off.

"Can chapter two begin after I finish my day's work, your humble-hired servant inquires?"

Ellen giggled. "Only if thoust will join me for a candlelight dinner in my humble abode at 8 p.m.?"

"That, I will accept most graciously, my sweet," Glen replied with a cocky grin, while kissing the top of her hand. "Now, about that bathroom."

"Oh yes. Of course"

"I guess I really do need to use it now," Glen smiled, while kissing Ellen on the lips.

"First door on the right. There are towels and washcloths in the closet, if you need them," Ellen informed, suddenly feeling shy again, even after being as close as two human beings could be moments earlier.

Glen bound from the bed nude, retreating to the living room for his clothes. He peaked around the bedroom doorframe, while standing in the hall. "You just gave me an idea," he said with a wicked grin. "Why don't we get a bath together?"

Ellen giggled, still lying in her bed under the concealment of the sheet. "How about tonight?" she beamed, feeling deliciously blissful and content as she looked at Glen.

"Before or after dinner?" he teased, liking the idea more and more.

"Your choice…surprise me," she said in a sultry voice, suddenly feeling as alive and happy as on her wedding picture.

Glen was no less radiant than Ellen was. To feel renewed again, with a woman in his arms, after so many months of being alone. His workday spun by at a fast pace, with Ellen constantly on his mind. The sandwich he had packed was eaten with one hand, as he continued to paint with the other. Even after their newly discovered intimacy they had just shared, Glen didn't want Ellen to think he wasn't living up to the deal that he had made with her. Nothing had changed with him concerning that.

Ellen was equally as high-spirited throughout her day. She

dusted and vacuumed before lunch, and changed her bed sheets to a sunny floral pattern of yellows, blues and greens. When the housework was all completed, she began her planning and preparation for the evening meal. It took her over an hour just to decide what to make Glen to eat. She considered barbecue chicken with fresh asparagus, or an oriental stir-fry, but ended her search when she came across an old favorite of her mother's – Beef Wellington. The asparagus would compliment it nicely, along with a Caesar salad and strawberry tart for desert. That, along with a special bottle of wine that Meg had given her last year for Christmas, would round off the menu.

They would eat in the dining room tonight instead of the kitchen. She wanted the mood to be just right. Ellen sat the table with her best linen tablecloth, wedding pattern china and crystal. Waterford candlesticks from her Aunt Nina, along with some Irises she had cut from the side of the house, completed the look.

Several times during the day she had caught a glimpse of Glen, but only waved and smiled at him. They both kept their distances, as if to add to the anticipated excitement of the reunion that the evening would unfold.

It was five o'clock and dinner was in the final stages of preparation. After having a cup of hot tea, Ellen decided it was her time just to relax and pamper herself until Glen was finished working. She soaked in a tub full of bubbles, and gave herself a manicure and pedicure. Her hairstyle and dress were chosen just as carefully as everything else had been for their "perfect" evening. She considered a French twist or braid, but ended up setting her hair on hot rollers, for a sexy, loose-flowing look. The dress was an aqua-colored slip style, with spaghetti straps and a sweetheart low-cut neckline that softly shaped and accentuated her bust line.

Ellen twirled around, while holding a hand mirror, taking in her entire appearance in the larger bathroom wall mirror. She only approved of her look once she chose matching cream-colored heels and aquamarine earrings that were her birthstones. She finished with several sprays of her favorite perfume, applying it to strategically to well-appointed areas of her body. She smiled back at her reflection, hoping Glen would be as pleased with the results as she was.

Ellen started pacing the floor at 7:45 p.m. The Beef Wellington and asparagus were cooked to perfection. She knew that by eight the asparagus would be soggy, since she had started it too early. Her only hope was to submerse it in ice water, re-heating it quickly right before serving. At 7:50 she lit the candles on the dining room table, and put the wine in a beautiful antique, silver ice bucket. At 7:55 she became quite impatient with the wait, resorting to peaking out from behind the kitchen curtains.

Glen was at the well pump cleaning up, and then he made his way to Eric's Mustang. The back seat held a clean t-shirt that Glen changed into. Ellen smiled as she watched him searching for a comb in the glove box. Once he found it, he meticulously combed his hair back in place, as he evaluated his appearance in the rearview mirror. It pleased her that he apparently wanted to look presentable, beyond the normal finger combing of his blonde locks. He took the steps two at a time, tapping lightly on the door that Ellen was more than anxious to open.

"Hi Ellen…Wow…do you look great!" he said with a pleased, wide-tooth grin as he took her in from head to toe.

"Thank you," she said graciously, casting him a warm smile, still giddy over the mid-day love making session they had just shared. "Come in. Dinner will be ready in a few minutes. All I need to do is a few last minute touches."

"Something sure does smell wonderful," Glen said while sniffing the air. "Is it you or dinner? Or both?" he teased, with a handsome smile.

"You decide," she challenged flirtatiously, as she went to the stove ready to turn the asparagus back on.

"There's no doubt it's you," he whispered from behind her, as he wrapped his arms around her waist. He nuzzled her neck, planting ticklish kisses behind her one ear. She turned in his arms wrapping her arms around his neck.

"Glen, I'll never get dinner on the table if we continue like this," she said gently.

"Would that be so bad?"

"No…. but I have been busy all afternoon trying to make you a nice meal," she smiled.

"You're right. I'll stop and behave myself," he winked. "That is, at least until dinner is over."

Ellen giggled as she stared at his handsome face. "Could I interest you in something cold to drink before dinner?"

"Iced tea would be great, if you have it."

"I just made a pitcher," Ellen answered as she served Glen the iced tea along with cheese dip and crackers.

Glen rubbed her arm as he drank heartily of the tea. She was still having a difficult time adjusting to this new level of intimacy and permissiveness between them. Even though she wanted it also, from almost the minute she first laid eyes on him, the newness of it would take some getting used to. She still felt somehow like she was cheating on Jack, or at least that he would be disappointed in her for being with the brother of the very man who ruined their future and lives together!

The anticipation of what was to follow after dinner was heavy in the air. Maybe it was too soon, Glen thought as they shared small talk and drank iced tea and ate the appetizer.

"I got to say something, Ellen."

"What's that?" Ellen questioned, finding it hard to answer with her mouth full of crackers.

Glen grinned, finding her irresistible. She looked like a little girl caught with her hand in the cookie jar, and yet an alluring woman all wrapped up in one package. He studied her with pleasure as he leaned forward with his hands crossed on the table in front of him.

"You told me to make the call about a bath. To be honest…I fantasized all day abut us getting one right after dinner, but you look too nice to be getting yourself wet."

Ellen returned the grin. "I could wash your back for you if you would like."

"I would love that," Glen said, while reaching across the table for Ellen's hand again. "What we just shared earlier was so perfect. I could hardly wait to see you again tonight."

"I kept feeling the same way all day," she admitted.

"I'm glad, Ellen. I want you to know that I don't want to rush things, and make you feel uncomfortable," Glen conveyed sincerely, kissing Ellen's hand reassuringly. "If I'm going too fast, just say so."

"No Glen, everything is fine. I … just haven't been with

anyone since Jack, and it takes time to adjust to a man again in my life …after being alone as I have been."

"Sweet Ellen," Glen continued, "I know I can't replace Jack and I wouldn't even try, but I do hope that we can continue to see where things go with us."

"One day at a time, Glen. That is how we will have to take things for now."

Ellen rose from the table bringing her hands to her hips. "Enough with the serious conversation! Dinner is ready if you are."

"I'm hungry and ready," he growled out playfully. "What can I help you with?"

"Not a thing, except maybe you could take the cork out of the wine bottle?"

The meal went off without a hitch. Glen was impressed with Ellen's ability to cook and serve a gourmet meal. It reminded him of the dinners his mother would prepare from time to time when special guests would come to visit. Samantha, on the other hand, always threw things together in a hurried manner, never taking the time to cook anything substantial and please Glen. Usually, it was hamburgers or hotdogs. Her kids were whom she chose to please.

"How about desert on the porch? The weatherman predicts pleasant temperatures the rest of the evening, and I thought it would be nice to sit outside."

"That sounds great!" Glen agreed with a smile, as he tried

to help her clear the dishes from the dining room table.

"Would you like coffee or more wine? I think there is some left in the bottle."

"Coffee would be nice, but I may take you up on the wine later," Glen replied as he stacked the dishes.

Ellen went to the refrigerator, and took out a crystal pedestal stand that displayed a luscious pastry, placing it on the counter, right in front of Glen. His eyes danced in pleasant surprise.

"I hope you saved room for desert. I made this strawberry tart today just for you."

"Mmmm…. Strawberry tart, how did you know that was my favorite?" he teased.

"I guess I'm a good guesser," she answered with a coy look, reaching for two plates and a knife.

The porch and night air were just as promised – cozy and pleasantly warm, without the sticky, hot humidity of earlier that day. Cuddles was enjoying his evening meal outdoors while Ellen and Glen sat together on the porch swing listening to the crickets chirping.

"I see what you mean about this swing. I could fall asleep out here."

"You better not," Ellen replied playfully, poking Glen in the ribs as she bent over to put her empty coffee cup on the porch floor.

Glen wrapped his arms around Ellen's waist, bringing her

back upright to hold in his embrace. "I didn't say I was going to now. I just meant…"

"I know what you meant," she giggled, resting her head on his shoulder. They sat quietly, without a word between them for several minutes, just listening to the night sounds and swaying to the slight movement of the swing.

"Hmmm…this is sooo nice," Glen whispered into Ellen's hair. "You smell so sweet and clean like a field of wild flowers."

Ellen felt hot again and lost in Glen's picturesque words. Memories of earlier and the time they spent together re-sparked the flames of desire for them both now. She turned to face his waiting lips that were warm and passionate in their intent. He kissed her fully and completely on the mouth, trailing smaller kisses along the side of her cheek and eyelid before stopping. They both sighed, holding each other closely, feeling totally content.

"How about that wine now?" Glen questioned huskily, staring deeply into Ellen's green eyes. The aqua marine earrings she wore complimented the shade of her eyes, somewhat lighter, but with the same intensity.

"I think I can manage that," Ellen answered, not really wanting to move from the comfortable position she was in. She reluctantly got up as Glen continued to hold and kiss the top of her hand. "You will have to let me go first…though."

"All right, but not for long…" Glen promised in a seductive voice, kissing the inside of her hand and touching it right in its center with his tongue, before releasing it. Her breath caught, somewhere in her throat, as she felt the intimate gesture that he bestowed.

Ellen found two clean wine glasses in the cupboard, and poured the bottle's remaining contents into each of them. Already she felt tipsy from the one glass that she had with dinner. Wine had the tendency to sedate her, and make her fall asleep. She would have to nurse the drink slowly if she didn't want to ruin the mood of the evening. On second thought, Ellen poured some of hers into Glen's glass, leaving her with only half of the problem to deal with.

"Here we go," she offered, extending a glass in Glen's direction. "Sorry it took so long, but I had to find some clean glasses."

"You didn't take very much," Glen observed, taking in the amount in each glass.

"I'm not a big drinker. This is plenty," she commented, as she found her place again beside of Glen on the swing.

"I don't drink much myself, at least since high school. One too many hangovers, made me wiser to the evils of the stuff," Glen confessed with a slight smile, as he took a sip of the contents. "I still like it though, from time to time. I just try to be more sensible now."

"That's how I feel also. Two drinks is my limit. Anymore than that, and I'm not responsible for my actions."

"Well in that case, maybe we should open another bottle," Glen teased, wrapping his free arm back around Ellen's shoulder.

"No, we shouldn't!" Ellen remarked adamantly, unless you want to help me to the bathroom in a few hours!"

"It can't be that bad?"

"Oh yes it is. Just take my word for it. You don't want to

see me in that condition!"

The night air was starting to cool down when Ellen and Glen decided to go back inside. They cleaned up the kitchen together, loading the dishes in the dishwasher and wiping down the counters, even though Ellen protested that Glen was her guest and that she could manage on her own.

"The meal and everything was great," Glen complimented again, as they sat in the living room paging through an old family photo album from Ellen's childhood.

"I can't remember how long it has been since I've had such a good meal."

"Thank you, Glen. It really was no big deal."

"Maybe not to you, but bachelors don't usually take the time or even know how to cook that well."

"What do you usually eat?" she inquired, sincere in wanting to know the answer.

"Oh, the usual…the normal single working guy menu – fast food, a frozen microwave dinner, or a sandwich. I can cook some, but I'm just too tired most of the time to do so. When I get home in the evening, I avoid making anything that involves a lot of work on my part."

"Albright's is a good place to eat when you want that simple country diner, homemade taste."

"I'll remember that, when I want to splurge," he chuckled. He already knew the spot, but he wanted to make Ellen feel she had offered a helpful suggestion. Eric frequented the place quite often. It was cheap and met his needs for a quick meal.

Ellen was flipping pages as they were talking, explaining every aunt, uncle, cousin and vacation she had been on; when Glen intentionally took the photo album out of her hands and laid it on the walnut coffee table in front of them. “I’m interested Ellen, but more interested in you at the moment,” he whispered, while kissing the side of her neck. “I would still love a bath, and I haven’t forgotten that you promised to wash my back,” he grinned playfully.

“I remembered too,” Ellen giggled, starting for the bathroom. She turned on the water and laid out a towel and washcloth, while Glen looked on. *She truly is beautiful*, he thought, as he watched her lovingly preparing his bath. His thoughts continued, as he considered the work clothes Ellen always saw him in - blue jeans and a shirt, unlike the formality of a dress like she was wearing tonight. He wanted to show her that side of him too. *An evening out was in order soon*, he decided.

Ellen turned and caught Glen staring, as he leaned against the doorframe with his arms crossed in front of him. “What?” she questioned with a smile.

“I can’t get enough of watching you.”

“Glen…” she said shyly, “Will I ever tire of your compliments?”

“I hope not,” he grinned, “Because there’s plenty more where that came from.”

“I think you can take over from here. Call me when you want your back washed,” she instructed, brushing past him with a quick kiss. “I’ll be in the kitchen unloading the dishwasher.”

Glen soaked leisurely for some time in the candle lit room that smelled of coconut. He felt relaxed from dinner and the wine, and just being with Ellen. *I could get used to this routine everyday,* he considered with contented satisfaction, staring at the pastel floral-pattern of the wallpaper. "Ellen sure likes her flowers," he chuckled to himself, dipping his head below the warm water, rinsing the shampoo from his hair. He was clean and ready for Ellen's touch. Already he was becoming hard with the anticipation of what lay ahead. "Ellen, your services are required," Glen beckoned in the same playful manner that they both acted out earlier in the day.

"Coming, me Lord," Ellen chimed back, following Glen's lead. Ellen entered, timidly opening the door as she peaked in.

"Me thinks, me back needs a good scrubbin' with a cloth, me lovely," Glen mimicked, in his best Cockney accent while scooping down in the water, looking for the washcloth.

Ellen could see every virile inch of Glen, as he handed her the wrung out cloth. It made her pulse quicken at the very site of him. His chest and hardened nipples glistened from the water falling in soft rivulets running down his muscular form. His legs were slightly drawn up, partially covering his manhood. She dipped the cloth back in the water, reaching across Glen for the soap. Every hand movement that Ellen made - that of taking the soap and rolling it around and around in the cloth until a frothy lather was made, he observed.

"Can you scoot up some?" she asked sweetly, as Glen honored her request. Ellen sat on the tub, and started rubbing his back first with meek light circular motions and then with bolder and longer, massaging caressing strokes, that left his back red.

"This feels so good, Ellen," he breathed contentedly with his eyes closed. "I think I could stay her forever," he whispered, enjoying the gift immensely.

"Wouldn't the water get cold?" she teased.

"Not if you were here to make me hot like you are now," he beckoned in a raspy voice, reopening his brilliant blue eyes, desiring other things other than to play around at the moment. He grabbed Ellen's hand that still held the washcloth, bringing it possessively down to his groin. "Wash me here, Ellen. I want to feel your hands all over me."

Glen looked at Ellen with passion-filled eyes and pulled her head towards him, claiming her lips in a powerful kiss, as she still held the throbbing shaft in her grasp. Glen's hands came up to Ellen's back finding and unfastening her zipper with one sleek movement. He lowered her straps off her shoulders, before the dress fell to the floor. She wore no bra but only her panties. His hand reached out to touch each extended nipple, tracing a wet path downward to the flame that was already burning between her legs. Glen began to massage her through the layer of thin fabric that was keeping them apart. Ellen finished undressing herself, lost to the rapture of his touch. Glen watched with sensual longing.

"I think I need to be more wet than I already am," Ellen offered with urgency as she stared at Glen. The candlelit room cast a sensual glow that was made for lovers.

Glen smiled. "I'm glad you see it that way," he answered with a sultry voice, rising to help her into the tub and into his waiting arms.

They kissed and caressed, each enjoying the pleasure the other one gave. Glen re-soaped the washcloth, washing Ellen's back and breasts, watching with extreme pleasure the erotic reaction he created in her. Their joining was sweet as Ellen straddled Glen in the soapy silky water of the tub. He suckled each of her nipples, as she cried out in ecstasy, throwing her head back in joy. He joined her in his own release, shuttering and holding her close at its completion.

"I never knew a bath could be so fun," she purred, lying on her side in the water, wrapping her leg around Glen's.

Jack and her were never so frivolous. The bed, and nowhere else, was for sex – usually once a week to satisfy a need. Not that it wasn't good between them, but there was never any room for discovery or spontaneity. She could already tell that Glen was a spirited lover. Her skin tingled with anticipation and excitement, at just the mere thought of what Glen would surprise her with in the future. This was new and exciting - an acquired art, but she was more than willing to learn, as long as Glen was the teacher.

"I guess we should get out and dry off. You're right, the water did get cold," Glen teased, kissing Ellen quickly on the lips. "I'll dry you, if you dry me," he bargained, while pulling her out of the tub, throwing her one of the two towels.

"You got a deal," she grinned, while reaching the towel behind him pulling her hands in opposite directions, try to dry his back, but still standing close. Glen copied her move.

"This is more fun that I imagined it could be," he smiled playfully, grabbing her around the middle tickling her the whole way to the bedroom. They ended up on the floor, in front of the bed, laughing until they cried – a tumble of wet bodies and towels.

They lay nude on their backs, staring at each other, still giggling with the newfound love that they had luckily found.

"I love you, Ellen," Glen whispered honestly and sincerely, as he touched her cheek tenderly

"I love you too, Glen," Ellen repeated, with the same heart-felt openness, not sure how this was possibly going to work out, and not caring for the moment.

It was two a.m. before Glen got home. Eric was already in bed, as Glen assumed that he would be. He was too tired to pack his lunch, as he usually did. He would grab something at The Quik Shopper on his way back out to Ellen's in the morning.

"Thank God, she told me not to be back at the farm until 8 a.m.," he said in relief. "If I keep up this routine, I'll have to stay in bed from utter exhaustion," he grinned with his hands clasped behind his head, as he stared up at the ceiling and fell asleep a contented man.

Chapter Fourteen

Eric was reading the paper at the kitchen table, as Glen entered the room, unable to stop yawning. "You're not at work yet?" Eric remarked in surprise, realizing it was unusual for Glen to still be at home at this hour.

Glen groaned, as he fumbled for the coffee and filters, realizing the coffee pot was empty. "Needed to catch up on some sleep," he muttered.

"Is little brother working as hard after hours as he is during the day at the farm?" Eric pried sarcastically.

Glen turned around, giving Eric a sly and yet tired irritated look. "I don't kiss and tell."

Eric wagged his head side to side in dawning awareness, clucking his tongue, with a gleam of curious fascination in his eyes. "If I were to guess, I would surmise you finally got some action with that viper. What you see in her, I don't have the foggiest…."

"Eric…stop," Glen, insisted, not feeling up to his morning jibes. "Don't mess in my business, and I won't mess in yours. Agreed?"

"Agreed…. Hey, I'm sorry bro. I was only joking."

"I know, but I'm really not up for it this morning."

"Point taken," Eric answered, with a defeated shrug, not wanting to get off the subject so quickly. "By the way, I'm leaving tomorrow evening for Toronto. I'll be gone a week, so as I told you before – use the car."

"I really appreciate that," Glen replied a little more warmly while taking a seat at the table, drinking from the hot steaming mug of freshly brewed coffee.

"You're welcome," Eric responded getting a refill on his cup also.

"I hope I can get a loan in a few weeks for a car of my own."

"What will you do in the meantime for transportation?"

"I guess take a taxi… You know how damn mad it makes me, when I think about this. I *do* have a car somewhere… and Samantha has it. *Now that's a viper, Eric!"*

Eric sighed with understanding. "When I get back to town, I'll take you to see my pal at Newton Motors – Stan Newton. Hopefully, he can give you a fantastic deal. He owes me a favor *big time* on a computer system I sold him a year ago. He got the whole package barely above cost, and in return he was willing to do advertising spots on the local TV and radio stations we came up with. He also put weekly promotions in several area newspapers. They gave credit to CWS for making their business more efficient to them and their customers. You know – joint partnership – Newton Motors and CWS together. And it worked. People came from further distances to buy cars, because Newton *is* very competitive. They doubled their car sales in three months, and the payoff was that it gave us some good leads too! I'll call Stan today and tell him to keep his eye open for something good for you."

"I'd appreciate that! I know it has probably inconvenienced you loaning me the Mustang. That is one fine set of wheels, Eric. I won't forget the favor. It means a lot," Glen acknowledged with sincerity.

"No problem. I know you would do the same for me, given the opportunity," Eric replied, while returning to the reading of his newspaper.

"Well, I gotta get going. I told Ellen I'd be out there at eight. Will I see you tonight when I get home?" Glen questioned.

"I have a date with Melinda. I may or may not be home, depending on how things go," Eric answered with a coy smile.

Glen returned the smile with a wink, walking towards the garage from the kitchen. "I guess then, it's better I don't see you tonight… See you whenever."

"Yeah, whenever." Eric replied, flipping to the sports section.

Glen could tell Ellen had been up for awhile. It surprised him that she wasn't still sleeping. After all, the time spent last night was exhausting, …at least for him. As he pulled into the driveway, he could see the laundry already hanging on the line, including the pretty floral sheets they had made love on before he left the night before. Glen knocked on the door…no answer…and again… no answer. "Hmm… I wonder what's going on. Maybe she's in the shower," he considered before walking away, ready to begin his day's labor.

He had completed the barn's painting the day before, now

it was time to tackle the driveway. Several loads of gravel would be needed to stabilize the fill dirt that he would put in the gullies. The purchasing of it, he would need to discuss with Ellen. Maybe over lunch, he hoped.

Glen discovered a wheelbarrow and shovel in the barn, and started loading stones and dirt that he found in a heap by the garden. It was heavy with stones, so he assumed someone had removed them from the garden, trying to make the ground more fertile for planting. Those same stones he would put to good use by filling in the gullies before the gravel was spread. *There has to be an object lesson somewhere in that,* he pondered.

Stones - causing problems for some – making solutions for others. Eric and Ellen – a problem, but hopefully for he and Ellen – the solution.

Glen skipped his morning break. Knowing he got a late start, and there was no sign of Ellen outside, he would work through lunch. *It is better to stay busy than to ponder why she is staying indoors*, he thought.

Ellen watched Glen from the side kitchen window. He was trying to fix the lane, and for the life of her, she couldn't figure our why the potholes bothered him so much. *I guess a smoother ride would be nice,* she considered, *and save on my shocks too.*

How would she tell him? Only three hours sleep had left her feeling restless and confused. Things were going too fast for her. Ellen knew she did care for Glen, and maybe even loved him, as she *claimed* last night. But after more agonizing thought she determined, it could be nothing more than a crazy sexual infatuation. Not a true form of real love like she had with Jack. After all, they hadn't had enough time together for it to be anything else but that. There had to be rules about this sort of thing. *Love takes time …* she concluded… not a fast, hot fury of runaway feelings like she was having for Glen, and he for her.

Yesterday had been so perfect, and it broke her heart now to think what she was thinking. After Glen had finally left last night, Ellen climbed into bed and lay awake long into the night thinking about all that had taken place between she and Glen in such a short period of time. As much as she hated to hurt Glen she knew she had to tell him she was having her apprehensions, and wasn't ready for such a serious relationship with him yet. She woke early, deciding that she would tell Glen that she still wanted to see him, even possibly date him if he agreed to her wishes, but she could not sleep with him for now.

How will I tell him? She continued to ponder in frustration. *Before the end of the day, I will need to explain my feelings…*she resolved. Glen will be disappointed, she knew, but there was no denying that things were not as they should be.

Glen took his chances and knocked on the door at noon. Ellen stood staring timidly at the door, willing herself to open it.

"Hi Ellen," Glen welcomed with a sunny smile. "I came by earlier and didn't get an answer. I guess you were busy or resting," he presumed optimistically, unaware of the coming blow.

"Oh…yes…I probably *was* in the shower," she acknowledged awkwardly, knowing she was telling a lie and feeling horrible for doing so.

Glen sensed something was amidst. "Everything ok?" he asked as he reached out to touch her arm.

Ellen gave a slight jump of retreat with the contact, as if she had just received an electrical shock. "Everything is fine. I am just in a hurry, and I am ready to leave and go into town for awhile," she replied nervously.

"Oh? I was hoping we could have had lunch together."

"It won't work today, Glen, but you're welcome to get out of the hot sun and eat in the kitchen or on the porch if you would like," she replied with an attempted smile.

"Alright…see you later?" Glen questioned, feeling somewhat disappointed that things weren't going to work out the way he had hoped. He reached out to give Ellen a kiss on the cheek, lingering a moment to be close to her.

She hesitantly reached out to touch his arm, knowing she needed to provide him with an answer. "Yes… we can see each other later, but it will be awhile until I'm home," she answered guiltily, knowing she was trying to avoid the inevitable.

"I'll be here," Glen answered with his brilliant blue, happy eyes that were beaming at her. Ellen knew that any single woman in Fillmore would die to have Glen smile at her in that way. *I must be crazy!* She screamed out in her mind, knowing what she was going to be giving up if Glen wasn't receptive to her wishes.

Ellen pulled away in the Saab, as Glen unpacked his sandwich he purchased on the way to work. He helped himself to a glass of iced tea in Ellen's refrigerator. He knew she wouldn't mind. Cuddles jumped up on the table meowing for a tidbit. "Are you sure your mom lets you up here boy?" Glen asked of the furry cat. He obliged the feline's request with a couple of torn pieces of turkey from his sandwich, which Cuddles devoured greedily, enjoying every last morsel with a final bath to his face and paws. Glen observed it all with chuckle, scratching the cat's head and ears after the ritual was complete.

If he couldn't have Ellen with him at the moment to keep him company, Cuddles was doing his best to suffice. "Oh, to have your life – one of being pampered all day long by a beautiful mistress such as yours, and to sleep whenever and wherever you please. You definitely have something special going on here, my boy." Cuddles squinted his eyes and yawned, jumping down and running to the living room, curling up on an overstuffed chair for a nap.

Glen made a quick trip to the bathroom, and then made his way into the living room to catch a glimpse of Ellen and Jack's portrait, and to reminisce over what they had just shared the night before on the couch. Curiosity caught Glen's eyes, as he noticed a large photo album lying open on the sofa. "This wasn't here last night," he observed as he sat down, putting the album on his lap. "Hmm…pictures of Ellen and Jack's wedding," he said with interest, thumbing through each one, realizing the happy and handsome couple they made. "I wonder why she was looking at these today…" Glen pondered with uncertainty. That thought plagued him throughout the afternoon, as he painted the mailbox and started to fix the pasture fencing. *Something was up.* He just sensed it.

Ellen was home by late afternoon and Glen was impatient to talk with her. "I think I've done enough for one day. Time to put my fears to rest," Glen spoke aloud in a determined voice, as he approached the house. There would be no cleaning up at the well pump this time. He was too anxious for the answers he sought.

Ellen was at the door on the first tap. “Hi, Glen.”

“Can I come in?”

“Sure…” she greeted with a shaky smile.

“Ellen, I wanted to talk to you about a few things.”

“Ok…” she answered with some hesitancy, not sure what was on Glen’s mind. “Would you like to sit down?”

“No, I’m fine,” he answered, firmly planted in her kitchen. “First, the lane - I filled in the gullies, but we need several loads of gravel to make a sturdier driving surface.”

Ellen was momentarily relieved. It wasn’t anything serious. “That’s fine. Do you have any idea on the price though?”

“I can call Monday and find out. I wouldn’t think over two hundred dollars, but I’ll check.”

“Let me make the call, Glen. I know who I have accounts with, and who will give me the best deal.”

“Alright. Then how about tomorrow?”

“What about tomorrow?” she asked suddenly crossing her arms in front of her.

Glen noticed the gesture. “I mean… do you want me here, working as usual?”

“Not on Sundays. *Of course, I thought you would have realized that.* I go to church and *I would never expect anyone to work seven days a week*,” Ellen stated a little too intensely.

“Hey, what’s wrong?” Glen replied, laying a hand on

Ellen's arm in a tender caring fashion. "You seem like something has been bothering you today. Did I do something wrong?"

"No…I'm fine, Glen. I just didn't get a lot of sleep last night," Ellen answered with a weak smile as she glanced at his hand still on her flesh.

"Well, I'm relieved that's all it is. You had me worried," he breathed with a sigh of relief, bending over to give her a kiss. Their lips met, but the fire of last night was no longer a hot molten flame. "Hey, I have an idea," he began, with arms still on Ellen. "Since I don't have to work tomorrow, why don't we make plans to do something?" Glen suggested in a hopeful tone.

"Sorry, but I can't," she answered timidly.

"It's no problem. I have loads to do anyway," he said, feeling slightly disappointed again, having the same uneasiness of earlier in the day.

"Glen about you not wanting to take pay for this week, I don't feel right about that anymore. You have done more in a week than I would have expected to be done in several weeks. You *deserve* the money."

"A deal is a deal, Ellen. I am a man of my word, and I would never accept the money. Although, next week is a different deal," Glen teased, giving Ellen a wink and another kiss on the cheek.

"Is there anything else?" Ellen reluctantly asked, as she broke free from the embrace, walking over to the sink.

"No, that's it," he responded, sensing the change in her again.

"Glen, something *is wrong.* I can't pretend," she confessed, turning to stare at him in a wide-eyed anxious way.

"Just say it!" Glen remarked in confusion, while sitting down in a kitchen chair uninvited.

She joined him at the table. "Things are going too fast for me. I do like you - maybe even love you, as I said last night; but we are moving too quickly, and I have to allow my head to catch up with my heart. Please don't be mad at me…" Ellen whispered with tear-filled eyes.

Glen absorbed each word, finding it hard to believe that they were coming out of the same woman that was alluring and hot with passion as he held her in his arms yesterday. Emotion-filled pain etched his face. "Does that mean you don't want to see me anymore?"

"Of course not!" Ellen blurted out in teary disbelief, reaching for Glen's hand. "I guess what I'm getting at is, I would like to continue seeing you casually at the farm, maybe even go out on a date from time to time, but without the intimacy of last night. Not that it wasn't wonderful, …because it was," she said with pleading in her eyes. "But, I need more time to sort out my feelings."

"*You need time?* Then I guess you got it!" he growled a little too abruptly, pushing the chair out and away from him quickly.

Glen hurried out the door, feeling a sense of humiliation. He apparently was further along with this thing than Ellen had been, he realized. He was in love with her, and rejected by the one woman he truly wanted. How would he cope without her soft and willing body that molded so perfectly against him, after he had experienced the ecstasy it brought? "Damn it, why did I run out like that?" he asked himself, while punching the barn door in pain.

Ellen sat on the living room floor hugging herself, while rocking back and forth and softly crying. Glen's knock interrupted her from her self-induced misery. "Just a minute," she yelled with a quiver to her voice, wiping her eyes quickly on her shirtfront.

"Hi Glen, …you're back," she said, with a mustered attempt at a smile.

"*Yeah, I'm back*," he answered with his hands in his pockets. "I'm sorry, Ellen. I just thought you wanted this thing as much as I did." He looked down at the porch, shifting his feet in defeat. "I know I shouldn't have reacted as I did…. leaving your house like that."

"That's ok," she answered, feeling suddenly guilty.

Glen looked up into her tear-stained eyes again, feeling as if someone had punched him in the gut. "I can't say it will be easy, but *I'll try* to back off. I can't deny that I love you, because I do," he choked out. "Unless you feel and want the same things as I do, it won't be right for either one of us," he added emotionally.

He reached for her, unable to control his desire to wrap her in his arms, and she did not resist his advances, wanting to be there, at least for that moment. They clung to each other, Ellen softly crying and Glen sighing with the impact of the moment; each lost in their own thoughts.

Glen broke the spell with a kiss to the top of Ellen's head. "I should get going," he breathed into her hair, breaking loose from their embrace.

"I will see you Monday, won't I?" Ellen questioned with

fear, looking into his eyes with uncertainty, not sure he was coming back.

"Yeah, I'll be back. I know you need me," he grinned, trying to lighten the mood.

"Have a nice weekend."

"You too," Glen wished. He waved and walked off the porch, leaving Ellen to stare after him.

The Mustang flung gravel, as he picked up speed, leaving the farm's lane. "Damnit, Glen, what were you thinking? She is right, things have gone too fast!" he muttered, realizing Ellen was being realistic. He knew he had to go about this in a totally different way, or he would risk the chance of completely losing her, and it hurt too much to consider that now.

Chapter Fifteen

Ellen was up with the birds. Sleep finally overtook her, because she was so weary from the lack of rest the night previous.

"Will it ever rain?" she asked, as she glanced out the window that was steamed up from the cup of coffee she held. The dry period was coming too early. Usually, it hit in late June.

She showered and dressed in a soft silk peach dress that was belted in the middle. She wore her hair loosely down her back, with a barrette securing a section at the top of her head. Little makeup was applied. Ellen didn't want to stand out pretentiously at church. She liked to blend in with the group, not drawing unnecessary attention to herself.

Church was a weekly event for Ellen; from as far back as she could remember. Her parents instilled the ritual within her, and her siblings - from the time of infancy until they all left home. It was not always a pleasant memory as a child, usually tolerated only by her parents' insistence; but now it was a thing of joy, bringing peace and inspiration, especially during Jack's death.

Her brother, to her parent's surprise, entered the clergy; but her sister was obstinate to religion and church even now. Ellen was in the middle of her siblings - not only in birth order, but also in the spiritual dimension of her life. She was never very close to Joe, her older brother, who was five years, her senior; but shared all the little-girl dreams with her sister Debra, who was two years younger than she was. Joe was in Florida now – married with two kids, and pastoring a large church with over a 1,000 members. Debra was in Texas. She married a doctor, and didn't have any children as of yet.

Ellen wondered if her sister was happy. Her mother had hinted that Debbie and her husband may have been having marital issues, but Ellen wondered if her mother was reading into things. Debbie never confided that truth, so Ellen could only speculate. She needed to call her sister. After all, it had been awhile since they last spoke. Maybe she would even shed some light on her current romantic situation, Ellen considered, while spraying perfume on both wrists. But she knew it was doubtful Glen would even be mentioned. That was something she wanted to work out on her own. The family had been telling her to start dating again for a year now, but they didn't understand the pain she still felt over the loss of Jack. Maybe Debbie's secrecy about her marriage wasn't so hard to understand after all.... They were a lot alike.

The minister spoke on love and forgiveness towards all men. Ellen felt as if a spotlight beam was signaling her out from the rest of the congregation, with the message intended only for her ears. Tears stung her eyes, as the last hymn was sung. *Why am I throwing my chance of happiness away with this man?* She pondered with a bowed head, as the closing prayer was being recited. *He loves me, and I want to love him back. God help me put things in perspective concerning Jack, and give Glen a chance. I don't want to hurt him or lose him....* she prayed silently, with her head still reverently bowed.

Ellen conveyed her polite good-byes to Rev. Rollands and her friends at church.

"Ellen, how are you?" Rev. Rollands asked, while shaking her hand warmly.

Ellen attempted a polite smile. "I'm fine, Pastor Rollands."

Rev. Rollands was graying at the temples and had kind eyes that spoke of sincerity and a caring nature. He had performed Jack's funeral and went beyond the call of duty, checking up on Ellen every day the first few weeks after his death. Ellen thought of him more like a father figure than a pastor. He was sincerely concerned for her well-being.

"I heard you finally found someone to take care of the planting," Rev. Rollands mentioned in a friendly way.

Ellen was reminded of Glen again. "Yes…I have, and he has gotten everything planted for me this week."

"That's wonderful, Ellen!" Pastor Rollands replied with a sincere, genuine smile, already extending his hand to the next person who was leaving the church.

Glen woke up too early. He had planned to sleep in until noon, but his inner body clock was set to early morning awakening. Now he was up, with nothing to keep him company but his thoughts. "What should I get myself into?" he said aloud, looking at the clock on the dresser and feeling bored. Yawning and rubbing the stubble on his face, he sat up and stretched both arms over his head. "Eric, probably didn't make it home last night, so that leaves me with no one to talk to or no place to go," he said in frustration, as he donned a pair of cutoffs. He made his way to the darkened kitchen, flipping on a light and the TV.

"Today, we will have a high of 90 degrees with mostly sunny skies. The low tonight will reach 65 degrees. Monday and Tuesday there is a slight chance of rain."

Glen listened to the local weather with interest. "That garden needs rain, or the seedlings will have trouble," he concluded while trying to consider what his main priorities should be for the coming week at the farm.

Already restless with the morning, Glen looked around the room. "This place needs some light," he observed, walking around the first floor, pulling up all the blinds. "Eric must think this place is a morgue or something."

Magazines laid in a cluttered heap, by an out-of-shape, recliner in the family room. Glen grabbed one on fitness along with his sunglasses, and decided to retreat to a lounge chair in the back yard. His thoughts wandered to Ellen, and their conversation from the evening prior. How he wished they were together now. *Who was she with at the moment?* Glen pondered. *She had mentioned that a friend would be coming to the farm.* He hoped it wasn't a male friend. That thought had never even crossed his mind before, at least, not until now. *Could there be someone else in her life that she had failed to mention?* Just considering the possibility was making him feel envious and jealous if it were true. He fantasized, thinking of them being together again; feeling that gnawing longing of wanting and desiring her. But reality spoke, reminding him of the rejection and hurt he was now feeling.

"Hey, wake up, you're getting a sunburn!" a familiar voice yelled, while throwing cold water in his face, jolting him from his dreams. Glen jumped up with a start, putting his arm up in front of his face like a shield.

"You son-of-a-bitch, Eric! What is your problem?" he

blurted out, looking at Eric in disbelief.

"Hey, take it easy! I was *just* joking around. I didn't mean to freak you out so badly," Eric said with a lack of sensitivity.

"Like hell, Eric. You intended on seeing a reaction out of me, and you got a good one. Are you happy now!" Glen asked with way too much intensity.

"I'm sorry, Glen… I didn't realize you would react like you did. I guess I got carried away," he laughed while shrugging off Glen's touchiness. "You seem edgy, is something wrong?"

"Is something wrong…? I seem edgy? Yeah, something is wrong. I'm in love with Ellen Harper, and I wish to God it would have never happened!" Glen admitted harshly.

Eric grabbed a patio chair and pulled it up to the lounge, finally paying attention. *"How the hell did that happen?"* he questioned sincerely, looking at Glen for the answer.

Glen sat back down, feeling his resolve collapsing along with his drooping shoulders. "We have become involved."

"Involved, as in *sexually involved*?" he ventured, in disbelief at the possibility.

"Yeah, you got it - sexually involved. She told me she loved me, and I told her I loved her too, and now apparently she has changed her mind."

"What makes you think that?"

"*I guess because she told me so*! Last night she said she still wanted a relationship with me, but not a sexual one. Things have gone too fast for her. I'm guessing she is still not over her husband yet," Glen stated matter-of-factly.

"I think its finally time for you to realize that there are more females in this town besides Ellen Harper. I have backed off up to this point, because I knew you wanted to get something going with her, but now that things aren't going the way you hoped, what's the problem with meeting other woman? How about you and I going out on the prowl when I get back to town?"

Glen looked at Eric in irritation and disbelief. "What about Melinda? I thought something was happening between the two of you?"

"Maybe I'm getting a little gun-shy myself. I don't know. The thought of being tied down to one lady scares the shit out of me! Do you remember me having a steady girlfriend longer than a couple weeks in high school, Glen?"

Glen continued to stare at Eric. He knew the symptoms. He had seen him like this before. "I guess I thought you would have *grown up* since then."

Eric laughed. "Ouch! I guess that's the cold water right back in my face, huh?"

"Take it any way you want. The pick of the liter won't always be around, Eric. You may regret it one day letting the good ones go."

"Maybe…"Eric said with a chuckle. "I need to ask a favor. Can you drop me off at the airport tonight and pick me up Friday around 7 in the evening?"

"Sure, whatever you need. You know what it means to me to be able to use the car."

"It's no big deal, Glen. Soon enough you will have your

own set of wheels. By the say, I did reach out to Stan, and he says he will start keeping his eyes open this week for a car for you. He says if he doesn't have anything, he will make some calls to other dealerships. I can tell Stan honestly wants to repay me for the increase in his sales. Now, what do you say about starting the day over on the right foot, and we'll make some lunch?" Eric suggested with a playful slap to Glen's leg.

"Sounds good to me," Glen interjected, feeling somewhat better now that Eric was finally home.

Omelets, with everything in them – except the kitchen sink – along with bagels and cream cheese that Eric had just picked up - satisfied their ferocious hunger.

"Melinda sure worked up a hearty appetite in me," Eric said between gulps of food.

"What kind?" Glen teased.

"Both," Eric laughed. "But then you wouldn't know about such things, little brother," he said with an ornery grin.

"I guess I just need to observe the *master of love* from afar, and learn your skillful ways," Glen sarcastically added while rolling his eyes.

Eric grabbled Glen in a headlock and spoke directly in his ear. "That's why we are going out Friday night when I get back to town, and I *won't* take no for an answer."

"You got a deal Romeo. Now let me go, so I can finish my eggs."

Ellen hurried home, throwing together a couple Greek salads before Megan arrived. She had called the night before to confirm their plans, and to let Ellen know Mike would not be joining them for the day. He had office work to catch up on, and Ellen was really happy it worked out that way. Maybe the subject of Glen would come up, if she got her nerve up to mention him. "This is silly," she said plainly, trying to erase the need to speak of him to Megan. "I don't want to talk to anyone about him, ever!"

"El, you here?" Megan asked, opening the front door without knocking.

"Come on in, Meg. I'll be out in a minute. I'm just putting some laundry away."

"Take your time," Megan answered while chomping on a wad of bubble gum, making her way to the living room, plopping down on one of the sofas. The photo album was still lying open on the couch. She picked it up, and gave a sympathetic smile to the picture of Ellen on her wedding day looking up at Jack. She closed it, opening it to the beginning, thumbing through each page. "You look so pretty," she beamed, glancing up at Ellen as she entered the room.

"Thank you," Ellen said softly, touched by her sentiment.

Megan patted the couch. "Sit by me.... Let's look at these together."

"Are you sure? I know I have bored you with a lot of my old pictures, including these, one too many times."

"No you haven't, and anyways, I love to look at wedding pictures.... especially yours."

Ellen looked at Megan, with tears stinging her eyes.

"What's wrong, El?"

"Oh, Meggg…. I'm so miserable!" she confessed, as she joined her friend on the sofa, reaching out for a hug.

"Tell me… what's bothering you. Are you thinking about Jack again?" Megan asked, genuinely concerned for her friend's wellbeing.

"Partly him and partly someone else."

Megan looked at Ellen in confusion.

"It's Glen Cummings."

"The guy helping you out around here? Eric's brother?"

"Yes… to all of the above," she admitted.

"Did he do something wrong? If so, just fire him," she resolved, not feeling the need to discuss it any further.

"It's not what you may be thinking," Ellen assured Megan. "We have grown close…. actually, too close this week."

Megan's eyes grew wide with understanding as she laid the photo album on the coffee table in front of her. *"Did the two of you make love?"*

"Yes…Megan. We did," Ellen reluctantly declared, while bursting into tears and bringing her hands up to her face.

"Honey, I don't understand why you are so upset?" Megan questioned, as she laid a hand on Ellen's shoulder trying to comfort her. "Isn't it about time you allowed yourself some happiness? If this Glen can supply it, what is the *big* deal?"

Ellen tried to regain her composure, wiping her nose with the back of her hand. "I'm not sure how I feel about him. I do know though, that I feel like I am cheating on Jack; and with a person he may not approve of, since it is Eric's brother."

Megan looked Ellen squarely in the eyes, taking hold of both of her hands, trying to gain her complete attention. *"Do you love him?"*

"I told him I did, but now I'm not so sure. I feel…I feel confused. I know he is hurt, because I told him we needed to slow down. Things have gone too fast for me."

Oh…I see..." Megan replied, sensing Ellen's insecurities about the past coming to the surface once again to interfere with her decision-making. "Well, if he really does care about you, he will be patient and let you work out your feelings," she said with a finality that was so much a trademark of her abrupt personality.

"That's what I keep telling myself, but I don't want to lose him because I am so mixed up!" Ellen exclaimed, beginning to cry again.

Megan reached out to Ellen and wrapped her arms around her, patting her back much like a mother comforting her hurting child. *"Stop worrying so much,"* she whispered and soothed tenderly. "If it's meant to be, he will be patient; and if he isn't able to understand, then it's better you found out now what kind of person he really is before you become too involved."

"You are such a good friend," Ellen said softly, hiccupping as they separated.

"We are best friends," Megan answered with a reassuring cheerful smile. "And I am sooo hungry. What do you say we go

out for lunch somewhere? I'll treat."

"Thanks, Meg, but I already made us lunch," Ellen answered with a smile, as she closed the photo album, putting it back on the bookcase shelf. "I hope Greek salads are ok?"

"They're my favorite. You know that, El," Megan replied eagerly, already making her way to the kitchen.

The afternoon progressed just as equally well for Glen and Eric as it did for Ellen and Megan. The guys caught an afternoon baseball game on TV, while Ellen and Megan decided on a walk. Ellen pointed out all that had been accomplished by Glen – the garden, barn, lane and repaired fences.

"He really has achieved a lot this week, hasn't he?" Megan commented, truly impressed with Glen's abilities.

"Yes, he has done a lot, and I wanted to pay him, but he insisted on our deal of a week of free work."

Megan looked over the pasture. "That's some guy, I would say. Do you ever think you will bring back the livestock?"

"I thought about it, but there's a lot of time and money involved. Glen and I never really discussed the subject to any real length, and I don't know if he has had any experience in this area. I guess I will mention it to him in the next few weeks. That is…if he stays around."

Ellen cast Megan a worried glance.

"Now don't start upsetting yourself again, " Megan consoled while patting Ellen's arm reassuringly. "Things will work out. I just have a good feeling about all this."

They spent the rest of the day preparing dinner together, just as they had done on numerous other occasions. An oriental stir-fry, that Ellen had considered making for Glen just two day previous, along with chocolate brownie sundaes, became the menu of choice after an inventory was made of the refrigerator and the pantry shelves.

Eric finished his packing while Glen showered and dressed. They decided to go to the Park and Dine Café before going to the airport. Diana approached while snapping her chewing gum in an annoying fashion. The tight polyester knit dress that was a size too small for her frame, only helped to accentuate her overly large breasts and shapely backside. Her hair was jet black, and she wore it in a tight bun secured on the top of her head, allowing a few loose tendrils to fall freely at the back of her neck. She applied entirely too much makeup, with the focal point of her appearance centering on the bright red lipstick that was badly applied.

"More coffee, Eric?" the waitress inquired, with a suggestive lift to her voice that hinted of being *willing to please* in and out of the diner.

"No thanks, Diana. Two cups are my limit. I don't want to be up all night," he winked with a flirtatious smile.

"And why not?" she teased, while sitting the coffee carafe on the cart beside of the table, bending over a little too far, giving Eric and Glen both an eyeful of her cleavage.

Eric grinned and winked at Glen, as they mutually admired the view.

"I have an important meeting in the morning. I need to be

sharp and alert."

Diana whispered with her toothy smile. "I bet you're sharp and alert now, aren't you Eric?"

Eric laughed, always amazed by her boldness that even set him back a notch or two. "You're never wrong, Diana," he added good-naturedly.

Glen looked on, fascinated with Eric's charisma and ability to attract and flirt with women. They were always putty in his hands.

"And who is this handsome devil you are sitting with?" Diana asked, turning her attention to Glen.

Eric didn't miss a beat, grinning from ear to ear with his hands clasped behind his head. "Sorry Diana, I'm not sure Glen wants to meet you. You may be more than he can handle."

"I'll speak for myself, thank you," Glen interjected, extending his hand to shake Diana's. "Glen Cummings, Eric's *younger* brother."

"Eric's younger brother, huh? Eric never mentioned he had a brother, let alone a good looking younger one at that," she purred. "Shame on you, Eric! I can see why you never spoke of him," Diana cooed, while returning her gaze to Glen, taking in his over-all physique from head to toe. "*A lot of competition…* I would guess, from the ladies."

Glen shifted restlessly in his chair, trying to remain cordial, smiling at her. Diana wanted him, he could tell, but only Ellen was on his mind.

"How did you guess, Diana?" Eric replied sarcastically,

"The reality is, Glen steals all of my girlfriends, and I couldn't handle him taking you away from me too."

She hoped there was truth to Eric's words. "You from these parts?" she asked, ignoring Eric, and turning her interest back to Glen.

He continued to eat his desert, unimpressed with the easiness of the woman. "Just moved here from Virginia," Glen mentioned, but without much enthusiasm.

Diana smiled seductively at him, suddenly feeling hot at the prospect of a new boyfriend, be he married or single. "I would love to show you around town, Glen. I'm sure Eric here, has been too busy to show you much of anything, with the way he comes and goes out of town all of the time."

Diana did have a point. He hadn't seen much of the town, other than a grocery, convenience and hardware store, along with a few other insignificant places. Glen smiled a cautious smile at Diana. "I may take you up on that."

Diana scribbled her phone number on the back of one of her order forms. Bending down she spoke softly, re-exposing her overly abundant bosom. "No need to leave a tip, sugar. A phone call from you, Glen, is tip enough," she breathed throatily, focusing in on her latest prey.

Eric was laughing, and coughing at the same time, trying to hide his humor with the situation. "Glen, I think we need to get going. I can't miss my flight."

"I'll see you, Diana," Glen interjected, rising from the table.

"Remember what I said, honey. I'll show you *anything* you want to see here in the area," she replied while winking and walking away, resuming the aggravating cracking of her gum. Eric left her a 20% tip, and Diana's phone number remained laying on the table.

"Hey, I'll be right back," Glen said, as he turned to go back into the restaurant.

"Forget something?" Eric asked with a smile, knowing full well what Glen was returning for.

"Yeah, I'll catch up with you in a minute," Glen replied, as he went back to the table and retrieved the note with her phone number scribbled on it. He looked it over, folded it in half, and put it in his pants' pocket. Diana watched him with a satisfied grin, from the dark confines of the kitchen's hallway.

The drive to the airport was twenty minutes away. Eric told Glen to "floor it" as he drove the Mustang. He was in a hurry to catch his flight, and needed to be dropped off at the front entrance as soon as possible. They had already wasted too much time getting caught up in Diana's flirtatious game.

"That Diana is a piece of work, isn't she?" Glen commented, while glancing over at Eric who was busy looking at his cellphone for last minute flight updates.

"Yeah, piece of ass…I meant work," Eric grinned, with a wink. He turned sideways to Glen, patting him on the shoulder with one well-intentioned brotherly move. "She would have you in a minute…you and I both know that. And I can guess what you went back to the table to get, and that's your business; but I gotta tell ya Glen, I can introduce you to a lot classier women than Diana. It's your call, bro. She offers a quick lay, if that is what you want." Glen remained silent, as he drove with a dead-set intensiveness.

"I don't want *it* or her!"

"Can't shake this Ellen thing, can you?"

"No, I can't, damn it! And don't need some two-bit whore to make me feel better for a few minutes either!"

"Take it easy," Eric replied, grabbing Glen's shoulder in a squeeze, as if to steady him with his emotions. "Getting this upset isn't going to make her come around."

"I know that, and I am sorry. I realize you are only trying to help, but the wounds are too fresh, and I don't need someone else screwing me up even worse right now. I hope you understand."

"Definitely, I do! But, I'm here when and if you change your mind.

"Thanks," Glen said, feeling suddenly regretful for allowing thoughts of Ellen to control his temper in such a negative way. "I'm sorry for getting intense," he added, as he pulled to the curb in front of the airport entrance.

"I'll be back in town on Friday. I'll call Thursday, to see if you want to meet me somewhere for a drink."

"Sounds good," Glen answered, as Eric grabbed his bag from the back seat. "Thanks again for the use of the Mustang."

"Don't mention it," Eric replied, running to catch his flight.

The time Ellen and Megan spent together was refreshing,

and just the change Ellen needed. Her friend always did that for her. She was like free therapy – always uplifting – making her see the optimistic side of any situation.

"How about a second sundae?"

"Are you kidding, El. I already have five pounds to lose. After today, it will probably be ten!"

"Oh what the hell, who cares about tomorrow – let's just live for today!" Ellen exclaimed gleefully.

Megan turned to Ellen in surprise, very rarely seeing that carefree side of her friend. "Who turned you into a philosopher? Earlier, you couldn't stop worrying, and now you want to say to hell with the world?"

"That's because of you being here," Ellen said sweetly. "See what good you always do for me."

"Compliments, compliments.... I know I'm wonderful!" Megan giggled with her infectious laugh.

"I *think* you are overdosing on sugar, Meg, because your head is beginning to swell," Ellen joked, pretending to be concerned by touching her head. "Maybe you need to fix it with another brownie."

"I think you are right," she agreed, acting intoxicated by the sugar. "But this time add a little extra hot fudge and whipped cream on top. I don't want to go into a seizure on the floor, or something, from a lack of sugar or fat."

Ellen laughed. "You are so crazy!"

"No worse than you are!"

They ate a generous second portion of desert, and then cleaned up the kitchen together.

"I need to get home, El. Mike has texted me twice, and I haven't answered. He will begin to wonder what happened to me."

"If you must," she resigned, hanging the dishrag over the kitchen sink faucet.

"I must…but we will do it again, and soon. Ok?" Megan promised, while looking into Ellen's eyes reassuringly.

"Whenever you can," Ellen answered. "Just call when you have some free time."

"I'll call you before that, silly," she replied, giving her friend a hug and kiss goodbye on the cheek.

Ellen hated to see Megan leave. She didn't want to be alone with her thoughts that were tormenting her now again. Glen was in a similar situation at Eric's house. Distance separated them, but their hearts and emotions were still joined. They lay victim to the other, finding sleep hard to come by, each replaying the mental recording of their time together. Newness…. Fear…Trust…. Discovery…Being lovers…. Fear again…. Ellen confused…Glen hurting…Thoughts turned to their day apart. Time spent with Megan…. Time spent with Eric…. And finally rest did come, but they were still with each other - in the dreams they dreamt.

Chapter Sixteen

The alarm sounded way too early once again, as Glen reached for it with his eyes half closed, haphazardly knocking the interruption off the nightstand. "Damn it! Where is that blasted thing?" he blurted out, fumbling for it in the darkened room. His throat was dry and felt like sandpaper. He wondered if he was getting sick. The lack of sleep, long hard hours of work, and this new development with Ellen, would do it he realized. *How will I deal with Ellen today?* He contemplated while lacing up his work boots. Not overstepping his bounds and remaining friends would not be easy. He felt overwhelmed with the whole situation. There could be no other way. He would have to avoid her, he concluded. At least for a while, until he could get a clearer perspective on how things would be between them now.

He would take his breaks behind the barn, totally out of her view, start using the outhouse again, and try to refrain from updating her on the progress made around the place. Things would come up, he knew, and then there was always the issue of the well pump. It was much too close to the house, and he knew by venturing in that direction, it would only tempt him to climb the steps and knock on her door. He would miss the welcome relief that the cold, underground water gave to him. He hated to do away with that, but he knew it was for the best. At least, when she was at home. It rejuvenated him, refreshing his spirit, giving him the stamina to continue with the day's work. He hoped she would find some time during the day to run errands, giving him the chance to still enjoy the reprieve he so looked forward to.

The house was quiet, just as Glen had grown accustomed to every day now. He went about his business, busying himself with the pulling of weeds, and turning on of the sprinkler system again. The tomatoes were wilted and would require watering on a daily basis now, at least until some rain arrived. The seeds hadn't poked through the ground yet, but within a few days he knew they would. He began to work on the pasture fence again, keeping busy with it until his mid-morning break.

There had been no sign of Ellen in the early morning hours. As much as he hated to admit it, he had been watching for her. He had hoped she would come to him with a change of heart, saying that she had made a mistake. But Glen knew she wouldn't at this point. Not now…but maybe one day.

Right before lunch, Glen was distracted by the sound of a diesel truck turning into the farm's lane. He stepped out from behind the barn, trying to figure out what was going on. Ellen was in the driveway motioning to the driver, giving him directions as to where he should dump a load of gravel he was delivering. It was as if she sensed Glen's presence. She turned towards the barn, and their eyes met for a brief moment. Hers held the same uncertainty he didn't want to see. Glen knew he should approach them, and confirm the amount of gravel the lane needed, but his feet didn't want to move.

"Ok, Glen, get your butt in gear," he mumbled to himself. He took deliberate long strides, meeting the two whose attention was now turned towards him.

Ellen made the almost too quick introduction. "Mr. Mummert, this is Glen Cummings. He helps me out around here."

"Glad to meet you, son," Mr. Mummert said, while

inhaling cigar smoke with one hand, shaking Glen's hand with the other.

Glen smiled; feeling better that someone was actually being friendly. "It's good to meet you too. I thought I should come up and confirm the amount of gravel needed for the lane. I figure three loads will do it." Glen looked in Ellen's direction for her approval, but she stared back at him blankly.

"That's what Mrs. Harper and I had been discussing before you joined us. I thought three would do it also."

Glen felt like he was intruding and fumbled with his words. "It sounds like you have things covered. I guess I'll be getting back to work then." Glen nodded at Mr. Mummert and began to turn and walk away. "Have a good day, Mr. Mummert, and sorry for the interruption," he added, glancing at Ellen, intending for the words to really be directed at her.

Ellen felt guilty, knowing the situation was awkward. "Thanks for your input, Glen," she yelled, stopping him dead in his tracks as he turned back around. "I wasn't sure if I should order two or three loads, but now that settles it – three it is!" she said, smiling hesitantly, trying to put him at ease.

"You're welcome. See you later," he waved, already making his way back to the barn.

Ellen watched him go, taking in his every movement, definitely distracted by his presence.

"Is he a good worker?"

"Huh?" Ellen responded, still in a daze. "You mean, Glen?"

Mr. Mummert laughed. “Don’t see anyone else around here, do you?”

Ellen was embarrassed. “No, I guess not,” she reddened. “He is an excellent worker, and had done a lot for me since he has been here. He finished putting in the garden, painted the barn, and is fixing the pasture fence. The gravel was his idea too. Glen thinks the lane has too many gullies, but it never seems to bother me,” she shrugged with a smile.

“Little lady, that lane of yours has needed to be fixed for years. I’m glad someone finally convinced you to do something about it, he bellowed with his hoarse-sounding voice. Coughing, he continued to draw deeply on the smelly cigar. “If you don’t mind, I may give Glen a call myself. I could use some help out at my farm also.”

Immediately Ellen felt possessive, taken back by the thought of Glen working for someone else beside herself. “Mr. Mummert, I can’t speak for Glen, but I really don’t see how he can fit another job into his already busy schedule. He is here from five-thirty until sometimes eight o’clock in the evening.”

“That weekends too?” he asked, blowing another smoke ring around his head.

“Saturdays, but not Sundays.”

“Oh, I see…” Mr. Mummert answered, feeling defeated. “Good help is always hard to come by.”

“I definitely know that from my own experience here at the farm. It’s my hope that Glen will decide to stay here for a long time,” Ellen replied with uncertainty.

“I guess you do,” Mr. Mummert answered with a knowing smile, as he swung his heavy frame up into the cabin of his dump

truck, huffing and puffing as he did so. "I'll be back shortly. You can mail me a check at your convenience."

"Thank you, Mr. Mummert," she waved, as he maneuvered the vehicle down the lane. Ellen thought of the kind old man's words – *Good help is hard to come by.* She didn't think of Glen as hired help. It sounded so beneath him. Glen's role was much more important to her than that, almost as if Jack was around again, breathing life into the place anew.

Glen wished he could read Ellen's mind. The episode with the gravel delivery had left him feeling despondent the rest of the day. *There was no need to approach Ellen*, he thought, as he hoed the weeds around the onions. "My opinion wasn't necessary. Face it, Cummings, you mean *nothing* more to her than a means to an end. You are an employee, and nothing else. She buys the gravel – you spread it!" *Stay away from her!* His mind yelled in silent despair, in answer to the words he spoke.

The week went by, day in and day out, in the same fashion. Glen, there early and Ellen, asleep - both doing a good job of avoiding the other. No rain.... The garden... Glen accomplishing his goals – spreading the gravel, fixing the pasture fence, as well as the weeding, hoeing, and watering of the vegetable beds. Ellen continuing to brood behind a closed door and curtains, always sneaking glances secretly at Glen, especially when he ventured close to the house, and usually when he was leaving at the end of the day.

Her hopes were dashed one day when she thought he was finally coming to the house, but instead he stopped at the well pump. It was an especially hot day and he was bare-chested and gleaming with sweat. Ellen's heart beat frantically at the raw site of him. He looked intensely handsome. His bronzed Adonis form held solid muscle that bulged in his arms and chest, as he raised and lowered the well pump handle. His hair glistened, and looked as if the sun had lightened it a shade since he started working for her. She also noticed his shorts that rode low on his hips displaying the starting fringe of his pubic hair leading down from his navel. She could feel her insides growing warm with desire as she observed him. He splashed himself quickly, submersing his head entirely under its stream. Once finished, he snapped his neck back, flinging water in a spray that even she could see from her hideout. He then turned abruptly, making his way back to his work.

As rejected as Ellen felt, she knew she had no one to blame but herself for what was occurring. Even now, feeling confused about her feelings, she never intended for him to avoid her totally. Ellen missed Glen. In the beginning of the week, she truly thought that they had reached a civil understanding when they talked the week prior. She assumed that he would continue to speak with her, but as the days drifted by, she realized that was not occurring. Still, she clung to a faint hope of optimism, trusting that time would heal the rift that was now between them.

The hoped for, seeking-out finally came on Friday, at lunch. Glen waved Ellen down, as she was ready to pull out of the driveway. She slammed on the brakes, delighted for the chance to speak with him again. "Hi Glen," she said with a smile, as she rolled down the car's window.

Glen forced a polite grin, keeping up his guard. "I need to ask a favor. Could I leave at 5, and be paid today instead of tomorrow?"

"Oh…. sure. I should be back by then," she replied,

suddenly feeling puzzled.

“If it’s a problem, just say so.”

“No…that’s fine,” Ellen answered half-heartedly, wondering why he was in such a hurry to leave. She hesitated, just stalling, waiting for him to say something else. He was silent as he shuffled his feet with his hands in his pockets and his head down. “Is there anything else then?” she asked, suddenly feeling very uncomfortable by the pause in the conversation.

“No…that should be it,” he answered, as he raised his gaze finding himself unable to take his eyes off her beautiful face. Their eyes locked, and said so much more than their words could convey, as they fought not to reach out and claim the other. Neither one was willing to put an end to the madness, and do away with the emotional pain that they were inflicting unnecessarily upon the other.

“Alright, then…I’ll see you later,” Ellen weakly replied, as she waved and drove away from Glen’s presence.

Glen followed the car’s smoke trail down the lane, until the Saab was no longer in site. “Why did she hesitate?” he questioned in frustration. He shook his head. “You’re grasping at straws, Cummings. It was probably just your imagination,” he concluded, returning to his work.

Ellen was back by four o’clock, after hurrying through her grocery shopping, a trip to the bank, and couple of browsing stops through some shops at the local mall. She was in need of a new bathing suit, but nothing seemed to be what she was looking for. She would have to drive to Lincoln in the next few weeks, and see what she could find there. Glen was still in the lane, spreading gravel, when she pulled in. “Where should I put the car?” she yelled from a distance, seeing the newly delivered load of gravel blocking her access.

Glen wiped his brow, and rested on the shovel handle. “Do you think you can steer it through the field, until you reach the finished area, and then work it back up on the lane?”

She calculated his request, considering the field and slight bank she would have to go over to reach the lane again. “Maybe I should just park it on the road,” she answered with uncertainty.

“I could drive it, if you would like,” he proposed, not sure what the response of the *Ice Princess* would be.

“That would be great!” she said with a smile, handling Glen the keys as he approached the car. Their fingertips touched for a brief moment, but the effect was scorching. Ellen consciously grabbed for the contact hand with her other, clutching them both to the front of her.

He noticed her action, but took it as a sign that he offended her even with his touch now.

“I’ll walk up to the house then,” she informed him.

“You really don’t have to walk,” Glen answered. “I promise I won’t wreck it,” he added flippantly. Glen walked around, opening the passenger door for Ellen, even before she responded. No answer was necessary on her part. Glen had already decided for her. They sat in silence, lost in thought. Glen slowly steering the Saab into the adjacent field, and Ellen staring out the side window, mesmerized. She was relishing in the smell of Glen – that of hard-working male, which she was coming to recognize and love. His presence was so near, and yet so far away.

She longed to touch him, but she didn't want to make things anymore complicated than they already were.

"There," he said. "Safe and sound, and not a scratch on her!" he smiled, while turning to Ellen, holding her gaze in his own. Glen's could feel his heart pounding. He wanted to let go of the steering wheel and bring Ellen to him in a passionate embrace, but thought better of it. "I'd better get back to work," he said slowly and softly.

"Yes…I guess so…" Ellen replied, feeling the heat also. "Thanks, Glen"

"You're welcome," he answered, as he left her still sitting in the car.

Glen returned to the pile of gravel with a newfound realization. Things were definitely *not* over between them, as much as they both attempted for it to be so.

Ellen met Glen at the well pump within an hour with his pay. She handed him an envelope. "It's all there…and then some."

"Then some?" Glen asked, looking at Ellen quizzically.

"You deserve more than the three hundred. I wish I could afford more, but I can't." Ellen stood still, waiting for him to open it.

Glen looked at the envelope's contents. "Ellen…. a deal is a deal, and three hundred is all I asked for and all I want." He handed fifty of it back in her direction.

Ellen looked disappointed. She knew intimacy was not what she wanted right now, but she did need Glen's help at the farm; and this was her way of letting him know how much she appreciated his efforts.

"Glen, please…" Ellen protested with her eyes.

"I don't know what to say."

"Don't say anything…. just take it."

Glen smiled, as he replaced the fifty into the envelope that she extended in her outstretched hand. "You're a hard lady to figure. I wasn't sure you even wanted me to come back this week."

Ellen felt hurt at his cold way of addressing her. "Of course I wanted you to return to work, Glen. Don't make this any harder on me than it already is," she pleaded with pain-filled eyes.

Ellen began to turn, but Glen grabbed her arm a little too roughly. He became suddenly angry, as he turned her back to face him.

"Just remember who's calling the shots here. My feelings towards you haven't changed. You've been bouncing my emotions around like a Ping-Pong ball, since I've known you. I'm trying to be patient with you, Ellen, hoping you will come to your senses, but I don't know if I can go on this way forever!" he gritted out madly.

Glen abruptly let go of her arm that he had moments before been applying too much pressure to. Ellen froze in disbelief with her mouth open showing her shock. She rubbed her arm and cried softly to herself as Glen spun out of the driveway spilling the freshly laid gravel into the field. He stared at the envelope, lying on the seat beside of him, with the money already half way out. "Three hundred and fifty dollars. I should have stuffed the extra fifty down her bra! That would have gotten a damn reaction out of her!"

Eric had called Glen the night previous to confirm his flight arrival. After the episode with Ellen, he was more than willing to join Eric for a drink. He was tired of feeling rejected, and maybe they would run into Diana. Even with Eric's words of warning about her, at the moment he didn't care. He knew she was probably like one of his typical troublesome girlfriends back in Virginia that had always caused him problems; but if anything happened between them it would only be for a *one-night stand.* He hadn't called her, but he hadn't thrown her number away either.

A quick stop home for a shower and to change clothes, was in order for the evening. Khakis, with a white polo shirt, were his choice. Glen appraised his appearance in the bathroom mirror. "Ellen Harper, if you don't want me, someone else will!" he said with hurtful determination, combing the last strands of hair back into place.

The terminal's flight schedule screen confirmed that Eric's plane would be arriving late. Glen hoped this wasn't an indication of a start to a bad evening. He approached a pretty blond with flawless skin that had a smile that looked plastered on, who was booking a flight for a passenger in front of him. It became his turn, and he flashed her his own dazzling smile. She returned her best "Miss America look", after glancing at his left hand to see if he wore a wedding ring.

"May I help you?"

Glen smiled at her again, continuing with his alluring spell.

“I hope so,” he winked, assuming she was single also.

She blushed for a quick second only, and was totally smitten with Glen as soon as she saw him approach. “What can I help you with?”

“My brother Eric Cummings is flying in from Toronto. His flight was due at six forty-five. I see from the flight arrival screen that the plane is now delayed. If I could have an update on that information, I would gladly appreciate it,” he said with a sly grin.

“I’ll see what I can do for you,” she quickly replied, before lowering her head to perform her search on her computer screen. Her fingers were a frenzy of activity, as she typed in the needed information. “Do you happen to know his flight number?” she asked, recapturing Glen’s eyes, as he now leaned over the counter.

“609”

“Ok….” She swore she thought she heard him breathe the word *sex* instead of *six*. The occasional interruption from a guy as outstanding in the looks department as Glen was rare, who crossed her counter. It was never easy for her to keep her mind on her work, when one as handsome as him finally came along. She smiled, as she raised her head with the requested information. “Mr. Cummings, your brother’s flight should be in by seven-thirty. The screen should now be properly updated,” she smiled sweetly.

“Thank you, Miss….?”

“Miss Newcomer…. Christina, that is,” she replied casually, wanting him to know her first name.

He smiled to himself with satisfaction. He knew he had a fish on the line, and yet he wasn’t really sure if he wanted to reel her in. Yet, it felt good to know that he still had his charm! *To hell with Ellen Harper!* Glen extended his hand. “Glen

Cummings, and the pleasure is all mine," he said with his sexiest sounding voice and smile that he could muster.

Christina swooned with delight as she grasped Glen's hand, being turned on by the feel of his callused male grasp that hinted of strength and hard work.

"Is there a coffee stand nearby?"

"Unfortunately there isn't, but there is a good restaurant around the corner. I'm on break in ten minutes, and I could take you there," she offered, hoping he would respond positively to her offer.

"That sounds great, but I better wait on Eric. We have dinner plans and he'll want to eat too."

"Oh…alright. To be honest, I totally forgot about your brother," she answered with a giggle and the same plastered-on smile.

"We plan to go out for drinks and dinner to a place I believe is called Leon's. Maybe, if you're free, you could stop by later and join us. That way, we can talk more later," he suggested with a wicked smile, not doubting for a moment that she would show up. He surprised himself. This wasn't like Glen to be acting like Eric, but Ellen had him wound up and aggravated. There wasn't an attraction of intellect going on here with Christina, as there was with Ellen; but he wanted to prove to himself that he was desirable to other females no matter what it took.

"I probably could swing by later. I know the place. It's great for dancing," she hinted, not paying much mind to the line of patrons behind Glen.

"We're back here too, ya know. Talk to your girlfriend when she's not working!" came an abrupt complaint from an irate fellow in the group.

Glen turned, suddenly realizing the extent of the holdup. "Sorry…. I didn't realize we had company," he confessed, turning back to Christina with a grin that was full of promise, charm and sex appeal. "I better get going. Hope I will see you later, and we'll dance the night away," he said with a wink and a promise, leaving her breathless, as she stared after him.

Eric arrived at seven-forty. Glen was anxious to leave the airport. A long day of work and now the wait with nothing to eat had left him pacing the floor, feeling very impatient.

"What's the big hurry, bro?"

"I'm just hungry."

"Then let's just grab a bite in the airport."

"No, that's ok," Glen, answered, picking up the pace. "I can wait. I'm just not good at standing around like this, but I'll be fine."

The ride to Leon's was animated with conversation of Glen and Eric's week.

"Things any better between you and Ellen?"

"As long as we keep our distance everything is good. Today though, I overreacted and grabbed the *Ice Princess* by the arm and told her what I thought of her attitude. It's hard for me to be around her, knowing I want our relationship to be on a different level than she does."

"The Ice Princess, huh?" Eric smirked with his typical sarcastic tone. "I never thought I'd hear you talking about her in that fashion."

"Oh, come on, Eric, you knew she had me pissed off at her before you left last weekend. I do have to admit though, that she did something that caught me off-guard today."

"What was that?"

"She gave me fifty extra dollars with my pay this week."

"She did that?" That's hard to believe!"

"I was surprised. I tried to give it back to her, but she insisted I keep it. She said I did more in a week than she expected from me in several weeks."

"She's probably right on that issue. Hey, and you know what? I bet she is just trying to thank you properly for giving her a good lay after a couple years of not getting any," he laughed, entertaining himself again with his own sick humor.

Glen glanced at Eric, who was grinning from ear to ear as he drove his Mustang. "You can cut the crap, Eric, any time now. That's bullshit, and you know it!"

"Hey, didn't we part this way?" I'll try not to get you stirred up anymore about Ellen.... deal?"

"Yeah, deal," Glen, sighed in frustration. "Just remember *she is a lady*, and I'd appreciate it if you would try to treat her with some respect when her name comes up."

"Ok, ok…" Eric said while biting his lip, wanting to laugh and make another rude comment, but decided against it. He looked forward to being with Glen, and there was no sense in ruining the evening over Ellen Harper.

Chapter Seventeen

They drove in silence for a few minutes, with Eric finally flipping on the radio to break the tension between them. The oldies station was playing again. All was forgotten by earlier words, as both brothers broke into perfect harmony singing a song from their high school days. Reservations hadn't been made at Leon's. They would have a thirty-minute wait until they could be seated.

"Let's hit the bar," Eric suggested. "We can start and end the night there. They have a great rock band that will be playing later."

"Yeah, that sounds good," Glen, agreed.

The bar was lively, with singles lining every available barstool and table. A barmaid, in a short black skirt and sequence tube top, approached the brothers. "May I help you guys?" she asked in a throaty, sexy-sounding drawl.

Eric flashed his charismatic smile. "We'll need a table in a little while doll, but we'll settle for the bar for now."

"I think I can arrange that," she said audaciously, turning to smile back at Eric and then at Glen. "Follow me," she motioned, swaying her hips suggestively as she made her way through the maze of bar tables and individuals who were crowded around a pool table.

Two beers later, they were seated in the dining room. Each decided on prime rib. Eric's was rare, and Glen's was medium-well.

"How was your week? Good things in Toronto?" Glen asked, as he scooped a chunk out of his baked potato.

"They're still considering my proposal. This one is *a hard nut to crack.* Usually, I can breeze through an agreement as lucrative as we are proposing, but not with these guys. They would sooner give the contract to a Canadian company, but they know that no one comes close to us. It will just take them awhile to review what everyone else is offering, and then they will call me."

"And if they don't?"

"And if they don't, they'd be fools. But that doesn't happen to me," Eric said smugly, looking at Glen with his over-confidence just oozing from his pores. "I haven't been turned down since my first year in this business."

Glen leaned into Eric, grinning broadly. "Is that the same with the ladies also?"

Eric chuckled. "My track record speaks for itself in that area too, but I don't stay around for the long term like I do with my computers. Machines are safer, Glen. You can always get rid of the old parts and make them like new again. Besides, they don't *demand anything* like a female does. If you don't feel like being with them for a few days or months, for that matter, they don't give a damn!" he said with a laugh, already acting loose from the beers he had been drinking. "I'm not good with female commitment…you know that, Glen. I'm the same… haven't changed," Eric answered with slightly slurred words. "Not any different in that area than when we were together in high school.

"That's too bad, Eric. I thought you and Melinda had something special going on. Aren't things different with her?"

"I thought so. That was, until we left for Canada. That's why I asked for your help with my rides to and from the airport. She's angry with me, and thinks we should see other people."

"What did you do now? Did she catch you playing with your computer?" Glen teased, giving Eric a playful slap on the back.

Eric started laughing with a loud intoxicated laugh. "Good one, Glen…. but nah that wasn't it. I called her by another name while we were making love."

"You did what?"

"Hey, what can I say… haven't you ever done that?"

Glen laughed. "No, I can't say that I have ever done that. I'd be pissed off at you too."

"She asked who Karen was, and I told her someone from a few months ago. She seemed to accept it. Then she calls me up in Canada with this emotional paranoid speech, thinking I am seeing Karen again on the side."

"Well, are you?" Glen asked pointedly.

"No, I haven't been. But now that Melinda has dumped me, maybe I should look her up again. She wasn't half bad looking, now that I think about it," Eric replied half in a drunken daze.

Glen took on a more serious tone, remembering anew what was happening to him personally. “Hey, don’t let her get away, if you think there is a possibility…”

Eric swung back on his chair. “I’m the last person who would go chasing after her. You know that, Glen,” he said nonchalantly.

The bar was filled to capacity, as they made their way back through the crowed room looking for a table. The band blared out a rousing beat that vibrated through every fiber of the their bodies. The music was way too loud for conversation, but that didn’t seem to stop the opposite sex from scoping out the territory for possible pickups. Someone smiled and waved at Glen, as if she knew him, beckoning him to join her. Glen realized, on second glance, that it was Christina Newcomer – the female from the airport.

Eric spoke loudly into Glen’s ear above the boom of the music. “That babe over there acts as if she *knows* you.”

“She does,” he smiled mischievously, already moving towards Christina’s table.

“Hi,” he yelled over the roar. “I didn’t know if you would show up or not.”

“What?” she questioned with her showy smile, unable to hear him above the noise.

Glen grabbed the seat beside of Christina. He leaned into her, repeating his statement a little louder. *“I said, I wasn’t sure if you would show up tonight or not. But I’m glad you did,”* he added warmly.

"Of course I planned to come. I wanted to see you again," she confessed.

"Hey, do you mind if my brother Eric joins us?" Glen asked, while pointing him out sitting across the room.

"That's fine with me," she answered sweetly, although somewhat disappointed, secretly wishing it were only the two of them.

Eric was leaning against a wall, looking around the room for a possible pick-up, when he noticed Glen motioning for him to join them. He reluctantly decided to intrude, preferring to be alone.

Glen made the introductions. "This is my brother, Eric. The one I was waiting on at the airport."

"Glad to meet you, Eric," Melinda gushed with a bright smile.

"The pleasure is all mine," Eric answered with his radiant smile, giving her the once over from head to toe with his appraising approval. He grabbed the seat opposite Christina and extended his hand to her.

"And Eric, this is Christina Newcomer. I mentioned to her that she should meet us here after she got off of work, and as you can see, she took me up on it," Glen said with a grin.

Eric flashed her the smile that he was famous for, and she responded in the same fashion that most women did – totally unnerved by the sex appeal he gave off with just one look.

Glen noticed the exchange. If Christina had been Ellen, Eric's flirtatious way would have irritated him; but for some reason, it didn't seem to matter with her. He passed it off as just Eric's way of relating to most women.

Ellen was happy that Megan had called her again, wanting to include her in on the plans for the evening. She thought she would be spending another Friday night alone at home, but Megan had insisted that Ellen join her and Mike for an evening out. *It had been so long....* she thought, as she waited on the front porch for them to pick her up. *There hasn't been a date or an evening out dancing since Jack*, she realized. She didn't initially want to go, but Megan begged her and said it would be fun. She hoped she wasn't making a big mistake. A car approached, as she was lost in thought, with the horn beeping her back to reality.

"Ready to party?" Megan yelled from her rolled down window. "Get in girl, it's time to boogie!"

"Oh Meg, really?" Ellen replied, shaking her head as she climbed into the back seat. "You are really full of yourself tonight."

"That's for sure," Mike chimed in, giving Megan a sly smile and quick kiss as he held the back door open for Ellen. "Meg tells me I'm the lucky guy who gets to dance with the two loveliest ladies in town."

"Megan, that's not necessary!" Ellen insisted, realizing what she was putting her husband up to for her benefit.

"Yes it is! You have no say so in the matter, and besides Mike wants to dance with you. *Don't you, Mike?"* Megan challenged, while giving him the eye.

"Ah...sure. Of course I do. I'd be pretty dumb to turn down a deal that good!"

"Thanks, Meg. Thanks, Mike. You guys are so sweet to me all of the time."

Megan turned to Ellen with a grin. "I love ya, but I only share Mike on the dance floor. He's mine after we take you home. You got that?" she teased.

Ellen giggled. "You are silly, Meg. What am I to do with you?"

"Just keep being my friend."

"Forever."

"Forever," Megan answered, while turning around with her arms extended over the seat to give Ellen a hug.

"Ok you two, don't start getting emotional on me. This is supposed to be a fun tonight."

"Point taken…I am glad you thought to include me in on your plans. Now let's go have some fun!" Ellen answered, as the merry trio made their way into Leon's.

The dance floor was full, with bodies pressed close, as the band crooned a slow love ballad. Mike led the group, as the hostess pointed to an empty table in the bar. She was trying to go over an unresolved controversial bill with a disgruntled customer, and wasn't able to show them to their table as she normally would have. The music was loudly playing with an inviting back beat that left Ellen feeling excited by the energy surrounding her. The only thing that could have made the evening more perfect for her would have been if Glen had done the inviting. *Oh well… maybe one day*, she pondered, as she glanced around the room at the happy couples dancing.

"Ellen, would you like a drink?" Megan shouted loudly over the noise.

"Oh, I'm sorry. I was watching everyone. What are you having, Meg?"

"A glass of Chardonnay."

"That sounds good. I'll have one also," Ellen yelled back with a smile.

"We're really busy, so it will be a couple of minutes," the waitress informed them.

"We'll be here," Megan answered, slipping Mike a grin. "How about you and I getting out there, so we can make sure that you remember how to dance? We wouldn't want you to get Ellen out on the dance floor and embarrass her."

"Speak for yourself!" Mike teased. "Remember I was voted the best dancer in my senior class."

"Yeah, yeah, you remind me of that every year at CWS's Christmas party," she said with a laugh.

Mike and Megan were tearing up the dance floor, doing different moves from the disco to the slide. Ellen smiled warmly at her friends. She longed for the kind of happiness that they shared again in her life, but she was so scared of it. Her thoughts wandered to Glen. He was so handsome, hard working, kind and a great lover. What more could she want? Why couldn't her heart override the hesitations of getting re-involved? Would Glen be around a few months from now? She doubted it. Maybe at best he would continue to work for her for a while, but surely another woman would come along to entertain him during his free time.

Fillmore had too many hungry, available females and very few eligible bachelors like Glen. *It was only a matter of time* she realized.

The drinks arrived just as Mike and Megan came back to the table. “That was perfect timing,” Ellen said with a laugh, as the two rejoined her. Mike was huffing and sweating as Megan and him sat back down. Megan poked Mike in his more-than-ample side.

“High School dance king, huh?”

“I try, Meg,” he panted heavily, still out of breath.

“I know honey,” she giggled, snuggling close to his side. “Your turn is next,” Megan reminded Ellen.

“Give me a minuet,” Mike interjected good-naturedly, as he was still trying to slow down his racing pulse, wiping his forehead off with the napkin in front of him.

Ellen felt sympathetic towards Mike knowing the role he was expected to play for the evening. He was over-weight, and not used to such a vigorous workout that his wife was demanding of him.

“Megan, I’m really just as content sitting here watching the two of you dance. I’m not much of a dancer anyway.”

“Nonsense, I know that isn’t the case, and you’re not getting off that easy!” she insisted.

“All right…. we’ve already been through this, but much later on in the evening would suit me just fine,” Ellen answered, smiling at her friend.

Ellen's *much later on* ended up being only a twenty-minute reprieve, just long enough for Mike to use the men's room and finish his drink.

"Come on Ellen," he hollered, looking more refreshed from washing the sweat off his face while he was in the bathroom. "The dance floor is getting cold."

She couldn't protest as Mike grabbed her hand, pulling her to her feet, mingling quickly amongst the other dancers. Ellen was a good dancer, and it really came easy with the exercising she did. Mike had her laughing, as he broke into "The Jerk*"* and "The Swim*"*. He wasn't an especially handsome guy, but he was one of the kindest men she knew. She mimicked his moves, and then twisted to the floor on a Chubby Checker, fast-moving twist number.

Everyone on the dance floor took their lead, breaking into every old dance move that they could think of. The room surrounding joined into the action by clapping and chanting, "Go, go, go!" with Megan being the ringleader. Ellen and Mike stayed securely to the middle. She shied away, feeling uncomfortable being in the spotlight.

"What's happening out on the dance floor?" Eric asked the waitress, as she brought another round of drinks.

"Oldies and Goodies showoffs! Everyone loves to see how many of the old dances they can remember."

"Sounds like fun!" Glen said enthusiastically, while taking in the action on the dance floor.

"To me also," Christina remarked pointedly, hoping Glen would take the hint.

He glanced at her and then at Eric, who was kicking him

under the table urging him silently on.

"Ah…would you like to dance, Christina?" Glen finally asked, not really feeling a strong desire to really do so.

"Yes!" she replied much-too-eagerly, already rising from the table. Just as Glen was getting up, the band announced a ten-minute intermission. "I guess we will have to wait awhile," he said with a feeling of relief.

"Yes…I guess so," Christina answered, looking disappointed.

Glen felt guilty for not being more receptive towards her, but it wasn't working. All he could think of was Ellen, and wanting to be with her instead of Christina.

That damn Glen, Eric thought, taking in the exchange at the table. *He's screwing up his evening with this woman. This sulking over Ellen Harper has got to stop! Once Glen is involved with someone else, Ellen will be yesterday's news. Christina isn't bad looking*, he concluded, taking in her overall appearance with a cocky grin. *Maybe I need to give them space, and he will figure this out for himself.*

Eric looked around the room, catching a glimpse of a pretty blonde at the bar. "See you two later," he said with a wink directed at Christina. "I think I see someone I know." The truth was he didn't know her *yet*, but he knew that would change shortly.

Glen was left alone at the table with Christina, and was suddenly at a loss for words. Conversation between them seemed easier at the airport. Now, neither one of them spoke, as they awkwardly took in the scenes of romance around the room. The band returned, and Glen felt committed to ask Christina to dance. "Do you want to *try* it again?" he beamed, with the same smile that won her over at the airport.

"Do you even need to ask?" she answered sweetly, as he led her to the dance floor by the hand. All was forgiven from his lack of attention, once he held her close in his arms. The female singer crooned a love ballad seductively, as the two of them swayed closely. Glen closed his eyes, pretending for just a few minutes that it was Ellen instead of Christina in his arms.

Megan and Mike returned to the dance floor, while Ellen was content watching and sipping her wine. It had been fun to dance with Mike, and she was glad she had accepted Megan's invitation. Maybe getting out like this wasn't so bad after all, Ellen decided happily. She glanced out on the dance floor noticing Megan and Mike wrapped tightly in a loving embrace. She smiled to herself, feeling happy for them and the love they shared. She considered herself lucky to have such loyal and caring friends. The smile stayed on her face as her eyes scanned the sea of other dancers. Everyone was holding their partner in such intimate embraces, including a very handsome couple to the far-right side of the floor. Shock registered on her face as her wine glass slipped from her fingers that were frozen in motion, spilling the contents on the table in front of her. It was Glen, with another woman! He was holding her very close with his eyes closed in the same intimate manner that Ellen had seen and experienced when they made love. He acted as if he were all-too-familiar with her.

Tears began to spill from her eyes uncontrollably, as she continued to observe Glen. He was occasionally stopping and breaking the closeness of their hold to smile and speak with the female. She seemed to be entranced with him, as Ellen knew anyone in her shoes would be. She didn't want Glen to see her there. She lowered her head, bringing her hand up to her forehead, trying to shield her face from him. She prayed that he hadn't already seen her dancing with Mike. She was humiliated enough to have to watch him. The thought of Glen knowing she was there, while he was dancing with someone else as she watched, was more than she could bear.

Megan looked over at Ellen and sensed something was terribly wrong, since she was hiding her face and dabbling her eyes with a napkin at the same time. "I think we need to get back to Ellen," Megan urged, speaking loudly into Mike's ear above the blare of the band's instruments.

"Why?" he questioned, looking at her puzzled.

"She seems upset," Megan answered, looking in Ellen's direction. They quickly rejoined her, realizing that her makeup was running, and she had apparently been crying quite a bit. They sat back down at the table, and Megan pulled a chair close to Ellen's.

"What's wrong sweetie?" she asked, as she touched her arm, trying to calm her.

"It's…Glen," she said nervously, inconspicuously pointing in his direction. "I really want to leave," she pleaded, begging Megan with pain-filled eyes. "I don't want him to see me like this…watching him."

Megan glanced in the direction that Ellen was pointing, and anger instantaneously flooded her every facial feature. "Who gives a shit what he thinks! He's the one looking like an asshole, by flaunting another woman in front of you already!"

Ellen felt bad for igniting Megan's temper. "I'm really not that strong to sit here," she replied weakly. "Try to understand…"

she said with a quivering voice, causing Megan to feel overwhelmed with compassion.

"Alright, let's go," she stated firmly with a look of determination, giving Mike the final word that was not to be questioned, when she made up her mind on something.

Mike and Megan tried to conceal Ellen as best as they could, huddling in close to surround her as she stooped low and walked from Leon's. Once Ellen and Megan were safely in the car, Mike returned to the bar to square up the bill. Ellen broke down sobbing, clutching her hands to her face.

"Ellen, he isn't worth it!" Megan gritted out bitterly. "Why don't you fire him tomorrow?"

Ellen hiccupped, trying to regain some composure. "Now Meggg…. I'm not sure I want to go to that extent. I need…his help, and after all, he really can date whomever he wants. I brought all this on myself anyways, insisting that I needed more space," she moaned in despair.

"Don't fool yourself, Ellen, and for heaven's sake don't take the blame for that jerk's actions! He's found himself another *flavor of the week* as soon as he realized that you wouldn't play house with him anymore."

Ellen barely spoke a word on the drive home, as Megan continued to vent her anger, giving her opinions about Glen and the *worthless kind of human being* he really was.

Mike was careful about commenting, not wanting to aggravate the situation any further. He was not one to pass judgment, since things weren't always as they seemed. Megan had caught him once in a compromising situation of his own, at a convention. He knew he was innocent, but Megan would not listen to reason, even threatening to divorce him. *Maybe this poor fool is a victim also.* Whatever was the case, even though it did appear to be bad, Mike would let the condemning rest solely on Megan's shoulders. She did enough for the both of them.

Ellen escaped Leon's and was safe from Glen's eyes, as she had hoped, but unfortunately not from Eric's. He noticed her sitting by herself, while Megan and Mike danced. He also noticed the change in her mood, and the tears as she watched Glen dancing with Christina. *"Good!"* he announced aloud, as he smiled with smug satisfaction taking in the whole scene.

"What's good?" his acquaintance for the evening questioned, as she rested her head on his shoulder while rubbing his leg, bringing him back to his present surroundings.

"Oh nothing," he beamed with delight. "I just realized a friend of mine finally got the girl up on the dance floor that he wanted to dance with all evening.... Can I buy you another drink?" he offered, trying to change the subject.

Glen danced several more dances with Christina, until he was reasonably sure he could politely claim exhaustion. It's not that he wasn't enjoying himself.... he was. It just wasn't that thrilling. The chemistry wasn't there. Try as he would, he couldn't free his mind. Ellen was there in his thoughts, even when he was dancing.

"I wonder where Eric got to?" he remarked absent-mindedly, looking around the room once they were seated again.

"Now do we *really* want your brother here with us?" Christina giggled, moving her chair closer to Glen's.

"I guess not," he relinquished with a polite smile, putting his arm around her in a perfunctory way.

Eric kept his distance. The evening wasn't turning out that well for him either. He knew he could go home with the bimbo who was attached to him like an octopus, but he just didn't feel up to it. Maybe because he had been away all week he was feeling disinterested and tired. *What else could it be?* He thought, as he excused himself, saying he needed to rejoin his friends.

"Mind if I join you guys again?" Eric asked with a flirtatious smile directed at Christina, already taking a seat and not really wanting an answer.

Glen was relieved that Eric came back. It would give him a good reason to excuse himself. "Christina, is it alright if Eric keeps you company for awhile?" he said while glancing in Eric's direction giving him the eye. "I need to use the men's room."

"Take your time," Christina replied, with her annoying inebriated giggle. "I'm sure Eric can tell me all about you while you are gone."

Eric faked a sarcastic chuckle. "We'll be fine. I'll tell her all about your bad points."

"Don't do me any favors! Everything he tells you Christina, will probably be an exaggeration, so don't believe a word he says," he grinned.

Glen made his way through the crowd, pausing in the hallway that led to the bathroom. He took out his cellphone and dialed Ellen's number. The phone rang twice before he hung up. "You fool!" he exclaimed. "She wouldn't want you calling her for no apparent reason at this hour!"

He was in no hurry to return to the table, realizing it was

only eleven o'clock. Glen wandered outside of Leon's, taking a seat at a cozy wrought-iron table for two, trying to kill some time. It was situated in an out-of-the-way romantic setting that was now dark and unused. The night was quiet, except for a nearby cricket chirping out a mating call. He welcomed the solitude. It reminded him of the farm, when he was alone working, lost in his thoughts. The noise and loudness in the bar he could take or leave. Mostly leave. Hopefully, he and Eric could exit shortly, without the awkwardness of a promised, future commitment to Christina.

Some time had passed before Glen rejoined the table. Christina and Eric were not to be found. He scanned the room for the familiar faces. He spotted them holding each other close on the dance floor just as she and Glen had done earlier. "What the devil!" Glen snickered in amusement, realizing Eric wasn't wasting any time, and Christina appeared only-too-happy to oblige.

He sat at the table alone, not really caring and almost relieved that they were dancing together. *Maybe she would offer to take Eric home,* Glen hoped if he suggested leaving. They were laughing and holding hands, as they approached the table.

"Sorry, bro," Eric confessed apologetically, as he pulled out a seat for Christina. "To be hon…est, we were tired of waiting on you! We had a couple more drinks and when you still hadn't returned we de…cided there was noth…ing to do but get back out there and dance," he continued in a drunken slur, winking at Christina.

"No problem," Glen answered sheepishly, now feeling guilty for staying outside for so long.

"What happened?" Eric said with a laugh. "I almost came looking for you. We thought may…be you were sick or fell in the pot or some…. thing."

Christina sat quietly, with her hands folded in her lap, just passing glances between the two handsome brothers, while an occasional ill-placed giggle irrupted.

"Aah, I'm sorry…. I started talking to someone who I met at the grocery store this week." He didn't care that he was lying. Making a good impression was the last thing on his mind at this point, and they were both too drunk to know if he was covering up anyways. *What is Ellen Harper doing to me?* He pondered with frustration. "If you don't mind, I'd like to get going."

Christina looked hurt momentarily thinking her evening was coming to an end, until she realized Eric wasn't getting up from the table like Glen was. He soothed her wounded pride by staying seated and wrapping an arm securely around her waist.

"Would you mind giving me a lift home later, Christina? Just because Glen is being anti-social doesn't mean I want to be," he said with eyes intent on romance, brushing his lips against the side of her neck.

Christina smiled warmly at Eric, realizing this brother was just as appealing, if not more so, at the moment. "I'm glad you asked. I'd love too!" she replied, a little too eagerly, very willing to help Eric out.

"Have a good time," Glen wished, giving Christina an affectionate squeeze to her hand, as he rose from the table. "Maybe we can do it again sometime."

"Sure…" she acknowledged. Even in her intoxicated state she knew that it was never going to happen again.

"Christina, I'm just going to walk Glen out, and I'll be right back. I promise I won't keep you waiting as long as he did, doll," Eric teased, bending over to give her a kiss before following Glen from the room.

"It wasn't necessary to walk me out."

"I know that dumb ass, but I thought I should tell you something before you leave, and I didn't want to mention it in front of Christina."

Glen shook his head, not even caring to address Eric's rude insult he just hurled his way. "Ok…go ahead, and spill it then."

"It's about Ellen Harper."

"What about her?"

"She was here tonight."

"What!" Glen exclaimed, not sure if he heard Eric correctly.

"You heard me. She was here with Mike and Megan Delaney."

"Who are they?"

"Friends of hers. I work with Meg. She can be an even worse bitch than her friend Ellen at times," he said with a laugh.

Glen was tired of dealing with Eric and his sloppy drunken behavior. The sooner he could get this conversation over with the better. "Why didn't you just tell me this earlier? I would have spoken to her."

He began to laugh boisterously. "I don't think that would have been a very good idea. Ellen, more than likely, would have thrown a drink in your face, and she would have probably kicked you where it hurts… real… bad," he grinned with glassy eyes. "But I'm telling you now, bro. I thought I should warn you," he added with an arm around his shoulder.

His breath reeked of beer as he over-pronounced each word much too slowly and with too much air. "She noticed you and Christina dancing, and didn't seem too happy about it either. She left the place crying, and I could have sworn that Mike and Meg were huddled around her, and she was crouching down low. It was obvious she didn't want you to spot her. I guess they thought you would never find out, except they hadn't counted on another Cummings' seeing the whole episode," he added with a laugh and a belch. "I'm *almost* positive they didn't see me."

"This is blowing my mind! She'll never get over this one!" Glen said, while shaking his head in disbelief at his streak of bad luck with Ellen. "Thanks for the warning. And Eric, be careful driving home," he added with concern.

"Anytime, bro, anytime," Eric interjected with a pat to Glen's back. "Hey, I'll see you tomorrow and I'll be fine," he called over his shoulder, already leaving Glen. "I need to get back to Christina before she thinks all Cummings' men are loads like Ellen does!"

Alone, Glen stood by the Mustang, tormented with his thoughts. To think that Ellen had been there, and to also know that seeing Christina and him dancing apparently upset her, left him feeling stunned by this new bad twist of fate.

She does care, he realized, *or she wouldn't have reacted in such a negative way.* What to do with the information was as puzzling as the problem. If Glen confronted her with it, things could possibly just get worse; and yet, if he kept what he found out to himself, he may never know if they could have worked things out. He kicked aside a rock that was near his feet as he continued to think about the evening. *I wonder if she would have danced with me? She was alone, without a date, with only her friends. I, on the other hand, had Christina. What she must of thought,* he pondered in frustration while looking up at the star-lit sky. *She probably is convinced that there has been someone else all this time, even while we were together.*

Glen lay in bed unable to sleep again, continuing to contemplate the situation. *Maybe I should call her or drive out to the farm,* he considered, while lying on his back staring at the ceiling of his bedroom. In the end, sleep overtook any immediate action. "I'll try to straighten this out in the morning," he sighed, rolling over to face another day's work in a few hours.

Megan would not calm down. Ellen felt a flood of relief when Mike finally turned into the now smooth farm lane. "I don't remember the lane ever being in this good of shape, Ellen. Did you have something done to it?" Mike questioned, trying to change the subject even as Megan continued to grumble to herself.

"Glen did it…He filled in the potholes with gravel," Ellen replied quietly.

Meg threw up her hands in frustration. *"Glen did it! Glen did it!* At least he did *something right*, that made you happy!"

Mike just stared at Megan in disbelief. The wine was

making her babble more than usual. He knew better than to take her on as an opponent when she was this upset; but he also knew that she would probably feel bad in the morning if she had an inkling of a memory of the aggressive attitude she was displaying now. Ellen had reached her limit with her too. It was rare that Ellen stood up to her over-bearing friend, but this was one of those times that she had heard quite enough. Megan wasn't being fair to Glen, and she didn't need any further input from her.

"*Megan,*" Ellen stated defensively, rarely calling her anything but Meg. "I don't want to talk about this anymore! Glen has been a good worker, and what he does with his personal life should really not be any concern of yours or mine, for that matter!"

"But, *Ellen*..."

"But Ellen, nothing. I've had a very stressful evening, and I don't wish to discuss this situation anymore tonight. I just want to go to bed and forget this night ever happened."

Megan felt guilty, knowing she had over-stepped her bounds. "I didn't mean to get you so upset. I'm sorry," she replied timidly, backing off considerably.

"You didn't," she said with a poorly attempted smile, lying to pacify her friend. "As I said earlier, I have brought this on myself. I chased him off," she admitted quietly, with fresh tears welling up in her eyes.

Megan's heart was breaking with compassion for her friend. She held back from blurting out more nasty remarks about Glen, turning her frustration towards Mike instead. "Mike, walk Ellen up to her door and see her in safely," she said curtly. "I'm a little tired and I think I will just sit here and wait.

"You don't mind, do you Ellen?"

"Not at all," Ellen said with a sincere smile, reaching over the seat to hug Megan's neck, resting her head lovingly on hers, before she got out of the car.

Megan reassuringly patted Ellen, not turning around to look at her. She wanted to keep her emotions in check.

Mike escorted Ellen to her door. "Do you want me to come in and make sure the boogie man didn't enter while you were away?" His attempt at humor did make her feel somewhat better.

Ellen giggled; Mike had a nice way of making her feel good even when she was feeling rotten. He had lifted her spirits on more than one occasion, especially after Jack's death. "That's ok. Any boogieman entering this house, Cuddles knows to claw to death," she smiled.

"That's good to know," he answered, suddenly turning more sincere in his intent. "You know, it may not be a bad idea to consider getting a dog. I have a friend who has a German Shepherd that just had a litter of puppies a few weeks ago."

Ellen was touched by Mike's concern for her safety. "I'm fine, Mike," she reassured with another smile. "I'm armed with an arsenal of deterrents just in case – ball bat, mace and a sharp kitchen knife…. and all under my bed."

"Ok…I got the message, you don't mess around," he chuckled, "But in case you change your mind, let me know. The puppies are free."

"Thanks, Mike," she added appreciatively. "It does mean a lot to me that you and Megan both tried to show me a nice evening."

“We know that,” he smiled, with compassion in his eyes as he turned to leave. Mike retreated a step, stopped for a moment, and then rejoined Ellen. “I’m sorry about Megan. She can get a little overbearing at times, as we both know. But you know she loves you, and she is concerned for your well-being.”

“Mike, there is no need to explain. Megan is like my sister, and I understand her motivations entirely. Although, I must admit that sometimes hearing the truth isn’t always the thing you want to hear when you are feeling bad. Sometimes it’s better just to drop it, and let it go.”

“Things will work out for the best,” he promised.

They waved their good-byes as Ellen stood on the porch, staring after the exhaust from the retreating car. She looked at her phone, and realized she had a missed call from Glen, and he had left no message. *Probably he called by mistake*, she thought. *Just like seeing him tonight…. one big mistake!*

She remained there for some time afterwards, just looking at the bright full moon, listening to the sounds of the night, while crying softly to herself.

Cuddles was waiting in the kitchen, a short distance away from the door standing guard, as if he overheard Mike’s comment about a dog. He was happy to see Ellen, rubbing against her legs as she walked into the room. “Miss me?” she cooed, bending down to scratch the cat’s head.

“Meoww…” he yawned back, running to the refrigerator, stopping dead in his tracks in front of it.

“I can tell that you’re hungry,” she said to her furbaby. Cuddles continued entangling Ellen’s legs, purring all the while, as she lovingly dished out the cat’s food, mixing the canned with the dry. "At least you care…" Ellen mentioned forlornly, distantly remembering the music… the dancing…. and Glen in the arms of another woman.

She needed to unwind and get a good night's rest. Glen would be coming in the morning, and she would have to face him sooner or later. A bath and a dreamy romance novel of *days gone by* lulled her to sleep, with fantasies of her knight in shining armor rescuing her. And there was her hero, with his handsome loving face – the face of Glen….

Chapter Eighteen

The uneasiness of the morning, and what was to unfold was on the minds of both Ellen and Glen.

If only I hadn't gone to Leon's last night, Glen thought, taking the lane slowly, hoping not to wake Ellen.

She heard the Mustang's engine though, and sat straight up in bed, as if a bolt of lightening had struck her on the spot. "Glen is here," she remarked, rising quickly and grabbing the pink terrycloth bathrobe that was hanging on a hook on the back of her bedroom door. "I won't give him the satisfaction of knowing I saw him at Leon's last night," she resolved, after a night of indecision.

She paced the floor of the kitchen, and randomly peaked out of the window, waiting for him to approach the house, but he didn't. Finally, she gave up, deciding to get an early start to her day.

Glen was pulling weeds from the garden, when he noticed the light snap on in the kitchen. *She's up early*, he observed, realizing that never happened since he began working at the farm. He hoped she wasn't sick, but he knew that possibility was far from remote. He guessed that last night still weighed heavily upon her mind, or maybe she had too much to drink.

They both kept busy with their morning activities – Glen, with the gardening and Ellen, with the housecleaning. Ellen vacuumed her bedroom carpeting. She could not erase from her mind the happy faces of Glen and the smiling, pretty young woman dancing intimately close in his arms. Reality finally registered, as she unintentionally pushed the vacuum into the dresser's leg. "Oh my, what have I done?" She dropped to her knees to survey the damage. "I can't believed I chipped the wood," she said in dismay. "My mother would have a fit if she could see what I did to Grandma's dresser."

She sat for a time on the floor, resting against the side of the antique, glancing around the room. Her eyes took in the eyelet lace that graced the bed and windows. The Victorian reproduction, floral-print wallpaper, she and Jack had chosen together. Jack…the memories of time spent with him in this room…. together…in this bed. And now Glen… and new memories spent with him here. *It was wrong*, she reasoned, *to think of Glen in the same manner as Jack.* It felt to Ellen like a desecration to their marriage bed, but she was growing weary from an unreasonable sense of loyalty to a dead man and a dead dream. She drew her knees up to her chest, clutching them close, resting her chin upon them. "I want him so badly!" she cried. "What stupid mistake have I made by sending him away?"

Through her hiccupping sobs, she heard a soft knocking on the front door. "Now who can that be? It must be Glen," she said with alarm, jumping up too quickly and catching her toe on the dresser foot, as if the furniture was returning the blow that the vacuum had inflicted just a few minutes prior. "Ouch!" she squealed, jumping up and down on one foot, looking at herself in the mirror. Her eyes were red from crying and her hair was in a disarrayed tumble. "Oh my… I look a mess. He'll know that I have been crying," she sobbed, blowing her nose on a tissue and combing the mismanaged locks back into a barrette. She rubbed both hands over her eyes, trying to wipe away the all-too-apparent evidence of the crying episode.

The knock sounded again. “Coming…” she yelled, making her way at a fast pace to the front door.

“Glen…. hello.”

“Ellen…hi. Can we talk, or is it a bad time?” He noticed the redness of her eyes, but wasn’t sure if she was sick or had been crying.

“It’s as good a time as any. Come in,” she offered, smiling timidly as she stood to the side, holding the door open for Glen to walk through.

“Ladies first,” he said, while returning the smile, motioning for her to precede him with his out-stretched hand. Ellen made no offer of something to eat or drink, which was her normal way. She had no desire to be polite, as she sat staring down at the table instead of at Glen, still feeling the pain of her torn and pent-up emotions. Glen was direct, wasting no time and getting to the point.

“Ellen, I know you saw me last night at Leon’s.”

“Why would you think that?” she asked, surprise registering on her face, as she looked up at Glen.

“Eric was there also, and he saw you there with your friends. He didn’t tell me any of this until after you left. If I knew you had been there, I would have come over to where you were sitting.”

“Glen, that’s nice of you to say that, but I really didn’t see either one of you there,” she lied, attempting a smile as she stated her half-truth, finding it hard to hide her pain. She hadn’t seen

Eric, and knowing now that he was there only made things worse.

Glen cleared his throat; suddenly feeling frustrated by her lack of honesty. His hands ran nervously though his hair, considering carefully what to say next. He looked deeply into her eyes desiring only for her to be honest with him. *"Ellen…I know you knew I was there,"* he said quietly, hating himself for making her disclose the truth against her will.

She looked alarmed, cornered like a child for trying to conceal the obvious.

"You saw me dancing with someone else, and it bothered you, didn't it?" he questioned softly, while reaching out to touch her arm, but drawing back, not sure of her reaction.

Ellen began to cry, feeling totally embarrassed by Glen's confrontation. She was feeling vulnerable at his truthfulness, never expecting him to be so open with what occurred. She dropped her head again with her shoulders heaving with anxiety.

His heart went out to her, wanting to hold her, but restrained his desire for fear of her rejection. "It's ok, Ellen," he consoled softly. "This whole thing between you and I has become totally crazy! The girl I was with meant *nothing* to me. I met her at the airport yesterday when I went to pick up Eric. She found out Eric and I was going to Leon's, so she met us there. It wasn't a date… She just showed up. I danced with her because I felt obligated to do so," he admitted regretfully. "Eric and her both kept throwing hints around about everyone dancing. I know it's not a good excuse, but I was upset with you for rejecting me. Damn it, Ellen, the whole time I was with her, I couldn't think of anything or anyone but you. I kept thinking – why can't I be with you, instead of her!" His face held a mask of frustration as he searched her own, waiting for her to speak.

Ellen's eyes met Glen's again, trying to absorb what he had just said to her. *He did still care!* Her heart was soaring with the possibility of another chance with him. This man that she loved! "I'm sorry I lied to you, Glen. I just couldn't admit…"

"I know," he interrupted, taking her hand finally in his own, squeezing it compassionately. There was no need for her to finish the sentence, and he didn't want to put her through any further pain or embarrassment. Relief washed over him, when she did not pull away as he held her hand in his own.

She became lost in his stormy blue eyes that were warm with affection. "I'm sorry for so many things, Glen, but mostly for my decision to set limits on our relationship as I did. I love you, Glen. I was so wrong," she breathed, with needed release.

"No, it is I who should apologize," he comforted. "You had every right to slow things down if you didn't feel ready to be as intimate as we had become. I acted childish, and I couldn't accept your rejection. I just didn't know how else to get over you without avoiding you," he admitted, feeling now that this whole thing was his fault. "I never stopped believing that one day you would come to me with a change of heart, but as the week progressed I was beginning to question if I was fooling myself. I hate to see you in pain from last night, but at least we are talking again. I love you too, Ellen," he said tenderly, taking her face between his hands, kissing her gently on each of her tear-swollen eyelids, trying to heal the hurt.

He captured her lips, savoring them softly at first, but with more aggression with each repeat of the intimate contact. They were in each other's arms in minutes, with Glen gathering Ellen close to him.

"I can't believe this is happening," Ellen sighed between kisses. "I thought we were over."

"Believe it, darling. I have thought of no one else but you, wishing and hoping for this time to come," he said heatedly, kissing her neck and earlobes.

"Glen, make me yours again," Ellen, pleaded urgently, reaching her hand boldly down to his pants, rubbing his hardness.

"Oh Ellen," he breathed in a raspy voice. "Are you sure?"

"I've never been more sure of anything in my life," she answered, pulling Glen to his feet, leading him without fear to the waiting comfort of her bed.

Hands and fingers were not fast enough. Clothes were in the way of the needed closeness they now longed for. Modesty was forgotten with the curtains still open. They were savagely starved for the sweet release they knew the other would bring.

With ragged breath, Glen carried Ellen nude to the awaiting bed, taking a hardened bud of her nipple into his mouth. He groaned deeply with satisfaction, finally realizing he was where he had longed to be for the last week.

Ellen's back arched up in response to the intimate contact. "Oh, Glen… it feels soo… good."

"Tell me what you want, Ellen. Don't be afraid, darling."

"Kiss me, Glen, and then use your imagination. I trust you to know what I want," she urged seductively.

Ellen's words and actions made Glen a savage with desire. Their probing tongues explored deeply into the other one's mouth, as Glen touched and fondled Ellen's breasts. Each caress spiraled them to new heights of longing. Ellen took the length of Glen's manhood between her palms, as Glen likewise delved deeply with his fingers into Ellen's slick, wet cavern of femininity.

"I can't take it anymore," Ellen pleaded as Glen trailed lingering kisses from her lips, to her breasts, to her abdomen, to her heated triangle of desire, igniting the flames until she burned and exploded with ecstasy.

"The day is still young, love, and we have a week's worth of catching up to do, so save your strength," Glen challenged enticingly, rolling Ellen to her side.

She no longer held back in her desires though, uninhibited in her actions. She gave Glen the same loving attention she had just moments before experienced, trailing kisses down his length until her mouth made contact with his male organ. She massaged and fondled him until he reached for her, ready for release. She straddled him, wrapping her legs around his own tightly, beginning a slow but steady rhythm that quickened in speed along with the beating of their hearts.

"I love you so much, Ellen," Glen moaned, wet with perspiration, and lost in the spell she had woven over him.

"I love you too," she echoed, bending over to kiss each of Glen's breasts, causing him to shiver with emotion.

He gathered her close, rolling Ellen beneath him, riding her uncontrollably with long deliberate, deep strokes that left her aching for more.

"Stop the madness in me!" she implored, wrapping her legs around his waist.

"Your wish is my command!" he hoarsely answered, as

they climbed the ladder of completion together, cascading back down amongst the falling stars.

"I could lie here forever like this, with you in my arms," Glen said in a dreamy distant way, after some time of just cuddling and touching the other.

Ellen sighed, "Me too…"

"I guess I should be getting back to work though."

Glen smiled and looked at Ellen. "I only thought we would talk. *This*…I never considered to be even a remote possibility," he whispered with pleased contentment.

Ellen grinned. "I guess we both got the wishes of our hearts today."

"Yes, I guess we did, he said happily, kissing her fully on her mouth.

She turned to snuggle closer to Glen's side. "I don't want you to go back to work today."

"What?" he questioned in surprise, raising her chin so he could look into her eyes.

"I want to spend the rest of the day together with you in a celebration."

"What are we celebrating?"

"Several things. You and I …Coming to my senses. But most of all, a release – a release from the past. I finally feel a sense of freedom to go on. That Jack wouldn't really mind us being together."

Glen propped up on an elbow looking down at Ellen as he played with a wisp of her hair. "Has that been weighing you down that heavily?" Glen asked in concern, suddenly enlightened to an explanation for Ellen's actions.

"Yes, it has…" she admitted with down cast eyes.

"It's ok…" he reassured, bringing her chin back up for a light kiss. "I respect your loyalty to his memory. I wouldn't want you to be any other way."

Tears swelled up in Ellen's eyes. Glen understood, and he hadn't condemned her for feeling the way she did. He had become, in the short time she knew him, like a gift from heaven. It felt right, as if Jack were granting his blessing for their relationship. Contentment and peace were apart of her now. This time Ellen would not let Glen go…

It was some time before they rose, just smiling contently between the light kisses that they couldn't stop giving the other, with only love and forgiveness radiating from their faces. There was no longer the feeling of being prohibited by the past or inhibited by the future. Their only desire was to be together.

"Let's go swimming today. There is a pond down the hill at the end of my property," she exclaimed with child-like enthusiasm. "I haven't done this since…. since before Jack's death."

"I'll do whatever you want, Ellen," Glen said softly, "But I am feeling a little guilty playing hooky and getting paid for it."

"Glen, you deserve every cent I have given you, and I know you are caught up with the garden. This is what I need now…to be with you," she confessed with sincerity.

Glen smiled understandably, happy for Ellen's change of heart that she was revealing her true feelings. "I don't have swimming trunks with me."

"I know," she teased, but no one can see us down there anyways. We will be in total seclusion."

"You naughty girl," he grinned, while tickling her ribs, making Ellen squeal with laughter.

"Stop it, Glen, before I pee myself."

"Ok, I can do that, but there aren't any guarantees I won't do other things to punish you."

"I can hardly wait," she laughed, jumping from the bed, running to the bathroom.

Ellen emerged, dressed in her new one-piece, royal blue bathing suit that she had just discovered days before in a lady's shop in the downtown shopping area of Fillmore. She spun around, wanting Glen's approval. He whistled and winked while nodding a yes that he liked it.

They made their way to the kitchen, and Glen looked on in open admiration, taking in Ellen's slim and trim athletic form as she poured and handed him an iced tea.

"How about I pack us a picnic lunch and fill a thermos with the rest of the tea?"

"Sure, but only if I can help you," Glen offered with a smile.

Ellen put Glen to work filling the thermos and packing pretzels and homemade chocolate chip cookies, while she made some ham and cheese sandwiches and cut up celery and carrot sticks. They packed the basket, throwing in a couple apples on second thought, along with napkins, plates and cups.

"There…we're done!" she said with satisfaction. "Except for a couple of towels and a blanket."

Glen grabbed the picnic basket and thermos, as Ellen made her way to the hall closet to get the other things. They walked hand in hand down the path to the place where Glen always wondered where it led. Today was the day he would finally find out – with the woman he loved and was coming to treasure.

Chapter Nineteen

Eric rolled over with a yawn, stretching his arms high above his head; taking in a woman's partially exposed nude back that was covered with a sheet. Her warm backside had been pressed intimately into his morning erection, and he knew there wouldn't be any resistance on her part if he reached out and woke her up; taking her again for probably the third time, if his memory served him correctly. That was, if he wanted to, and he didn't. It was all coming back to him now, along with the intense pain of a hangover and whom he was with. The smiling, perky-nosed Christina Newcomer; the one Glen had ever so conveniently dumped on him.

Not to say that she wasn't attractive, or even pleasant company, but Eric wasn't on the prowl right now for a meaningful relationship. Alcohol had dulled his senses, as it had in the past, helping to bring about the fulfillment of his immediate needs. Now his need of the moment was to get out of this awkward situation that he found himself in, as quickly and with as little of a scene as possible.

Eric gingerly lifted the sheet, slowly uncovering his nude frame while sliding from the bed as quietly as possible, hoping not to rouse the sleeping female. Christina began to stir, stopping Eric dead in his tracks.

"Mmmm…. Eric, is that you?"

"Aaah…yeah it is, but I need to get going. I have an appointment with someone this morning," he explained hurriedly.

Christina sat upright, exposing her breasts as she digested Eric's words. "Will I see you later?" she asked demurely.

"I'm too busy today, doll," he muttered, while finding his clothes and dressing hurriedly.

"How about tomorrow then?" she questioned anxiously, already sensing Eric's rejection.

"I don't think so," he replied, suddenly feeling guilty from his lack of manners. He looked at her with a fake pretense of a smile. "I'll try to call you in a few days." That was all the better he could come up with. Eric had no intentions of ever calling or getting in touch with her again.

"Good bye, Eric," Christiana replied sadly, with the same apprehensive feeling that she had felt towards Glen the night before. "I'll be waiting to hear from you," she called, as he slammed the door behind him, leaving her alone in her own house.

"Damnit!" Eric yelled, realizing his second problem of the day. "Glen has my damn car!" There was no way he was asking Christina for help, and showing her where he lived. He was relieved he hadn't given her his cellphone number either. Walking home or calling a cab, were his only options. He knew Glen would be at Ellen's working, and he probably had his phone turned off even if he did try to call him. It was only five miles, so he decided walking would help clear his head.

The distance was more than he anticipated, as he sat on the curb nursing not only the pain in his head, but his tired and aching feet. *Italian loafers were not made to stand up against such abuse*, he determined, as he glanced up and down the familiar neighborhood street. *Only a mile and I will be home…* he thought with relief, as he started walking again. "Glen and I have to have a serious talk about finding him a car. This is ridiculous and my good will gesture needs to come to an end!" he moaned aloud realizing he was limping more than walking.

"Hi stranger, need a lift?"

"Oh no!" Eric exclaimed quietly to himself under his breath, not wanting to glance up for fear it was Christina that was following him. But curiosity won out, realizing the voice rang of familiarity.

"Oh…Melinda…hi…I didn't expect that it was you."

"And *whom* did you expect it to be?" she questioned in an accusing tone.

"Not anyone in particular," he said with a convincing smile. "But to be honest, not you either."

She felt the same sense of hurt as she felt a few days earlier from Eric's lack of commitment. "I can leave you here, if that is what you would like," she informed him cynically knowing he was in pain.

"No, *please* don't do that," he said in desperation while holding on to a stop sign pole, realizing the thought of a ride sounded very inviting.

"Okay… I guess it isn't out of my way to go past your house," she added in a theatrical tone of indifference, deriving much pleasure from watching him suffer. He was really at her mercy, and this was a first for the great Eric Cummings.

She glanced at her watch and feigned another complication

in taking him home. "Eric, I really *do* need to meet someone in fifteen minutes. I think this is going to rush me."

Eric wasn't giving up that easily. "Melinda, I wouldn't ask if I didn't really need a lift. My feet are killing me and Glen has my car. I called a cab, but I must have given him the wrong street address where I was at because he never showed up."

Melinda knew the second part of his statement was probably a lie, but the site of him being vulnerable and practically begging her for a ride, tugged at her heart's strings. She wanted him in the car next to her, even if it was only for a short ride to his house. She smiled at him, tearing down the wall between them.

"Get in. I'll take you home."

"Thanks, Melinda," he said, while hurrying to get into the car, breathing a sigh of relief. "How have you been?" Eric asked, taking in the site of her face that looked more beautiful than he remembered.

"I've been just fine. Staying busy at work as usual."

"And your evenings?" he asked with a coy smile, over-stepping his bounds as he always did.

"My evenings? Oh, I guess you could say that they are as usual too."

Eric snickered, as he looked down at his shoes, realizing her flippant way was as appealing as she was physically. "Ok, Melinda, let's stop beating around the bush. Are you seeing someone else?"

"Someone else? What is that supposed to mean? No, I'm not Eric! Not that it is any business of yours!" she declared, while slamming on the brakes several houses away from his own. "But I think if any questions are to be asked, I should be the one asking them of you! I know you have been *seeing someone else*, as you put it!"

Eric chuckled as he turned to look at her. "Oh you do, do you?" he replied, finding amusement in her jealousy. "And how would you know that?"

"I have my ways of finding things out, and I don't know what you think is so funny," she answered, getting madder by the minute by his egotistical attitude that needed to be lowered a notch or two.

"Ok, Melinda, enough of these silly little-girl games that you are enjoying playing with me," Eric replied haughtily, while squarely looking her in the face. "We are mature adults, and here is the truth, whether you like it or not. I *have been out*, and *will continue to do so* until I feel the need to be committed to one person. Possessiveness and jealously are turn-offs to me. I answer to *no one* but myself. I stopped doing that when I left my parent's home years ago. I'm sorry to say this to you, but apparently you have made more out of our relationship outside of work than you should have."

Melinda's face turned bright red at the humiliating, tactless and harsh words that Eric had just hurled at her. She hated herself even more for giving him any satisfaction at seeing her crumble by his insults. "I guess you are right. I have made more out of our relationship than I should have," she reluctantly confessed, wishing she had never offered him a ride. "But be assured, you don't need to worry about that happening again, Mr. Cummings. From here on out, our relationship is *strictly* business and *nothing more*! Now *please* get out of my car, because your ride is over! This taxi takes you no further!" she announced harshly with her voice trembling uncontrollably.

Eric looked at her in disbelief. “Take it easy, Melinda. I’m getting out,” he stated with alarm, knowing he had ignited a dangerous fuse in her. He opened the door quickly, barely having enough time to jump out of the way of her fast advancing car.

Melinda squealed away rapidly. “You asshole!” she yelled while pounding the steering wheel. Once out of ear range she cried openly, wishing she had run him down in the street. “I may love him, but it stops now!” she vowed. “He doesn’t *deserve* my love!”

Eric felt like a real bastard for what he had just done to Melinda. He was falling in love with her, and he didn’t want to admit it to either himself or to her. True commitment to one person was as foreign to him as the blisters he now carried on his feet. Shutting the whole thing down seemed to be the only sensible thing to do. Melinda deserved someone more stable than he was. In the long run, he was doing her a favor, whether she could see that now or not.

Chapter Twenty

"Watch you step!" Glen warned, stepping over a tree root that was sticking up high enough for someone to trip over. Ellen smiled, appreciative of Glen's protectiveness.

"There's a nice spot right over there by that grove of cottonwood trees where we can lay our things," she gestured, pointing in the general direction.

"Lead the way," he said with a laugh, following her to their destination. They dropped the items, and laid the blanket under the trees.

"Do you want to eat or swim first?" Ellen asked.

"I'm hungry, but a good swim would sure feel good since it is so hot out already."

"I was hoping you would say that," Ellen yelled, racing to the water's edge.

Glen called after her. "What about skinny dipping?"

"Later," she answered, diving quickly into the chilly but exhilarating water's depth. Glen was swift to follow.

"Whew, is this cold!" Ellen yelled, swimming towards Glen. "I wasn't thinking, but it is just the beginning of June. Maybe we should have waited a week or two yet."

"Don't be a sissy. It feels great!" he teased, meeting Ellen where they were still able to stand.

She wrapped her goose-bumped arms around Glen's neck, whispering in his ear. "I'm glad you decided to join me."

"I'm glad you asked," he answered, bringing his lips down to her waiting ones for a searing kiss.

"Are you cold?" she questioned, feeling a shiver of a chill running through him.

"No…it's you babe," he breathed. "Your kisses bring that reaction out in me," he said with an alluring smile that made her breath catch from the sight of him.

Ellen's eyes shone with happiness as she gazed into Glen's, that were shining back at her warmly. They clung to each other tightly, as she rested her head on his shoulder, listening to the water lap up around them.

"This is heavenly. Let's stay here forever - just like this."

"I'll stay here forever, but I would like to do more than just stay here like this. I could think of more fun ways to pass the time other than just hugging."

"Why don't you show me?" Ellen challenged, growing bolder with each renewed encounter.

Glen smiled devilishly, lowering Ellen's bathing suit from her shoulders to her waist, planting kisses on all her bare areas, while caressing each breast and sucking deeply on each nipple, bring them to firm peaks of hardness. He played with each breast as if he were a potter molding clay. "Now isn't this more fun than just hugging?" he teased, bring his head back up to Ellen's view.

"Do you need to ask?" she breathed heavily, already lost to Glen's magical touch.

Words were forgotten as he totally removed her suit, throwing it to shore. She unzipped his cutoffs pitching them to shore also, a short distance away from her bathing suit. Ellen wrapped her legs around Glen's waist, interlocking them behind his back. His hands reached out to grasp her buttocks as she guided his firmness into her opening. "Ride me, Ellen," he passionately requested, bracing with a wide stance as his feet sunk deeply into the thick soft mud on the bottom of the pond's floor.

She obeyed willingly, riding him fierce and hard throwing her head back while bracing her hands on his chest. "Oh Glen, I'm coming," she moaned, lashing out with wild abandon.

"Me too, honey, me too…" he answered, out of control with the moment. They clung tightly to each other, shuddering with a climatic finality, and then held each other for some time afterwards, trying to regain a normal breathing pattern once again.

"Whew…" Glen exhaled, feeling winded. "I don't know if I have the strength to swim back to shore after that," he teased with a hint of real truth to his words.

"Maybe I need to give you mouth to mouth resuscitation," she mocked, adding to their fun. Glen burst out laughing, splashing Ellen playfully. "So that's the way you are going to be," she threatened between mouthfuls of water, trying to act serious. She dove under the water and then reappeared, exploding quickly like a hidden rocket behind his back, attempting to push his head down to the bottom of the pond. And then just as quickly, swimming the short distance to the shore, scrambling to the grassy knoll finding the place where Glen's cutoffs lay.

"What are you doing?" Glen asked, still disoriented by Ellen's sudden maneuver.

"What does it look like?" she prodded, holding the jean shorts up like a trophy. "Remember playing the game "Hide and Seek" when you were a kid?"

"Yeah…" Glen answered, suddenly feeling apprehensive as to what Ellen had in mind. "What are you *getting at*, Ellen?" he asked, with dawning awareness, not sure he liked what she had in mind.

"You'll see," she answered in a prankish manner. "I just thought it might be fun for us to play that *fun* game again." With that, she tossed the shorts with all her might, far above Glen's head into the pond. They landed with a loud splash and then sank below the surface.

"Ellen!" he yelled, half in disbelief and yet tickled by her cute way of flirting. "What do you expect me to do now? I do have to walk back up to the house later, you know."

"I know, I know," she mocked, while shaking her head from side-to-side and clicking her tongue, pretending sympathy for Glen's predicament. "I guess you will just have to hope I don't throw your beach towel in there too."

"Ellen, you wouldn't."

"Wouldn't I?" she teased, bending down to grab the towel.

Glen wasn't taking any chances. He swam at a break-neck pace to shore, turning only briefly to orientate himself where his shorts went down, for future reference. "So… you think you are funny?" he yelled, while running and tackling her down on the beach blanket.

"I would say that you look especially funny, and yet strikingly sexy right now."

"Oh really," Glen blurted out, acting as if he was mad. "I'll show you funny," he answered, while straddling Ellen and holding her arms high above her head with one hand, and tickling her all over with the other; planting ticklish kisses down the column of her neck. "Unless you beg for forgiveness, I will just have to continue with this form of torture, and then get your suit, and throw it… and then throw it…" Glen said with hesitation, trying to locate the perfect place. "Up in that tree over there," he added while pointing to the spot with one hand but still holding her secure with the other.

"You wouldn't!"

"Oh yes I would!" he announced triumphantly, calling her bluff.

"Ok, I'm sorry," she giggled, as he still held her constrained. "I'll help you find your cutoffs, as soon as I get my bathing suit back on. I know where I threw them."

"No thank you. I'll find them myself. You may throw them out further, and only make the problem worse."

Ellen wasn't sure if Glen was being serious now, and she was feeling suddenly worried that maybe she took things too far. She gave him a troubled frown.

"Fooled you! I'm just kidding!" he yelled, diving back in to the pond with a running leap.

Ellen laughed, enjoying the game immensely, rejoining him in the water. She felt young and carefree again. After several failed attempts, Ellen discovered his shorts. "Here," she said with panting, broken speech, still worn-out from diving under the water so many times. She swam to him, handing Glen the drenched shorts. "I won't ever do that again," she promised.

"Don't say that! Just think of all the fun we would have missed today if you hadn't come up with that fun game of "Hide and Seek" that we played," he replied with a grin. "And just remember, paybacks can be nasty."

She smiled at him reassuringly, "I think I'm up for the challenge."

He gave her a quick kiss. "Can we eat now? All this swimming has left me starving."

She watched Glen slip the wet jeans back over his slick tight form. Even this action brought waves of excitement that started a burning between her legs again. He was a perfect specimen of a healthy male - her healthy male. She liked the sound of those words.

They ate the lunch that they packed together in its entirety, and then dragged the beach blanket out from under the shade of the trees, and placed it on a soft grassy patch of grass, catching the rays of the afternoon sun.

"I can't remember the last time I did this," Glen mentioned warmly, while they lay on their stomachs holding hands, staring into each other's eyes.

"What do you mean? Laying out in the sun?"

"No, I mean swimming, a picnic, and *you know.*"

"I *know what*?" she grinned, rolling to her side to await the answer.

He smiled back at her in his cute nasty-boy way. “Well, hopefully, we won’t let this blanket go to waste.”

“I hoped that’s what you would say,” she answered softly, meeting his lips for a kiss.

Their lovemaking was as bold and brazen as the hot-searing sun that they enjoyed together. In the aftermath of the passion they shared, Glen leaned back on his elbows, glancing cautiously around at his surroundings.

“What’s wrong?” Ellen questioned with concern.

“It’s ok,” he said with a reassuring smile. “I just hope you are right and no one can see us out here. Because for all we know they are filming an X-rated movie, and we are the stars.”

“Oh Glen, don’t be silly!” she said, while shaking her head and looking at him like he was crazy.

“You never know…what might be lurking in the woods,” he replied in a low scary voice, while grabbing her quickly and pretending to bite her neck.

“Glen, stop it! You’re silly!” she giggled, trying to get away from his playful embrace. “I think we should get back up to the house, because I want to check on Cuddles.”

“Nonsense, you are just scared.”

“I am not!” she adamantly replied, with her hands on her hips.

“Yes, you are. Admit it,” he teased, picking her up in his arms while running back to the pond.

“One more swim and then we will go home.”

Home…. Ellen liked the sound of those words. Not her home alone, but their home together. She would hold to that dream now… as she clung to Glen’s neck. Maybe one day, may one day…

“Glen!” she screamed. *“It’s cold!”*

He dropped her like a sack of potatoes with a loud splash into the refreshing sparkling pond, bringing her back to reality.

Chapter Twenty-One

"The hamburgers are just about done," Glen yelled through the kitchen screen door to Ellen, who was busily putting the side dishes of corn on the cob, baked beans, and potato salad on the table.

"Ok Glen, I'll be right out with a plate for them. Everything else is ready," she called back to him. Ellen pushed the screened door aside with her elbow, juggling a platter and spatula with one hand and the rolls with the other.

"Why don't we eat outside?" Glen asked with a smile, while placing each burger in a roll. It's such a nice day to do so."

"I guess we can do that, but the patio furniture is dirty and it will take awhile to clean it up."

"We don't have to sit at the table," he grinned. "The porch swing or the front porch steps would suit me just fine."

"That sounds fun! I guess we can just keep the food in the kitchen though, and make up our plates from there."

"Whatever is easiest," he answered in his easygoing manner, trying to keep the evening as simple and carefree as possible.

They ate leisurely, not in a rush for their second picnic of the day to be done with as quickly as the first. The day had been too perfect for words, each moment and sensation a thing to be savored before the sun set, putting the day to rest. The taste of the food, the smell of the country air, and the persistent longing that they held for each other, were more pleasant than any words spoken. There was a new freedom, with no more holding back in restraint and confusion – only free to soar like the last few birds flying overhead back to their homes for the night.

"Mmmm… everything was so good, Ellen. You sure are a good cook," Glen complimented with genuine heartfelt praise, before taking the last bite of his hamburger.

She smiled at him lovingly, removing a crumb of food that was still on his chin. "Thanks, Glen. It was easy with your help."

"You did most of the work. How about a walk after dinner?"

"I could use a walk," she gestured, with her hands patting her over-extended abdomen. "I ate too much, but then I always seem to do that," she giggled.

"I don't know what you are talking about. You had only one plate and I had three!"

"But my plate was filled to the brim!" she confessed.

"You need to keep up your strength, especially after all that exercising we did today," he said with a sly grin.

"I think my energy level can manage just fine with a few less calories, even with such exhausting activities," she replied with a playful scolding look.

"Yeah, you're right. Ok the real truth is…you did pig out."

"Glen…" Ellen replied, looking at him questionably.

"Just kidding," he joked, running off the porch. She followed close behind, pretending to be hurt by his words while chasing him.

"That's *some way* to talk to someone you claim to be in love with."

He stopped the game, reaching for her and enfolding her in his arms. "I'm sorry," he whispered against her hair. "I was just kidding. We Cummings have a real problem with that. We tease the people we are closest to, but sometimes they don't realize it isn't to be taken seriously."

"I know you were only joking," she smiled with longing written all over her face, gazing deeply into Glen's blue eyes.

"Good," he answered, meeting her lips for a passionate kiss. "Up for that walk now?" Glen asked, already finding it hard to concentrate on anything but making love to Ellen again.

"Sure," she smiled, grabbing his hand. He led her around the garden, updating her on the growing process of each different plant, and then he walked her by the pasture fence and the barn. He was proud of his accomplishments and yearned for Ellen's approval. If she were pleased, he would be happy. And after today, he knew that she was happy. There was no longer a doubt in his mind.

"Everything looks so great, Glen, and the vegetables are further along this year than they were last year at this time. I'll be able to get the produce stand running quicker than I have in the past," she added with satisfaction.

"Where do you put the stand?"

"At the end of the lane. People all over town know about my stand. It helps to pay the bills."

"I guess it does. Where do you store it?"

"It's in the barn against the back wall, under some tarps. Do you want to see it?"

"Sure. I noticed the tarping, but I never thought to look beneath it. I guess I have been too busy with other things around here."

Glen opened the heavy, newly painted barn door that still hinted of the pungency of the new paint. Ellen entered first, while Glen wedged a block of wood beneath it and the floor, giving more light to the already dimming room. The smells of hay, turpentine and paint filled the air. New and old mixed together, creating an overwhelming heady aroma.

Ellen reached for the light's pull cord that was dangling from a rafter overhead. "That's better," she remarked, already throwing one of the tarps from the stand. Glen helped her with the other two remaining ones.

"Wow, what a stand!" Glen observed with admiration.

"Yes, it is nice," Ellen, replied. "Jack had it built by a carpenter in town. We only used it one season, before he died…" she said with downcast eyes.

"I'm sorry," Glen consoled, wrapping an arm around Ellen's shoulder.

"It's fine," she said with determined newfound strength. "I wanted the stand more than he did anyway. CWS kept him busy. I wanted this as my diversion."

"I see…."

She broke free of Glen's hold, totally absorbed in studying each board of the structure. "It needs some tightening, Glen," she pointed out, showing him several loose boards. "Do you think you can do the repairs, and have it sanded and painted in a week?" Ellen asked optimistically, while glancing up at him with hope-filled eyes.

"I think I can manage that," he answered with a warm smile, not wanting to disappoint her. "But none of the garden's produce will be in by next week."

"I realize that, but I can start out with some baked goods and homemade bread. Then before you know it, the spring onions and lettuce will be in. After that, everything else will just start ripening. It's that way every year."

"Yeah, you're right," he replied with a little sadness to his voice.

"What's wrong?" Ellen questioned, trying to look in Glen's eyes for the answer.

"I don't know," he mumbled, scuffing up the dust on the barn's floor with his foot. "I guess I'll just miss seeing you while I'm working. I can see it now, everyone from town will be keeping you company instead of me," he added as he stroked her face lovingly with his thumb.

Ellen was touched by his honesty. "Oh Glen, we will always have the evenings," she said sweetly.

"That's true," he smiled, feeling only half-convinced.

"Also, I do have a "Sorry I'm Closed" sign that I hang on

the front of the stand whenever I need to be in the house."

An idea sprung up as Glen grabbed Ellen, holding her close. "I guess you will need to put that sign out a lot," he grinned playfully.

"If I do that, I won't make any money, Mr. Cummings," she giggled, relaxing in Glen's embrace.

"Yeah, I guess you're right, but long lunch hours may need to be in order."

"I think that is workable," she teased, reaching up on her toes to plant a quick kiss on Glen's lips.

"I need more than that," he beckoned in a husky voice, engulfing her mouth with his own in a searing kiss that left Ellen feeling weak.

"Are you ready to go back to the house now?" she asked slowly, finding it hard to speak. "I need…to put the food away, and…do the dishes."

"Those things can wait," he answered heavily, picking her up in his arms and carrying her to a pile of soft hay in an adjacent corner of the barn. "Wait here," he instructed, as he removed the block of wedged wood from under the barn door. The dimly lit room and the streaks of light still poking through the barn's walls, cast a seductive aura surrounding Ellen. Glen paused, just taking in the beautiful picture she made while lying in the hay. He made his way back, reclaiming her with a passionate embrace. Glen began to unbutton her shirt.

"In here?" she questioned apprehensively, honestly surprised that he wanted her so soon again.

"Why not?" he smiled, already pulling her shorts and

panties down from her hips. His shorts were soon to follow. Ellen observed his muscular form and bulging manhood already hard with desire. Would she ever grow tired of this man? She knew that would never be the case in her lifetime.

He walked to a nail hook on the barn's rough interior wall, and removed a soft, flannel long-sleeved shirt that he had left there in case it was cool on any given morning. "Here, roll onto this," he beckoned, as he smoothed out the soft fabric with his hands.

"You make me feel like a princess," she whispered, as she obliged Glen's request.

"You are a princess. My princess…" he said, while straddling her on all fours. "I have fantasized about us doing this in the barn for days now."

"You have?" she smiled in surprise, still amazed with the secrets that Glen was revealing.

"Yeah…and everything we would do right here in the hay, with no one to see us except for a few mice and bats maybe."

"Bats and mice!" Ellen exclaimed with a start, while sitting up and taking Glen with her. "Maybe we should go back in the house."

"Oh, come on," Glen insisted, nibbling on Ellen's neck. "I'm here to protect you," he reassured, wrapping his strong arms securely around her waist. "No man or beast would dare harm my Ellen," he promised, while continuing to kiss her neck, laying her slowly back down in their nest of love.

"Glen, you make me feel so wonderful," she said with emotion, while framing his face with her delicate hands. He turned his face into her palm, kissing and licking it erotically.

"Make me feel wonderful, Ellen," he challenged, lowering her hand to his erection. She loved the feel of him, velvety smooth but oh so strong. He likewise relished in her feel – slick, wet and tight, wanting to feel each pulsating sensation. Her hands guided him into her opening once again, ready to receive the gift of his affection. The hay spoke beneath them, as the urgency of each intimate caress and movement intensified. "Oh, Ellen…" Glen proclaimed exuberantly, as each muscle of his body became hard, rigid, and perspired from the vigorous workout.

"Oh, oh yes…" Ellen echoed, giving way to her own glorious release.

They lay side by side on the shirt now tangled with hay. Glen smiled at Ellen, as he lovingly picked pieces of the hay from her hair. "You look so beautiful like this."

"Glen, you're too kind," she answered with a doubtful look on her face. "I know that isn't the case."

"To me it is. Don't take me wrong, you look great dressed up; but this earthy, healthy look, I like best."

Ellen blushed. "I think you would tell me I looked beautiful if I were covered in mud."

"Maybe…" he teased with a quick kiss. "How about on the first big rain we find a big puddle and get naked and make love…? You know…" he grinned, "Like they did at Woodstock."

"Glen, you are crazy!" she cajoled, secretly considering the idea to be potentially fun.

"I know I'm crazy – crazy for you!" he replied, wrapping her tightly in his embrace.

Several kisses later, Ellen's intentions could no longer be dissuaded. "Don't take this wrong, Glen, I would really love to stay here all night wrapped in your arms; but I do need to get back to the house. Cuddles has probably helped himself to all of the leftovers."

"Smart cat," Glen winked, as he got out of the hay, brushing the straw stubble from his body.

"Put on your shorts," she ordered, with mock sternness, throwing them at Glen.

"Ok, your highness. I can see you tire of your love slave."

"Never!" she answered adamantly, with a smile. "See you in the house. Don't be long."

"I won't," he said warmly, as he watched her leave the barn.

Cuddles was curled up on one of the floral living room sofas, fast asleep. The food sat untouched, just as it had been left before Ellen and Glen had taken their walk. She felt cheerful and content, even as she went about the not-so-pleasant task of scraping the food from the dishes and loading them in the dishwasher.

"You should have waited on me to help you," Glen whispered in Ellen's ear, giving her a little jump. He wrapped his arms around her waist from behind, planting small kisses against her neck.

She giggled from Glen's touch, turning to touch him with wet hands. "I wash dishes everyday, Glen, and actually enjoy it.

But thanks for the offer."

"I never heard of anyone enjoying washing dishes, but hey, if that makes you happy I won't interfere. But can I at least wrap up the food on the table and put it in the refrigerator?"

"That would be nice," she said with a smile, turning back around to get to her task at hand.

They worked well in the kitchen as a team, putting everything away in neat order within minutes, being just as efficient at this as they were at making love.

"Feel like sitting on the swing or maybe relaxing in the living room?" Ellen inquired, as she hung up the damp kitchen towels, slinging them over the oven door handle.

"The living room sounds great, since you asked."

They chose the same sofa where the wedding album had been laying out. Glen was happy it was no longer there where it had been several days before. He felt cautious too. *What if she turned on him again?* Although, things seemed so perfect now, it could be unfortunately different tomorrow. Being this attached was dangerous, since his love for her was growing every day. If she changed her mind now, he didn't know how he would handle it.

"So was the barn everything you fantasized it would be?" Ellen asked inquisitively, with a gleam in her eye.

"And more," Glen answered contently, snuggling close to Ellen on the couch.

"It was nice…" she sighed. "I never ever considered

making love in such a musty and dirty place, but I guess I feel different about that now."

"You guess?" You still sound skeptical."

I don't mean to be," she giggled against his chest.

He kissed the top of her head, breathing in deeply of the lingering scent of hay that still reminded him of their time just spent together in the barn. "You know, Ellen, we can really do it anywhere, as long as we use our imaginations."

His husky sensual words gave her delightful chills.

"And you know hay isn't so dirty as long as there is something covering it."

"Yes, I guess you're right."

She loved Glen's spontaneity. He was so different from Jack.

"Ellen, can we discuss something that has been on my mind for quite some time now?" Glen knew he was treading on dangerous territory, but he felt that the discussion with Ellen had to happen.

"Sure.... Glen," she answered cautiously, unsure why he was suddenly acting so serious.

He hesitated, not sure it was the best time or place; but decided it may never be an ideal situation. "It's about Eric. This thing with him and Jack has been hanging between us since we met. Don't you think it's time we talked about it?"

Ellen's heart and pulse began to quicken. *Was it time?*

Why did Glen have to bring this up right now when things were finally on a good track between them and the day had been so perfect? "If that is what you want, Glen…" Ellen answered in a resigned fashion, pulling away and casting her eyes to the floor.

He grabbed for her chin, reclaiming eye contact. "Hey…. I can see you're in pain. It's time to *stop* this pain! I love you, and I want *anything* that divides us to be put behind us."

"I'm not sure if just by talking about this, will I *ever* change my feelings about Eric."

"It may, if you see both sides of the coin."

"What do you mean?" Ellen questioned.

"I mean, Eric has spoken to me about Jack and the situation, and the picture he paints sheds a somewhat different light on the subject."

Ellen suddenly became defensively ridged, with her legs crossed and hands grabbing for her opposite arms tightly. "What exactly has he told you?" she asked sternly.

Glen picked up on her mood, but proceeded with caution anyways. "He told me of a friendship that he had with Jack and with you on occasion, for that matter. He said that you and Jack would go out with him and a date from time to time."

"That's true…we did do that, and we always had fun together," Ellen had to admit.

"But, Eric also spoke of work and what went on there."

Ellen exhaled nervously, still allowing Glen to continue even though she was finding it hard to control herself.

"According to Eric, Jack did a very good job for CWS but

not apparently good enough for Peter Winston's standards."

"That is not true!" Ellen insisted adamantly, with much emotion in her voice.

"Please Ellen, calm down," Glen urged with gentleness, placing a steadying hand on her arm. "Let me finish."

"Alright," she conceded, trying to regain her composure.

"What Eric told me was that he was out-performing Jack in sales and with being more aggressive with customers and management for that matter. Eric was always going beyond what was expected of him to search out new customers, and Jack was holding back, not showing the same drive. Peter noticed and advanced him. Jack, on the other hand, had a job change too. And we both know it wasn't considered to be a promotion."

"This isn't fair, Glen…" Ellen protested in defeat. "You don't know Jack! He was a good man, and it's because of Eric that he is dead!"

"You're wrong, Ellen," Glen insisted, grabbing her by the arms and turning her to face him. "Eric was very upset by Jack's death. Remember, they *were* friends."

Ellen began to cry, lowering her head again in frustration and embarrassment. "He…. he… was devoted to our marriage, and me" she whimpered. "He may not have had the drive and determination of Eric, but that's because he felt… that his marriage was just as important."

"And that is wonderful, Ellen," Glen reassured. "Any man lucky enough to have you in their life should have felt that way; but you can't blame Eric for Jack's death because he had different priorities than Jack did. That's business and the way of the world. If you want to blame someone, blame Peter for only wanting the best for his company. He had a decision to make, and I'm sure it was a real tough one that he wrestled with. According to Eric, Peter thought the world of Jack also; but in the end, he had to decide who was the better candidate for running his company. Face it Ellen, there is too much competition in the business world and survival is the name of the game," Glen added realistically. "A company can be on top and exist today, and be destined for bankruptcy tomorrow if the wrong people are making the decisions."

Ellen was trembling all over with emotion. "Why do you have to rub this in so badly on me right now?" she asked with pain-filled eyes.

Glen felt sick inside. He didn't want to hurt Ellen, but he knew she had to hear the truth. *"I don't want to hurt you,"* he said with heart-felt emotion, but it's unfair to chastise Eric any longer. *He does not hate you, Ellen.* He just doesn't understand you. Eric wasn't *responsible* for Jack's depression. Jack was - and he should have gotten help. Maybe a job change was in order. Who's to say."?

"It isn't as easy as you make it sound, Glen," Ellen replied with a stubbornness that showed in the set of her chin. "I tried to tell Jack that maybe he should talk with someone," Ellen admitted, "But he felt he could work things out on his own. Remember, Fillmore is a small town. That was the last thing he wanted getting out, that he felt the need for psychiatric help. He worried that if CWS found out about his feelings, he could have been taken out of management completely or may have even lost his job."

"Ellen, I can't honestly say what would have happened to Jack if he would have revealed his true feelings. Eric acts as if

Peter is a reasonable boss though, and he probably would have supported Jack, if he would have just gone to him." Glen considered his next words carefully, fearful of Ellen's reaction. "Do you really think the car accident was truly an accident?"

"What are you implying, Glen?" she questioned in stunned disbelief.

"I think you *know* what I am asking."

Ellen pulled away, turning her back to Glen. *"I...don't know,"* she answered quietly. "It hurts too much to think he would do such a thing. To leave me…all alone… to suffer," she said in a distant state of consideration and realization, with intensity etched on her face. Those same morbid thoughts had crossed her mind on more than one occasion, but she shook them away as quickly as they surfaced. She felt mortified to even ponder them.

Ellen began to sob again, with her whole body shaking uncontrollably.

Glen's hands came up to her shoulders. The space he had given her moments earlier was no longer needed, as he reclaimed her in his protective arms. "My dear sweet Ellen, I am so sorry," he whispered against her hair. "I know this is killing you, but it's time to put this bitterness to rest."

"I just have been sooo… confused by this whole thing," she confessed between hiccups.

"Ellen, please turn around," he requested earnestly. "Is it worth it any longer? Can't you find it in your heart to consider the possibility that Eric is not to blame here?"

Ellen slowly turned, still diverting her eyes from him. "Oh

Glen," she cried, falling into his arms. "Why did Jack do this to me?"

"God only knows..." he breathed, while smoothing the tear-soaked strands of hair away from her face. "I'm asking you again, Ellen, with all the love I hold for you. Will you please give my brother another chance?" he pleaded with intensity, as he waited for her response.

Ellen was quiet for some time, knowing the words Glen wanted to hear, and yet hating herself at the same time for feeling her resolve breaking. "I will try..." she answered, barely above a whisper. "That is all I can promise for now."

"Thank you..." Glen breathed with a sigh of relief, kissing the top of her head. "I know what I put you through with this conversation wasn't easy. Thank you for opening up to me."

They held each other for some time. Glen comforting and soothing Ellen, with loving massaging caresses to her back, arms and face. She needed to be nurtured, as a parent nurtures a child. She knew Glen meant her no harm, but it still hurt to face the truth. Deep inside she had already considered the words Glen spoke, many nights before he even said them now. During the day, she could keep her mind preoccupied with the work around the farm, but the night left her free to wrestle with her thoughts. If what Glen was saying was true, she felt ashamed of herself. It would be hard to undo the damage, even if the opportunity presented itself.

"How about something to drink?" Glen suggested, hoping to change the subject and boost Ellen's spirits again.

She attempted a smile. "What would you like?"

"Anything," he answered with a kiss.

"I have wine, coffee, or tea. What sounds good?"

"I could use a glass of wine."

"Me too," she confessed, suddenly feeling a little lighter.

"Good," he said, pulling Ellen to her feet. "Let's stop all this depressing talk and get back to a happier subject, like you and me," he said while nuzzling her neck with a ticklish kiss.

Ellen laughed, "I agree – just don't tickle me," she answered good-naturedly, wrapping her arm around Glen's waist.

The wine tasted sweet as they sat in the kitchen, trying to rekindle the earlier mood of the day.

"So what's up for tomorrow? Can I see you again?" Glen inquired warmly.

"You know I go to church on Sundays. Why don't you join me?"

Glen hesitated. He hadn't attended church in several years, except for his father's funeral. "Ah…I don't know, Ellen. I'm not much for getting involved in something like that."

"You never went to church?"

"Sure… my parents took us when we were at home but I haven't been there for awhile."

"Oh…. I see," Ellen answered, suddenly realizing another real difference she hadn't considered between them.

"But, if it means that much to you, I guess I can give it a try."

"You will?" she beamed, happy and surprised at his change of heart.

"I will, but getting there may be a problem."

"Why is that?"

"Because I can't borrow Eric's car forever. He probably will want to use it tomorrow himself."

"That's no problem. I can pick you up."

"Ellen.... I have my pride you know.'

"Reality has to overcome your pride in this case. Just remember that my pride was put through a real test tonight also," she reminded him. "The subject matter may be different, but we all have to face the facts at times," she answered with a thoughtful smile.

"I guess you're right, but my parents taught me from little on up that there were certain things men do and women do. The guy always picks the girl up, and should open and close her car door."

"You will perform all those gallant and cavalier things soon enough, once you get a car of your own," she said with a teasing smile. "After all, every girl likes to feel special; and as far as that car door thing goes, you already have that down to a fine science now," she said with a giggle.

"Talking about a car, Eric and I plan to find one this week. So a couple of evenings I will be tied up with him, unless you want to go along."

"That's ok. I would only get in the way. It's better you and Eric figure that out on your own."

Ellen had lied. She would have loved to have gone car shopping with Glen, but not if Eric was included in on the deal – which he was. This was going to take some time to adjust her way of thinking where Eric was concerned.

Glen leaned back on the kitchen chair, balancing on two legs, stretching his arms high above his head. "I guess I'd better get going. Talking about Eric has made me realized he is probably pretty upset with me about this time. I'm usually home by now, and he may have wanted to use his car tonight."

"Alright," Ellen resigned, wishing they could still spend more time together. "I'll walk you out."

"You're sweet," he said with a kiss to her forehead, "But I'd rather you stay in the house and lock the door behind you," he insisted. "That way I know you're safe and sound."

"Glen, nothing is going to happen to me out here. I never worry about my safety."

"Well, I do," he said while putting an arm around Ellen's shoulder and pulling her protectively into his embrace. "Things can happen anywhere, no matter where you live."

"I'll be fine," she reassured, enjoying the security of being wrapped in his protection.

They walked together to the kitchen door, avoiding as long as possible their final good-byes of the day. Glen wrapped his arms lovingly around Ellen's waist, breathing in deeply the smell of her hair that still hinted of the hay and their lovemaking of earlier in the barn. He shuddered with the memory, feeling aroused again, wanting only to reclaim her and the feel the hotness of her heat again.

"Glen, it has been a wonderful day. I don't remember when I ever had so much fun."

"I feel the same way. I hate to leave you and go home," he breathed passionately.

"Then don't," she challenged with sensual eyes.

"You know I must, or I may not have a place to live in come the morning," he reluctantly added.

"That could be remedied."

Glen smiled, making no comment, but feeling a sense of total contentment. He didn't want to read into the meaning of her words. He reached for Ellen, holding her lovingly in his arms, kissing her with all the passion the day had held for the both of them.

"Oh Ellen, we should stop, or I *won't* make it home," he whispered, while rubbing her breasts through her blouse, bringing the nipples to hardness again.

She moaned with the pleasurable awareness of the contact, finding it hard to speak. "We always have tomorrow."

"I'll hold you to that," he replied huskily, consuming her with another knee-bending kiss. "I'll call you in the morning about church, and let you know if I can use Eric's car or not."

"I'll be waiting…" she promised, as they kissed their final goodbye kiss of the night.

Chapter Twenty-Two

Eric scraped the charred blackness from both sides of the grilled-cheese sandwich that he had attempted to prepare for his dinner. That, along with a can of tomato soup and a beer, would have to suffice, he decided.

"That damn Glen is going to hear it from me when he gets in! Can't believe his phone keeps going to voicemail. This car business is getting out of hand," he muttered to himself in an irritated manner while finishing up the salvaging job of his meal.

He ate the mundane fare in a perfunctory manner as his thoughts wandered to Melinda. "Why did I have to screw this up?" he said aloud in frustration. All day, after getting back to the house, he considered calling her. But he knew she probably would hang up on him and not listen to what he had to say. *She definitely deserves better*, he resolved. *What's the problem in just forgetting her since she is like the others?*

Eric knew the answers already, without question. She wasn't like the others. She was bright, beautiful, and a great lover. They worked in total harmony in the office almost reading each other's minds. And most of all, she genuinely seemed to care for him. He was growing weary with the mental process of telling himself that he couldn't be in love with her. *Being with someone else, as I did last night, has nothing to do with love,* he rationalized.

"Hi Eric," Glen greeted jovially, while walking up to the kitchen table. "You look a million miles away."

Eric glanced up from his soup bowl, with a streak of anger crossing his face. He was in dire need of a shave and shower, and his eyes were bloodshot and darkened with circles from a lack of sleep. "I wish I was. By myself.... all alone... and with my *own* car," he gritted out sarcastically.

"Hey, I'm sorry," Glen, offered defensively, while taking the seat opposite Eric, suddenly feeling very guilty. "Ellen and I lost track of time."

"Ellen...Ellen and you, huh?" Eric said with an intoxicated slur, as he took another long swig from his fifth can of beer. "You still wasting time with that chic?" he questioned harshly, while holding the beer can at an askew angle almost spilling the contents all over the table.

"Eric, you're drunk. Watch your words!" Glen warned. "I just put up with this crap from you last night!"

"You're damn right I am drunk, and pissed off too! Could it be that I'm mad because I never seem to have my car anymore?" he shot out irrationally.

"Where's that shit coming from? I didn't think it bothered you so much, but I guess I was wrong!" Glen declared while slamming the chair against the table, leaving the room in a huff. "Don't worry, I'll find my own transportation in the future."

Eric wiped the back of his hand over his mouth, after finishing and crushing the can of beer that he had been working on. "You're not telling me anything I don't already know. And remember whose house you're in also," Eric yelled, as Glen retreated up the hall steps to his bedroom.

"What an asshole!" Glen mumbled in frustration, as he collapsed on his bed, feeling extremely pissed-off and misled by Eric. *I wouldn't even be in this situation if it weren't for Samantha*, came the spinning reality back again to haunt him. She messed up everything in his past, and was still affecting his present. He vowed that another day wouldn't go by without a plan for getting his own vehicle.

Eric stumbled up the darkened steps trying to feel his way to the bathroom. "Shit!" he growled, as he bumped his head into a wall, rattling the lighted sconce in its path, almost knocking the globe to the floor.

It was some time until the racket died down and Eric made his way to bed. He gave a loud belch and turned out the light, cursing the world and everything around him.

Chapter Twenty-Three

A new day…. Sunday, and Glen was up early. He donned some running shorts and a pair of sneakers, and decided a good jog was in order. He had a need to clear the cobwebs of emotion that were still fresh in his mind from the night before. Eric's words had hurt. He felt confused, not even sure if his brother really wanted him staying at his house, let alone use his car anymore.

The three-mile run did Glen some good. It gave him time to consider the good and the bad of what was going on. One thing was for certain, he was in love with Ellen, and he knew she loved him too. It was more than evident now that time was of the essence. He needed a car and maybe a place to live. Last night had confirmed that. These things were problems, but hopefully he could work the problems out without damaging the brotherly relationship he and Eric had just renewed.

"Hellooo…" was the sleepy response to the ringing and answering of Ellen's phone.

"You up sleepy head?"

"Glen?"

"Yes, who else would it be?" he teased.

"Ellen sat up in bed, wiping the sleep from one eye. "I'm sorry, my alarm wasn't to go off for another fifteen minutes yet.

I'm not a morning person.

He laughed. "I *know*."

"I'm waking up now, though," she replied sleepily with a yawn.

"Hey, my tired girl, the reason I'm calling is to see if we are still on for church."

"It starts at eleven o'clock," she muttered somewhat incoherently.

"I take that to be yes?"

"I would like it very much if you would go with me. You know that, Glen."

"Then your wish is my command," he answered warmly. "There is one problem though. I will need a ride."

"Eric won't let you use his car?"

"No, he won't. I think he wants me to make sure I remember whose name the title is in. But really, I can't blame him. He's been more than accommodating."

"Did you two get in a fight?" Ellen asked, sensing something was amidst.

"Not really much of one, since Eric didn't have me as a willing participant. But let's just say he strongly voiced his opinion."

"*Oh, I see*.... So does that mean you would like me to pick you up?"

Glen felt awkward. One day Ellen would never need to be picking him up again. He would make sure of that! "Yeah, I guess…" he said quietly. "Since I have no other way of coming to get you today."

She tried to make light of the situation, secretly feeling sorry for his dilemma. "Be ready at ten fifteen. I'll honk the horn."

"Alright. I love you, Ellen."

"Love you too," she answered sleepily as she closed her eyes to another ten minutes of rest.

Glen showered and dressed, choosing navy pants, with a blue and white striped shirt and a geometric print tie. He adjusted the knot, giving himself the final once over. His appearance met with his approval, but not in a haughty conceited way. If anything, he took his good looks for granted, never seeing himself as more than average.

Ellen pulled up in front of Eric's house, being right on time to the minute. There was not a need for her to blow the horn since Glen was on the front porch waiting.

"You look great," he grinned, opening the front passenger's door.

"Thank you. So do you," she blushed, as he leaned over to give her a lingering kiss.

She was dressed in a sleeveless summer print of blue, yellow, green and raspberry that complimented her trim figure. She wore her hair in a braid that was twisted into a bun at the nape of her neck. Gold earrings, necklace, and bracelet adorned her with simple but sophisticated elegance. She was Glen's breath of sunshine and beauty, after a cloudy night with Eric.

“Everything ok now?” Ellen asked, while giving him a quick look of concern as she pulled away from the house.

“Nothing has changed,“ he answered softly, resting a hand on her shoulder. “But then I haven’t seen the grump today.”

Ellen glanced at Glen, feeling sympathetic to his plight. “Even though I have had my feelings about your brother, I hate to see the two of you having problems.”

“Don’t worry, love,” he consoled, giving her shoulder a squeeze. “We will work it out.”

“I hope so,” she added sweetly, with a supportive smile that tugged at his heart.

They drove a short distance to the church, which was downtown on Bradford Street. The building was of moderate size, with red brick façade and stained glass windows surrounding it. A steeple, that housed a bell, rang out merrily to all that entered its sacred dwelling.

“Hello, Ellen, it is good to see you today,” echoed a cheerful voice from the entry foyer. Walter Evans was the name behind the voice and the greeter for the week.

Ellen reached out to shake his hand. “Walter, it is so nice to see you too. This is my friend, Glen Cummings.”

“Glad to make your acquaintance,” he said warmly, reaching out two hands to shake Glen’s one.

"It's good to meet you too, sir," Glen replied sincerely, feeling touched by the older man's friendliness.

"I hope you enjoy the service today, and you will come back and visit us again."

"I think I will do just that," Glen answered with a warm smile, while taking Ellen by the hand.

They made their way into the sanctuary, being stopped several times by those curious few onlookers who wanted to meet Glen. Mr. Miller from the hardware store was there, along with a clerk from the Quick Shopper.

Several single female members standing in a group nearby stared with outright jealously at Ellen and her handsome companion. "Who is *that* guy, and how did Ellen Harper get so lucky?" they asked each other in utter fascination and envy.

To Glen's surprise, he enjoyed the service more than he thought he would. Pastor Rollands spoke on the Ten Commandments and the need to obey them. Glen knew he fell short in that particular area, especially the one about keeping the Sabbath Day holy. *If this makes Ellen happy and she wants me to start coming here with her, I think I can make it work,* he thought, as he gave her a brief but loving grin.

Ellen felt at peace with Glen and her surroundings. To be with Glen and hold his hand, while sharing in the church experience she had come to adore, was very touching to her. Even Jack hadn't been a regular attendee like she was. He had gone several times a year – mainly on holidays – to appease her. For the most part, there was always something else he wanted to do; be it golf, yard work, or even a workout at the local gym.

Glen and Ellen walked hand in hand out to the Saab, after

introductions were extended to a few more of the congregation before they said their polite good-byes.

Ellen handed Glen the keys. "Would you like to drive?" she asked, realizing numerous eyes were still on them, being sensitive to his male ego.

"I would love to," he replied gratefully, taking the keys from her and unlocking the passenger's door for her. "Name the place. I'm taking you out to lunch."

"You are?" Ellen giggled, delighted by his surprise.

"Yes, I am. So where do you want to go?"

"Well.... there's the diner or Albright's, or a nice place in Hastings called The Lantern House, which is about thirty minutes from here. All of them have fairly nice menus."

"I've been to the first two, so why don't we try the Lantern House?"

"That's fine with me, as long as you don't mind the drive."

"I welcome the drive, as long as you're here to keep me company," he said with a lazy smile as he leaned over to give her a tender kiss. Several of the church ladies still gazed at them, as they pulled away feeling blissful and in love.

The sky was a beautiful shade of azure-blue, with billowy clouds, lazily drifting overhead. Cows and horses serenely grazed in the pastures, as the drive wound them through the scenic Nebraska countryside. Wildflowers dotted the horizon sporadically, causing a frenzy of color, like an artist's pallet.

"It's so beautiful out here, Ellen. Almost like a picture."

"I know…" she said dreamily, while staring out the window in wonder. "That's one of the nice things about driving out here."

"I can see that," he agreed.

The scenic landscaping gave way to a small town, with a few houses popping up on the horizon. "It's just ahead, Glen. On the left," Ellen mentioned, while pointing in the general direction.

"Ok, I see it," he answered, steering the car into the adjacent parking lot.

The white clapboard structure, with its contrasting burgundy trim, was decorated in a warm and homey manner. Each window contained an antique lantern that was kept lit throughout the entire day. The inside smelled of eucalyptus leaves and cinnamon, from the many dried flower arrangements hanging creatively from the beamed ceiling rafters. The tables and chairs were authentic antiques, originating from English pubs.

The front door opened to a hostess stand that was situated in a large foyer. The many Sunday churchgoers were uncomfortably standing shoulder to shoulder in the crammed room, since the place did not contain enough benches for everyone to sit down until a table was available.

"Your name please?" the hostess asked.

"Glen Cummings."

She glanced at him sternly as she wrote down his name.

"A quiet table for two would be nice," Glen requested, with his best heart-stopping smile, but the matronly woman wasn't impressed.

"It will be a forty-five minutes, and there's no guarantee on a quiet table location with a crowd like this. Still interested?"

Glen looked to Ellen for her input. "Is that ok with you, sweetie?" he asked.

"That's fine," she whispered. "It's worth the wait."

"I'll take your word for it," he grinned.

"We'll wait."

"May I help the next person please?" the hostess bellowed, glancing to the couple in line behind Glen and Ellen.

"How about a short walk outside until it is our turn?"

"Sounds good to me," she agreed, linking her arm in Glen's and making her way to the front door. "There isn't too much to see out here. I know, because I've had this wait before."

Glen wondered with whom. *Probably Jack*, he surmised. "It doesn't matter to me. As long as we can walk and be together, the scenery doesn't matter much."

They passed many houses along the way that varied in style. A couple of them were of wood clapboard, just like the restaurant. Some were brick, and a few more were encased in vinyl siding. Each was modest in size with well-kept lawns and landscaping. The small community seemed to take pride in what it had. Children played happily in their yards - several on a swing set, and a few tossed a basketball into a net. The focal point of activity for the day seemed to be centered upon an unorganized neighborhood baseball game, being played in a vacant field behind the elementary school. From a distance, Ellen and Glen stopped to observe. Two kids argued if the one was tagged out or not.

Glen chuckled warmly as he took in the scene. “I remember those days in my neighborhood. Eric always stole base and usually the game ended up in a fight with everyone going home. My mother, without fail, would come outside wondering what all the commotion was about. After awhile though, she didn’t even have to ask. Eric always gave her a good song and dance, but she would never buy into it.”

“What’s your mother like?” Ellen asked curiously.

“She’s great - a mom and a friend. She has always supported me no matter what is going on in my life.”

“That’s wonderful, Glen. My parents are a lot like that also.”

“Yeah…I know it is wonderful. I guess I didn’t always realize how special she really was though. You know…it’s easy to take things for granted like that…. like so many people do. That was…until my dad died a few years ago.”

“Glen, I’m sorry.”

“Thanks, but I’m fine. I have finally come to terms with his death. I hated to see my Mom alone after all the years they shared together, but things do have a way of working out.”

“How’s that?”

“She’s dating an old friend of my parents who lost his wife also. They discovered each other at a support group meeting for those people losing a loved one to cancer.”

“How nice for your mother,” Ellen replied with understanding.

“I think so too,” he smiled. “We all just want to be loved in this world." Glen bent over to give Ellen a tender kiss. "Thank you for loving me."

Her eyes welled up with tears, but this time they were being shed with happiness. The moment was so special. "It is I who should be thanking you, after all that I have put you through."

"Shhh..." Glen added, putting his index finger to her lips. "Not another word. Those days are behind us now." Glen glanced down at his watch. "We better get back to the restaurant. Our table should be ready by now."

"Ok," she resigned, already wishing they could just stay where they were for the rest of the afternoon.

The lunch was as enjoyable as the walk that they had just taken. It was their first real date away from the farm, and the time passed by all too quickly.

"That was some meal, Ellen. I am stuffed!" Glen commented, while grabbing his stomach as in pain.

Ellen moaned. "I know what you mean. I feel like I just had Thanksgiving dinner! I won't be able to eat another thing all day."

Glen chuckled heartily at Ellen. "I wouldn't go that far. I think I could sneak in a sandwich before the day is up."

"If you say so," she giggled, while shaking her head in disbelief.

"Are you ready to go home, or would you like to drive around some more?"

Ellen was so fond of Glen's consideration and his desire to make her happy. "How about we see just a little more of the scenery? I hate for the day to end. The sky is just so blue."

"I know what you mean. I don't want it to end either, Ellen," Glen replied, feeling alive and confident that all the obstacles seemed to be finally melting down between them.

"There is a road up ahead - on the right - that I always like to take when I am out this way. A person has a collection of totem poles he has carved, sitting out in his front yard. It had become quite the local tourist attraction."

"You're kidding!" Glen remarked with amused curiosity while making the turn.

"No, it's true, and each one of them is so unique – some serious, some funny, but all a work of art."

They drove along what seemed to be a deserted road, until they rounded the bend, giving way to the spectacle that Ellen had described. Two other cars sat with their motors idling while the people inside the vehicles pointed and stared in amazement. As Glen and Ellen approached, the other motorists hesitantly departed after taking a few pictures, allowing them the same access to enjoy the simple entertainment they had just witnessed - but this time up close and personal.

"This is unreal, Ellen!" Glen stated with childlike fascination. "I guess my favorite is the one over there with all the monster faces."

"That seems to be the hardest one he attempted; but look over there at that one," she said while pointing. "I always thought that one in particular was the prettiest."

"That figures," Glen teased. "You like flowers and I like

monsters – go figure!" he added, while leaning over to give Ellen a quick but loving kiss.

The merry pair made their way back to the farm – full, but content with the time they had just spent together. Without so much as a slight jar or side-ways motion, the Saab sped back the road to the farmhouse.

"The lane is way too smooth now. I miss the bumps," Ellen remarked with mock arrogance, turning to Glen to wait for his reaction.

"Your car doesn't seem to agree," he replied with a grin, keeping his eyes aimed straight ahead.

"Ok, you made your point," she conceded, poking him playfully in the ribs before getting out of the car.

"Sore loser," Glen yelled, rubbing the tender spot where the contact had been made.

"Who's the *sore* loser?" Ellen emphasized with a coy laugh, as she struggled to get the side porch door open to her house.

Glen was soon to follow cornering her in the kitchen. Had a little trouble with that key, huh? Afraid I was going to pay you back for that rib jab?"

"Glen…. don't be getting any ideas," Ellen challenged mischievously as she broke free of his constraint, rolling up the dishtowel into a tight rope, threatening to snap it at his legs.

"Ellen, you wouldn't?"

"Oh, wouldn't I?" she beckoned, taking on a low cat-like

prowl, extending the towel at an angle in his direction. "Remember the lake yesterday and your shorts?"

"Don't remind me," he said playfully. Glen's eyes darted quickly around the room, hoping to find a makeshift weapon of his own. Without any luck, he opened the drawer behind his back, searching with one hand while keeping his gaze fixed on Ellen. "You like cornering your prey, don't you, Ellen?" he teased.

"You could say that," she smirked, closing the distance between them. "Especially when the prey happens to be such a fine specimen."

"Not so fast, Amazon woman," he yelled dramatically, extracting a rolling pin and holding it in front of her view. "Let the games begin!"

Ellen's eyes widened with surprise, as she began snapping the towel wildly, attempting to take in a few low blows to his legs. But Glen was too quick for her, matching each one of her snaps with a block from the wooden dowel. One to his upper torso caught his free hand as he grabbed the tail of the swinging, stinging snake. He reeled Ellen in, dishtowel and all, wrapping her securely around the waist with the cloth weapon; brining her back to rest against his chest.

"I guess this wild animal will have to drag such a worthy opponent back to his cave now," Glen breathed in a worn-out breath against Ellen's ear, while planting feather light kisses down her neck.

Ellen giggled and shivered at his touch. "You are so silly, but I do love your silliness," she confessed, turning to face Glen in the towel belt that he had crafted and had her willingly entrapped in.

They held each other as both of their weapons fell to the floor, lost in the power that each held over the other.

"I'd better get home. I still have that episode on my mind from last night. Hopefully, Eric and I can make amends and put this car thing behind us."

"What will you do about work tomorrow?"

"I guess I will call a cab."

"That's silly. Why don't you spend the night here?"

Glen smiled warmly at Ellen, feeling touched by her generosity and also her willingness to take this new step in their relationship. "Don't tempt me, Ellen. You don't know how good that offer sounds, but I think Eric and I need some time tonight to go over a few things."

"If you insist," she resigned, releasing her arms from around his waist. She walked across the kitchen to the desk, stopping to pick up her car keys and purse. "Do you want to drive or should I?" she questioned, holding the keys up for an answer.

Glen walked over to meet her by the desk. "Ellen, I'll call a cab. I don't want you running me clear into town," Glen protested, while trying to dial a cab company from his cell phone.

"Oh no you won't. I won't hear of it!" she insisted, while taking his phone and hanging up on the person who just answered. "No cabby is driving my boyfriend home!"

Glen began to laugh. Ellen was being so cute. "Come here silly," he beckoned, while wrapping his arms securely around her waist again. Words were forgotten as he kissed her tenderly. Ellen felt a warmth spread throughout her, settling low in her abdomen.

"Glen, we should stop," she whispered. "Or Eric may be in bed by the time you get home."

"I know…" he admitted reluctantly, feeling a familiar hardening in his loins as he nibbled on her ear, sending shivers of desire down her spine. "But he isn't nearly as fun to be with as you."

"Glen…. we *must* stop, even though I don't want you too," Ellen sighed heavily, finding it nearly beyond her capabilities to turn him away.

"Ok, ok…. you're right. I do need to get going," he hesitantly agreed, resting his forehead on her own, not wanting to let her go.

The lights were on downstairs, as Ellen and Glen approached Eric's place.

"Good luck with your talk," Ellen wished, as she watched Glen silently staring at the house.

"Thanks. Everything will be fine," he reassured, turning and leaning towards her for one last kiss goodnight. "Drive carefully. I'll call you later to make sure you got in all right."

"I'll be fine, Glen."

"I know that, but I'll sleep better knowing you're home safe and sound."

Ellen smiled tenderly at her wonderful caring man. "I am so lucky to have you."

"The feeling is mutual," he answered with a playful wink, throwing her a kiss before closing the car door.

She pulled the car slowly away, as she watched his every move. His hand reached for the keys that were hidden in his jacket pocket, unlocking the front door with ease. He caught her staring, as he turned and waved a warm good-bye before closing the door behind him.

The sound of a TV show was echoing down from the upstairs bedroom. Glen climbed the steps, hoping Eric was still awake. He peeked around the corner to find Eric with his hands clasped behind his head, propped up on several pillows, chuckling warmly at the screen that entertained him.

"What's on tonight?" Glen asked with an apprehensive smile, hoping to break the ice between them. Eric was startled by the unexpected intrusion.

"Oh…hi, Glen. When did you get in?" he inquired, while unclasping is hands and sitting up straighter in the bed.

"Just now. I heard the noise up here, and figured you were still up."

"Yeah, I am, but I was just ready to call it a night in ten minutes."

"Before you do that, could we talk a minute?" Glen asked, while entering the room and taking a chair beside of the bed.

"I'm pretty tire, Glen," Eric answered thoughtlessly. "So let's make it quick."

"Quick it will be! About the other night…."

"No need to even talk about the other night. It's over," Eric said with a yawn.

"Maybe for you, but I think the truth finally came out, and we need to talk about it."

"What truth was that?" Eric smirked, finally making eye contact with Glen.

"You know what truth I'm talking about. The car and my overuse of it."

"Don't worr…"

"Eric, let me finish," Glen emphasized firmly, needing to make his point. "I know I have over extended myself, taking advantage of your generosity, but I didn't mean to. I can move out tomorrow…"

"Move out?" Eric repeated a little too loudly, swinging his legs around to the side of the bed. "I don't want you to move out. Hell, you just got here a few weeks ago."

"How can you say that when you made it clear last night that I am taking too much from you?"

"Look," Eric began as he scratched his head and yawned again. "I was drunk and I said things I didn't mean. I was out of control – plain and simple – no other explanation."

"Maybe so, but the car issue *is the truth.* If the tables were turned, and I had loaned you the car, I wouldn't want to be at home without it when I needed it either."

"I guess…" Eric conceded. "But this car thing can be worked out."

Glen was touched by Eric's willingness to still help him. "I'm sorry Eric, for all the hassle I've put you through. Starting tomorrow, I'm going to take a cab to work until I get a car."

Eric sighed, rubbing the day's growth of beard-stubble on his face. "I'll make you a deal. Take a cab tomorrow and be home early – say around six o'clock – and we'll go car shopping. I'll give Stan a call, first thing in the morning, and hopefully he will have a few nice possibilities we can choose from."

"I really shouldn't be buying a car right now. The money is going to be a problem."

"Let's not worry about that for the moment. We'll figure something out, and it will be my pleasure to loan you the money. Now, I don't want to hear another word about it or we will be arguing for another hour and I'm beat. Goodnight. I'm going to sleep *now*," Eric announced with finality. "I'm tired, and I have a full schedule tomorrow."

"Alright, whatever you say," Glen resigned, throwing his hands up in the air. "I will see you at six." Glen walked from the room, but turned back in the doorway. "Thanks, Eric."

"No problem. Hey can you get that light?" he asked with another yawn.

"Sure," Glen answered, snapping off the light leaving Eric to his slumber.

Chapter Twenty-Four

The tapping of the shade against the window frame woke Glen before the alarm did. He hoped the breeze would continue throughout the day, giving him a welcoming reprieve from the heat. He showered and dressed in his usual attire – cut off blue jean shorts and a cotton t-shirt. Today it would be the sleeveless variety. Glen knew the weather forecaster predicted a hot one. He threw a pair of khakis and a baby blue golf shirt into a duffel bag. He planned to change at Ellen's after work. No need to embarrass Eric around his business associate friends. He would try to put his best foot forward for the car salesman.

Glen quietly shut the door and locked it, not wanting to disturb Eric at this early hour. It was only four o'clock, and Glen wanted to make sure Ellen got an honest day's work out of him, even if he had to arrive an hour earlier than usual. The "free times" he had spent with her, were weighing heavily on his conscience now. If he was going to take out a loan of money from Eric to buy a car, he wanted to know that he could repay every penny, and that he had worked hard to earn it.

The cab driver was talking loudly on his walkie-talkie as Glen approached the vehicle.

"Glad you came out," the cabby grunted out matter-of-factly. "Didn't want to beep the horn and wake your neighbors."

"Glad you didn't," Glen mentioned, as he opened the front

passenger's door and climbed in the seat.

"Where would you be off to so early this morning?" the middle-aged, unkempt cabby asked, taking in Glen's lightly clad appearance.

"I work on a farm out off of Route 161. Ellen Harper's place."

"Ellen Harper…?" he pondered reflectively. "Yeah, yeah, I know of the gal. She's the one who lost that husband of hers a time ago. Not too much gets by me in a small town like Fillmore," he bragged.

"Is that so?" Glen answered absentmindedly, not feeling awake enough to want to communicate.

"She still has that farm, huh?"

"Yeah, she does. And I am there trying to make sure it stays that way."

The cabby turned towards Glen again, considering his words. He had a couple teeth missing on the one side of his mouth and his breath reeked of coffee.

"She sure is a pretty young thing. Can't believe no one has ever taken up with her."

Glen chuckled to himself, knowing the driver was prying. "Maybe Mrs. Harper doesn't want someone *taking up with her*. Maybe her farm and cat are all she wants in her life."

"Her cat?" he questioned with interest.

"Yeah, she has this cat she is real attached to. I'd keep my distance though, because he is *real big*. Probably as big as a small mountain lion and when I think of it…."

"Think of what?" the cabby interrupted with an anxious manner.

"When I think of it, maybe that's what it really is," Glen interjected in his best acting role. That cat has the *longest claws* I have ever seen on a domestic. I've seen him rip into an animal like a bear would, and he uses a telephone pole near the house as a scratching post. He has big shards of wood pulled off the thing. Probably could tear into someone real good if they ever tried to mess with the *lady of the house*."

The cabby gulped uncomfortably as he glanced at Glen again, envisioning the gruesome scene in his mind.

"She also talks about getting a real big watch dog someday soon. You know, the killer variety – shepherd, pit bull, or one of those doberman pincher types. Let me tell you buddy, I do my job, keep my distance, and leave when I'm done for the day. The contact is minimal, except when she hands me my pay."

The cabby noticeably swallowed again, clearing his throat for a reply. "Thanks for the warning, pal. Me and the guys down at the tavern have brought her up from time to time after a few beers. Boy, will they think different now! I'll be honest, I had considered calling on Mrs. Harper one of these days, since my wife and I have been separated for some time now, but I steer clear of that kind of trouble. She sounds like a real wacko!"

"You're probably smart to have come to that conclusion," Glen concluded with mock sarcasm, as he paid the driver and bid him a triumph goodbye.

When the driver was long out of view, Glen erupted into a

loud sidesplitting laugh, just imagining the upcoming conversations at the tavern about the strange Ellen Harper and her evil cat. Glen gathered his wits, knowing he had a long day ahead of him. As he walked by the quiet, dark house, making his way to the barn, thoughts of Ellen evaded his mind with the same yearning that he had felt the night before when they were together.

"Oh Ellen…" he lamented with concern. "I don't want anyone making the moves on you, especially an opportunity seeker of the likes of that scum!"

Glen wanted to wake her and take her in his arms again, possessing her body, mind and soul. Cuddles was probably curled up beside of her, presenting the pretty picture that he longed to be more and more a part of. But the commitment of work was his priority now, and must always take center stage. His desires for passion would have to be suppressed until the workday ended.

The garden was dry, as he expected it would be, but the plants were continuing to grow. Everything had finally sprouted. The most crucial time was now. The seedlings needed to be nourished and babied until they were stronger and more mature. He hoed out the weeds that had taken root over the weekend, meticulously cultivating and aerating each individual plant. When he was satisfied with the results, the sprayer heads on the sprinklers were strategically readjusted and turned on. An arc of water fanned out to kiss each plant with much needed nourishment. The leaves danced to the beat of the droplets, tapping out a quiet rhythm before slipping to the awaiting ground surrounding. Glen surveyed the scene with a feeling of admiration. The humming whisper from the spray of water that each sprinkler brought forth, made him feel so calm and at peace with his environment. He was satisfied and happy, content to let the moment last, for at least a few lingering moments.

"Hi.... caught you daydreaming?" came a petal-soft feminine voice, which interrupted the spell he was under. Caressing arms wrapped around his waist from behind, stirring him back to reality. An arousing hunger instantaneously overwhelmed him at the feel of the familiar, loving embrace. Glen turned, engulfing her lips with his own, needing Ellen's nourishment as much as the seedlings needed the water.

"You're up already. I hope I didn't wake you," he said thoughtfully, while holding her face in his hands.

"Not you, but pesky Cuddles. I guess spring fever has hit him, because the bright sunshine streaming through the window had him balancing on my windowsill while he meowed loudly. He wouldn't stop until I let him out."

"He's one heck of a cat!" Glen chuckled, remembering his earlier conversation with the cabby.

Ellen was still in her nightgown that was peaking out from her terry-cloth robe that she wore. The matching scuffs were not nearly sufficient enough to guard against the abuse of walking outside, especially around the rocks and dirt of the garden.

Glen took in every inch of Ellen's appearance that was already causing a tightening in his groin. "Are you trying to seduce me and take me away from work?" he asked in a sultry voice.

"I'm always trying to seduce you, honey," she replied flirtatiously with a hand on her hips. "But I just really wanted to say hello."

"Well I'm glad you did," he added, while brushing the trace of dirt from her face that his work gloves had placed. "I needed to talk to you anyways."

"What about?" Ellen asked, as they walked back to the porch.

"About Eric. I got a chance to talk to him last night. He was still up when I got in."

"That's good," Ellen said, as they sat on the swing.

"We straightened things out between us, and he wants to meet me at six o'clock tonight so we can go car shopping. If it is alright with you, I would like to leave early today."

"Glen, I can't believe you are even asking me for permission. Of course you can leave early."

"Ellen, you know I would never take it for granted that you are my employer," Glen expressed sincerely, while holding her hand. "I will always remember where the line is drawn here. I am trying to take the job seriously and not mix business with pleasure all of the time."

"Thank you, Glen," Ellen offered with a smile, as she leaned towards him, kissing him on the cheek. "I already know that, and that's one of the many things that attracts me to you. Feel free to leave however early you need to."

"I figure somewhere between four-thirty and five o'clock, I should head out. Just so you know, I got here an hour early today."

Ellen just shook her head, never ceasing to be amazed by Glen's integrity. "That was not necessary. You are probably exhausted already."

"Not really. If anything I am hyped-up about the car," he

grinned.

"Well, I hope today will be your lucky day and you will find just what you are looking for."

Glen reached out and took her into his embrace. "Ellen, I have already found what I am looking for several weeks ago. The car will only make life easier, but that isn't anything compared to finding you."

She smiled up at him feeling happier than she had felt for the past two years. "Glen, I love you so much," she answered with tears of happiness filling her eyes.

"I hope so, because I can't imagine a day without you anymore, Ellen. I love you too with all my heart," he replied earnestly, as he made her melt from the heat of the deep kisses that he showered upon her.

Ellen stayed busy the rest of the morning, while Glen ventured into the barn and decided it was time to tackle the job of tightening and fixing the produce stand. After taking the tarps completely off the stand, and then folding and laying them to the side, he stood back staring at the heavy object.

"This isn't going to be easy to move," he realized as he looked around the barn trying to find a solution to the problem at hand. He ventured around the musty hay-strewn room, looking for something to solve his dilemma. In a neglected area of the barn, a jack and cart with wheels were stored, looking as if they hadn't seen much use in awhile. "Maybe this is what was used before. It wouldn't hurt to give it a try," he mentioned aloud as he considered how the items could be utilized in solving the problem.

He slipped the jack under one end of the stand and started

cranking it up until the desired leverage was reached, before sliding the awaiting cart under the end. He needed to place a few concrete blocks that he also found in the barn, under the same end. These would provide the additional support needed until he could hoist up the other end to secure the cart. Never did he consider the extent of the undertaking that it would take to lift the produce stand onto the cart by himself, but he accomplished it with determination and the creativity of using the jack. Asking Ellen to help was not even an option in Glen's mind. He would never ask that of her. He secured the stand to the cart, with several heavy ropes crisscrossing them back and forth, finishing the job by tying the ropes to the cart's handle.

Glen eyed the tractor, that up until this time he had not attempted to use. "Hope this thing is all right," Glen said as he circled it, looking for any telltale signs of an apparent problem. He discovered that the key was in the ignition. Climbing onto the tractor's seat, he gave the key a turn as he pushed down on the clutch and gas pedal. A grinding click was all he heard. He adjusted the choke and tried to start it again. This time a few muffled chugs and a pop followed by a puff of smoke from the muffler occurred, and then the engine died again.

Glen sighed, resting his palms on his forehead, leaning on the tractor's steering wheel. His determination resurfaced, as he gave the tractor a playful tap on the engine's cover. "Come on Bessie, don't fail me now, just when I'm getting to know you." Glen turned the key again, and this time contact was made, as if the tractor understood Glen's plea. A few weak sputters and then full engine power was achieved. The tractor roared loudly, coming out of its slumber. "I knew you could do it, Bessie!" he exclaimed triumphantly, giving the tractor another pat of approval, as he backed the machinery up to meet the cart's handle.

Ellen was busy hanging up her laundry outside, when she heard the old familiar noise of the tractor that had sat idle for almost two years. Only when the pastures were being utilized and the livestock was still there, did it get used. "I can't believe he got it running," she said with amazement, as she hung up her last pair of shorts.

Glen slowly steered the tractor out of the barn with the produce stand following on the cart. Ellen watched with her mouth hanging open, observing the spectacle with delight. "I would deny it if I hadn't seen it. How did he lift that heavy thing?"

Glen could see her expression, as he proudly rode the tractor while waving at her, as if he were in a parade. He stopped the tractor near the well pump, and turned the engine off. Glen jumped down and was grinning from ear to ear, as Ellen approached.

"Is it ok if I leave it here? This would be an easy place for me to work on it."

"Sure," Ellen said with the amazed look still etched on her face. "But how did you possibly move it all by yourself?"

"Genius, sweetheart, genius! Your boyfriend is no dummy. I found an old jack and it worked very nicely, as you can see."

Ellen giggled, with the realization of how proud Glen was of himself. She didn't have the heart to admit to him that everyone else, who had moved the produce stand, had also used the jack. The difference was - no one attempted to move it without help, as Glen had just done.

"You are so clever," she praised. "But how are you ever going to get it back down now?"

Glen looked puzzled and bewildered by her statement, not

giving a thought as to how he was going to accomplish that. He scratched his head for a second, staring at the stand that was now balanced strategically on the cart. "If I got it up there with the jack, I'll take it down the same way," he said with a determination written all over his face.

"How about I get dressed quickly, and I will help you?"

"Thanks, Ellen, but I can manage on my own," Glen yelled from behind, as he made his way back to the barn for the jack.

"See you later," she shrugged, walking towards the house. There was not any point in arguing with Glen. It was already becoming apparent to her in the short time that she knew him, that when he made up his mind there was no changing it.

Glen was just as resolved to see the produce stand secure on the ground, as he was to hoist it up on the cart. Ellen watched from behind the kitchen curtain, as she had done so many times before. She didn't want to embarrass him by making it obvious she was watching, so she kept her distance within the house. It was hard for Ellen to understand why his male pride was coming through on something as minor as this; but if it was that important to Glen for him to do this thing on his own, then so be it, she would respect him for that and not interfere.

The whole procedure took less than an hour and Glen was quite exhausted, but satisfied when he was finished. He submersed his whole head under the well pump. The cold water snapped him back to attention, as he shook his head up and down, sending a spray of water all over the produce stand and Cuddles, who had decided to take a nap on the new fixture in the yard.

"Didn't mean to frighten you, boy," Glen admitted

apologetically, as Cuddles scampered off the stand, from the wetness that startled him from his slumber. The whole scene tickled Ellen. She was falling so deeply in love with the man, and life was more than wonderful right now.

"Lunch is ready," Ellen announced, as she brought out a tray piled high with a variety of delectable delights. Glen broke into a pleased, wide-toothed smile of approval, as he finished finger combing his hair back in place.

"What a nice surprise, but I did pack my own."

"Ok…that's fine. I'll just have to sit out here and eat all this by myself, while I watch you *enjoy* your bag lunch," she teased, sweeping her hand above the tray in a displaying-type motion as if she were a model on a game show.

"Oh no you won't!" he laughed. "My baloney sandwich can just be fed to the trash can today, as far as I'm concerned! It's not often I get *real food*."

"I'm glad you changed your mind," she commented warmly, as they sat on the porch steps eating a plate of fried chicken, macaroni and cheese and cole slaw. "I had wanted to invite you to dinner tonight, and since I now know you are going car shopping, I figured we could still have our lunch together."

"Thank you," Glen smiled appreciatively. "You know I would have accepted the invitation in a minute, if this car thing hadn't come up."

"I understand totally," Ellen replied, while biting into a crunchy chicken leg. "I am so happy this is finally happening for you."

"I am too…. but I guess it *still* bothers me when I know that I have a good car out there somewhere that rightfully I should be using now. It kills me to think that I have to buy something all over again that I worked so hard for only a few years ago."

"I still can't believe someone would just up and take your car like that," she commented while wiping her mouth with her napkin. "Can't you try to call the police again about it?"

"As far as they are concerned, the subject is pretty much closed. Samantha probably sold it for the parts, and probably my car has been disassembled and doesn't even exist anymore."

Ellen felt so heartsick for Glen. *What kind of woman would do such a cruel thing to such a kind man?* She thought.

"Well, what happened, can't be changed," she said emphatically, while rising and putting their finished plates on the tray. "And all you can do now is live for the present and look forward to the purchase of your new car," she said with a sunny smile.

"It won't be new."

"You know what I mean, Glen."

"Yes, I do, and…. and I'm sorry. Life just doesn't seem fair when things like this happen."

"Glen," Ellen stated firmly, while holding onto the tray. "We *all* go through things. Look at me, and my pre-conceived attitude that you asked me to work on and try to change concerning Jack's death."

"You're right, Ellen. I really don't get into this frame of mind too often. I guess today is just making me remember," he said while taking the tray from her. “If you get that door, I’ll take this to the kitchen; and then I got to get back to work. Although I must admit that the thought of spending the whole day on the porch talking, and maybe doing a few *other* things,” he added with a grin and wink, “Sounds a lot more appealing.”

Ellen smiled, reaching up to kiss Glen over the tray. “You work too hard, you know that?”

“Yeah, at everything but loving you, because that comes easy for me,” he answered, returning the kiss that fed his soul.

The afternoon passed by quickly as Glen hammered a few nails here and there and sanded the produce stand down to a smooth base, ready for the paint when it would be applied. As he worked, he thought of Ellen’s words of the morning and at lunch. Those words of getting what he was looking for, and those words of living for today. *She is so profound*, he thought, as he sanded down an edge of a corner. *I may not have the car I want yet, but I have truly found the woman I want to spend the rest of my life with.* Ellen…he loved, and he didn’t want to lose her. One day, when the time was right and he felt he was more financially secure, he would ask her to marry him. Glen could no longer imagine his life without her.

“Ellen, may I use your bathroom?” Glen asked as he held the bag of clothes he had brought from home. “I need to change.”

“Of course, Glen. And use the shower too, if you want.”

“Are you sure?”

“Glen…don’t be silly!”

He bent forward towards her, giving her another kiss. “I wish I were staying for dinner. It’s been too long since we made love,” he whispered against her neck. “I miss you.”

Shivers of delight fluttered down Ellen’s spine. “I miss you too,” she said quietly, but there is always tomorrow.”

Glen smiled lovingly into her playful green eyes, giving Ellen another kiss. “I won’t forget you said that.”

“I hope you won’t,” she said with a playful slap to his backside, as he disappeared into the bathroom.

After a shower and shave, Glen entered the kitchen with his duffel bag in hand, looking handsome and well-polished in his outfit.

“Need a lift into town?” Ellen inquired over her magazine. “I noticed you didn’t have Eric’s car today.”

“Yeah, I took a cab out, and I’ll just take a cab home.”

“No, you won’t!” Ellen insisted sternly, while laying the magazine on the table. “I need to go into town anyway and do my grocery shopping, so I won’t take no for an answer.”

“Who am I to argue with such a lovely lady?” Glen grinned, while sitting at the table and squeezing Ellen’s hand.

“Well that was easier than I thought,” Ellen answered in surprise, expecting a debate.

“Why would I want to argue when I get the chance to be with you a few more minutes?”

“I’m glad you came to that conclusion, since I totally agree,” she giggled with satisfaction, rising to grab her purse and grocery list.

As they pulled up in front of Eric's place, Glen had to smile. He loved Ellen, and the woman she was in and out of the bedroom that she was now displaying. She made his veins pump with desire even in simple acts of kindness such as this.

"*Are you sure* you don't want to join Eric and I?" he offered, as he pulled her into his embrace rubbing the sides of her face with his thumbs. She shuttered at his touch as his mouth found its willing target of her lips once again.

"I'm sure, she breathed heavily, finding it quite difficult to pull away from the overpowering sensual affect Glen was having over her.

"I would love your input," he teased, as his hand sought the warmness between her thighs. Even with the restriction of her clothing, her breath caught at the sudden contact, as if a spark ignited her to life. At that moment, she only wanted to please him, but her disillusions and the pain of the past won again.

She pulled away from his embrace, bracing her hands against his chest. "It's better if you and Eric handle this on your own. But thanks anyways," she replied meekly, seeing the disappointment in Glen's eyes. "If something doesn't work out tonight though, I promise I will go the next time."

"Alright…" he replied hesitantly, finding it hard to believe that after just having their talk the other day, she would still be acting this way. Glen could read between the lines. It wasn't going to be easy to convince Ellen to ever be around Eric again.

Chapter Twenty-Five

The house felt especially quiet and empty, as Glen waited patiently for Eric to show up. He looked at the clock as he drummed his fingers repeatedly on the counter, realizing how over-anxious he was becoming. It was only quarter of six, and Eric wouldn't be home for another fifteen minutes yet.

The door opened and slammed in one quick motion. "Sorry I'm late," Eric, yelled, as he dashed up the hall steps, leaving Glen to stare after him. "Be down in a minute, after I get out of this suit."

Glen paged absent-mindedly through a sports magazine waiting on Eric to reappear. He hoped it wouldn't take overly long to reach a decision about a car. Maybe there was a chance he could still head back out to Ellen's for the evening. He had really hated to say goodbye to her. He knew if he hadn't left when he did, they would probably be lying in each other's arms after exhausting sex. But the car had to be dealt with, and that was the priority now. *Samantha again….* Would he ever stop hating her for what she had done to him?

"Ready to go?" Eric asked, breaking through the pensive silence.

"You bet," Glen answered enthusiastically, laying down his magazine, ready to join Eric at the door.

The drive to Newton Motors was only two miles from Eric's house. They rode with the top down on the Mustang, as the late afternoon sun still warmed them and the wind whipped playfully through their hair.

"I spoke with Stan today and he called me back after lunch with three real good possibilities, and possibly a fourth, if a trade-in deal goes through before we get there."

"That's good. What style and make are they?"

"He didn't really go into that. He just said that they had low mileage and had been well maintained.

"As long as it gets me around, I don't really care."

"Well, I care," Eric, grinned. "You gotta keep up that Cummings playboy image, you know. We can't have you driving around in something that you would see mom in."

"If you say so, bro," Glen sighed, rolling his eyes. "I wouldn't want to ruin your studly reputation."

"No, I guess you wouldn't," Eric laughed good-naturedly, as he parked the car in front of the used car section of the car dealership. Since I do a good enough job of ruining it myself."

"It can't be that bad."

"You know it is.... but enough of this talk. Let's go look at some cars!" Eric offered, playfully slapping Glen on the back.

"You got it!" Glen answered, as the two of them made their way into the show room.

The stale smell of cigarette smoke lingered in the air as Mr. Newton talked his sales pitch to a potential client over the office phone. He recognized Eric, and motioned for Glen and him to take a seat on the cheap leatherette sofa opposite his desk. "I'll be off of here in a minute," he whispered with his hand over the receiver. Eric and Glen smiled and nodded back politely, hoping the wait wouldn't be too long. "Yes, Mrs. Collins…. Yes, I think we can come up with that price as a trade-in on your vehicle. Let me get the paperwork together tonight and we can finalize things by tomorrow, if that is alright with you."

Eric enjoyed seeing Mr. Newton at work. A true salesperson – just like himself. He admired the way he reeled in his catch, giving a false sense of allusion that the customer was in charge, while all along it was him guiding and orchestrating the decision. "Good…good… tomorrow then. Around nine…that's great…see you then," Mr. Newton concluded, as he hung up the phone. "She's a hard sell, if you know what I mean," he chuckled, with a deep belly laugh, as he extinguished the half-smoked smoke.

They smiled and nodded back in polite understanding.

"So, you're in the market for a car, huh?" Mr. Newton asked, as he leaned back in his chair with hands clasped behind his head, studying Glen in the process.

"Yes, I am," Glen, acknowledged with a smile.

"Stan, this is my brother Glen that I told you about."

Stan Newton extended his hand over the desk in Glen's direction. Glen rose from the couch, meeting the outstretched palm, shaking it firmly. "Glad to make your acquaintance, Glen. I hope we can fix you up with something."

"I hope so too," Glen answered sincerely, knowing Mr. Newton would probably reel him in also before it was all over.

The three ventured around the massive car lot, taking in the possibilities.

"This one is real nice. It only has 30,000 miles on it. It's a real beaut," Mr. Newton said, with admiration in his voice as he glided his hand over the freshly waxed finish.

"Good engine?" Eric asked.

"Never a problem. We've serviced from day one."

"Why did the owner get rid of it then?" Glen asked with concern.

Stan Newton chuckled again, re-evaluating his selling tactic. The *worriers* were the hardest ones to convince. "There's no problem, Glen. He's just one of those fellows who likes a new car every couple of years, and you're just one of the lucky fellows there to collect on his extravagance. You couldn't go wrong with this car."

Glen felt the fish hook in his side. Mr. Newton had his interest. The other two cars that he had showed him were all right, but they had the Sedan-image that Eric convinced him to avoid. This car, on the other hand, was sporty. It breathed young-at-heart with its rear spoiler, sky-blue paintjob that matched his eyes, and a sunroof. However, the farm and the practicality for hauling needed to be considered. His choice had to be based not only on his job, but also on the possibility of a life with Ellen that he hoped for in the future.

"Wasn't there a fourth choice?" Glen questioned with curiosity.

Eric and Stan both sighed in unison. It was getting late and everyone was feeling hunger pangs.

"Yes…there is," Mr. Newton said hesitantly, "but it was just brought in a few hours ago, and we haven't fully checked it over yet. It's a Bronco with 4-wheel drive. It's practical, but may not have the look you are after."

"It's just what I am after," Glen said with keen interest. "Could I please see it?"

Mr. Newton chuckled heartily. "I'll be happy to do that, but there's no guarantee that the mileage and condition are up to par."

"I understand, but this will be perfect for my needs if everything checks out."

Eric knew what was up. A rugged vehicle able to withstand farm lanes and pastures, hauling, dirty shoes and clothes. It was a future with Ellen Harper and her farm. Eric could see the handwriting on the wall, and he wasn't sure he was happy about the direction that Glen was going. He shook his head and smiled to himself. *Oh well….* he thought, *it's his life. He's doing better than I have done for myself in the romance department.*

"Here is it, Glen," Stan Newton announced as they were walking. He pointed the way to the vehicle in front of them.

Glen was immediately impressed as he strolled around the Bronco, taking in every square inch and running his hand over the paint job as Mr. Newton had done.

"Can I climb in and look it over?"

"Sure. Help yourself," Mr. Newton answered, confident now of a sale. "I'll be right back with the keys. They should be at the front desk on the peg board."

Glen climbed in, situating himself comfortably in the driver's seat, as Eric followed suit, climbing up into the front passenger's seat beside of him. He watched Glen intently memorizing every detail of the interior of the vehicle.

"Don't you want something with more image-appeal?"

"No," Glen answered firmly, giving Eric the eye for a few seconds, not giving a damn about his image at this point.

"Ok…just thought I'd ask."

Mr. Newton returned with the keys, handing them to Glen through the driver's window. "You and Eric can take it for a spin if you would like. I have some paperwork to finish up in my office, so you can keep it for half an hour or so – if that suits."

"Thanks, Mr. Newton. We'll take you up on that," Glen replied with an appreciative smile.

"Just stop in my office when you are done, Mr. Newton added while lighting up another cigarette. "I'll try to get some additional information for you before you get back."

Glen carefully pulled out of the car lot, making his way onto the main road. He turned on the radio, pressing the search button until he found the oldies station.

"So what do you think?" Eric asked, curious, but already guessing Glen's reply.

"It's just what I wanted!" Glen announced with a pleased smile, as he increased the speed, flooring it outside the city limits.

They laughed, feeling carefree, like they were two teenagers again out joy-riding. Glen was in control again – *healed* – just knowing he would be his own man again, with his own vehicle. Eric was giving him the solution to getting his self-worth back. He felt freer than he had felt in months.

"So, is this the one you want?"

"I would say a definite yes, unless Mr. Newton finds something out about it with the mechanical end. The mileage is good, the interior looks almost new, and I would have picked out the same color blue if I had the choice."

"Well, that's great, Glen! Stan will be glad to know that you decided on something so soon, and he can close this deal tonight," Eric grinned, giving his brother a pat on the back.

"I don't know how I can ever thank you enough, Eric," Glen voiced with much sincerity, feeling overwhelmed with gratitude.

"You would do the same for me," Eric replied, not doubting his words for a second. He glanced at his watch, realizing they had been gone for quite awhile already. "Stan is probably wondering where we are. We have been gone for over 40 minutes."

"Has it been that long? It seems like only ten to me. I could have driven around all evening!" Glen replied in amazement.

Eric chuckled good-naturedly, pleased to see his brother so happy. "Soon enough you can be driving around all evening. Let's get back and tell Stan we have a deal if everything else checks out. Then, it's time to work on the price. But I'm sure I got that covered."

Mr. Newton was waiting patiently when Eric and Glen returned. Glen dropped the keys on the desk. "Sorry we're late. I just didn't want to bring it back," he confessed.

"So you like it then, son?" he asked, as he glanced up from a contract that he had just finalized.

"Yeah, it's great!" Glen said with a wide-toothed grin.

"Does that mean you want it then?" Mr. Newton questioned with a raised brow.

"That all depends on you, and what you found out, if anything," Glen answered apprehensively.

Stan Newton shifted his weight, leaning on the desk, ready to present his sale-pitch. "The vehicle is only 3 years old and a trade-in for a newer model. Nothing major has had to be done on the mechanical end except tune-ups. The people that owned it didn't use it hard, only to commute back and forth a short distance to work. No vacation travel or heavy use such as hauling."

Glen was thrilled with the news.

"What about the price?" Eric asked. It was his time to get involved.

Mr. Newton cleared his throat, while shuffling the papers on his desk. "Well Eric.... Glen..." he began, addressing them both. "The Bronco is worth $15,000 but for you I can make it $10,000."

Eric shifted his feet. He wasn't satisfied with the pricing. He took care of Mr. Newton with a top-of-the-line computer system, and now it was his time to repay. "Stan, are you sure that's the very best you can do for my brother? He needs a car, but I know this is more than Glen intended to spend."

Glen shot Eric a concerned and frustrated look. He hated to have Eric speak on his behalf, and more than that he hated to rely on him for the money. His pride was suddenly feeling shot down again.

"Maybe we should look elsewhere, Eric," Glen interjected, wanting to speak for himself. "I don't want Mr. Newton thinking we are taking advantage of his time or his generous offer." Glen looked at Mr. Newton who was studying him intently. "Thanks for all that you tried to do for me, Mr. Newton, but Eric is right, I can't afford $10,000."

"Ok… ok…" Mr. Newton said in exasperation. "I like you kid, and this one will be on me. Eight thousand, and I definitely can't go a penny lower."

Eric's face flashed a triumph grin. "You're more than generous, Stan. What do you think, Glen?" That price sounds unbeatable to me."

"It does to me too," Glen beamed, in disbelief that things were going to work out after all. "You got a deal, Mr. Newton," Glen confirmed with a handshake. "How can I thank you enough?"

"Thank me by buying your next car here. That's thanks enough. Son, I can remember a day that I had a hard time paying for a car. Sometimes it's good to remember those times. Keeps you humble, if you know what I mean," he said in a gruff, but pleasant-sounding loud voice. "Hey, and Eric, you can buy your next sports car here also," he cheerfully added. I think you are due for a new one within the year."

"That's a given, but I can do one better than that. I would like to upgrade your printer for free. The clarity on a new laser printer that I am now using and will offer you, will do incredible things for brochures that you could print up. I can make that trade tomorrow, if you would like."

Mr. Newton seemed pleased. "You got a deal," he answered, standing up to shake Eric's hand and then Glen's again. "I will need a day to get the paper work together on the Bronco since it is getting late, and then you can pick it up tomorrow after 6."

Eric wrote out the check for eight thousand dollars while Glen signed his name to several papers. He couldn't believe that things were working out in so many good ways for him - Ellen, and now this. Things were all at once looking up.

"I'm at a loss for words. I still feel like I'm dreaming that I'm getting the Bronco, and I still can't get over the fact that you are helping me to this extent. Thanks, Eric," Glen expressed with heart-felt appreciation as they made their way back to the house.

"Glen, it's my pleasure. I was worried though, that we weren't going to get it that cheap. That is one heck of a price, don't you think?"

"I am very pleased. Mr. Newton is being more than generous," Glen said, as he balanced a pizza in one hand, slamming the car door with the other. "You know we do need to work out the payments I will be making to you."

"It's not necessary to discuss that tonight," Eric answered as he unlocked the door that led into the house from the garage.

"I really *do* want to discuss it," Glen insisted as he placed the pizza on the counter while Eric got out a couple plates.

Eric knew that there was no sense arguing. "Ok, ok Glen, what do you feel comfortable paying, and how often? I really don't even need the money right now," he confessed.

"I have my pride, Eric, and I *need* to do this, starting with my next paycheck."

Eric tore into his third piece of the chewy pizza crust. "Whatever you want to do is fine with me."

"How about fifty dollars a week? I should have it paid off in three and a half years at that rate, and maybe sooner if I get extra cash."

"That's fine, Glen, and if you ever feel too strapped for cash we can just postpone the deal for awhile."

"That won't happen," Glen, replied firmly, as he threw his used paper plate away. "Thanks again, bro. I owe you big time," Glen added warmly.

"Oh get off it," Eric answered with slight embarrassment. I didn't buy you a house or set you up in business. It's the least I can do. After all, you do your fare share of house sitting while I'm away."

Glen grinned and shook his head. "Whatever you say, but it still means a lot to me." He left Eric sitting in the kitchen watching *a comedy sitcom*, and went to his bedroom to call Ellen.

"Hello?"

"Hi, beautiful."

"Glen?"

"Who else would it be?" he chuckled. "I wanted to call you before I went to sleep, just to tell you the good news."

"Well, tell me," Ellen asked with excitement in her voice.

"I found a car."

"That's great, Glen!"

"Well, not a car exactly, but a 4-wheel drive Bronco SUV. It's in great shape, and the price I got it for is way better than I thought it was going to be."

"I am so happy for you," she answered sincerely.

"I am happy too, Ellen."

"Will you be bringing it to work in the morning?"

"I wish I could, but it's not ready yet. But by tomorrow night, it will be ready. So I guess Thursday it will be all mine! He added with pride.

"I can hardly wait to see it."

I can hardly wait to show it to you, darling," he whispered. "I love you."

"I love you too."

"Good night, Ellen."

"Good night, Glen. I'll see you in the morning."

Chapter Twenty-Six

The taxi ride out to Ellen's was alive with chatter from the same driver who had picked Glen up the day before.

"Went to Del Ray's last night. Told the guys there the story about that Mrs. Harper."

"Oh yeah?" Glen snickered with amusement.

"Yeah… they said she sounds like a real nut case, and if they ever see that mountain lion of hers they're gonna shoot it."

Glen's mood became suddenly irate, tired of playing the game with the loser. He turned to face the cabby, speaking in a low growl. "If I were you *buddy*, I would tell my friends at the bar to *think twice* before doing something as stupid as that! Mrs. Harper minds her business and doesn't need any trouble from nosey busybodies who are trespassing on her land! If I were working at the time and caught anyone there without good intent, I would have to call the sheriff."

"No need to get in a huff over this," the cabby said with a rise to his voice. "We just thought this would be doing everybody a favor, including you."

"You thought wrong," Glen interjected sternly. "I keep my distance, but I am there to protect Mrs. Harper, her property, and her possessions. I'd stay away if I was you, and I'd tell the guys at the bar that too. *Got it?"* Glen demanded adamantly.

"Yeah…sure…" the cabby answered with confusion. "Don't need any trouble, that's for sure."

"Glad you see it that way," Glen interjected sarcastically. "Keep the change…"

"Thanks, pal."

The cabby looked down at the money in his hand. He cocked his head to the side with a dazed look on his face, as he stared at the bills to cover the fare, and realized the tip was only an additional penny. "The hell with you!" he yelled as he pitched the penny from the retreating vehicle.

Glen walked away, grinning with smug satisfaction, never turning to look at the trail of exhaust. His blood was still boiling at the thought of someone harming Ellen or Cuddles. He hoped the cabby and his friends were history, or he would have to break them in two.

The produce stand was covered in a fine smattering of dew that glistened brightly in the morning sunshine. Glen realized that he should have covered it with a tarp the night before. Now he would need to wipe it down and let it dry for a couple hours before giving it a coat of paint. In one corner of the barn, he found a stack of old, but clean towels, folded neatly in a wooden crate and ready for use.

"These will do," he said, while grabbing a stack and heading back out to the wet stand. Several damp towels and a splinter in his thumb later, he completed the task at hand. "Damn, does that hurt!" he moaned, trying to bite the aggravator out of his flesh. "Maybe Ellen can remove it when she gets up," he grimaced to himself, glancing up at the still quiet house.

He missed the intimacy they had just shared a few days prior. Too many unavoidable distractions had kept them apart. Just the thought of her set his loins on fire. He wanted her now, even though he had made a commitment to himself that he wouldn't let this happen during the workday. Never had he knocked on the door before and woke her up, but today would be the first. He was impatient to be with her again. It had been too long.

Ellen opened her eyes abruptly to the sound of the soft tapping on the door. At first she thought she was dreaming, but knew otherwise as it continued.

"Who can that be, Cuddles?" she questioned, to the one-eye-opened cat, curled comfortably at the foot of her bed. Ellen grabbed her robe, thrown over a spindle on the footboard, and glanced out the window. *No car*, she thought. *It still must be Glen*, she concluded happily to herself, smiling warmly. She hugged the robe around herself, as she ran to the front door in bare feet.

"Who's there?" she questioned timidly, with an ear pressed to the wooden door.

"Ellen, it's me, …Glen."

Ellen threw back the door, happy to greet her bronzed Adonis. "Glen, come in," she invited, as he wiped his boots briskly on the porch mat.

"Sorry to bother you so early, but I got a splinter in my thumb and it's killing me. Can you get it out for me?" he questioned, faking a pained expression.

Ellen giggled at his little-boy charm. “Of course, silly. Have a seat, and I’ll find a needle in my sewing box.” She sterilized the needle with some rubbing alcohol, before taking Eric’s hand and placing it in her lap. “This may hurt a little,” she said softly, bending low over his thumb to see exactly how deep the splinter was embedded.

“Ouch!” he groaned, milking it for all it was worth.

“I’m sorry,” she said, smiling sympathetically, as she looked up into a pair of his play-acting, baby-blue eyes. One more prick with the needle, and then she extracted the splinter with tweezers. Antibacterial ointment and a bandaide followed. “Good as new,” she cheerfully admonished, giving his thumb a loving kiss, as if he were a little child. Glen returned the smiled, reaching out and pulling Ellen onto his lap, wrapping is arms securely around her.

“My lips need the kisses more than my thumb does,” he whispered, possessing her mouth in a fierce deep kiss. Ellen’s mouth responded with equal ardor, her lips parting to accept his tongue, as hungry for Glen as he was for her.

He picked her up in his arms, carrying her to the bedroom, laying her on the bed. I need to get back to work, but I need you too. It has been too long,” he groaned with passion, as he quickly tore off his clothes.

“I know, darling. I’ve dreamed for the day that you would come to me like this,” Ellen beckoned, already alive with passion.

Their unclothed bodies clung to each other, sending Cuddles scampering off the bed. Words were forgotten as touches were re-familiarized and lips were locked in ecstasy. Glen suckled each of Ellen’s nipples to a hardened bud, as she arched in delight.

“I can’t hold off any longer,” he said with yearning.

"I want you too," she answered with shallow breaths, as she pulled Glen down on top of her.

Their union was as wonderful and fulfilling as it had been the first time that they had been together. Every time now was like that for them, so alive with intensity and desire. They lay together, slick with a sheen of wet, much like what Glen had just removed from the produce stand. It was quite some time until their breathing took on a more normal rate. The feeling of wanting to return to slumber had to be resisted by both of them as they lay locked in the other one's embrace.

"I should get back to work," he whispered softly, as he brushed his lips against her face.

"Do you have to?" she pleaded with eyes that spoke only of love.

"I do," he answered gently, kissing her forehead as he slid from the bed grabbing his clothes.

Ellen loved to see him nude. The tanned skin against the white creamy concealed skin that displayed the power of his manhood always left her senses as well as her pulse racing. As he dressed, she watched his muscles flex as he lifted each leg to put his jean shorts back on. She never dreamt she would find love again, and with someone so perfect in physique was an added bonus.

Glen bent over the bed giving her one last kiss. "Come out and visit me if you get the chance later. I'll be painting the produce stand."

Ellen smiled warmly, touching her hands to both sides of his face. "Is there any question? Of course I will be out to see you."

Glen returned the look of mutual affection as he gave her one last kiss. He adored the woman.

The stand had dried sufficiently and Glen decided to paint it the same white that was already on it. There was an adequate amount of the color still left from painting the barn.

Ellen appeared with a pitcher of iced tea and glasses, just as Glen was finishing the top shelves that would hold some of the vegetables. "Does it meet your approval, Madame?" he asked with a fake French accent and a bow.

She giggled happily. "It looks wonderful! How about a cool drink and a break?"

"I think I can spare five minutes for such a lovely lady," he answered with his breath-taking smile as he wiped off his forehead with the back of his hand.

They sat on the porch steps together as Glen took deep gulps from the glass.

"You know, Glen, I don't expect you to work so hard. A five minute break is hardly sufficient."

"I know that," he smiled. "But I already had a nice and quite adequate break this morning," Glen added with a wink. "I want to keep on this, because I need to get going at a fairly decent hour tonight. I don't need to leave as early as I did last night, but my car will be ready, and I want to pick it up."

"You're excited, aren't you?"

"You know I am, Ellen," Glen said with pride. "This takes a lot of pressure off of me."

"I know it does," she replied with tender understanding while patting his hand. "Why don't I make us an early dinner and I will drive you to Newton's. Then we can pick up your car together."

Glen hesitated, thinking of Eric. "Well…. I guess I should call Eric first and let him know of those plans. I think he planned on taking me over there himself to pick it up."

Ellen felt totally embarrassed. "Oh…I'm sorry Glen. Just forget I even mentioned it."

Glen wrapped his arm around Ellen's shoulder, pulling her close to his side. "Don't read into things. I would much rather be with you," he reassured. "I'll just give Eric a call and let him know that I can pick up the Bronco without him."

"Are you sure?" she asked. "I didn't even think about Eric."

"I'll just give him a call now, and then we'll have an answer. Ok?" he grinned while grabbing her chin.

"Ok… but I can just as well stay at home tonight. The last thing I want to do is make a problem with you and Eric."

Glen helped Ellen to her feet before he grabbed the tray with the empty glasses and pitcher. He placed it on the counter in the kitchen, and then retreated to the porch to call Eric.

Chapter Twenty-Seven

Computer World Systems was a flurry of activity. The office pool of secretaries was busy typing in orders and dealing with the phone customers and their many questions. Not many complaints came across the lines fortunately. Each computer system sold was of superior quality. Eric made sure of that.

Melinda's morning had gone rather smoothly. She felt better than she had felt in days. An early morning workout at the gym, and an invigorating whirlpool had made her come alive with energy. She was even finally beginning to deal with her pent-up anger and resentful feelings towards Eric. She had considered quitting her job, since it was hard not to encounter Eric everyday when her secretarial duties beckoned her into his office. But he remained businesslike and civil, not even mentioning anything personal. Initially, it was a source of pain. She almost hoped he would say something – anything intimate – when they were alone; but he didn't, and that wasn't like Eric. So Melinda would go on alone and single again, she decided with new resolve, as she began her busy day at CWS. After all, Eric Cummings wasn't the only gorgeous, successful hunk in the sea, with a personality that ignited her like a scorching flame.

"Melinda?"

"Yes, Eric," Melinda answered over the intercom, snapping out of her daydream.

"Will you pull the Rosano account and bring it to me? He just called and wants a break down on those figures again."

"Sure, Eric. I'll be right there." Melinda still called him Eric. She couldn't imagine herself going back to calling him Mr. Cummings. That formality had stopped after the first week of them working together. Eric insisted on first names, and she liked it that way.

Melinda pulled the file from the current perspective sales drawer, and made her way to Eric's door amid the stares of the other female employees. It never ceased to amaze her how they always focused their attention on her, when she prepared to enter Eric's office. The probing stares made her feel as if illicit sexual acts were always going on between them behind the closed door. She could only imagine what the rumormongers were saying. Melinda didn't care though. It was only jealousy anyway. Any number of them would have gladly traded places with her for one night in Eric's bed.

Eric sat back in his chair with his feet crossed and propped up on the desk. He spoke loudly, staring intently at the ceiling. "Yes, Mr. Rosano, I think we can do that. My secretary is here now with those figures," he acknowledged, giving Melinda a smile as she entered the room with the file in hand. He made her feel nervous, as he did everyday. This day was no exception, with the charisma and sex appeal that was so much a part of his nature. His presence just breathed searing hot desire.

She laid the file on his desk, opening it to the very page of information that Eric needed. She turned to leave, but Eric tapped the desk loudly with his pen, causing Melinda to turn back around in surprise. He motioned for her to sit down on the sofa opposite his desk. She looked confused, but obliged his request, thinking that maybe he needed to ask her questions about the account information. Her stomach twisted in a tight knot, as she watched him openly consume her with his piercing eyes. She felt like a cornered animal being sized–up before the kill.

Eric stared intently at Melinda, taking in her entire appearance, as the conversation continued between he and Mr. Rosano. She was trim, fit and tan – outfitted in a black suit that emphasized each shapely curve of her body. He missed her. *Why did I have to screw this relationship up so badly?* He contemplated.

Melinda nervously glanced around the room while he continued his conversation, making unintentional eye contact with him from time to time. It unnerved her that Eric was still observing her intently with an amused playboy grin on his face.

"That's right…aah-huh…. yeah, sure. Call or email me with any questions…."

She sighed heavily, realizing he was succeeding in flustering her, and he was well aware of it too. Wanting only to escape his non-verbal advances, but knowing that was an impossibility, she diverted her eyes, keeping them glued to his hands that were busy shuffling the papers on his desk. *Those hands*, she thought…. how she missed those wonderful hands and the mastery they had over her.

"We are anxious to wrap things up also, Mr. Rosano…" *Her breasts look wonderful….*

That curl of hair that hits his collar….

"A week from Thursday? As far as I can tell, from looking at my calendar, that will work."

I want him…

I want her… "Alright, I will see you then. Remember to call me if you need anything else before our next meeting. Goodbye, sir," he ended, with his triumph over-confident ego ready to explode again. Mr. Rosano was putty in his hands and Eric knew it. The deal only needed signatures. Everything else was a given. Eric put down the phone, as he lowered his legs to the floor, sitting upright in his chair again. "Melinda…. we need to talk."

Melinda's heart began to pound frantically in her chest, as she raised her eyes and locked them with his chestnut brown ones. The tone of his words was different somehow. She knew this wasn't going to be directly about work. This was going to be personal. She hoped Eric didn't intend on convincing her to leave Computer World Systems. He knew she would never file charges against him for sexual discrimination since the attraction was mutual.

She shifted restlessly on the sofa, re-crossing her legs in the opposite direction, finding it hard to find the words to speak. "What do we need to talk about, Eric?"

"I think you already know the answer to that," he replied, as he scrutinized her every movement and word. "Things are so screwed up between us, and I don't like it."

"Your choice of words couldn't be more appropriate," she said mockingly, gaining confidence with her rage. "You did *screw up*, and with someone else besides me, unfortunately."

"Melinda, your sarcasm doesn't become you," Eric replied with stone-faced seriousness. "I was wrong, and I know I am an ass-hole, but I want another chance to prove I can be faithful to you."

Melinda began to laugh in anxious disbelief. He never gave up. "Eric, you don't owe me anything. And as much as I haven't wanted to admit it, I have finally accepted the fact that you will never be totally faithful to one person."

Eric closed his eyes, sighing heavily with the statement she had just imparted. He couldn't deny it was very realistic and truthful. "You're right, Melinda," he said with total heart-felt sincerity, as he gazed deeply into her eyes again. "I can't refute the charges that you lay before me, because up until this point, that has been the way I have always handled my relationships," he added with deep regret. "But Melinda…" he began, as he threaded his fingers together and rested them under his chin, while resting his arms on his desk as if he were weary. "I have been doing a lot of thinking, and I want things to be different with us. It would tear me up inside if I knew you were doing the same deceptive things to me that I have done to you in the past. Maybe I don't know the first thing about love, but I think I'm smart enough to know that when you love someone you're not supposed to do those things."

Melinda shook her head in frustration, glancing down at the floor and then back up at Eric. "What are you saying, Eric? Are you saying that you think you love me?"

Eric hesitated; knowing that the declaration that she wanted clarification on was a big step from him in word and action. "That's exactly what I am saying, Melinda, and I want a chance to prove that to you. I love you," Eric replied genuinely, while rising from his desk and making his way over to her.

Melinda's heart was pounding wildly; feeling like it was ready to leap from her chest. She knew his words were melting the wall of protection that she had attempted to shield herself with. He approached her, attempting to sit down on the couch, but her hands reached out to brace his chest and stop him at arm's length. *"I can't handle you playing with me, Eric.* I want a man who is devoted only to me. I will not lie - there is definitely chemistry between us when we are together, but it has to be more than the physical for me now, Eric. Do you understand that?"

Eric's eyes were smoldering embers-of-desire, but they held honesty and love too. "Forgive me, Melinda. I am a self-centered ass, but thank God, I'm not so stupid that I don't know a good thing when I see it. And you are the best thing that has ever happened to me. I have been miserable without you. I swear I won't screw up this time.... *if you just give me the chance!"*

Melinda's worried eyes smiled up at him, as her hand reached up to touch the side of his face. His lips brushed over her fingertips making her sigh breathlessly. "I want to give you that chance, Eric. Please don't disappoint me this time," she breathed softly, being pulled helplessly into his amorous trance and embrace.

"I won't, darling," he promised barely above a whisper, as he enfolded her in his arms. He possessed her lips, luxuriating in the feel of them. His tongue teased the inside of her sweet luscious mouth. She hesitated, but relinquished, meeting his tongue with her own. He groaned with desire, pulling her closer into his embrace. Melinda was lost. She knew her defenses and reserve of just an hour ago were being broken down. She loved him too, and had never stopped. Her mind wrestled with the thoughts of the other employees just on the other side of the office door; and also the thought of the pain that he could still cause her in the future, if this was just him screaming out for immediate gratification.

"We should stop, Eric," she whispered, pulling slightly away to gaze into his eyes.

"We will stop for now, but promise me you will meet me tonight for dinner."

"Eric… maybe we should give this some time. A day or two…."

"Melinda, please…" he pleaded as he ran his hand seductively up her jacket sleeve, and then brushed over the side of her breast. He was already hard with desire and wanted nothing more, at the moment, than to strip off her skirt and hose and do it to her in his office before she changed her mind.

"Alright, Eric… but nothing more will happen beyond what we just did," she replied adamantly, giving him a look of warning. "We should take things slowly, just to make sure you really want what you say you do."

"You got a deal," he winked, while smacking her backside lightly as she walked from the room. Eric raised his arms high above his head, stretching out his spine, breathing a sigh of relief that he had another chance to prove himself to Melinda. He gazed out the wall's length of windows that over-looked an expanse of land that was soon to be developed into surrounding businesses. He would miss the solitude of CWS being alone without neighbors, with only a grove of trees in the distance; but life held its changes, even in small towns like Fillmore.

Tonight will be special, he promised with a contented smile. They would kiss again, and if he had his way, they would do much more. He savored the thought of being totally fulfilled and sated with her in his arms, before the evening was over. The office encounter was just a preview of what would hopefully unfold between them. Eric was happy and content with Melinda's change of heart. Being faithful to one woman was foreign to him, but he looked forward to proving to himself, as well as Melinda, that he was up for a new challenge. He was miserable without her – plain lonely and bored when he wasn't working. Things had to be different between them this time, he knew, or he would lose her forever. No one else would enter the picture this time. Eric would make sure of that.

Chapter Twenty-Eight

"Eric.... you have a call on line two. It's your brother...."

"Thanks, Melinda," Eric replied brightly, turning quickly to pick up the phone. "Glen what's up?"

"Nothing major, but I did want to talk to you about tonight."

Eric felt like he had totally blown it. He had forgotten about Glen and how important the evening was for him. The car would be ready. If he cancelled his plans with Melinda, it may get her apprehensions back into full swing again.

"Tonight.... oh yeah.... what time do you want to meet?"

"Well about that... I was wondering if you would mind if I picked up the Bronco on my own with Ellen. We were going to make a date out of it."

Relief flooded over Eric. "Sounds perfect! Although, if it were me, I could think of a more romantic setting for a date; but to each their own, bro," he said with a chuckle.

"Little do you know about what qualifies as romance. There's nothing like a good old-fashioned joy ride that leads to *other* things."

"If you say so," Eric resigned. "Have a good time and I'll see you later. On second thought.... maybe you won't. I may not be home tonight."

“Business?”

“Not tonight, bro. Romance, hopefully, is in the air for both of the Cummings’ brothers.”

Glen worked intently for the rest of the afternoon, finishing the painting of the produce stand. The fresh, pungent paint covered the stand in a glossy shine. Glen hoped Cuddles didn’t get any ideas of jumping on it now. He felt he should warn Ellen to keep the cat inside for the day.

“You need some help?” Glen yelled, as he saw Ellen taking down her laundry from the wash-line.

“I’m fine,” she answered sweetly, as she glanced in the direction of her handsome man with his paint-splattered hands. He cleaned them swiftly, making his way to Ellen’s side.

“Talked with Eric about tonight,” Glen mentioned, as he bent down to pick up the full laundry basket.

“Is he going with you still?”

“No, but you are,” he grinned.

“Oh?” she beamed with happy surprise.

“Actually, Eric seems relieved that he doesn’t have to go with me tonight after all. He has a date, and didn’t want to break it.”

“Well that is just perfect! I’ll make us a quick dinner and then we can go pick up the Bronco.”

“Sounds good to me, but don’t go to any big trouble.”

"How do burgers on the grill and pasta salad sound?"

"Just great!" Glen answered enthusiastically, as he carried the laundry basket to the porch door. "By the way, Ellen," Glen said with a turn. "It may be a good idea to keep Cuddles in overnight so he doesn't jump up on the produce stand."

"That may be a problem, since he doesn't use a liter box that often; and he is used to going outside whenever he wants to."

"Well, then I would be keeping an eye on him. If he walks on it, he will have sticky paint all over him, and the stand will show a trail of cat-print marks."

"I'll try to keep an eye on him," Ellen promised. "But you know how bad boys can be - they just don't cooperate when you want them to."

"Are you implying *that I* am a bad boy?" Glen grinned playfully.

"You are *my* bad boy," Ellen answered with flirtatious eyes while pointing at his broad chest. "And I think *bad boys* can be a lot of fun when they are as loving as you are," she confessed, grabbing both of his cheeks in a playful squeeze.

Glen wrapped his arms around Ellen holding her tight. "This bad boy enjoys loving you immensely," he replied with a husky voice, swooping down to engulf her lips in a searing kiss that left her knees weak.

"I'm convinced," she gushed. "But anytime you feel the need to remind me just do so."

Glen's response was a series of mind-boggling kisses that led to the postponement of all thoughts of food for close to an hour as he carried her to the bedroom in his arms.

Dinner and the cleanup of the kitchen were completed before Glen and Ellen drove to Newton Motors. They worked well as a team. Ellen made the pasta salad while Glen flipped the burgers on the grill. After dinner, Ellen washed the dishes and Glen dried them.

"There's a space over there," Glen pointed, as Ellen parallel parked perfectly in a space between two cars. "This shouldn't take too long," Glen grinned, as the two of them walked hand in hand to Mr. Newton's office.

"Take however long you need," Ellen re-assured with a smile, as Glen knocked on the office door.

"Come in," a voice boomed from behind a wooden door that separated them.

Glen opened the door, standing in the doorframe with Ellen by his side. "Hi, Mr. Newton, I'm here to pick up the Bronco. Is everything ready to go?"

"Come in, Glen," Mr. Newton exclaimed loudly. "And bring that pretty lady friend in with you." The car salesman rose to the occasion, extending his hand to Ellen. "You look familiar to me, little lady."

"I'm Ellen Harper, sir. We probably passed in the grocery store or something," she replied politely.

"No.... somewhere else," he answered contemplatively, trying to place her. "Did you ever buy a vehicle off of me before?"

"I'm sorry to say that I haven't," she confessed with a smile.

"I'll figure it out probably after you leave," he answered, laughing good-naturedly. "It always happens like that."

"So, is my car ready?" Glen asked anxiously again, hoping to get Mr. Newton thinking about his business instead of Ellen.

"Umm…yes. It is ready. All I need is one last signature on this form, and you'll be all set."

The signature was signed and Mr. Newton gave hearty handshakes to Glen and Ellen one last time.

"The Bronco, I believe, is parked beside the doors of the service center."

"Thanks, Mr. Newton for everything," Glen said sincerely. "I know you gave me one heck of a deal, and I appreciate it."

"No problem, Glen. Any brother of Eric's deserves a deal. He's done a lot for us. All I ask is that you buy another car from me one day. Preferably new the next time," he added with a hearty chuckle. "And in the future, call me Stan."

"Alright…. Stan," he replied with a pleasant smile, trying the name out for size.

Glen unlocked the passenger's door for Ellen. "Your chariot awaits, Madame."

Ellen giggled. "Thank you, kind sir," Ellen replied in her best-attempted southern drawl, as she climbed up on the seat.

Glen sat quietly for a minute in the car, sighing deeply as he clutched the steering wheel. "I can't believe it's actually mine," he whispered intensely, turning to stare at Ellen.

"I know, honey. I am so happy for you," Ellen said with kind understanding, as she patted the top of his hand that was closest to her. "It'*s yours* and you *deserve it*! So enjoy it."

"I plan to, Ellen," he beamed. "And I'm especially happy that you are here with me sharing all this," he smiled.

"Well show me what this thing is made of," Ellen challenged, breaking the seriousness of the moment.

"Ok, but you better buckle up," Glen warned playfully, as he backed the Bronco out onto the street. Ellen laughed loudly, as Glen roared down the road causing the curious bystanders to stare after them.

"I hope you don't get a ticket for this hot rod display."

"Ellen, you know this isn't a hot rod," he emphasized, thinking about Eric's playboy image remarks again. "And," he grinned, looking at her mischievously, "If I would be so unfortunate as to get a ticket, it is quite obvious that you know everyone around here anyways. That pretty face of yours will talk me out of any trouble I could possibly find myself in."

"Is *that so?"* she giggled.

"You know it is," he grinned, grabbing her knee, making her squeal with delight.

They rode through the countryside for several hours, happy and content, enjoying the last glimmers of daylight on the horizon. The Bronco took the farm's lane with ease.

"Don't say it, Glen. I know, I know, the Bronco is so *glad* the lane is fixed."

Now it was Glen's turn to laugh. "My lips are sealed," he replied, bringing the vehicle to a stop in front of the farm house."

"I think I like your lips better unsealed," she said with passion-filled eyes.

Glen reached over the seat to kiss her, parting her lips as his tongue entered her mouth in a long and deep kiss. Ellen sighed under the scorching heat of their embrace. "Definitely unsealed is better.... Would you like to come in for some desert?" she asked.

Glen smiled teasingly. "What do you have to offer?"

"Homemade cookies and ice cream."

"Sounds delicious, but I'd much rather have you for desert," he confessed, while brushing his lips against the pulse point of her neck."

Shivers of desire ran deliciously up and down Ellen's spine.

"You can have both you know," she answered breathlessly.

"You got a deal," he whispered back, still planting kisses along the column of her slender neck. "But the ice cream and cookies can wait until much later," he smiled as they quickly ran in the house hand in hand. "And remember, we need to pick up the Saab later."

"The Saab can sit until tomorrow," Ellen added without hesitation, as she removed her t-shirt, throwing it in Glen's face on her way to the bedroom.

Chapter Twenty-Nine

The day was winding down at CWS for the busy 8 to 5 time-clock watchers. Everyone appeared to be gone except for the typical few executives who lingered on, sometimes late into the evening. Eric was one of those executives. He had no need to leave at any particular time since there usually wasn't anyone or anything to answer to outside of CWS. Sometimes, and more so lately, he wished that these circumstances were different. *A long-term commitment to something other than this job might be nice after all*, he had decided of late. And why, when his mind went in that direction, Melinda entered his thoughts, he did not know; but she did possess the traits of a person that he could spend the rest of his life with.

"Hi Eric," Melinda greeted pleasantly, entering his office with her purse and blazer swung over her arm. "Do you want to pick me up at home, or do you want me to wait here for you?"

Eric smiled, happy to see her again, even though it had only been a couple of hours since they were last together. "I just wrapped things up for the day. I'll get my briefcase and we're outta here," he grinned.

Eric grabbed for Melinda's hand, bringing it to his lips for a kiss as they got on the elevator. "Where would you like to go to eat?" he asked thoughtfully, bringing their still clasped hands back down to his side.

"You decide. It really doesn't matter to me."

"We could drive to Grand Island and go to Pierre's if you would like."

"That sounds wonderful!" Melinda replied happily. Eric remembered it was her favorite place to eat.

The drive to Pierre's was animated with conversation of CWS. They spoke of the busy weeks of work that they had been going through, as well as the project that needed to be completed the following day. Eric found a parking space close to the front of the restaurant, and walked around to open Melinda's door. He extended his hand, offering to help her from the Mustang before walking with his arm wrapped securely around Melinda's waist. She was somewhat taken back, but did not resist his advances.

They were placed at a romantic candlelit table, off in a secluded corner. Melinda was pleasantly surprised to find out that Eric reserved the table in advance, calling apparently from work earlier in the day. Beside of the table, a bottle of champagne was waiting, chilling in a silver decanter. A waiter dressed in a black tuxedo poured each one of them a generous libation after Eric sampled and approved the offering.

"Perfect!" he announced with gusto as they ate their salads, Eric poured the remainder of the champagne into Melinda's glass and his own, and then he ordered a bottle of red wine to be served with the main course. "I think the Rosano account is all wrapped up. He sounds very pleased with what we are proposing."

"Eric, you know *they all are pleased* with what you have to offer them."

Eric smiled, finding Melinda especially beautiful in the soft romantic glow of the candlelight. “How about you, Melinda, do you like what I have to offer as well?” Eric asked pointedly, bringing the glass of champagne to his lips, waiting for an answer.

Melinda blushed, caught off guard by his apparent bold advances he was making. “Eric, it was always good with us,” she said quietly. “But unfortunately, a lot of other women can say the same thing,” she remarked without hesitation.

“Do we *really* have to get into this again?”

“I guess not,” she replied somewhat apologetically. “I’m sorry. I do want the evening to go well between us,” she smiled.

Eric looked relieved. “So do I,” he added, reaching over to give her a kiss as he grabbed her hand giving it an affectionate squeeze.

The wine was served with dinner, which included a French dish of veal in cream sauce and chocolate soufflé for desert.

“Can I get you anything else this evening?” the waiter offered, efficient to every detail.

“Not a thing for me,” Melinda replied with a smile, feeling totally relaxed and satisfied.

“Me neither,” Eric added. “Give our compliments to the chef. He always does a superb job.”

“Yes he does,” Melinda agreed, with much enthusiasm.

They walked to the car hand in hand again, while Eric

unlocked the car door for Melinda.

"It's been great being with you tonight," Eric confessed, as he sat gazing at Melinda, with a reply on her part remaining in silence. Desire flooded his eyes as he became enthralled by her loveliness. His hand reached out to touch her shoulder, and instinctively she jumped slightly at the contact. "I want to see you again. Are you willing?"

Melinda felt vulnerable. She desperately wanted to be with him, but she didn't want to feel the pain again either from his rejection or from the breakdown of his respect and trust. She knew his track record. It was no secret to her or anyone else that knew of him, that he was a womanizer and had broken many hearts along the way. She hated to be numbered amongst his many conquests that he had probably made broken promises to also. Maybe his admittance of love, like he had proclaimed earlier in the day, was a line he threw out to other women in last-attempt desperation, when his relationships were falling apart. She had never heard that to be the case, but it was certainly something to be considered.

"I would like to see you again, Eric, but I'm not so sure it's a good idea."

"*And why not?*" he asked with a raised brow, dropping his arm down to his side in defeat.

"Eric, you know how I feel."

"Yes, I do, but I'm resigned not to let things turn out the same way again. You mean too much to me. You gotta believe that, Melinda."

"I really *do* want to believe that," she said with downcast eyes. "But I also don't like being made a fool of."

"Believe it, Melinda. I want only you," he promised, as he raised her chin and put his free arm around her shoulder again.

"Oh, Eric…" Melinda sighed, raising her eyes to be instantly locked with his. "I'm tired of the fight. Maybe it is the wine talking, but I want you too, Eric, and if you screw up this time – so help me God – I'll get someone to break your legs."

Eric grinned and shook his head while touching his fingers to her lips to silence her. "If you break my legs, it will be hard to make love to you. And that's what I want tonight, Melinda," he propositioned. "To make love to you until we are thoroughly and totally exhausted. Let's just be good to each other, and put the pain of the past behind us and start over. I want *only you. Only you…*" Eric reassured, reaching out, attempting to do his best and kiss her doubts away.

"Oh, Eric, as hard as I been trying to tell myself this isn't wise to be involved with you, I can't stop loving you," she moaned, lost to his magic.

He thanked God for his good fortune. He was *actually* getting another chance with her. "I love you too, Melinda. Say you'll stay with me tonight," Eric whispered. "Let's go down the street to the Dexter and spend the night together. I want to hold you and make love to you until the sun comes up."

"Eric…" she breathed. "You make it so difficult to say no."

"Then don't. Please, just say yes," he beckoned, letting his hand drift to her breast.

"Alright," she conceded with her pulse quickening from his touch. "Take me to the Dexter, but I will need to be home in time to change my clothes for work."

"I understand," he teased with mock seriousness. "We wouldn't want someone at CWS to actually think you would wear the same clothes to work two days in a row."

Chapter Thirty

The romantic fulfillment of the night before gave way to a morning of contented souls. Melinda lay in the arms of Eric, feeling very much in love and where she wanted to be. Ellen also was in the arms of Glen – safe and secure – wishing he would never leave.

Glen had spent the night, attempting first to call Eric, wanting to let him know that he wouldn't be home – but without luck. Eric, on the other hand, didn't even think about Glen. His phone was turned off. He was too lost in the passion of rekindling his love with Melinda.

Glen's bare torso slid from the bed as he pulled back the curtain from the window. The sky was gray and heavy with the falling rain. *Thank God….* he thought. He turned to look at Ellen as the pleasant reminders of the night before replayed in his mind. She was still asleep and had only moved slightly when Glen decided to leave the comfort of her bed. She looked so beautiful and peaceful with a contented smile etched on her face. Cuddles was curled up at her feet, and the disruption was stirring him back to life with a yawn. Glen chuckled to himself, watching the pampered pet that was almost like a child to Ellen. This was the scene he had longed for every day since he arrived at the farm, and now it had come true. He was with her, but an agreement of work on the farm beckoned him out of the fantasy.

Glen could see the produce stand from the window. Ellen had

watched Cuddles closely the night before, keeping a careful eye on him when she let him out. The paint would be dry by now, so Cuddles was off of his restriction. Cuddles meowed loudly, and Glen turned with a start.

"Shhh… Cuddles. You'll wake her up," he admonished quietly just above a whisper, as the cat squinted his eyes shut as if he understood the reprimand. Glen grinned and shook his head, as he looked at the pampered feline whose life was that of constant spoiling. "What a life," he whispered with an amused smile, as he crawled back into the bed, causing the mattress to sink in the middle and the bedsprings to squeak. "Ellen, darling," he beckoned playfully. "Can we talk a minute?"

"Hmm…" she sighed, rolling over to gaze at him through sleepy, half-opened eyes. "What's wrong, Glen?" she said with a fulfilled happy smile.

"Nothing, my love," Glen continued, kissing her lightly on the tip of her nose. "But, it is finally raining and I don't know what you want me to do until it stops."

Ellen smiled. "I guess we will just have to spend the whole day in bed."

"Ellen, be serious," Glen, answered, while propping himself up on one elbow. "I can't accept your money, and just lay around and do nothing."

"Oh, *you will be doing something*, sweetie," Ellen replied seductively, as she pulled herself up on her elbow too. She touched her fingertips to his lips and sketched lazy circles from there to his forehead and back down again. "You will be my love slave and that will be worth every cent that I pay you."

Glen grinned, lazily setting his gaze on her exposed cleavage that was peaking out from the sheet. "Ellen… you tempt me beyond belief, but you know how I feel about this."

"Yeah, yeah, Glen, I know," she mocked, as she rolled her eyes in feigned indifference.

Glen looked at her, not sure if she were being serious or not.

"I was only teasing!" Ellen giggled, replying in a singsong fashion. She sat up in bed looking at him seriously, trying to make her point. "There is plenty that you can help me with inside the house. I want to start baking items and freezing them for the produce stand. You can help me with that. I also need to do some spring-cleaning around here. Walls need to be washed and so do the windows. And the basement needs to be cleaned out. So you see, there are plenty of indoor activities to keep you busy, especially since the idea of being my love slave doesn't seem to appeal to you," she said with a pretend pout and sad-looking eyes.

Glen laughed, rolling Ellen on her back as he returned to his place beneath the rumpled sheets. He climbed on top of her, holding her arms to her sides. "I never said I didn't *want* to be your love slave, it's just that my conscience won't allow it. At least that is, not for long," he grinned sensuously, planting kisses down the side of her neck.

Ellen giggled loudly, trying to pull loose from Glen's hold. "Stop it Glen, before I pee myself!"

"I don't care if you pee yourself. It will only give me another job of washing the sheets."

"Glen, that's disgusting!" Ellen gasped, while continuing to giggle and hiccup all at the same time.

“Ok, ok, I’ll stop,” he said. “But only because I love you so much,” he added warmly while rolling on his side taking her in his arms.

Ellen turned suddenly soft natured and reflective. “I love you too, Glen, with my whole heart,” she added, while acting out the thing she dreamed of doing from the first moment she observed Glen doing the same. She reached up, combing her fingers through his hair with both of her hands, before kissing him passionately on the lips.

It was Glen’s undoing, as he groaned deeply before fusing his body with her own, bringing them together in a climatic pinnacle of oneness and completion before the responsibilities of the day began.

The clock’s alarm blared with a shrill that brought disgruntled sighs from Eric and Melinda both. “It’s time to get up sleepy head,” Eric urged softly, as he kissed the top of Melinda’s head. She rolled more securely into Eric’s embrace.

“Do we have to?” she moaned, wanting only to stay in this safe, peaceful haven all day.

Eric felt content too. “I know how your feeling darling, but you know the busy schedule that awaits the both of us at CWS. And have you forgotten so soon the wardrobe change you *wanted* to make?” he added good-naturedly.

Melinda was up with a start. “Beat you to the car,” she yelled, as she ran to the bathroom with her wrinkled suit and underclothes in hand.

The rain continued to fall at a steady pace throughout the day. The smell of banana and apple bread baked in the oven, as Glen washed down the walls in the dining room.

"That smell is driving me crazy! I hope I get a sample, Ellen!" Glen yelled out to her playfully, as she was busy preparing the next set of bread pans for the oven.

She grinned to herself as she smoothed the batter in each pan. "When you have a minute, come out to the kitchen and you can test if for me."

He returned the scrub cloth to the bucket, and peaked around the kitchen door opening. "I'll make a minute for a deal like that!"

Ellen smiled warmly, enjoying immensely the closeness of having Glen in the house with her all day. Ellen had sliced a piece of both the banana and apple bread, and laid it on a pretty china plate, that was outlined in a border of pink, blue and yellow flowers. "I also made some coffee. Would you like a cup?"

"That sounds wonderful," Glen replied with a sparkle in his eyes. "But you didn't have to go to so much trouble for me."

"No trouble. And besides, I need an expert opinion before I sell this to my customers."

Glen tasted each delicate tasty morsel, finding it hard to suppress his groans of delight.

Ellen watched, staring at him in eager anticipation on the edge of her seat. "So what do you think?"

"You can't already tell?" Glen laughed. "It tastes great!"

"Just great?" she teased.

"Great… wonderful…. marvelous…. out-of-this-world," he over-emphasized, causing Ellen to giggle.

"You are so silly!"

"And so are you," he chuckled, finishing off the last bite of banana bread and his coffee. "Where are you going to store all the loaves until the produce stand is open for business?"

"I have a chest freezer and an upright too in the basement. The bread isn't as good as fresh out of the oven, but it sells anyway. I have been doing this for 3 years now, and once the stand is open, I try to bake some pies every day too. I don't like to freeze them though. I also plan to bake cookies and cakes. I don't put icing on the cakes until I take them out of the freezer the night before. It seems to work pretty well."

"It sounds as if you have it down to a science. What do you do with the things you don't sell?"

"I take them into town every few days to the local shelter. Those homeless souls always seem to appreciate it."

"Ellen, you are so kind-hearted," Glen interjected warmly.

"I know you would do the same, Glen."

"Yeah, I would, but that doesn't make what you are doing any less special. There are not enough caring people in the world who give freely of themselves for the needs of someone less fortunate."

Late into the afternoon, Ellen continued to bake and Glen completed the scrubbing of the walls in the last of the three bedrooms. Ellen continued baking while Glen took a twenty-minute break to eat a quick lunch.

"You work too hard, Ellen," Glen observed, while finishing his turkey sandwich. It doesn't hurt to stop from time to time and catch your breath."

"To be honest, I'm not even hungry after snacking off of one of the loaves of apple bread all morning, she replied with a smile. I am stopping for the day though. I have baked twenty-four loaves and that's enough for one day."

Glen began to grin, balancing backwards on two legs of his chair. "I'm finished also. What would you like your love slave to do for you now?"

Ellen began to giggle. "Well, since it is still raining, and there isn't much left to do today, I guess you can go home; that is…unless you would like to join me for a little nap since we *both* worked so hard," she said seductively. "I thought that maybe we could begin where we left off this morning."

Glen got up from his chair, reaching over to take Ellen in his arms, looking at her intently. "I'm not wearing out my welcome, am I, since I have been here since yesterday?"

"Glen, you should know better," she scolded good-naturedly, looking into his dreamy sky-blue eyes. "It has been wonderful having you so close to me. It is so hard to say goodbye to you at the end of the day anymore. I will miss you until I see you again in the morning," she admitted quietly.

"I feel the same way, Ellen. But I want you to call the shots. The last thing I want to do is rush your feelings before you are ready." Glen's eyes were heavy with a flood of emotion engulfing him. "I miss you too when I'm away from you. I love you so much!" he declared, engulfing her mouth in a fierce, all-consuming kiss.

Their lovemaking was just as fierce and consuming, each giving and receiving the pleasure that was becoming second nature to them. Glen held Ellen close, as their breathing returned to a normal pace.

"I know now that it was fate the day you walked up to the farm and found me sleeping under the oak tree. Things this wonderful just doesn't happen everyday to people. I feel so lucky to have you in my life," Ellen said sincerely, with misty eyes.

Glen sighed, feeling very content. He kissed her reassuringly as he pulled her close to his strong bare chest. "It is I who is the lucky one. Never did I imagine that looking Eric up would bring me to the girl of my dreams; and you are that…. dear, sweet Ellen," he said between kisses to her neck.

Ellen shivered pleasantly, rising up on one elbow. "How about dinner, and ….if you would like…you can spend the night again," she offered, while drawing lazy circles over his chest.

"I would love to, Ellen, but I should really get home. I need to change clothes and go over a few things with Eric; but if you ask me that same question tomorrow night I would be better prepared to stay, and the answer would be yes."

Ellen smiled. "I understand, but you can't blame a girl for trying."

"The girl can try as often as she wants," he teased. "Believe me, it's harder to say no than yes to offers this good."

As Glen dressed, Ellen slipped on her bathrobe and made her way back into the kitchen.

"Be right back," she yelled over her shoulder. Ellen's hands were full as she entered the foyer, carrying both a loaf of the banana and apple bread. "For you and Eric," she smiled, handing them to Glen. "I hope he enjoys it as much as you seem too."

Glen smiled back appreciatively. "This is so nice, Ellen. I know Eric will love it, but to be honest, I hate to share it with him," he confessed with a wink. Her sudden outpouring of generosity towards Eric surprised him. In small ways, the barriers were beginning to come down.

"That's why I gave you two of them, silly. There should be plenty for two hungry Cummings' men."

"I guess we'll just have to make it work," he teased, as he leaned over to give her a tender kiss goodbye. "See you tomorrow, honey. Try to go to bed early and catch up on your sleep, because if it rains again, I'll be knocking on the door in the morning."

Ellen giggled. "I have something for you," she explained as they walked together to the kitchen. She opened a drawer and pulled out a key and gave it to Glen. "Use this," she instructed sweetly while grabbing his hand and placing the key in his palm. "I've wanted to give you this for some time now."

Glen smiled happily. "Are you absolutely sure?" he questioned, feeling touched by another sentiment of kindness and trust that was being freely bestowed upon him by Ellen.

"Do you need ask?" she replied sincerely, "If it's raining, come in and either crawl into bed with me or start washing the inside of the windows. I'll have the cleaner and rags sitting on the counter."

"Now that's a real hard call," Glen answered sarcastically. "If this is a test, I really can't decide which one of those two choices would be the right thing to do." He shook his head with his hand resting on his chin, trying to act as if he were in serious contemplation about the situation.

Ellen laughed. "Oh Glen, you are so silly! You decide, and then surprise me in the morning."

"That will take some real consideration tonight, but I'm sure by tomorrow I will figure it out. See ya!" he winked, leaving Ellen standing at the door laughing merrily, tickled by his constant wit and humor.

Glen was in the Bronco and already out of the lane, when realization clicked.

"Back so soon? Did you change your mind?" she challenged playfully, as she reopened the door to Glen's knock.

He leaned forward and gave her a kiss. "I would like to claim I did, but I just remembered that we need to pick up the Saab."

"Oh…. that's right," she answered with her hand to her mouth. "It totally slipped my mind with the busy day we have had," she admitted with sudden awareness of her forgetfulness.

"Hurry and get dressed, and we'll go pick it up."

"Alright," Ellen called over her back, as she ran to the bedroom quickly finding her discarded pair of shorts and a t-shirt.

The Saab was still where they had left it the night before. Ellen was grateful Mr. Newton hadn't had it hauled away.

"I'll see you in the morning," Glen whispered while leaning over to kiss Ellen.

"Do that," she winked, as she made her way to the Saab.

Glen waited until Ellen was safe in her car, and then he drove away. Their horns blared out good-byes in unison to each other, creating a unique two-part harmony.

Eric was in the kitchen, cleaning up after himself from the mediocre attempt at making dinner again.

"There's food left in the fridge if you're hungry," Eric offered nonchalantly.

Glen laid the two loaves of sweet breads on the counter directly in front of him. "From Ellen," he announced proudly.

"For me?" Eric asked in surprise.

"Actually, for the both of us," he explained. "She's starting to bake bread for her produce stand, and she wanted to share some of it with us."

Eric didn't hesitate. He still remembered Ellen's cooking, and her wonderful baked goods. She was always an excellent cook. He grabbed the knife, cutting a slice from both loaves, sampling some of each. "Hmmm…tell her I said thanks, and that the bread is delicious. She sure knows how to bake, Glen."

"She sure does," Glen said slyly, grinning from ear to ear.

"The bread, bro. I meant the bread."

Both of them laughed and talked about the last couple of day's events as they ate together.

"I tried reaching you last night, but I didn't get an answer. I wanted to let you know that I wasn't coming home."

"Oh?" Eric answered, somewhat surprised, looking up before eating his last bite of bread.

"I stayed at Ellen's"

Eric began to chuckle in earnest. "I see…. I see…. You and she are really becoming an item."

"Yeah, well where were *you* last night?"

Eric shook his head from side to side, chuckling to himself. "Ok, touché. I should have known better then to rib you. I was with Melinda. I confess - we had an evening that wasn't meant to end. So it didn't!" he grinned.

"Melinda, huh?" It was Glen's turn. "She *actually* would even consider giving you another chance. Is she crazy?"

"Yeah, I guess she is," Eric said with a broad grin. "Crazy in love with me!"

"Heaven help her!" Glen exclaimed in jest, slapping him on the back.

Eric turned to face Glen, his tone and actions becoming suddenly serious, wanting to make his point. *"I'm not going to blow it this time, Glen. She means too much to me,"*

Glen was surprised by Eric's words; earnestly hoping it was genuine, for Melinda's sake. He had never seen his brother act this way before when it came to a woman.

"At a loss for words, Glen?" Eric questioned. "I don't know why. It's obvious that you apparently feel the same way about Ellen, so why can't it happen for me too?"

"I'm sorry, Eric. It definitely can happen for you. That is, if you truly want it too. But there is one big difference between you and I, and our female relationships up until this point. I don't have any trouble staying faithful. I want only Ellen. Since I've moved to Fillmore, no one has or will take her place. Can you honestly say that it will be that easy for you and Melinda?"

"I don't know…" Eric answered pensively. "People are different, Glen. Not everyone does things the same way, but I know I need to change. I'm not happy with the way I've been acting up until this point – as you say – with my female relationships. I guess we all have areas of our lives we need to work on. For some of us, we figure things out at a younger age than others do. Melinda is good for me, and I think I really do love her."

Glen squeezed Eric's arm in an affectionate brotherly way. "Hey, I didn't mean to come on so strong. I hope you do work things out this time with Melinda. She must be doing something good for you, because I've never heard you talk so seriously about a female."

After dinner, Glen showed Eric the Bronco and took him on a ride through the country.

"Handles real well, Glen. You made a good choice."

Glen grinned, looking over at Eric. "I consider that a real compliment coming from a die-hard, Mustang convertible junkie."

Eric laughed, bobbing his head in amusement. "Hey, a guy can change his mind about a lot of things, not just women! See what good you have done for me since you have moved in," he added warmly.

“Yeah, I can see that,” he shot back sarcastically. “Seriously though, you made this all possible for me and I can’t thank you enough.”

‘I know that, but now it’s time to just accept my *gracious generosity*, and get beyond it.”

“That attitude will do it real quick!” Glen laughed, as he floored the Bronco, making a U-turn with the dust flying, heading back to town.

Chapter Thirty-One

The rain fell steadily and the windshield wipers slapped out a constant rhythm as Glen drove through the early-morning fog. He felt so alive, even on such a dreary day. *No cab, no borrowed car, just free without commitments; that was, except willingly to Ellen,* he thought warmly. It was too soon to feel this way, his common sense warned him, but his heart told him otherwise. He was sure she felt the same way. One day they would marry, have children, and stay on the farm forever. More and more Glen was determined to see that happen.

The front porch steps he took easily even though the slight squeak of the wood sounded his presence. His hand instinctively went into a fist position, ready to knock on the door, but then he remembered the key that Ellen had given him the night before. He reached in his jean's pocket reclaiming his key chain. He thumbed through as many as five unidentifiable keys that he had a hard time remembering what they had been used for, until he came upon Ellen's. The lock didn't want to turn easily, until he tried pulling the door towards him while he turned the key at the same time to the left.

The house was silent, and he knew Ellen was asleep. He stood in the foyer, quietly debating which direction he should head for – the kitchen or the bedroom. The cleaning supplies were right where she had promised they would be, on the counter, neatly placed in a bucket. He sighed as he grabbed the metal bucket handle, swinging it down to his side while carrying it to the first kitchen window. He sprayed the cleaner on the glass, watching it drizzle as it made contact with the bottom pane, much like the rain that was falling softly on the outside of the glass.

"*This is crazy,*" Glen said aloud in frustration. He hurried and wiped the liquid with a paper towel until it was free of its original dull film, before washing his hands at the kitchen sink. He looked around, trying to find a towel to dry them, but impatiently opted for his blue jeans instead as he tiptoed at an energetic pace to Ellen's bedroom.

The door was open, and he noticed that she was lying on her side with both hands tucked together under her face, as if she were posing for a picture. To him, she looked like an angel in her white satin gown. Her lovely auburn hair with its soft waves, fell seductively over one breast. A wisp of it that moved every time she breathed, crossed over her lips making Glen ache to kiss her. His loins grew hard with pounding desire as he worshipped the goddess that he was free to gaze at with abandon.

He quickly removed his clothes, crawling into bed beside of Ellen. It amazed him how he could do that without waking her up. She was such a sound sleeper. Glen lay on his side facing Ellen, just staring and studying her every facial feature. Her skin was slightly tanned from being outdoors a lot, but still soft and smooth, without a flaw anywhere. Her lashes were long and dark and her lips were full and velvety, just begging to be kissed. Glen was in heaven, just lying there quietly without interruption, mesmerized by Ellen's beauty. He blew gently at the playful wisp of hair, causing Ellen to stir and instinctively rub her hand across her face and nose. Glen chuckled softly, blowing again lightly. Ellen rolled on her stomach, turning her head away from him. Not to be defeated, Glen crawled across her back, straddling his weight above her. He blew on her turned cheek and she fluttered her lashes, finally sensing his presence.

"Glen…?" she questioned dreamily.

"Yes, love. Who else?"

"I knew it was you all along," she said sleepily, as she turned over again on her back smiling up at him warmly. He responded with a series of ticklish kisses to the right side of her neck. Ellen giggled merrily and tried to push him away, but without much success.

"I didn't feel like washing windows quite yet, so I'm here to keep you company," he offered enticingly.

Ellen smiled serenely, finally opening her eyes fully, gazing at the vision of the magnificent male perched above her. "You can wake me up everyday like this, as far as I am concerned. That is, as long as you don't tickle me."

"You got a deal," he replied huskily as he bent down to kiss her passionately on the mouth. Ellen could feel his aroused hardness pressing persistently between her thighs. "Why don't you let me remove that pretty gown that is keeping us apart?" he breathed.

Ellen sat up and unfastened the three tiny pearl buttons that barely held her bosom intact. Glen's hand reached inside the opening, caressing one of her breasts and then the other with equal attention. "Oh Glen…. as soon as you touch me like that I melt every time," she moaned.

The gown was off in one swift movement, and their bodies quickly entwined together in unison with intimate touches. Their breathing was ragged as Glen brought one nipple into his mouth suckling it to a hardened peak while Ellen's hand stroked the throbbing erection between Glen's legs.

The joining of their bodies took on a wild flurry of delight as each arched and cried out in release. They lay quietly afterwards in each other's arms, still fascinated with the total power and fulfillment that they were able to give the other, time and time again.

"We shouldn't always be doing this you know," Glen, said with half-sincerity.

"And why not?" Ellen asked apprehensively, as she looked into his sky-blue eyes.

"Because I feel guilty. I should have maintained some self-control and washed the windows instead. If I keep this up, I won't be able to accept pay for the week."

"Glen, don't be silly," she said with exasperation.

Ellen was growing weary of having to convince him on a daily basis anymore that she was ok with their love making sessions occurring at some part of the workday.

"You gotta get over the guilt about the time we spend together. After all, who else is monitoring this except for me?" She questioned with a smile as she propped herself up an elbow. "I don't care at all. Our relationship is more important to me than what you get done around here."

Glen was touched. "I'm glad you feel that way, but I do have my scruples."

Ellen patted Glen's arm. "I know, I know, but just take it that on rainy days those are take it easy, bonus days."

"But…"

"Shhh…" Ellen insisted, bringing her finger up to Glen's mouth to silence him. "Not another word about the subject. You can clean the windows now if it makes you feel better," she laughed, as she reached for her gown that was lying at the bottom of the bed.

"I'll do just that," he snapped back playfully, grabbing his clothes also and putting them back on.

Glen washed the windows as Ellen fried eggs and bacon and had coffee brewing. She approached the dining room with a potholder in hand.

"How about some breakfast?"

"Thanks, but I already had some before I left Eric's."

"And what was that, coffee and toast?"

"Actually, just coffee," he replied while wiping a streak from the window.

"It will be ready in five minutes," she winked. "I'll set you a place."

The day sped by quickly with Glen completing all of the indoor windows and even finishing the sweeping of the basement. Ellen busied herself with her daily housework, and then changed her clothes so that she could go into town.

"How about running into town with me for awhile? I need to

pick up a few things at the grocery store and run a few errands," she mentioned to Glen who was still busy with his work.

"I think I will stay. I'm on a roll with the windows, and I want to finish them on the outside." Glen kissed Ellen a sweet goodbye, patting her lightly on her backside. "Don't be too long. I miss you when you are away," he winked.

"I won't, honey," she replied, reciprocating the pat.

Ellen beeped the Saab's horn noisily as she drove down the lane on her return. Glen ran down the porch steps to greet her as she brought the car to a stop.

"Could you help me with the groceries, pleaseeee….?" she asked with as sweet of a voice as possible.

"My pleasure," he answered, grabbing two bags, leaving Ellen with only one to carry.

"I hope you don't have plans for dinner because I bought a couple steaks for the grill."

"I never turn down steak," Glen smiled, helping Ellen unbag the groceries on the kitchen table. "I'll stay for dinner under one condition."

"What's that?" Ellen asked, as she placed the canned goods on the pantry shelf.

"That you let me take you out to dinner tomorrow night?"

"I never turn down an out-to-dinner invitation," she grinned. "You got a deal."

They dined in the kitchen on steak, baked potatoes, and tossed salad. Ellen turned on the stereo, finding a station that played romantic dinner music and she lit a candle, placing it in the center of the table. The room cast a sensuous light, and love shone brightly in each of their faces as they laughed and enjoyed the other one's company.

"Everything tastes delicious, Ellen."

"Thanks, Glen," Ellen answered happily, as she chewed a tasty morsel of the grilled steak. She loved his compliments that were so free flowing anymore. "I have a video I rented that we could watch tonight. It is a romantic comedy."

"That sounds good to me, as long as we can snuggle on the couch," he grinned.

"The couch or maybe even the rug," she added with a suggestive tone and a lift to her eyebrow. "And I'll even make popcorn too!"

Glen leaned forward, giving her a kiss that hinted of other intentions besides finishing their dinner. He pulled away, taking a deep breath, trying to get a grasp on his raging desires that were already burning out of control. "We better stop if you really want to watch that movie."

Ellen smiled warmly into his eyes. "Let's go make the popcorn together," she said while extending her hand towards his.

Ellen taught Glen the fine art of popcorn making. She measured out the corn and he measured out the oil.

"This little bit of oil, and all that popcorn will definitely work?" he questioned, as he poured the last tablespoon of oil into the popper."

"You got it!" she laughed, putting the clear plastic cover on as they waited, watching the show of dancing corn kernels.

Ellen poured two glasses of Coke, and handed Glen one of them. "By the way, your money for the week is on my desk, in an envelope with your name on it. Just for future reference, I'll always put it there, Glen. I don't want to make this pay thing a big deal. I know how awkward this is already becoming for you."

"Thanks, Ellen," he replied with a sense of relief, realizing that she was trying to make the situation as easy as possible for him. It's just taking me awhile to sort out the business from the personal.

"You'll figure it out. I have confidence in you," she smiled warmly, with love-filled eyes.

The movie made them laugh, but the popcorn war held the most excitement, as each of them dodged the fluffy white bullets that the other one threw from behind the barricades of furniture.

"I give up," Ellen yelled from behind the popcorn-strewn couch.

"Chicken – buck, buck, buck," Glen cackled. "Giving up so easily? You surprise me Ellen. I didn't think you were a quitter," he emphasized with cocky arrogance.

"I know when I am defeated," she answered, with a secret smirk, knowing she wasn't finished with him yet. *Let him be lulled into a false sense of security,* she thought with a wicked smile, as she quietly picked up two handfuls of the scattered popcorn holding it securely.

"Ellen, I still have a half-of-a-bowl left," he said with little-boy disappointment.

"Well, that's too bad," she announced timidly, still communicating from behind the couch. "There's probably two bowls of popcorn that need to be picked up."

"If that's all you're worried about, I will pick it up all by myself if we can finish our war."

"Ok, Glen…fire away," Ellen resigned willingly, while standing straight up from behind the sofa, becoming an easy target. She was finding it harder and harder to say no to this playful man-child that she loved.

"You're making this too easy, Ellen. Pick up some of that popcorn off of the rug, throw it at me, and then duck… Don't just stand there!"

"No…. that's ok, Glen. I'll just stand here and let you throw popcorn at me until your heart's content," she replied with fake resignation.

"You win," he announced. "I'll start cleaning this up now."

"Oh, Glen," she laughed, running out from behind the couch with her hands behind her back. As she brought them forward, Glen thought for a split second that she was going to embrace him, but instead she threw both hands of popcorn in his face.

"You brat!" he yelled, throwing her playfully to the ground, landing in a heap along with her beneath couch pillows, popcorn, and newspapers. He gazed tenderly into her eyes after the wrestling had subsided. "You know, I haven't ever felt this happy."

"I know what you mean. I feel the same way," she confessed,

reaching out to brush her hand across his whisker-stubbled cheek. “I didn’t think something this wonderful would have ever happened for us.”

He kissed her forehead, pulling her closely into his embrace. “Let’s use this rug. I haven’t been able to think of anything else since you first mentioned it.”

“What about the popcorn?” she grinned flirtatiously. “I believe *that’s* been on your mind also.”

“Ok, you and popcorn. What can I say,” he answered with a fake egotistical lift to his voice.

“You can say you love me, you turkey.”

“I’m a turkey now, huh?” he questioned, while taking her face between his hands, grinning intently with his effervescent smile.

“Yes, you are,” she giggled.

Glen’s mood turned suddenly reflective, serious in its intent. “I love you with my whole heart darling, and even more so that we can play like this and feel young and carefree.” He kissed her tenderly and yet deeply, as his tongue parted her lips and plunged deeply into her mouth. “What do you say about the rug?” he whispered huskily.

“I say… the rug will feel better with the popcorn brushed off of it,” she answered, still with a tender smile but also with ragged breath.

“I was hoping you would see it that way,” he grinned, as he brushed the popcorn quickly out of their path, and then rolled her onto her back and kissed her urgently.

Sometime later, feeling sated and satisfied, Glen leaned up on an elbow to stare at Ellen. Their clothes lay in a heap now, mingled in with the other items on the floor. Ellen was near sleep, lying on her side, pressing her hip invitingly into Glen's side. Even now, a surge of desire shot through Glen again, just by her simple unintentional action. He cherished the moment – just to be able to gaze upon her perfect nude body, fully exposed to his view, watching her freely at his leisure again.

"Hey sleepyhead, wake up," he whispered, tenderly kissing the hair near her temple and rubbing her arm.

"I don't want to," she moaned sweetly, rolling towards him, throwing the same arm that he was showering attention on, across his chest.

He smiled, knowing he would inevitably have to leave soon. "Ellen, let me carry you to your bed. I need to get going because I have things to do at home tonight."

He wanted to pay Eric and he needed clean clothes for work the next day, and also clothes for going out to dinner with Ellen in the evening. "I'll see you in the morning," he breathed into her hair as he held her close for one last kiss goodnight."

"I wish you didn't have to go."

"I know, but I must."

Glen dressed, and then carried her to the bedroom, placing her lovingly on the bed while covering her up to her chin with the bedspread.

"Sleep well, darling. I'll lock the door behind me."

"Alright, Glen…" Ellen whispered softly, already drifting into contented sleep.

The house was quiet and dark and the garage empty, as Glen pulled into the adjacent parking space beside of Eric's.

"He must be with Melinda again," Glen concluded, as he flipped on the light switch in the kitchen.

The kitchen was clean, meaning Eric hadn't been home for dinner either. He pulled out the fifty dollars that he owed Eric for his first car payment, and laid it by the coffee maker. He scribbled a note and laid it beside of the money.

Eric,

Here is the first payment on the Bronco. Oh, and by the way, I know you don't want to hear this again, but thanks!

Glen

Glen laid the ink pen down that he was just holding and reread the note that he had just written. He chuckled warmly to himself, still in disbelief by Eric's generosity. He felt extremely happy and content. Life was good.

Chapter Thirty-Two

The persistent ringing of the phone stirred Ellen from slumber, instead of Glen's presence, which had been the case for the last few mornings.

"Hellooo…" came the sleepy response from Ellen.

"Did I wake you?" Megan questioned.

"Yes…Meg, you did – but that's ok. I needed to get up. What time is it anyways?"

"It's eight o'clock, and I'm sorry for waking you, but I thought you would be up by now."

"I usually am. I just feel so tired for some reason."

"You're not sick, are you?"

"No, I have been feeling pretty good, actually. Just overly tired in the morning lately, but I have been keeping later hours than usual. You know me, Meg, I have never really been much of a morning person."

"Take vitamins, El. They give me extra energy. Maybe they will help."

"Meg, I'm not sure I want the same amount of energy you have," she giggled.

"Ok, El…"

"You know I love ya, even if you are hyper."

"I'm not *that* hyper! But, I'll let that pass. Anyways, I called to see how you've been doing; other than tired, what else exciting is happening in your life?"

"If you're wondering about Glen, things are perfect between us. He couldn't be any sweeter or more caring. Things are very good for us," she sighed contentedly.

"That's great, Ellen. Keep this up, and there will be a wedding on the horizon."

"I don't think we are to that point yet, but the thought of spending the rest of my life with Glen *does* sound wonderful! We are just so compatible."

"What about Eric? Have you worked out your problems with him?"

"Not really, but I'm trying to be more civil towards him. I had Glen take him some banana and apple bread the other day."

"That was nice."

"Well, you know me, Meg, always the sweetheart," she said sarcastically.

"Oh yeah, *right*."

They both laughed heartily with mutual understanding. Moodiness visited both of them from time to time. It was no secret to either friend.

"So what's been up with you?" Ellen asked light-heartily.

"Not much… Business as usual in the office, and an occasional evening out with Mike from time to time. I guess that's why I called. I miss you."

"Oh Meg…. I'm sorry. Come over whenever you want. I meant to call, but I have been somewhat side-tracked."

"Hmm…. interesting. I thought his last name was *Cummings* not *side-tracked*."

Ellen giggled. "Oh, Meg, you are so silly."

"El, don't worry your pretty head over me. I'm really fine. We just need a girl's night out soon when you can get away from Glen."

"You got it! Check your schedule and we'll plan something soon. Ok?"

"Sounds good to me. I'll call you back in a couple days."

"Alright. Take care, Meg."

"You too."

"Bye."

"Talk soon. Bye."

Ellen peaked out the window. The rain had stopped, and the sky was clear and blue again. She could see Glen in the garden hoeing out the weeds. Ellen already wished that it was still raining so that Glen would be in the house with her again.

"Guess who?" Ellen teased, covering Glen's eyes with her

hands from behind his back.

"Well let's see. Could it be Amanda?"

"*Amanda?"* Who is Amanda?" she demanded, feigning jealousy.

"No, I'm sorry, my mistake. Not Amanda – Sarah, right?"

"*Glen!"* Ellen shrilled in frustration. "You know it's me."

Glen started to laugh uncontrollably, turning around to face his vixen. "Of course, I knew it was you, but I just love to tease you anyways," he said with the famous Cummings' wide-toothed grin, as he wrapped her in his arms. He leaned down and kissed her passionately, causing them both to sigh from it intensity. "I'm not playing today, Ellen," he announced with determination.

"*Oh really?"* she answered skeptically, pulling away from him, placing her hands on her hips in a saucy stance, tempting him once again with her laughter and dancing emerald eyes.

"He looked at her cautiously, knowing she was capable of overwhelming his emotions and logic at the snap of her slender, beautiful fingers. "Ellen.... please let me work today," he smiled with a lop-sided grin. "I *feel* like have been on a *paid vacation* the last few days, and now it's time to get down to serious business outdoors."

"If you insist. I won't get in your way today," she answered, pretending to pout with her lips puckered out and her arms crossed over her chest.

Glen laughed heartily, bending over at the waist clutching his stomach from laughing so much.

"What? What's so funny?"

“You, silly,” he replied, walking over to take her in his arms again, giving her a light kiss in the process. “If you can’t stand to be away from me, find a lawn chair and sit out here while I work. I would love the company.”

“That’s alright. I have plenty to do indoors,” she said awkwardly, feeling suddenly like a young schoolgirl with a major crush.

He grinned, tickled with her girlish behavior. “I hope you will take a little time for me today,” he added, lifting her chin to his view.

“Of course I will,” she answered fondly, already looking forward to the breaks they would share together during the day. She looked into his sky-blue eyes and reached up to give him a tender kiss. “I love you,” she whispered softly, while running her hands purposely through his hair. Glen closed his eyes with the heady sensation of her touch. “You know you did do a lot for me indoors this week that I never find time to do.”

“I guess it just doesn’t seem like *real* work to me.”

“Glen, you sound so chauvinistic! Working indoors is hard work for a man or a woman.”

“I’m sorry, I didn’t mean to come off like that. I just know what you hired me to do, and that was to primarily take care of the garden and farm.”

“Then work your fingers to the bone, my lord, and I will be in thy castle if thou desirest to see me later.”

“Lunch would be nice, my lady fair. Can you join me?” he said with a pleasant smile.

"It will be ready at noon."

"I brought mine, Ellen. Sorry," he answered somewhat sheepishly, feeling badly at disappointing her at every turn.

"You really do mean business today, don't you, Glen? Fine, I'll meet you under the oak tree at 12:00 with my bag lunch too."

The morning went by quickly as he finished weeding, and then he moved the produce stand down to the end of the lane where it would stay until the close of the produce season in the late Fall. Ellen met him, as promised, under the majestic oak that welcomed them with its cooling shade.

"I love this tree," Ellen sighed. "It always makes me feel so at peace with myself when I am beneath it," she added as she sat crossed-leg, taking a bite out of her chicken salad sandwich.

"I know what you mean," Glen agreed, as he looked skyward to the many leafy branches that covered both of them like a giant canopy. "It feels like instant air conditioning. Sometimes when I'm hot, I rinse off at the well pump, and then sit under the tree. I feel so relaxed with the breeze blowing, I have to fight the feeling of taking a nap."

"Maybe you should sometime," Ellen suggested with a smile. "I have taken a nap under this tree on several occasions, and it is wonderful!"

"Sometime I probably will, but not intentionally," he grinned, as he finished his ham sandwich. "By the way, Eric loved the banana and apply bread. He told me to thank you. I think you really surprised him."

"*I'm sure he did,*" she replied knowingly. "I'm glad he liked it. And I promise that you will be sick of it by the end of summer, after I send home about the tenth loaf."

"I don't think I could ever grow tired of your cooking," Glen said sincerely. "I brought clothes to change into for tonight. So if it's ok with you, I'll shower and change here."

"You know it's fine."

"Eric told me of a good French restaurant that he and Melinda went to the other night. I thought we could try it, if that's alright with you?"

"Anything is fine. I love French food."

Dinner was wonderful, as well as the remainder of the weekend. Glen went to church again with Ellen, and they enjoyed another romantic interlude at the pond.

The weeks that unfolded took on a routine pace, but one that Ellen and Glen came to feel very comfortable with. Their love was growing and becoming stronger everyday. Ellen's tears had ceased weeks ago and were replaced with only laughter and contentment. She was feeling free of the past and its misery that was so much apart of her for the prior two years. Glen was spending the night more often, and the produce stand was open for business. Ellen was constantly busy with her customers, and the daily baking. Glen became her necessary set of second hands, setting up the stand in the morning and tearing it down in the evening; clearing out those items that were no longer sellable, and delivering them daily to the local food bank for the needy. After much discussion and preparation of the barn, Ellen and Glen agreed on the return of some of the livestock. They would start with cattle. The plans were set for him to pick them up the following day.

"Thank you, Mrs. Carter," Ellen offered politely, as she placed the money that she had just received into the metal container that held the cash for the day. "Those green beans were just picked this morning, and I know they will be delicious!"

"Everything you sell is delicious, dear. That's why I always come back," the sweet elderly lady replied, who stopped to buy produce every couple of days.

Glen smiled warmly at Ellen as Mrs. Carter pulled away. He leaned his shoulder against the side of the stand watching her with pride and admiration. "Everyone loves you. Do you know that?"

"I try to please," Ellen answered with a giggle, as she straightened up the corn display that Mrs. Carter had left in a disheveled array.

"I wish you would come with me tomorrow, Ellen. Are you sure you can't close the stand down for a day, and join me to pick up the cattle?" Glen asked as he walked towards her.

"I can't Glen. You know I would love to, but this is the peak of the produce season," Ellen explained sweetly as she laid her hand on top of Glen's. "My customers rely on me, and I really can't afford to lose a day's business right now. After all, that's what is paying for the cattle."

She would never mention it to him with his sensitivity of being paid by her, but the produce stand paid his income too. Taking time off in the middle of the summer was almost impossible. It was the money she lived on, and kept her going months after the produce stand was closed down for the season.

Glen turned Ellen around to face him, taking her chin in his hand. “You can’t blame a guy for trying,” he said with a smile, placing a light kiss on her lips. “It will be lonely riding in Mr. Miller’s cattle truck without you.”

“You’ll be fine,” she reassured. “Especially after you pick up the cows. Their mooing will keep you company,” she giggled.

“How about keeping me company for the rest of the evening then?” Glen asked, with a seductive look in his eyes. “Let’s get a shower together and dry off in bed.”

Ellen returned the look of desire, before glancing at her watch. “The stand should stay open ten more minutes.”

“I need to put a few garden tools away, but it shouldn’t take anymore than ten minutes. I’ll be back to help you drop the canvas over the front of the stand, and then we can walk up to the house together. Deal?” his eyes twinkled.

“You have this all figured out, don’t you?” Ellen said with a playful gleam in her eyes.

“You better believe it! I have to keep the lady entrepreneur loosened up. You know what they say about all work and no play,” he grinned.

“Boy, have the tables turned in the last few weeks. I remember when it was me begging you to stop working. See how does it feel?” she challenged brazenly.

“*I see…*” he smiled, looking at her tight-fitting tank top cleavage that was totally exposed to his view, as she bent over to pick up a basket of tomatoes.

Luckily, the typical last straggler customer of the day never showed up, as Glen secured the final knot on the canvas covering. All of the baked goods had been sold, and Glen had made his shelter run earlier in the day. What remained, was only the produce that could still be offered the next day.

Ellen counted out the container of money, separating the coins from the bills. "$268.27," she announced proudly, as she wrote the amount in her daily ledger, sealing the money in a zip lock bag with a deposit slip enclosed for the bank.

"That's twenty dollars more than yesterday, isn't it?"

Ellen smiled broadly. "Yes… the stand is doing so well this year. And I have you to thank for that, Glen," Ellen said sincerely.

"Ellen…you *know* you could have done it without me."

"No, I couldn't have. And you *know* that too. I always had to close the stand down whenever I needed to go into town or the house in the past. I am staying open a lot more hours now, and it is showing with the profits. I truly appreciate all your help."

"I want to help, Ellen, in any way I can. It makes me happy to make you happy," he said as he rubbed her cheek with the back of his knuckles.

Ellen smiled lovingly as they walked hand in hand into the house. "Glen, my days are all happy now that you are in my life. I am so glad I decided to give into my bitterness and hire you…. and I'm also glad that you came back a second time and made me a deal that I couldn't refuse," she confessed with tears welling up in her eyes.

"It was fate, Ellen. We were meant to be together."

"I think so too," she answered while looking at him tenderly.

"Would you like something to eat? I have a casserole in the refrigerator that only needs to be reheated in the microwave for about 10 minutes."

"Dinner can wait. I have other things on my mind right now, and it isn't food."

"But aren't you hungry?"

"Hungry for you," he said passionately, as he engulfed her mouth in an all-consuming fiery kiss.

Their shorts and t-shirts came off quickly as they allowed the invigorating water of the shower to refresh and renew them. Each washed the other, causing shivers of delight and desire to ignite them, as they massaged and caressed each part of the other one's body.

Glen dried Ellen off with a big fluffy white, terry cloth towel, as she lay on the bed staring lovingly into his handsome tanned face. He was still glistening wet from the shower's water that clung to his skin, extending his nipples from the chill in the air. His hair was rumpled in a sporadic pattern of every-which-way that was very appealing and sexy in a roguish sort of way.

"Don't you want me to dry you off also?" she questioned.

"No time for that," he said in a ragged breath. "I want and need you so badly right now, Ellen," he added, as he grinded his hips more intimately into contact with hers.

Glen threw the towel from the bed as he captured her mouth in a heart-stopping, heat-searing kiss. Ellen's head swooned with desire, as their tongues met and tangled in a lover's dance. He entered her swiftly, surrounding her waist with his arms.

"Glen…" she moaned, as her eyelids fluttered – lost in passion – wanting only to wrap her legs around him tightly. It was his undoing, and more than he could handle. Glen's thrusts were deliberate and intense, finally culminating with his groans of pleasure, releasing the seed of his being within her.

"I'm sorry I didn't take things a little slower. There are times I just can't control myself, Ellen. You overwhelm me with such uncontrollable desire," Glen confessed as his breathing took on a more normal pace again.

Ellen smoothed a strand of hair away from his face that was still damp from the shower. "Don't ever apologize," she admonished sincerely, as she turned on her side to stare at him. "I wanted you just as badly, and besides, we have the whole evening."

Glen smiled, as he took Ellen into his arms again, "Will I ever stop loving you?"

"I hope not," she admitted quietly. "I don't think…. I could survive now without you."

"Yes, you could, Ellen. You don't give yourself enough credit for being the strong woman that you are," Glen answered, taking her chin in his hand. "But if I have anything to do with it, you won't ever have to be put in the position of being without me."

He felt the need to admonish her – to help her recognize the strength she had deep within herself. He never wanted to see her feeling weak and vulnerable again like she was when he first met her. She was such a different person now. Almost like a bird let out of a cage, free to fly. "Ellen…. I want to ask you something," he said, as he began stroking her arm.

"What is it?" Ellen asked apprehensively, sensing Glen's

nervousness. He hesitated, sighing before he began again.

"I feel so unworthy of you. My income is way below what it should be, and I'm not saying that to make you feel badly. I know that what you give me is all that you can afford, and I wouldn't even take that if I didn't have some bills to pay."

"Glen…" Ellen interrupted, not sure where his words were leading too.

"Please let me finish, Ellen," he answered as he stared at her, sincere with determination. "What I am trying to say is, I didn't plan to fall in love with you like this."

"*Oh?*" Ellen responded, feeling suddenly on the defensive again, as if another Cummings' was ready to destroy her.

"Ellen, what is wrong? You look upset."

"Go ahead and say it! You realize things are too serious between us, and you are quitting and I will never see you again," she exclaimed while sitting up and grabbing her face with the palms of her hands, tears beginning to swell up in her eyes.

"Ellen, where is this coming from?" Glen questioned in disbelief, as he sat up, putting his arm around Ellen's shoulders, removing her hands from her face. "I am going nowhere darling," he reassured with a kiss to her temple.

"Then what are you trying to tell me?" Ellen asked, looking at him in total confusion.

"I am just trying to say that I had no idea I'd fall so quickly for you. I hoped that one day I would be more financially secure before I brought this subject up, but the truth is…Ellen…. I don't want to go home to Eric's anymore. I don't want to leave your bed after we make love, and I can't stand my own cooking after eating and enjoying yours so much."

She giggled softly, amused at his banter, not knowing or understanding where all his words were leading. Ellen looked up into Glen's sincere eyes, hoping to find the answer.

"Please, Ellen," he continued while grabbing her hands in his own. "*Will you marry me?*"

Ellen felt an enormous sense of relief flood over her as if the ocean waves washed away every emotion of doubt. "*You are asking me to marry you?*"

"*Yes...*" Glen answered softly with a smile of uncertainty, suddenly feeling as apprehensive as Ellen had felt seconds earlier.

"Of course I will marry you," she cried out happily, as she wrapped her arms tightly around Glen's neck.

"You worried me there for a minute," he breathed against her neck with a sigh of relief. "I thought maybe you didn't want to marry me."

Ellen looked at Glen with joyous tears streaming down her face. "We are both silly aren't we, for assuming the worst."

"Yes we are," Glen, replied with a smile and a kiss to the top of her hand. "But why are you crying, Ellen?"

"Because I am sooo happy," she assured Glen, as she kissed him lovingly on the lips. "And as far as you worrying about money, stop worrying. Life is fine now, just as it is. We have each other, and this farm. And besides, the livestock will increase our profits if all goes well."

"All will go well, Ellen. I will make sure of that!" Glen

promised. They pledged their love one to the other, and made love again; but this time in an unhurried fashion, before drifting off to sleep into sweet contented bliss.

Chapter Thirty-Three

The smell of bacon frying woke Glen from his slumber. The alarm clock that he had set for 5:00 A.M. had been turned off. It was almost 5:30 and he rolled over to gather Ellen in his arms, but to Glen's dismay, there were only cold empty sheets.

"It's time to rise and shine," she greeted cheerfully from the bedroom door. She was dressed in her pink terrycloth robe with the string pulled tight, which only helped to accentuate her already shapely figure.

"I can see that," he observed with a devilish grin, observing his erection sticking straight up through the sheet that was barely covering him up to his waist. "But you shouldn't have let me sleep. Mr. Miller will wonder where I am, since I told him I would be at his store at 6:30 sharp."

"You will be fine," Ellen replied assuredly, fighting the urge to return to the bed after observing the powerful and handsome male laid out in front of her. "After all, my husband-to-be needs a good breakfast before he sets out on a trip that will shape our future together."

"I guess an offer that sweet I can't turn down," he said with a wink, as he strolled naked to her side and placed a light kiss on her lips. "I'll be out in fifteen minutes after I grab a quick shower and get dressed."

They dined together at the kitchen table, as they enjoyed their meal and the pleasant morning breeze that was drifting through the open window.

"More coffee?" Ellen offered, as she rose to get the carafe.

"Better not, hon. I really need to get going," Glen answered, as he got up to meet Ellen across the room. "Put that pot down, so I can give you a decent kiss goodbye," he said with a wide-toothed smile as he reached his hands around her waist, putting the coffee down for her.

"Never goodbye, Glen. I hate those words…" she said with a forlorn look in her eyes.

"Hey, why so serious this morning?" he asked while grabbing her chin, bringing her downcast stare up to meet his eyes. "I'm not going anywhere, ever! We're talking only a few hours away from here. Anything longer than that and you will always go with me. Produce stand or not. Deal?"

"Deal," she grinned, trying to dismiss her uneasiness.

"Why so melancholy today?"

"I don't know…. I just feel apprehensive for some reason."

"About what? Everything is perfect. I just asked you to marry me last night. Don't you remember, or did you change your mind?" he teased, still holding her securely in his embrace.

"Oh Glen, don't be silly. Of course I remember, and there is no way I would change my mind."

"Then don't be gloomy. Everything is fine."

"You're right. I'm just being silly. Please drive carefully, though," she added, still feeling her uneasiness.

"I will. I have my whole future to come home to. I love you, Ellen," he said tenderly, as he kissed her firmly on the mouth, memorizing its softness and taste, and then he hugged her securely one last time.

"I love you too, Glen. With my whole heart…."

Glen pulled into the parking lot, finding Mr. Miller waiting at the store, just as he had promised.

"Sorry I'm late," Glen confessed, bringing the Bronco to a stop beside the large cattle truck.

"Five minutes don't count as late," Mr. Miller, answered good-naturedly as he took a sip from a large mug of coffee.

"I really appreciate you letting me use the truck. Are you sure I can't give you some money for its use?"

"Filler ir up with gas. That'll do. Anytime I can do something nice for Miss Ellen, I am on board. She's had a lot on her since her husband's death."

"I know she has, but things are going to be different now."

"How's that?" Mr. Miller asked with interest.

Glen brightened with a smile, hesitant, but wanting to tell someone his good news. "I asked Ellen to marry me last night, and she accepted. You're the first person I have told," he confessed with a grin full of pride.

"Well congratulations, son," Mr. Miller offered wholeheartedly, patting Glen's back a little too firmly. "My missus will be happy to hear the news."

"Not as happy as I was when Ellen said yes," Glen chuckled.

"So when is the happy occasion taking place?"

Glen quietly contemplated the question before answering. They hadn't even talked about a date. "Soon, I hope," he answered with a pleasant smile. "We need to figure the details out yet. When I get back to town, Ellen and I will have to talk about that. I guess we were so caught up in the moment, we didn't even think about a wedding date," he replied thoughtfully as he climbed up into the cabin of the big truck, waving Mr. Miller a fond goodbye, leaving him to stand amidst a cloud of dust from the gravel-filled parking lot.

Ellen placed several loaves of banana and apple bread neatly in a row by the potatoes that had just been dug up by Glen that week. The produce stand was keeping her as busy as ever. It would be harder today to take her breaks in and out of the house, since Glen was gone. She had come to rely on him in so many ways.

"He asked me to marry him…" Ellen said dreamily, with a contented smile etched on her face. "Mrs. Glen Cummings. Mrs. Ellen Cummings. Ummm…. I like the sound of that," she happily declared to herself, as she raised her awning to the first customer of the day.

"Morning, Mrs. Harper. I'm here to buy some of your delicious banana bread."

“I’m glad you like it, Mrs. Blutcher,” Ellen replied warmly, ringing up the purchase of the two loaves that she bought on a weekly basis. “The potatoes and corn are fresh also, if you would like some of them too,” she added.

“Thanks, Ellen, but not today. But, I’ll be back in a few days,” the friendly woman answered as she dropped the two loaves into her canvas tote that she carried with her wherever she went.

Several other customers arrived, buying the potatoes and corn that Ellen pushed, along with other items from the plentiful bounty on display. It was eleven o’clock; the customary time Ellen hung the closed sign on the produce stand. She dropped the awning, securing the ropes loosely in place.

Most everyone in town knew her hours. The stand wouldn’t be open again until one o’clock. Except for the occasional persistent patron who just had to purchase something during those off hours, no one came up to the house. This was her time to do her housework, laundry, and additional baking. Glen’s presence though, was making it harder for her to stick to the routine, especially when he tempted her with another session of their intense lovemaking. Today though, there was no excuse for getting her indoor work done.

As she placed two more loaves of banana bread in the oven, a steady tapping sounded at the front door. “Who could that be?” she said aloud, as she laid the potholders down on the flour-strewn kitchen table. “It’s too soon for Glen to be back. It must be someone wanting something from the stand,” she concluded.

She washed her hands quickly at the sink, drying them on the way to the door. Ellen opened the door to a woman staring at her. She was caught off guard by the stranger - not someone Ellen had seen before. Average in height and weight, a brunette with brown eyes. She was fairly attractive, but not exceptionally so. She wore a skirt that exposed a good portion of leg, and a short-cropped shirt that exposed her midriff. She carried an infant in her arms, balancing the child on one hip. By her side was a young girl, who sucked her thumb with one hand, and held to the woman's skirt hem with the other, rubbing it between her fingers like a security blanket. Mucous drained from the girl-child's nose, intermingling with the thumb, while she sucked. Both children appeared noticeably unkempt, with uncombed hair, and clothes that could stand a washing.

"Mrs. Harper?" the woman began, causing Ellen to be puzzled that she apparently recognized or had heard of her.

Who was she? Ellen thought. She was second-guessing whether she had seen her before and had forgotten.

"I'm sorry, do I know you?" Ellen asked, with a polite mannerly smile, trying to place her.

"No, you don't. But I *know* you, and I would like to talk to you about something real important," she replied with a slight southern drawl.

"Aah…sure," Ellen answered, somewhat apprehensive, walking out to the side porch. "We can sit and talk here," she motioned to the swing. "And the kids can play. There isn't anything that they can really get in trouble with."

The woman put the toddler down, and the baby began to cry. "Now don't start that, Tommy. Mommy can't always hold you," she remarked indifferently, as she tried to push the hair out of his eyes. "Elizabeth, play with your brother," she instructed, as she removed a small toy from her oversized, canvas carryall bag, and handed it to the boy.

"So what do you want to talk with me about?" Ellen questioned, anxious to get back to her work inside.

"I don't know where to begin," the woman shifted restlessly with downcast eyes. "I guess I just felt the need to come here, and set you straight on a few things."

"And *what* would those things be?" she asked, feeling suddenly very uneasy.

"Me, my children, their daddy, and my husband."

"I don't even *know* you," Ellen said with irritated amazement at the woman's comments.

"Maybe not me or my children, but I *know you know* my husband."

Ellen began to laugh nervously in disbelief. Apparently this woman had mistaken her for someone else, or had the wrong address. *Although, she did call me Mrs. Harper*, she thought with worry. "Whom may I ask is your husband?"

"*Glen Cummings*," she stated matter-of-factly without so much as an ounce of emotion crossing her face.

Ellen registered shock, like she had never felt before. A blow worse than Jack's death was doubling her over in disbelief, like a knife wound to the stomach. She was feeling dead and yet alive all at the same time – caught in a state of limbo – unable to speak or move, but she knew she had to. This woman's words and their implication were cutting her beyond belief, but she still needed clarity to their meaning.

"What did you say?"

"Glen Cummings. He is my husband, and these are his kids – Elizabeth and Thomas," she said with a wave in the children's direction.

"*His children…*" Ellen muttered quietly, in astonishment. "And you…what is your name?" Ellen bit out rudely as she held on to the arm of the swing for support.

"My name is Sa…man…tha," she answered, with an ill-controlled victor's smile. "Has Glen ever mentioned me?" she asked sweetly.

Ellen's stomach was revolting with the feeling of nausea. She wanted to run from the porch, and regurgitate in the grass the contents of her breakfast, but she had to maintain her dignity – what little bit was left of it.

"Yes…he has…but he never said that he was married to you. Just together…living, I mean…. living together." She was having a hard time formulating her thoughts. The words were not flowing easily.

"That doesn't surprise me in the least. Just like Glen to forget *such an important detail*. And what about *our* kids? Did he fail to mention them too?" she smirked, looking piercingly into Ellen's eyes.

"He mentioned that *you* had children, but he never said that they were his," she replied, getting up from the swing and walking over to the railing to rest upon it instead.

"*Well, they are his!*" Samantha hissed, much too dramatically. "And I thought you had a right to know the truth about Glen and his life with me, before you got too involved and hurt. I know Glen is quite the looker, always turning ladies heads, but he *always* comes back to me after he is done with his newest girlfriend."

Ellen's head was in a whirl. How could this all be possibly happening? He had just asked her to marry him last night, and she had said yes, for heaven's sakes!

"What did you do with Glen's car?" Ellen asked bitterly, knowing the answer to the question really didn't even matter at this point, but she was having a hard time staying focused.

Samantha was caught by surprise. "Aaah…if you mean *our* car, it is parked in your driveway," she commented straightforwardly, covering her tracks very carefully. This added bit of information just deepened the assault that was being inflicted upon Ellen. The full impact of the truth was finally registering.

Everything he had told her was apparently lies fabricated for the purpose of hurting her. Maybe even Eric was a part of the whole farce. She could hear it now – *Glen, since you are having trouble with the wife, go check out the widow Ellen Harper who lives out in the country on a farm. She'll be good for a couple months of a free roll in the hay until you can patch things up with Samantha. Not only will you be getting your jollies, but you'll be helping me get even with the bitch for smearing my reputation in the mud around town.*

Tears were begging to flow from her eyes as she imagined the hateful plot that they devised against her. She didn't know at that moment, whom she hated more for the pain she was experiencing – Glen, Samantha or Eric.

"And how did you locate him, and me for that matter?" she ventured scornfully, resolved anew not to break down with tears in front of this woman.

"His mother," she said plainly. "She told me that he had

moved to Fillmore, and was living in with his brother." Tommy began to crawl back into Samantha's arms as she shifted him restlessly to her other hip. "I went to Eric's house, but no one was home. A neighbor told me where Glen worked, and all about you…and him. She was really quite helpful," she said with a triumph cruel look again. "So where is Glen? His kids are really anxious to see him, and so am I. We have a lot of catching up to do."

"Where's my daddy?" Elizabeth chimed in. The child's innocent but sincere question made tears of resignation swell up in Ellen's eyes. She could not allow this Samantha to get the better of her, although the bitter reality of the situation was becoming all too apparent. Not now, at least. Not for her to see.

"He is *not* here. He is gone for the day, and I don't expect him back until later tonight."

"Well, *that* is a problem."

"*Yes, it most certainly is*. I am busy, and I don't have the time to continue this conversation much longer. Maybe you should contact Eric and he will let you wait at is house until Glen gets back. He works at Computer World Systems. I get the point of your visit, and as hard as it is for me to accept that you are speaking the total truth, apparently Glen has misled me. Anything else you have heard is purely gossip and speculation. And as far as future rumors go, I don't think you will have anything to worry about. I plan to terminate Glen's employment immediately. If there is one thing I can't tolerate is someone who lies and is deceitful."

Samantha's face was jubilant with the feat that she had just accomplished. "I'm sorry that you feel that way, but more than likely Glen will want to quit working for you anyways, once I tell him about all the job openings back home."

Knowing it was better that she left well enough alone, did not stop Ellen from asking one last punishing question. "Samantha, has Glen really done something like this before?"

"Unfortunately for the trouble it causes our family, he has done this several times in the past. But I love him anyways," she replied demurely with bright and happy eyes. "And he *always* comes back to me."

"*Oh…I see*," she answered, with the pain of dawning awareness etched all over her face. Well, good luck to you and him both…and your family," Ellen wished quietly and with much effort, as she rose and made her way back to the screen door.

"By the way, can you give me Glen's cellphone number?"

Ellen was surprised by Samantha's request. "Why don't you have that?" she asked.

"Ummm, he changed it once he moved out here."

"Ok… I am sorry that he did that; but no, I do not feel I'm at liberty to share that with you. Maybe Eric will do so. Goodbye Samantha, I have nothing more to say," Ellen breathed, shutting the screened door as well as the heavy wooden door, locking it behind her. She sighed heavily, letting the weight of the door hold her frame up, as she shook all over and began to sob uncontrollably.

After several minutes, Ellen made her way back to the kitchen window, peaking secretly out from behind the curtain. Samantha opened the back door of the car letting both children crawl in. *No car seats or seat belts were present or being used,* Ellen observed. It would be different if they were her children. Ellen shook the thought from her mind, just as quickly as it entered, feeling repulsed by Glen's deception anew. Glen and her would never have children together! She was devastated. In less than 24 hours, she was happier and sadder than she had ever felt in her entire life.

Chapter Thirty-Four

The air was alive with excitement as the auctioneer rattled off the raised ante from the bidder for the cow up for consideration. Five people were in the bidding against Glen. He knew his limit and what the maximum was that he wanted to spend. This wasn't something new for him, or his first time at a cattle auction. Although it was a first for him at making the decision on his own. A farmer in Virginia had taught him the art of purchasing cattle, when they had attended livestock auctions together. But this was a different part of the country, and the way people did business. Ten cows were already purchased. His goal for the day was 25 in total. If all went as planned, he would double that number in a few months. His goal was to own a large herd of beef cattle in the next few years; but financially, this was all he and Ellen could afford for now.

"Over here," Glen yelled, above the auctioneer's call.

"Sold to #112," was the loud reply, when no one counter-offered the bid that Glen made.

Glen was in high spirits, knowing he handled the purchasing of the cattle better than he guessed he would. There had been some concerns on his part, that he may not remember all the things his friend back in Virginia had taught him to look for when purchasing a cow - a healthy coat, bright eyes, good muscle tone, and one that was not too scrawny were all-important considerations. Only 14 more cows needed to be bid on, until he could be on his way back home to the woman he loved and cherished. His future… Ellen Harper.

Ellen's tears continued to fall freely, as she frantically ran around the house. She pulled the half-baked banana bread loaves from the oven and emptied them in the trash, and then smashed up a whole can of wet cat food into a bowl on the floor for Cuddles. Her clothes were already packed. She didn't even care about the selection she had made. A few shorts, jeans, t-shirts, pajamas, underclothes, bathing suit and a jacket were all she planned to wear and need anyways. She quickly added a few toiletries, knowing that she could borrow or buy anything she had forgotten.

The unexpected call to Denver was quite a pleasant surprise for her mother, as Ellen announced she would be arriving that day for an extended visit. Her mother questioned if everything was all right, but Ellen hid her emotions well. She had decided that over the phone wasn't the appropriate way to tell her mother what had happened, since she hadn't shared that much about her life with her recently. It would take a lot of effort, but she needed to gain some self-control before seeing her mother and father. The last thing Ellen wanted to do was fall apart in front of them. They had already been called upon once before, to weather the storm of Jack's death. She would just have to find the strength in herself, she resolved. She just had to….

All bases were covered, except for the farm and Cuddles. Hopefully, Megan would take care of the cat, but what would happen to the farm? "Glen…" she breathed. "He is coming back with the cattle," she remembered in distress. There wasn't anything she could do, but write him a note. The farm could rot in hell for all she was concerned. Maybe Megan would know of someone who could tend to things.

“Good morning. Computer World Systems.”

“Yes, is Megan Delaney in?”

“One minute, please.”

“Megan Delaney. May I help you?”

“Megan, it’s Ellen.”

“El, what up?” Megan said with a smile.

“Megg…. I feel horrible,” Ellen sobbed, gulping as she attempted to speak.

“Sweetie, stop crying. I can’t understand a word you are saying.” Megan answered with concern.

Ellen blew her nose, and then began again.

“I’m sorry, Meg. I am going to Denver for a long time…. to visit my mother and father…. And I need you to watch Cuddles for me.”

“Slow down a minute!” Megan interjected in exasperation, having a hard time formulating what was happening, and the sudden need to leave. She cupped her hand over the receiver, keeping her voice low, so no one else in the office would hear her. “Why are you leaving, with the produce stand in full swing and as good as things are right now between you and Glen? Is something wrong with one of your folks?”

“No Meggg…. My parents are fine. It’s Glen.”

“What about Glen? I thought everything was perfect between the two of you.”

“I thought so too. That was… until today,” she moaned, with

tear-filled emotion.

"What did he do to you now, Ellen?" Megan asked aggressively, in her overprotective, sisterly way.

"You won't believe this, and I am still having a hard time grasping it myself; but his wife was here today looking for him, and he has two kids."

"No freakin way!" Megan said in disbelief, shaking her head. "I can't believe this! Are you sure?"

"I heard it right from her, and I saw the two children."

"Was Glen there?"

"No…he has been at a cattle auction all day, and is still there. And to tell you the truth, Meg, I never thought I would say this, but maybe it was a good thing that he wasn't here; because I think I could have done him bodily harm if he had been. He had mentioned her to me several times before though, but he only said that they had lived together only. Nothing about marriage or kids. He claimed that she ran off and stole his car, but she was there with the car and acted quite surprised when I asked her where Glen's car was. She said *their car* – plural – was in my driveway. She acted unaffected by my questions, not as if she had something to hide. She said they got in a fight, and Glen had a habit of running off with other women and then returning to her. Beyond that, I thought it was strange that she asked me for Glen's phone number, and I did not give it to her. I knew she was irritated with me, but I just couldn't do it."

"Well don't you find that weird, Ellen, that she didn't know her own husband's phone number?"

“Yes, I did, but she claims he changed it once he moved to Nebraska.”

“Well, Ellen, if what she is saying is true, Glen is nothing but a lying cheat, and scumball.”

“I know… Meggg…that is why I need to get away from this whole mess, and try to get my head on straight.”

“I feel so badly for you, and of course I will watch Cuddles, but what about the farm and the produce stand and the cows? And what about Glen? If he doesn’t know any of this has happened, what is he to think when he gets home?”

“Meg, I just can’t think straight right now. The farm and Glen can go to hell for all I am concerned!” she exclaimed, while the sobbing began again.

“Ellen, honey, you gotta calm down. It isn’t doing you any good to get this upset over a jerk like him. I must be honest; I can understand your feelings about Glen, but not everything else. The farm is your whole life. It is your livelihood. Now that you are on to the bum, he will be out of your life, and you will still have something of value to hold on to.”

“It’s not that easy. Things have changed, Meg. You see…Glen just asked me to marry him last night, and I said yes.”

“Oh no…” Megan replied in astonishment.

“Now can you understand my desperate situation?” she whimpered helplessly. “I thought I was totally and madly in love with the most wonderful and perfect man for me on the planet, and now that dream is shattered. The farm had become us together – a joint project with mutual dreams that we both shared. Without him, life here on the farm is just a horrible reminder of my loss – first Jack, and now Glen. How much should one person have to tolerate?" she cried out in despair.

"You go be with your parents, El," Megan encouraged with overwhelming compassion, as she resigned herself to the fact that her best friend was leaving for an indefinite time period. Mike and I will take care of things. He grew up on a cattle farm, and I know we can handle things. Would you mind if we moved in for a while? At least until you are back home or you know what you want to do. I think it would be a lot easier."

"Meg…of course you can stay at the farm. I hate to put everything on you and Mike though. I just feel I can't cope. I need a break."

"Whatever you want, El. Don't worry about Cuddles either. I will take care of him."

"Look, I gotta get going. My plane takes off in 3 hours, and I still have some things to finish up. I'm going to leave a note for Glen on my kitchen table, but I'm not mentioning where I am going. *Please* do me a favor, and don't tell him where I went. *Will you promise me that, Meg?"* I could not bear it if he tracked me down. I don't ever want to see him again!"

"If it means that much to you… sure. I only hope I can control myself around him. If I don't cause Glen bodily harm, Mike just may, after I tell him what is going on."

Even though her heart was breaking, she still loved him. Her heart ached at the prospect of someone hurting him. Letting go of her feelings completely for Glen wasn't going to be an easy endeavor.

"Megan, I only want him out of my life, not dead, for gosh sakes! The last thing I need is for you or Mike to have a problem because of him. It isn't worth it. So *please* behave yourselves in front of Glen."

"I will, sweetie. I promise. Take care of yourself, El. And remember always that Mike and I love you, and we will always be here for you whenever you need us."

"I love you too," Ellen, whimpered, as the flow of tears began to stream down her face again. "Thank you for being here for me right now. I'll never forget this, Meg. I will call you soon, and let you know how I am doing."

"I'll be waiting to hear from you. Take care, El."

"I will try…bye."

Ellen gave Cuddles a much-too-firm hug goodbye. The cat seemed to sense something was up, watching her inquisitively as she cried. He always was more loveable and followed her around the house more when she was upset about something. Now, was one of the most utmost of those times. "Mommy will miss you," she whispered against the cat's face. "Megan will take good care of you, and I promise I will be back."

Cuddles answered with a faint meow, as he sniffed Ellen's tear-soaked cheeks. She released him to the ground, grabbing her suitcases in return.

"Oh damn!" she exclaimed with exasperation, remembering the note she still needed to write to Glen. "Two hours until my flight. I gotta hurry," she said, as she scribbled what she wanted to say to Glen on a sheet of paper from the notepad on her desk.

Glen,

I am going away for an extended period of time. Megan and Mike will be staying here to take care of Cuddles and the farm. I am releasing you from your employment responsibilities. I met your wife Samantha, and your two children today. She apparently hopes for reconciliation, and she even feels that the possibility of a job exists for you back in your hometown. I am the last person to be a home wrecker. I *will not* be responsible for the breakup of your marriage, or for you leaving your children. I cannot understand why you had to hurt me like this, and lie to me to the degree that you did. It would have been better if we had never met. I am a victim of your charms, and for that, I hold myself responsible. But in the process, you have left me feeling shattered and a helpless shell of a person. I never want to see you again. Good luck fixing your marriage with Samantha.

I do mean that sincerely.

Ellen

P.S. I guess I was right all along about the last name Cummings!

The flight to Denver was uneventful and routine. Luckily, Ellen was able to sit in a seat without anyone beside of her. She needed the solitude of time alone to reflect. The majority of the flight she cried, with her face turned towards the window, feigning sleep whenever a stewardess approached. The sound of the pilot announcing their arrival in Denver was all that was needed for her to sit upright and get her wits about her.

"Mother will be waiting," she said aloud, as she wiped every trace of tears from her eyes. She looked at herself in the mirror of her compact, realizing how swollen and blood-shot her eyes had become. "Mother will know. What am I to do?" she moaned, as she grabbed her purse and headed off the plane.

Marie Meadows sat in the airport terminal, watching the planes take off and land. She was sophisticated in appearance as well as demeanor. Her color-treated, dark brunette hair was upswept in a French twist, secured with an antique pearl comb. She was thin in build, and wore a linen cream suit with a floral print scarf that was tucked into the V of the suit's neckline, along with cream pumps and a handbag that matched. She anxiously awaited the arrival of her daughter, whom she was extremely worried about since the phone call of earlier in the day. Something was wrong. Marie just knew it. Ellen never came home except for the holidays.

She grabbed her purse, clutching it beneath her arm, as she made her way to the baggage claim area since Ellen's plane had just landed. She would feel a lot better once Ellen explained the mystery of the visit.

"Hi, Mom," Ellen waved from a distance, as she approached her mother with her best attempt at cheerfulness.

Marie hugged her daughter soundly. "It's so good to see you, honey," she said while giving Ellen a kiss on the cheek.

"It's good to see you too, Mom," Ellen replied with a quiver in her voice.

Marie sensed something was terribly wrong as they waited together by the conveyor belt, but refrained from asking with so many passengers surrounding them. "Do you have much luggage?"

"Just two bags, besides my carry-on that I have here," she answered quietly, trying to maintain her resolve in front crowd.

Marie looked at Ellen as they waited, and could tell she had been crying. Her mind raced with concern as to what was bothering her daughter so much that she felt the need to come to Denver. They each pulled a bag, walking the short distance to the parked, black with gold-trimmed Cadillac.

"This is the new car you told me about, isn't it mother?"

"Yes, honey. I just love it! Your father is so good to me."

"He certainly is," Ellen agreed, smiling a sad smile, as she stared at her mother's beautiful face that always spoke of happiness. She felt that same happiness less than 24 hours earlier. *How could things have turned around so drastically?* She questioned. Fate was just not good to her. Tears began to stream down Ellen's cheeks. She turned her face away from her mother to look out the window.

Marie pulled the car off of the road still clutching the steering wheel as she began her speech. *"Something is wrong, Ellen. I don't want to pry, but I am so concerned. You have never been good at hiding your tears from me."*

Ellen turned back around to face her mother. "I am sorry…I didn't want to get you involved in all of this so quickly," she burst out, beginning to sob again uncontrollably.

Marie looked confused and very concerned. "It's ok," Marie assured, patting Ellen's arm. "I am your mother…you can tell me anything."

Ellen gulped and looked painfully at her mother. "Mom, do

you remember Glen that I told you about?"

"Yes, that's the one who has been helping you out at the farm, right?"

"Yes, that's right. Well, things have gotten serious between us. I fell…I fell in love with him, and he claimed that he was in love with me also. He asked me to marry him just last night, and I said yes."

"Well that's wonderful, Ellen," she said in a congratulatory way. "But why the tears?" she asked in puzzlement.

"Because his wife and children showed up this morning at my doorstep. She felt I had a right to know about them. Mother, I was totally humiliated and devastated! How could he have deceived me so badly?"

"Was Glen there at the time?" she questioned gently.

"No, he wasn't. He was at a cattle auction buying what was to be the beginning of the return of the livestock to my farm. *It was our dream together!"*

"Ellen, I am so sorry," she offered, patting her hand. "But did you consider that this woman could be lying? After all, Glen wasn't there to defend himself."

"I thought a lot about that, from the time she told me her tale. But she showed me his children, and she said they missed him greatly. The girl even told me that she missed her daddy. His wife was even driving the car he claimed that she stole from him. She acted as if they had only had a meaningless fight, and she was there to convince him to come back home to Virginia. He's done this to other women before, mother," Ellen said in an anguished tone.

"Did she tell you that too?"

"Well, yes…"

"It still could be a lie somehow, even though the evidence points against him."

"I don't think so, mother. He had spoken of her, but he claimed they had only lived together. Why would she lie? Glen could have been at the farm today. She had no way of knowing he was gone. It was just too believable. I *can't*…break up a family!" Ellen exclaimed with a rush of new tears dampening her eyes. "And maybe Glen intended to dump me after awhile anyways, making me the greater fool."

"Oh, my baby," Marie comforted, wrapping Ellen in her arms. "I can see why you are so upset. I only hope this woman didn't see an open window of opportunity, and used it to her advantage, especially since Glen wasn't there to defend himself. But if your instincts are correct, and you truly feel this man has deceived you, I share in your grief and pain."

"Mother, my instincts are right. I know it…I just know it!" she insisted.

"Shhh…" Marie whispered into Ellen's hair, as she continued to hug her daughter and pat her back. "You are home now, and this whole horrible chapter of your life will pass too. You are so beautiful, strong and young. You are a Meadows and a survivor," she said at arm's length while trying to cement the message in Ellen's brain. "Believe in yourself! You know your father and I will let you stay here for as long as you would like. I'm so glad you decided to come home," she continued, as she gazed steadfastly into her child's eyes. "I wish the circumstances were more pleasant, but we will make the most of it."

"Oh Mother, thank you. I knew things would be better once I saw you," she hiccupped.

Marie smiled, kissing Ellen on the cheek. "Dry your eyes, sweetie. We will be home in 10 minutes, and daddy is grilling steaks for us for dinner."

"Dinner's on," Howard Meadows announced happily as his family joined him by the pool.

Marie and Ellen made their way to the flagstone patio and the awaiting table that was already set with plates. The swimming pool glistened and beckoned, as they sat under the shade-giving umbrella, admiring the view.

Marie had quickly filled her husband in on Ellen's plight, while Ellen was in the bathroom. He promised Marie not to mention anything unless Ellen brought up the subject.

"Daddy, I really can't eat a steak this big," Ellen insisted, as her father placed a large New York Strip on her plate.

"Nonsense, darling. Eat what you want. The dog will enjoy the rest," he said with a grin.

"I'm sorry, but I just can't waste food," Ellen replied despondently, as she cut a very small portion from the steak, placing the rest back on the serving platter. "You know, I donate some of my baked goods and produce to a homeless shelter in Fillmore. There are a lot of people who are without food, and I always try to remember that."

Howard just stared at his wife, not knowing what to say next.

“That’s wonderful dear, that you are so generous in your community,” Marie answered for him, as she moved the meat away to the other end of the table.

“Honey, there are grilled potatoes and salad too,” Marie offered, as she passed Ellen the side dishes.

Ellen took a very small portion of each, barely touching what she did eat, once it was on her plate.

“Not hungry?” Howard asked as he glanced up at Ellen, and heartily finished off his large steak.

“Not really, dad,” Ellen answered, barely above a whisper, as she played with her food, poking and sliding it around the plate with her fork, much like a child. “I’m not feeling well.”

Ellen looked in Marie’s direction. “Mother, did you tell him?” she asked pointedly.

“Yes, I did,” Marie, admitted sheepishly, imploring her husband for support. “But, there is not any need to talk about this anymore until you want to.”

“Thank you, mother,” Ellen said in relief.

“I just need a good night’s sleep, and I just don’t want to think about it anymore tonight, but I promise we will talk,” she said with a weak attempt at a smile as she looked at her dad.

“It’s ok, honey. Whenever you are ready, I will be here to listen,” her father offered with concern.

The tears began to stream down Ellen’s face again. “I love you both so much,” she cried out in desperation, casting glances from one and then to the other of her parents.

They were both by her side in seconds, as she wrapped them in her embrace, kissing and hugging them – never wanting to let them go.

"I will see you in the morning. I just want to go to bed now - back in my old bed and in my old room."

"We understand sweetie," Marie consoled gently, hugging and kissing her daughter in return.

Howard gave her a sound bear hug, sending her on her way with his own words of wisdom. "Get a good night's sleep, and I'm sure things will look different in the morning."

Ellen smiled fondly at her father. "Thank you, daddy. I certainly hope so," she replied quietly, as she made her way back into the house through the french patio doors.

Chapter Thirty-Five

Glen pulled into the farm's lane, just as the sun was dipping below the horizon. The fading, burnt-orange circle, promised another hot and sunny day to follow. Twenty-five cattle had been purchased, and the money that he estimated he would need to spend, came in far below what was expected. *Ellen will be happy with the news*, he thought. The scene of her waiting, hopefully in bed with nothing on, aroused a sexual hunger in him that only she could quench. It surprised Glen to see a car parked beside of Ellen's in the driveway.

"What's Megan doing here?" he contemplated aloud with disappointment, realizing that he and Ellen wouldn't be alone after all.

"Hi, Megan," he greeted, making his way to the kitchen, where the only light in the house was turned on. "Where's Ellen?" he questioned, with a pleasant smile. "The truck is loaded down with cattle, but I couldn't wait to see her. I just wanted to say hi to her before I put them out to pasture."

Mike walked from the bathroom, joining them in the kitchen. He looked at his wife whose face was etched with anger, like he had never seen before.

"*She's not here!*" Megan hissed out aggressively at Glen.

"But her car is here."

"Yes, it is, but she isn't here because a taxi came to get her," Megan snapped.

"Where is she? Is something wrong?" Glen asked in confusion.

"You better sit down. Maybe we outta talk," Mike suggested diplomatically.

"What's wrong, damnit? I'm not sitting down, and I want some answers, now!" Glen replied sharply, with both hands planted firmly on the table. "Where is Ellen? Is she ok? And what the hell is wrong with the two of you? You act as if I killed someone or something."

Daggers of hate flew out of Megan's eyes. "*Killing someone*, I think at this point, would be easier to deal with than this!"

"*What the hell are you talking about?*" Glen yelled, raising his arms to the ceiling in utter frustration.

"We are talking about *Ellen*…Glen. *We are talking about Ellen*," she explained very succinctly. And I, for one, am *sick* of this pathetic game you are playing. You have hurt my friend to the point of utter devastation, and she doesn't deserve it!"

Glen shook his head in total disbelief, wanting to wake up from the apparent unfolding nightmare. "Megan, I just asked Ellen to marry me last night, and she said yes. Then I spent the night with the lady of my dreams, curled in my arms. After which time, I awoke to a delicious breakfast, prepared by that same lovely lady, and we kissed fondly goodbye. I told her I would see her this evening after buying cattle intended for our future together. Tell me how any of that would be devastating to her?"

Megan glared angrily at Glen, as Mike just sighed and looked on. "It's not what happened last night or while you were with

Ellen this morning. It's what happened after you left today. Ellen received a visitor, or should I say…. *visitors*. Namely, your wife and two children!" Megan shot out distastefully.

"*My what?* I am *not* married, and I sure as hell don't have any children!"

"You may have fooled Ellen, but *don't* play the same coy game with me!" she warned. "We are on to you, Glen," Megan gritted out starting to rise from her seat.

"Now, calm down," Mike interjected, patting Megan on the shoulder making her sit again. "Getting this upset is not going to solve anything. Glen needs to know what is happening so that he can decide what he must do."

"Thanks, Mike."

"Don't thank me. Let's get one thing straight. I am on Megan and Ellen's side, but I can see this isn't accomplishing much of anything by having a shouting match."

"Ok…please explain to me what is going on," Glen resigned, grabbing a seat and taking his head in his hands. He was feeling suddenly sick and defeated. It did not take much for him to see that his world was falling apart right before his eyes.

Megan began pacing the floor, almost stalking Glen as a cat stalks their prey. "Ellen told us that a woman came here today looking for you. Apparently, your brother's neighbor told her where she could find you. She informed Ellen that you two had just had a little spat and she was here to make up; and to let you know that your two kids missed their *daddy* terribly," Megan seethed, with her arms crossed in an accusatory pose, stopping right in front of Glen for his reaction.

"I'm not married to anyone, Megan. *I swear it*!"

Megan clapped her hands slowly. "*Bravo, Glen.* You had me going there for a moment. I was almost convinced by your *fine acting job*," she mocked sarcastically.

"Get off my back, Megan!" Glen gritted out in irritation. "What was this woman's name anyways?"

"*Sa...man...tha*!" Megan hissed out like venom.

"*Samantha*?" Glen screamed out in disbelief, jumping off his chair. "Why that conniving little bitch!"

"So you *do* know her?"

"Yeah, I *know her* alright! But I only *lived* with her in Virginia. And the kids are not mine! I swear it! I told Ellen about Samantha, and she knows I was never married to her!"

"Well, if that is the case, then why would she come here? She could have found you here at the farm today, and that would have blown her story. Anyways, she was in your so-called *stolen car*."

She did steal my car, damnit!" Glen exclaimed, losing his patience with Megan as he pounded his fist firmly on the table, making the salt and peppershakers rattle. "And I don't know why she came here, but all I can say is, she is *very* lucky. *Very lucky indeed*," he emphasized with marked hatred. "If I had been here, she never would have gotten away with any of this crap. It's all a bunch of sick, twisted lies! She ruined my life once, and she isn't going to get away with it a second time! I love Ellen, and I need to talk to her, and clear this whole mess up. So tell me where she is."

"She doesn't want to talk to you, Glen. I absolutely am not going to tell you where she is!" Megan blurted out with determined stubbornness that was so much a part of her nature.

"I can't believe this," Glen responded in total disbelief. He looked in Mike's direction for assistance, feeling totally beaten. "How about you, Mike? You can't be buying into any of this!"

Mike sighed, not wanting to admit that he was beginning to feel somewhat sympathetic towards Glen. He had to wonder if Glen was really telling the truth. "I think you already know the answer to that, Glen. As I said before, I must stand by Megan and Ellen."

"She left a note," Megan interjected matter-of-factly. When Glen and the cattle truck had been heading up the lane, Megan had quickly grabbed the note and put it in her jean's pocket. She had wanted the opportunity to yell at him first, before handing the note over to him. Now that she was satisfied with her degree of ranting and raging, she relinquished the letter freely pointing it in his direction.

Glen grabbed it from Megan opening it quickly, reading it over twice, while absorbing each word in frustration. "I can't believe this! I love Ellen, and yet she still wants me to leave. *I know this farm*! You two can see that. The produce stand is in full swing, and the garden and cattle are a full time job. *I need to be here!*"

"Glen, Samantha is at your brother's. Why don't you go talk to her? Maybe you won't want to come back here after you see her and …the kids," Megan said in a calm but sarcastic voice.

Mike lightly pinched the back of her arm, warning her silently by the gesture to behave herself.

"I *will* talk to Samantha, and I *will* be back after I get this mess straightened out!" Glen yelled, heading for the front door. "Oh, and by the way…" he added with an edge, staring boldface at Megan, "The cattle need to be put to pasture; and if I really am the liar you are making me out to be, I would let the two of you handle the job. But I do have a conscience, and I will take care of them just as I had planned. You tell Ellen that I love her, and this whole thing is bullshit! I'm not giving up on us! You tell her that!" he yelled out with much emotion as tears moistened his blue eyes.

Glen slammed the door causing the knickknacks to rattle, while he jumped off the porch, skipping the steps entirely.

"Whoa, is he mad," Megan breathed out uncomfortably, pacing the floor again.

"I hope Ellen is right. That is all I can say…" Mike interjected quietly, as he took a seat at the table again.

Megan was steaming as she pulled the chair out beside of Mike. "I can't believe you said that. Of course Ellen is right! I know my friend, and she wouldn't just throw her whole future away, and her happiness with it, if she wasn't right."

"And I *really* want to believe that," Mike emphasized sympathetically while patting Megan's arm. "The conclusion you and Ellen have come to is probably correct, but Gold help us all if Ellen assumed wrong."

Chapter Thirty-Six

Glen fought back the mist of tears that kept covering his eyes, as he led the cattle from the truck into the awaiting pasture that was to become their new home. He ran the water from the garden hose into the trough. All that was left for him to do was return the truck to Mr. Miller's store. It was nearly impossible for him emotionally to pull out of the farm's lane. The thought of doing so, maybe for the last time, almost tore his heart apart.

"*Damn that Samantha*!" he said aloud, as he turned the Bronco out on the road, away from Mr. Miller's store. "I should have pressed the police to do more when she messed with me the first time! I won't be easy on her after this!" he vowed, pounding the dashboard in confirmation.

Glen pulled into the driveway of Eric's. No sign of his old car, Samantha, or her kids. *What is going on?* He thought. The dark house made it apparent to Glen that Eric wasn't home yet either. He fumbled for his keys, opening the screen door, trying to locate the door's lock. A note fell to the step, which had been wedged between the two doors. He flipped on the living room light and realized it was a note from Samantha.

Dear Glen,

I am here in town, staying at the Good Night Motel. I miss you, and so do the kids. Please come see us.

Love,

Samantha

Glen fumed angrily, feeling his blood pressure rise as he read the note. He crumbled it tightly in one clenched fist throwing it in the trashcan that was in the kitchen. The thought of physically hurting her crossed his mind, but only a passing thought was all that he would allow. He would never stoop to her level, and resort to violence.

The drive to the Good Night Motel was only a few minutes away. The elderly female clerk at the front desk was very willing to give Glen all the information that he requested.

"Yeah, a woman and her two kids, like you're describing, checked in this afternoon. I'll call her room and you can talk to her if you would like," the desk clerk said with a pleasant voice.

"I'd rather surprise her," he replied, with his best attempt at a friendly smile. "It's been a while since I last saw her, and I know she will *be thrilled* if I just knock on the door."

"Well…alright," the senior grey-haired clerk reluctantly agreed. "It's not really our policy to do this, but you seem sincere enough. You're not a mass murderer or anything are you?" she said good-naturedly. "Wouldn't want to lose my job," she laughed.

"I don't even step on spiders – if that helps," Glen grinned, striving for joviality.

"Good enough. The number is 214. Hope you surprise her."

"*Oh, I will,*" Glen chuckled bitterly, as he made his way out of the office and to Samantha's room.

Samantha heard the knock on the door, and gave her hair a quick brushing before she ran to open it. The children were sleeping, and she was glad for that. It would give her a chance to hopefully spend some quality time with Glen. She just had to convince him that she and the kids loved and needed him, and that he needed and missed them just as much. She knew he had always said that he would like to have kids of his own one day, and there was no question that he was always so kind and loving to her children, just the way a *real* father should be.

"Hello, Glen," Samantha greeted with as cheerful of a tone and smile as she could muster.

"Hello, Samantha," Glen gritted out between clenched teeth, looking as if he was ready to explode.

"Come in, Glen. The children are sleeping though, so we will need to be quiet," she added with a whisper.

Thomas and Elizabeth snuggled together in one of the double beds that Samantha had pushed up against a wall. Glen glanced at the sleeping cherubs. They looked so peaceful as they slept. He felt a wave of compassion for them, knowing that they didn't have a choice in being around such a twisted mother for the rest of their youth. He could escape, but they were stuck with her.

"This isn't a social call, Samantha, if you haven't figured that out by now. The crazy shit that you just pulled today on Ellen Cummings, out at her farm, is more that I thought *even you* were capable of! I never thought I would say this, but you are destroying my life again!"

He took a step in her direction, wanting only to grab and squeeze her arm hard, but reconsidered. The children started to squirm in their sleep from the obvious rise in the noise level.

"Glen, keep your voice down," she warned anxiously.

"Let's take a walk outside, Samantha. The kids will be fine for a couple of minutes if we stay right in front of the room."

Samantha looked worried. She knew Glen was furious with her and the evil gleam in his eyes was frightening her. She grabbed her room key, and they made their way to a low brick wall that bordered the parking lot.

"Aren't you going to sit down?" Samantha questioned, as she pushed herself up on the wall.

Glen remained unmoved, with his anger boiling just below the surface. "I don't think so…I'd rather stand."

"All right…. so why are you so mad at me, Glen?" she mewed sweetly, in her best Virginia drawl, trying to lighten him up.

"Don't play the innocent with me, Samantha. I *know* what you said to Ellen Cummings. She is hurt beyond belief. That woman thinks I am a liar, and it's all because of you!"

"I just told her the truth, Glen."

"*The truth*! You call us being married and having two kids together the truth!"

"Alright, that was stretching things. But it *was like* we were married, and the kids *were like* yours, when *we were* together. And the subject of marriage did come up a time or two between us. To be honest, Glen, I truly thought we would have been married by now."

Glen laughed heartily in disbelief. "Samantha, I hate to say this, but *you* were the one to bring up marriage. It was never me. I knew a marriage between us would never work. All we did was fight. We had nothing in common once the infatuation was over between us."

"Sex was good for us, Glen. We could still have that, and hopefully we could grow together and be closer in the future."

"Never, Samantha!" he cruelly replied. "Not in this lifetime! You lied to Ellen, and you know it! If I knew where she was right at the moment, I swear to God, I would drag you there by your hair and force you to tell her the truth!"

She shivered at his severe comments, hating them almost as much as his piercing glare. "Glen, please calm down," she said with an over-emphasized southern drawl. She reached her arm in Glen's direction, but withdrew it quickly, back to her side, after viewing the murderous scowl on his face. "Sometimes, we do things when we are desperate. By you not being there at the farm when I got there, proves to me that God is looking out for us, and we are meant to be together. Don't you see that, Glen?"

Glen shook his head in disgust. "The only thing I see, lady, is a sick person who needs some real help. And my car – I can't believe you stole my car, and now you act as if nothing ever happened! What ever I saw in you, I have to wonder where my mind was."

He started to pace, running his hands through his blonde locks with a nervous gesture. "God, if only I knew where Ellen was right now. I can only imagine the torment and betrayal she has to be feeling. And what if I had been there today at the farm…then what would you have done?" Glen asked, looking at Samantha for answers.

"I would have asked Ellen if I could have spoken with you…I guess I wouldn't have gotten my chance to tell her my story in that case. I was lucky."

"*Lucky – you call that lucky?"* he gritted out. "You are *not lucky*, Samantha. As far as I'm concerned, in case you were misled, *we have no future together, and I resent you for meddling in my life again*!"

"You really think you love this person, don't you?"

"Yes I do, but you would never understand the kind of love we share. There aren't deceit and lies, and cruel acts that try to control the other person, unlike the pattern that always seemed to exist with us. I love her so much, Samantha, that I had asked Ellen to marry me just last night, and she had said yes."

Glen paced back and forth in front of Samantha unable to stop raking his hands nervously through his hair.

"You say there aren't any lies or deceit between you, but why don't you know where she is right now?" she interjected meekly, knowing she was treading on dangerous territory by igniting his temper anew.

"I don't know where she is because of you, damnit!" he screamed. "After the stunt that you just pulled, she is gone, and no one will tell me where she is at. But by damn, I will find her!" he yelled adamantly, kicking up some stones.

Samantha's expression hinted of the hurt that Glen was inflicting upon her, but she was still determined not to give up so easily. She had seen his temper flare before, but she was always able to soften him up in the past when she wanted to. The stunt of running off with his car, she realized, had been a bad mistake.

There had been an evening when she decided to go barhopping with her girlfriends, and Glen was left at home to babysit. She had told him she was going to a Tupperware party, and called later to say she would be staying at a friend's house that had just broken up with her boyfriend and needed comforting. Little did Glen know that she was calling from a local motel, lying in the arms of a guy she had just met at the bar that night. The stranger made her drunken promises of owning a large construction company 100 miles away, and that he wanted her to come and live with him. She bought into it – hook, line and sinker.

Back home, two days later, she convinced Glen to catch a ride to work with a friend. She claimed she wanted to go birthday shopping for him. Instead, she packed her bags and left town with her two kids and Glen's car. Once she arrived, she happily ran to the front door of her "one night stand" knocking repeatedly, as her kids looked on from the car. He opened the door looking shocked, remembering he had unfortunately given her his address. He reluctantly allowed her to enter with the children in tow, remembering the night they had had. She connived her way into spending the night, and soon the one night led to many nights. Her lover was tolerant, since she didn't disappoint him in the bedroom, even if the spare baggage of her children staying there was part of the deal. Samantha had a way of convincing even the most seasoned of bachelors that she could make them happy – at least sexually.

It took several weeks, but Samantha finally caught on that the construction company was nothing more than a small operation that did driveway sealing. The jobs were sparse, and the incoming money was almost non-existent lately since she showed up. She cried her eyes out one afternoon when her new boyfriend came home drunk and knocked her to the ground when she complained that there wasn't any food in the house to make dinner that evening. Not one to stay when she knew an opportunity wasn't materializing with a man; she wiped her tears and began planning for her exit. She realized at that moment what she had thrown away by giving up on Glen. "He may not be rich," she said to herself, as she sat on the bed contemplating what to do next. "But he did work consistently, and was nice enough to my kids and me."

Samantha called her mom, as she had done when she first left town, but this time it was to instruct her to not keep Glen away and to answer his questions if he called, and to find him and smooth the way for their reconciliation. Samantha called several days later to hear the news that Glen had left town and no one knew where he was.

Feeling totally frustrated and helpless, she knew she had to find him, so out of desperation she called Glen's mother several months later, explaining that she had made a big mistake, and needed to find Glen and speak to him. That was when she learned that he had left for Nebraska and was staying with his brother Eric.

She left at the next opportunity, when her fling was on one of his sealing jobs. She found $200.00 in one of his dresser drawers that she stole. She packed up all of her clothes and the children's, throwing them into garbage bags quickly; and placed the kids in the back seat of the car, sleeping at rest stops along the way, with only five hours of sleep at night. She made the drive in only two days to Nebraska.

Existing on the raw energy that drove her now, Samantha listened to Glen's biting words, trying to coax him back into submission, as she had done so many times in the past. "Glen, you feel this strongly about her because you have only been around her, and no one else at that farm. It's what you have grown used to. But, I know if you came back to Tommy, Elizabeth and I, we could work this out. I will never do something stupid again, like leaving you and taking the car," she promised with a sweet drawl, reaching out to touch his arm.

Glen gritted his teeth again, drawing back as if he had been touched by a hot scorching iron, firmly in disbelief by her persistence and her attempt at any physical contact. "*Sa…man…tha!* Let me say this as clearly as I can, without any misunderstanding. First of all, *never touch me again, like you just did!"* he informed her in disgust, brushing off his arm as if something was still on it. "*You* will never do something stupid like leaving and taking my car again, because I will *not* be giving you that chance to do so ever again! With or without Ellen in my life, you and I have no future together!" he stated plainly. "Our relationship was over long before you ever stole my car. That was just a final act to confirm to me that I wasn't wrong about you. I know now what you had been doing behind my back all of those nights when you were out, and I was home with your kids. You sicken me, Samantha!" Glen spat out, stinging her with the venom of his words.

Samantha hung her head in defeat. She knew it was over. Glen was never going to make amends with her. Too much bad blood was between them, and she had no one to blame but herself.

Glen sensed that reality had finally sunk in with her, as she looked up at him with tear-filled eyes. "I will do you one big favor. I won't turn you into the police department. This bullshit that you told Ellen - of me leaving my car with you, I could disprove easily. I filled out a police report on you, and my mother is my witness to that fact. It only amazes me that the police haven't caught up with you up until this point. I ought to take the car and leave you high and dry, but I hate to see the children riding a bus the whole way back to Virginia."

"I'm having to make car payments for the Bronco that I am driving now, and I resent it like hell!" he yelled out, making her cringe with fear. "I could really use the money I am earning now towards more important things, but instead it goes towards a car payment that I shouldn't have to be making. So I am putting you to the test, Samantha," Glen added with biting smoothness. "Take your chances. I'm on to you, and you know it! Go home…keep the car…. and hope the authorities don't catch up with you. Or better yet – hide the car away – as you have probably done up until this point; and see how long it takes until your *luck*, as you say, runs out."

"Glen, you wouldn't actually want to see me in prison away from my children, would you?"

"No, Samantha, I wouldn't wish that on anyone, but you do have another option," he advised, feeling as if she were finally listening and taking him seriously for the first time since he had met her. "Go home, and take my car back with you and turn it in to my mother – once you get there. I'll drop the charges if you choose to do that. Whatever you decide, we have no future together, Samantha. Get that straight!"

" But the children, Gleeenn…" she drawled, still clinging to a dead hope.

"Your children, Samantha. *Your children* – from the two fathers who fathered them! I'm truly sorry that I wasn't their dad, because I would have done right by them, but you know the truth. So stop the fantasy!"

Samantha began to cry hysterically, hoping for one last

attempt at Glen's sympathy. "You…. are so cruel, Gleeenn…. I only wanted to love you."

Glen began to laugh in amazement at her shallow, much-too-late forthcoming words. "No, you didn't, and you know it! You just love having a man around who can pay your way. I still can't do that to the degree that you would have ever been satisfied with, so why are you sniffing around here? You'll meet someone else, probably even before you get back to Virginia. There is no use in pretending – you know it will happen. And besides all that, I don't really care how you feel about me, because I don't feel the same way about you. I'm in love with Ellen Harper, and I want no one else in my life now or in the future. I can't make it any clearer."

"Goodbye, Samantha," he said with finality. "I'll call the motel in the morning, and make sure you have checked out. If not, I'll be calling the police. I do wish you happiness," he said sympathetically, as he turned and walked away.

He could still hear Samantha softly crying to herself, as he got into the Bronco and drove off, heading for Eric's once more.

Chapter Thirty-Seven

Morning arrived, and for all concerned, sleep did not come easy. Mike and Megan were up at their usual six o'clock.

"What are we going to do, hon, about the farm?" Mike asked, as he poured himself a bowl of cereal.

Megan was busy making coffee for the both of them. "I don't know," she answered, as she dumped the water into the top of the automatic drip coffee maker. "I kept asking myself that same question over and over again last night, but without any real conclusion. I thought about asking off from work for a week or so, maybe even taking an extended leave of absence."

She stopped to stare at him, carefully considering her options. "You know we can afford it, Mike."

"If that's what you want to do, I will back you on your decision, but you have never taken off of work like that before. Are you sure you would be happy if you were off work for an extended period of time?" Mike asked, concerned for her well-being. "You job is so much a part of you."

"So maybe it's time I try something new," Megan replied with determination, as she poured them both a cup of the aromatic brew. "I always wanted to see what it was like to be home doing all the domestic things. Ellen is like a sister to me, and I *won't* allow this farm to fold while she is getting her head together. She'll regret it the rest of her life if she loses everything when she wakes up from this nightmare. She has to have some kind of future without Glen. This farm has always been that constant, and by damn, if I'm going to let her give it up while she isn't thinking straight!"

"You are one heck of a friend, Meg," Mike acknowledged as he added sugar and half and half to the coffee in front of him.

Megan smiled at her dear friend and husband. "What about a wife? Am I one heck of a good wife, also?" she teased, while leaning across the table for a kiss.

"That and more," he added, while kissing her warmly on the mouth.

"I'm going to call into work at 7:30 and let them know I won't be in for the week. If I don't hear from Ellen by the end of the week, or she doesn't change her mind and come home, I'll need to be asking off for a longer period of time at that point. I just don't want word of this getting back to Eric. You know how gossip flies around the office. I will just have to go to Peter and ask him to keep this confidential."

Mike patted Megan's arm. "Meg, I think that is being unrealistic. Even if word doesn't get around the office, Glen will surely tell Eric what is happening, and that we are helping Ellen out."

"Megan sighed. "Damn, I didn't think about that! Oh well, that just adds another complication to this whole mess," she said with a shake of her head. Eric likes me though. I don't think he would intentionally try to make problems for me at work just because I am trying to help Megan out."

"Putting that all aside," Mike pointed out with concern, "I don't know how we can possibly do all that needs to be done around here. It takes a lot of physical strength and determination to take care of this farm."

"Glen and Ellen managed, and we will too," she answered with absolute certainty. "I know your insurance company needs you, Mike, so I am going to make some calls today. Hopefully, I can get someone to help us. I look at it this way," she said while raising three fingers. "#1 – we need to keep the cattle fed and watered. #2 – we need to pick the vegetables from the garden. And #3 – we need to keep the produce stand running. Everything else can be put on hold for a while. I checked Ellen's freezer, and she has about 30 loaves of her banana and apple bread in there yet."

"I feel guilty leaving you here alone today while I go to work," Mike confessed as he stood up and put his bowl and cup in the sink.

"*Don't feel that way, Mike,*" she stated firmly. "I understand how busy you are," Megan added as she began to draw a sink of sudsy water to clean up their breakfast dishes. "I'll be fine. Just bring dinner home tonight, ok?" she said in somewhat of a worried tone.

Glen rolled and tossed all night long, wishing Eric had made it home. He really needed to talk to his brother and he wasn't answering his phone even with several voicemail messages being left to call him back. The whole episode continued to gnaw at his insides, not giving him any peace. None of this should be happening, and now it was dawn. He wanted to be at the farm working. *Megan and Mike can't keep things all together*, he thought. *They have jobs for heavens' sake! The place will fall apart*. Those feelings haunted his every thought, along with the devastation and confusion of losing Ellen.

Glen grabbed a pair of shorts and made his way to the kitchen. His first order of business for the day was to call the motel where

Samantha had been staying. It was only 7 o'clock but he hoped she was long gone.

"Hello," he began, as the motel clerk greeted him good morning. "Has room 214 checked out yet?"

"Hold on please. No, that room is still occupied. Would you like me to connect you to that room?"

"Yeah.... sure," Glen answered, feeling the level of irritation building to a crescendo in him again, from her still being in town.

"Hellooo..." came the sleepy response from Samantha.

"Pressing your luck, huh?" Glen gritted out harshly in disbelief that she was still there and sleeping.

"I *am* leaving, Glen, within the hour. Have a heart," she replied wearily. "I have a long drive ahead of me, and I didn't sleep too well last night. I needed at least a few hours of sleep before I got on the road."

"Excuses, that's all it is," he bit out, feeling no sympathy for her after what she had done to Ellen and him.

"One hour, Samantha. That's all I am giving you! If you are not gone in one hour, I call the police. And remember what I said about the car. Call my mother when you get back to town. I will call and alert her to your impending visit. If I were you, I would take what I am saying seriously and leave my car with her. If not, suffer the consequences, when the law catches up with you!"

"Gleennn?" she pleaded, with her best southern drawl, knowing her hope was fading fast.

"Goodbye, Samantha. I have nothing more to say to you. It

was all said last night."

Glen called in exactly one hour. Samantha Wallace was packed and gone. He then called his mom, hating to get her involved in the whole ugly mess.

"Hello…? Glen is that you?" Robin Cummings asked surprised to hear from her son whom she hadn't heard from in several months.

"Hi Mom. How are you?" he asked, feeling better in seconds for hearing her cheery voice.

"I'm just fine, Glen. How are you?"

"I've been better, I must say. Look, something is going on right now, and I could really use your help."

"Anything, Glen. What is it?" she asked with concern.

"It's Samantha. She came here to Fillmore with her kids and my car."

"I was afraid something like this would happen sooner or later, since she and her mother both have been inquiring into your whereabouts! Her mother called me first, and I told her that I didn't know where you were and she didn't press the subject." She chuckled somewhat as she continued. "I hated to tell a little lie, Glen, but I was trying to protect you."

Glen had to smile at the honesty and sincerity of his mother. *It was a pity that Samantha didn't even have a fraction of the integrity his mother had always reflected to those around her*, he pondered with remorse.

"I think God will forgive you for telling a little white lie this one time, Mother," he answered good-naturedly. "It was for a good cause. You just tried to protect me."

"I know that, Glen, but I'm also not proud of myself for what I did several weeks later," she confessed with regret echoing in her voice. "Samantha called me in time also, as I just said. She claimed she had changed and was a different person since losing you. She went on to say that she held herself solely responsible for the many mistakes in your relationship. I was truly shocked and taken back by the sincere way she was acting. It was my undoing when she said she wanted to personally apologize to you, and return the car. She asked me to not contact you because she wanted to surprise you. I thought that would make you happy, even if you sent her away after she had returned your car. From the sound of your voice, I can tell something is wrong. I'm sorry, Glen, if Samantha's visit is the cause. I truly did mean well."

"I know that, Mother," he consoled. "I must say though, that I never dreamt she would show up like she did," he replied despondently as he spooned some scrambled eggs onto his plate that he just cooked.

"Listen, I am not upset with you mother. Samantha is manipulative, and she has conned a lot of people. She is a pro at playing the innocent. She did have my car with her, and since I just bought another vehicle, I told her to drive the car back to Virginia, and drop it off at your house. I hated to see her kids have to ride the whole way home on a bus," he admitted, with the same softness that had gotten him in over his head in the first place with Samantha.

"Once my car is back in your possession, I want you to sell it for me. But we will talk about that in a few days. I also advised her that if she doesn't do this, I would call the police and put them on alert again about the car."

"I am so sorry you have gone through all this," his mother comforted.

"Mom, you haven't heard the worst. What Samantha did to me in Virginia was bad enough, but what she pulled yesterday was beyond anything I thought she was capable of."

"What did she do?" his mother asked with genuine concern.

"She went to the farm, where I was working. While I was away, she told the owner that I was married to her, and that her kids were my kids too."

"That's a typical Samantha move."

"Yes, but there is more. The owner's name is Ellen, and her husband died a couple years ago. I had been there helping her with the farm work and we had become involved. Mom, I just asked her to marry me two days ago, and she said yes," he interjected with forlorn emotion, remembering the tender moment that he spoke the words of promise and endearment to her, holding her in his arms while they were in Ellen's bed together.

"Now over this, she ran off and doesn't want to see me anymore. She left a note telling me it was over between us, that I was fired, and that I should reconcile with Samantha and the kids. Ellen's friends won't tell me her whereabouts, even though they know where she is. I love her, Mom, and I can't believe she bought into Samantha's bag of lies. It hurts me to think that she didn't even hang around long enough for me to tell her my side of the story," Glen confided sadly, while running his free hand through his hair.

"Son, I am so sorry. Would you like me to come to Nebraska for a couple of weeks and stay with you and Eric? I could make you some nice home-cooked meals."

"Thanks, mom, but that isn't necessary. I'll be ok. And besides, I need you there to take care of the business of getting my car back, and then I want you to put it up for sale."

"That's the least I can do. As far as this Ellen girl goes, I don't know what to say, other then it's good that you found out early rather than a couple years down the road that she has a problem with trust. You will be all right, Glen. You are stronger that you realize sometimes."

"I'm in love with her mom. I have never felt about someone like I feel about Ellen. I *won't* give up on her that easy. It has only been a day since she has left. I'm still praying that she will come to her senses."

"Then I will pray for that too," his mother comforted. "I love you, Glen."

"I love you too, Mom. And thanks for everything. I will call you in a few days or you should call me once Samantha stops by. Whichever comes first, since I promised her I will drop the charges if she does what is right."

"I'll be in touch, Glen."

"Thanks, Mom. Hopefully, this will all work out for all concerned."

Chapter Thirty-Eight

Ellen tossed restlessly throughout the night. When she finally did fall asleep, horrible nightmares kept haunting and waking her. Glen was kissing Samantha and holding their children. In another dream, he was laughing at Ellen while he pulled away in his car, bound back to Virginia with Samantha and the children in tow. The last dream episode tormented her the most - Jack was talking to Glen, and then they began beating each other up. Eric joined in, and they beat Jack to a bloody, hardly recognizable, lifeless pulp. The two brothers stood over the dead man, continuing to kick him in the ribs, laughing uncontrollably.

Ellen bolted straight up in bed. She screamed out in fear, her heart racing wildly in her chest, beating out of control. Beads of perspiration clung to her skin as she clutched the covers up to her chest with tight fists.

"Are you all right?" Marie asked with alarmed concern, as she came quickly to Ellen's side.

"I'm fine, mother. I just have been having horrible nightmares."

"You poor thing," Marie comforted, while sitting on the bed and wrapping her arms around her daughter. "It will get better, honey. I promise. You have just had a very difficult time."

"I hope so, mom," Ellen whispered, feeling the tears cascading down her face again. "I can't even escape him in my sleep."

"Let's give it a few days, and if you aren't sleeping any better, I think you should go see Dr. Fairchild. Maybe he will prescribe you a mild sedative."

"Mom, you know how I feel about taking drugs if I don't have to."

"I know darling, but maybe in this case you do need something. On any account, let's not worry about that now. Why don't we go to the kitchen and I'll make you a cup of herbal tea and honey?" she offered, with a pleasant smile.

"That sounds wonderful, Mom," Ellen agreed, as her mother helped her into her robe, and they made their way arm in arm to the kitchen.

Glen was relieved that Samantha was finally gone. Now the order of the day was to talk with Eric. He hadn't said anything about going out of town on business, and he hoped that he would be in the office.

"Good morning, Computer World Systems. How may I direct your call?"

"Is Eric Cummings in?"

"May I tell him who is calling, please?"

"His brother, Glen."

"One moment," the receptionist replied as she put him on hold.

"Mr. Cummings?"

"Yes, Sharon."

"Your brother Glen is on the phone."

"Thank you, Sharon," Eric replied, realizing he hadn't returned Glen's calls as he had intended to.

"Hi Glen, what's up?" he greeted jovially.

"A lot. I need to talk to you, as soon as possible."

"You sound upset."

"I am, and I have been trying to reach you since last night."

"Sorry, bro. I spent the night at Melinda's, and my phone died. When I got your messages today, I knew I couldn't call you for awhile… been busy at work."

"Yeah…I get it. Is there some way I can talk to you in person, and not over the phone?"

"Sure…. how about in 45 minutes at The Park and Dine?"

"That won't work. I want to have total privacy."

"Ok…how about I come home then?"

"I'll be here waiting."

Eric was home within the hour. He knew something must be terribly wrong. Glen was always at work by this time of day. He hoped it wasn't their mother. Eric knew he needed to take some time off, and visit her. It had been too long. Eric found Glen in the kitchen, with his shoulders bent over the kitchen table. His face was riddled with emotion. "Glen, is it Mom?" Eric asked with concern.

"No… as far as I know, she is fine. But I'm not," he answered, looking up at him with a pained expression on his face.

Eric pulled up a chair, giving Glen his full attention.

"What's going on?"

"Ellen Harper…it's over between us, and I lost my job," he uttered, while hanging his head.

"That bitch!" I warned you she was mean and an uncaring person."

"Don't jump to conclusions, Eric," Glen said defensively, as he raised his eyes to stare directly at his brother again. "She's the victim here, and I guess…. in a way… so am I."

"*What could you possibly mean by that statement?*" Eric asked in amazement.

I picked up cattle yesterday for Ellen, and I was away from the house until nightfall. During the day, Ellen received a visitor, or should I say several visitors. It was Samantha Wallace and her two kids."

"Samantha? What the hell does she want?" Eric asked in irritation.

"She apparently decided to screw up my life even more than she already had in Virginia. Ellen's friends - Mike and Megan Delaney, who by the way are staying out at the farm, informed me of all of this after the fact. Ellen is gone, and she wants it kept a secret as to her whereabouts. She left a note for me. Here, read it, and them maybe you will better understand what Samantha is truly capable of."

Glen handed Eric the note from Ellen that he had stuffed in his jean's pocket. Eric read the note, raising his eyebrows and shaking his head in disbelief. "That Samantha is a real sicko. You know that?"

"Of course I know that! Apparently though, Ellen hasn't come to the same conclusion. It's so damn unfair that she won't even give me the courtesy of an explanation. Samantha must have laid it on pretty thick for her to just up and leave like this."

"Doesn't surprise me any. Ever since Jack's death, she doesn't think straight. Everyone in town knows that. But, what about Samantha, did you ever catch up with her?"

"Yeah, I did. Last night she left a note in your screen door for me, and it said she and her kids were staying out at the Goodnight Motel. As soon as I read the note, I went to the motel and tracked her down. I told her this fantasy of hers had to end and we didn't have any future together. Can you believe she was driving my car that she had stolen?"

"Where is it now?"

"I told her to drive it home."

"You did what!" Eric exclaimed in total disbelief, considering the possibility that Glen was losing it mentally too.

"Now wait a minute. I don't need an extra vehicle at the moment, and I wanted to see her leave as quickly as possible. I do have a heart, Eric. Didn't want to think of her kids on a bus."

"But Glen, you probably won't ever get the car back now," Eric said while loosening his tie and pacing back and forth, trying to sort the whole mess out in his mind.

"My instincts tell me different. I told her to call Mom when she gets back to Virginia, and to turn the car over to her. She knows the police will be hot on her trail if she doesn't do things my way. I warned her that the charges would only be dropped when she takes the car to Mom's as soon as she gets back to town. So, in a sense, I am testing her, to see if she does the right thing now that I am giving her the chance. I think she is *really* scared, Eric. I fear I could have done her some bodily harm if I wouldn't have gotten hold of my emotions," he said with a far-off bitter look.

"After that tale…you and I both," he agreed, just shaking his head in astonishment.

"I told Samantha she was lucky I wasn't there when she showed up. I would have set the record straight, right in front of Ellen and her both. But such wasn't my luck, and now I am without my job and my fiancé."

"Fiancé?"

"Yeah. I know it sounds ironic, but I had just asked Ellen to marry me the night before this happened, and she said yes. And now this…it's just too unbelievable!" Glen replied, shaking his head in frustration as he began to pace the floor. "And her friends are being very protective of her. That farm won't make it without me!"

Eric sighed, trying to focus and absorb all the events that had taken place in the last couple of days involving his brother. "It sounds like she has no sense of trust. She could have at least waited to talk to you before she just up and left."

"Eric, she is so fragile. This thing with Jack's death and you, and her feelings now towards me have probably led her to believe that we both wanted to make a fool out of her, and see her hurt. It all adds up to me being the villain here. I wouldn't be surprised if she assumes that I have just been playing with her. And yes…even though I'm sure you don't understand – I do love her. That damn Samantha!" he breathed with bitter regret. "Why did she have to do this?"

"Who knows…?" Eric answered pensively. "But don't worry, bro. No matter what happens, I will be here for you. You still have a home, and the Bronco. Don't worry about paying for it right now until you find another job. I'll ask around. Maybe someone will know of work somewhere. We Cummings' need to stick together."

"That's why I called you, Eric. I was feeling so alone and uncertain about things. I did call Mom, and I filled her in on everything, and she said she will call me back once she hears from Samantha."

Eric reached out, and squeezed Glen's shoulder. "You know you're not alone. Look, I gotta get back to work. I have a pressing meeting, but let's get together for dinner."

"Eric, I really don't want to go out anywhere."

"Fine then. I'll bring dinner home to you," he informed, with a sympathetic smile. In the meantime, look through the want adds," Eric, suggested, handing Glen the local paper. "I'll be home at six with steaks and beer," he yelled over his shoulder, while running for the door with his cellphone ringing in his ear.

Chapter Thirty-Nine

The want ads were filled with several possibilities of things that Glen thought he could do until something better came along. A farmer was looking for a ranch hand for a large cattle farm, a convenience store was looking for a night clerk, and a local factory was looking for an assemblyperson for parts.

"It's something," Glen said aloud, as he circled the three ads that caught his eye. "Hopefully, this will be temporary anyways, at least until Ellen comes to her senses."

He called all three listed numbers, getting an answering machine at the ranch, and a reply to pick up an application from the other two. He figured he would stop by the Quik Shopper, since it was the first stop on the way. "Is your manager here?" Glen asked with a friendly grin, as the clerk blushed and giggled.

"Mrs. Moore, a man is here to see you," the clerk announced over the speaker that was directed to the back room. Mrs. Moore poked her head out from behind the office door.

"May I help you?"

"I'm Glen Cummings, ma'am. I just called about the night shift job that is available. I was told to come in and pick up an application."

"Ah, yes. *Yes…*" she answered, as she took in his handsome and strong physical appearance. "You can come back here to my office."

“It’s ok, Caroline. Let him come back,” she instructed the clerk behind the cash register.

Glen entered a small, cluttered office, and took a seat by the desk that was scattered with papers. Mrs. Moore shuffled the papers off of her desk and chair, repositioning them to a large stack that was sitting on the floor by the file cabinet. Glen had to chuckle to himself at her apparent frustration for having nowhere to work or sit as he glanced around the cubbyhole of a space. He couldn’t even imagine where she was working or sitting before he entered the office. Probably, the very chair he was now sitting on.

She breathed heavily and readjusted her bra along with her t-shirt that had the store logo printed on the front of it, before she sat down. *Her apparent large bosom and rolls at the abdomen probably came from snacking on one-too-many hotdogs and bags of chips while working*, he surmised. Her face was warm though, with kind eyes that were etched with dark circles and lines that read like a book telling the tale of an uneasy life and not much sleep. “So you want a job working here, huh? And *why* would that be? You don’t look the part of the average Joe wanting a job from me,” she commented, as she lit up a cigarette. She inhaled deeply, studying him purposefully, curious and waiting for his response.

Glen shifted his weight, and cleared his throat. “I *need* a job. I have done this type of work before, and I don’t mine staying up all night.”

She studied his face intently, astute to his sincerity. “You’re not on drugs or a drinker are you?” she asked in a scrutinizing way.

“Heavens, no!” Glen replied with a nervous laugh.

“Well, I won’t put up with that, and if I find out you are a addict you are out!”

"No…not my issues at all," Glen said with silent frustration, thinking that coming there may have been a bad idea after all.

Mrs. Moore shifted in her seat that creaked, and inhaled deeply again on the cigarette that was half-way smoked. "Well now that we got that out of the way, I just thought you would want to know it pays more at night. Do you know that?"

Glen shifted too, running his hands through his hair. "To be honest, I didn't even give it much thought," Glen answered, wishing he was outside at the farm about now breathing in the fresh air instead of the stale smoke that was lingering in the office like a heavy fog.

"Are you gonna stick around, or is this just a stepping stone until something better comes along?"

Glen cleared his throat again. "That's hard to answer. All I can tell you is that I will be loyal to the job while I work here, and if and when I decide to quit, I will give you ample notice to find a replacement for me."

"I guess I can't expect no better. No one makes it here long, especially on the night shift. You're hired," she stated matter-of-factly, as she took another long final drag off her cigarette before squishing it out in the ashtray. "Can you start tonight?"

"Tonight? I'm hired?" Glen was caught off guard by her quick decision.

"Don't act so surprised," she smiled with a grin that displayed a couple teeth missing on the one side of her mouth. "Yeah, you're hired. Oh, and by the way, I can't afford to do a back ground check or drug test on you, so hopefully you have a clean record?"

"I'm clean…" he smiled at her. "But I need a night before I start working."

"I guess I can swing that," she hesitantly agreed to, knowing she had to cover his shift for the evening. "Tomorrow night then. Ten to six-thirty in the morning – those are the hours. Five days a week."

Glen reached out to shake Mrs. Moore's hand. "Thanks. I really appreciate it," he said, attempting a warm smile. This wasn't something he was especially looking forward to doing, but the reality of needing the money was constantly in the forefront of his mind right now.

"Don't disappoint me," Mr. Cummings. "We just had to fire a man who could never show up to work sober."

"I won't disappoint you, Mrs. Moore." Glen rose from his chair extending his hand in her direction. "Thank you so much for hiring me, and please call me Glen," he said with a friendly handsome grin.

Mrs. Moore rose from her chair, grabbing on to her desk for support. She blushed and cleared her throat as a small smile lit up her craggy exterior once more. "Glen…then," she said awkwardly, knowing it was going to take some time to get used to working with someone so handsome. The last thing she wanted to do was make a fool of herself and drool over him, especially in his presence. She always portrayed a hardened image with her employees, and she knew if she weren't careful he could bring out her soft side.

She coughed and cleared her throat, excusing herself as she shuffled from behind the desk. "I need to check on things in the store. Sometimes Caroline gets behind," she muttered. "I'll see you tomorrow evening, *Glen*," she said with a slight flutter to her eyelashes, acting like a foolish schoolgirl with a crush on the new boy in her class.

Chapter Forty

The cows were grazing nearby, as Megan pulled green beans from the garden's vines. She wiped her sweat-beaded brow with her dirty, sticky hands that already had several cuts on them. She was quite the spectacle, with mud smeared all over her forehead. *Just the tomatoes yet*, she thought wearily, as she reached for a wicker basket nearby. She couldn't believe how tired she felt already, and it wasn't even mid-morning yet. She had a new respect for Ellen, and what she had to go through to maintain the farm, just from several hours of exerting herself physically. A sedentary desk job was by no means preparation for such strenuous labor. A customer drove up the lane, honking her horn repeatedly, as she noticed Megan.

"Where is Ellen? I need a few things from the produce stand," the overbearing lady demanded, as she took in Megan's disheveled appearance and her dirty face.

Megan stood up, much too quickly, feeling a sharp pain land suddenly in her lower back. She grabbed the spot with her hand and moaned, as she came to her feet. "She's away for awhile…. on a vacation." The pain continued and she grimaced. "I'm watching over things…. while she is gone."

"Oh, *I see…*" the customer remarked cynically, surveying her surroundings.

Megan had a sneaking suspicion that the old crank would be reporting to Ellen all of her inadequacies upon her return.

“I need a loaf of apple bread, 3 tomatoes, and 6 ears of corn.”

Megan continued to massage her lower back, beginning to feel the pain ease somewhat. “I’m a little behind on things today,” she confessed, feeling the need to be vindicated as she walked towards the lady. “Could you possibly come back this afternoon, let’s say after 1 o’clock? To be honest, I haven’t even opened the stand up yet for the day,” she admitted with a sheepish smile. “But, by one o’clock it will be in full swing.”

The stern, scowling-faced woman was not sympathetic. “That *will not* suit my schedule. I need those items *now.* And, I *know* if Mrs. Harper were here, she would see to it that I got what I needed!”

Megan was secretly fuming, as she attempted a cordial smile. “I will need ten minutes, if you can wait,” she answered between clenched teeth that conveyed a plastered-on happy face.

“I will be *waiting* in my car.”

Megan shook her head in disbelief, as she went back to the garden for the requested items, and then headed to the house for the loaf of apple bread. “*Only for you, Ellen,*” she said beneath her breath, as she met the cantankerous old soul back at her car.

The lady rolled down her window, handing her the proper change. “The amount is right. I know, because I buy the same things every week,” she remarked with a stern face.

“Thank you. Come again,” Megan replied sarcastically, not giving a damn if the money was right or not. She was just happy to see her go.

Once the dust had cleared from the lane, Megan made her way

to the produce stand. She took a good long look at it. A canopy was tied securely to the front of the structure. Megan struggled to release an over-tightened knot that didn't want to budge. She finally freed it, bringing the canopy up over an extending frame, tying the cords to it in completion.

The produce from yesterday was still in its bins. Megan picked through the contents, pulling out the several overly ripened and rotted items out of the mix. "*What do I possibly do with all the extra?*" Megan asked herself, feeling totally frustrated and inadequate as the minutes were ticking by. She considered the freshly picked produce as well as those things that would be a couple days old tomorrow. "*Should I throw it away or reduce the price and still try to sell it? Maybe I should call Ellen. No, I can't bother her over something as trivial as this, after what she has been through,*" Megan resolved with new determination.

She stared at all the freshly picked produce sitting in baskets behind the counter. She hated to admit it, but already she knew that this endeavor was more than one person could truly handle. "*I'll just have to call Glen. I shouldn't, but I will.*" Megan reluctantly dialed the number, finding it scribbled on a scratch piece of paper that was thumbtacked to the bulletin board above Ellen's desk. The phone ran, and Glen answered it.

"Hello, is this Glen?"

"Yes…it is." His heart jumped at the sound of a female voice calling his name, and for a moment he thought it was Ellen.

"Glen, this is Megan, and I need you to answer a question for me," she hurriedly explained.

"What's that?"

"What do I do with all the old produce?"

Glen sighed, and then hurt registered again. He had hoped Ellen had come to her senses, and that Megan had called on her behalf. "It needs to be taken to the homeless shelter on a daily basis. I can pick it up for you if you would like."

"Thanks, Glen, but I couldn't pay you to do that. I would never ask you to do anything around here for free. Thanks for the info though."

"Any word on Ellen?" he interjected quickly, not giving her a chance to hang up.

"No, not a thing."

"Well, if you hear from her, will you give her a message from me?"

Megan shifted restlessly. "Well, that depends Glen, on what the message is. You know her wishes, and you know I will do everything to protect her right now."

"*I know that!*" he stated defensively. "Tell her, Samantha is gone. I told her to leave, and to take her lies with her! Tell Ellen that I still love her, and if she just would give me a chance to explain…. I would prove to her that Samantha is lying."

"I'll tell her Glen…if and when she calls," Megan answered hesitantly.

The phone call ended abruptly with Megan hanging up with a curt goodbye. Glen sat at the table again, just pondering their conversation. An idea came to him from Megan's unintentional silent pleas of needing assistance.

"*Megan can't pay me. I worked at the farm for free before, and I will just do it again! Surely, she won't turn down free help,*" he said jubilantly, as he got into the Bronco, and drove off towards the farm with a renewed sense of optimism and hope.

Ellen awoke to the smell of cinnamon rolls baking in the oven, which was one of her mother's specialties. The warm tea of earlier, was sufficient in relaxing her back into several more hours of fairly good sleep. She yawned, stretching her arms high above her head. Sitting up in bed made her fell suddenly light-headed and nauseous. Briskly she ran to the bathroom, barley making it to the toilet in time to heave up her stomach's contents.

"*Oh no,*" she moaned, "*I'm getting sick on top of everything else!*"

Marie knocked on the bathroom door. "Are you ok, dear? I heard you running."

"I'm fine, Mom. Come on in," she said, as she wiped her face with a wet washcloth. "I just feel sick, and I threw up. Probably stomach flu."

"Or maybe this whole ordeal just has your stomach upset from your nerves."

Ellen attempted a weak smile as she looked at her caring and concerned Mother. "Whatever it is, I'm sure I'll feel better in a few hours."

"How about a cinnamon roll? I baked them especially for you, honey."

"Mom, you are the best, but I really don't think I can handle anything to eat right now, but maybe later," she answered with an appreciative but weary smile.

"That's fine. We'll just pop one in the microwave and heat it up when you are up to eating it. I must admit," Marie confessed, "That I had hoped we could have gone shopping and had lunch today, but there is always tomorrow," she added, as she helped Ellen back to bed.

Ellen sighed, feeling nausea returning again. "I think another time would definitely suit me better, mother. Maybe I should just stay in bed for a while until this thing passes. I think I will just try to rest and read."

"I have a stack of magazines, and a couple of novels you might enjoy."

"Anything, mother.... anything," Ellen breathed, as she pulled the covers up under her chin, hoping the nausea would soon pass. By the time Marie was back with the promised reading material, Ellen was fast asleep.

Glen could see the produce stand in the distance, and its cheery, yellow canopy flapping in the bright afternoon sun. As he parked the Bronco off the side of the road, Megan was busy straightening the bins. She turned with a start, and was totally surprised at the site of the familiar, handsome tanned face walking towards her.

"Glen.... what are you doing here?" she asked in astonishment, dropping a tomato, splattering it to the ground in a spray of red pulp and seeds.

"I'm back, Megan," he said firmly, "And here to work."

"Glen, this is silly," she said with a nervous chuckle of

disbelief. "You know how Ellen feels about things."

"Yes…I do. But also, I know you have a job, and even though it is wonderful that you would do all this for your friend, this is a lot to ask from any one person."

"It needn't be your concern," she said stiffly, as she turned her back to him again, trying to wipe the seeds from her pants.

"Megan…please, listen to reason. I am willing to work around here for free."

"For free?" she repeated, momentarily in shocked amazement. "Oh, I get it, you're trying that trick again?" she interjected with a smirk on her face. "What now – you think you are going to score with me also, even though I am married?"

Glen snickered, and shook his head at her is disbelief, recalling her ability to be endlessly rude. "You are a spitfire, aren't you?"

Megan arched her eyebrows in warning as her hands went to her hips in self-defiance. "Ok Glen. Let's just consider what you are saying. Yes, I must admit if you worked here, it would make things a helluva lot easier on me – this is true – but what about you? Don't you need money to pay your bills? And what about Ellen? She would never forgive me if she found out about this!" she said while waving a yellow squash in the air.

Glen grinned slightly, being entertained by Megan making quite the scene with tomato all over her and the squash being waved in his direction like a sword for her protection. "First of all, Megan, I already have another job working nights at the Quik Shopper five nights a week, so money isn't the issue. Which means, I can put in some hours here during the day, and on weekends. And second, just don't tell Ellen that I am helping out.

I still love her, and I figure in time she is going to realize that this whole thing has been a misconstrued lie told by a sick person to benefit herself and herself only. What Ellen doesn't know, for the time being, can't hurt her."

"Yeah…I can see you sorting things out that way. I guess that was your attitude when it came to Ellen not finding out the truth about Samantha."

"You *really* want to *insist* on hitting below the belt, don't you Megan?"

"You *deserve* everything you are getting!" she shouted angrily.

"Whether I *deserve* it or not will hopefully be decided one day once emotions calm down, but in the meantime, let me get back to the business of holding down this farm. The livestock especially need my attention," he pleaded.

Megan felt her reserve crumbling. Glen was there; ready to assist, and she didn't know what to do with the cows anyways. The local farmers she called couldn't help, and they were short-handed themselves.

"Ok, Glen…you got a deal," she conceded reluctantly. "But damn it, if this thing back fires and it causes me a problem with my friendship with Ellen, you will *pay dearly* and wish you never heard the name Megan Delaney!"

"I'll take my chances," he said, with an ever-so-slight grin. "Now let me get started. The first thing I need to do is get this old produce to the shelter," Glen commented, as he grabbed a few empty boxes off of the ground behind the stand.

Megan hesitated, but then grabbed a box also and helped him fill and load the vegetables into the trunk of the Bronco.

"*Thanks, Glen…*" she breathed, as he drove down the lane slowly and headed towards town.

He waved a pleasant goodbye before departing, while Megan stood staring at him with her hands back on her hips.

"I must be crazy to trust him, but thank God for the help…thank God."

Glen arrived at the shelter, feeling a real sense of victory, though small that it was. He knew if he were to figure out where Ellen was, the first step would have to be at regaining Megan's trust. Hopefully in time, she would see him in a more positive light, and realize Samantha had been lying.

The matronly, plump lady that sat at the front desk of the Fillmore City Shelter was busily shuffling papers and talking on the phone to a woman who apparently needed some comforting. A friendly smile of recognition crossed her face, when Glen entered the room with a large box of produce in hand.

"I'll be with you in a minute," she whispered, with her hand over the receiver, instantly recognizing the familiar face of Glen.

"Take your time," he grinned, as he took a seat and thumbed through a magazine until she was done with the troubled caller.

"Well hello, Glen. We thought maybe you were away on vacation."

"No vacation. Just had some personal things to attend to the last couple of days. I'm really sorry to be late," he echoed. "It just couldn't be helped. Where would you like these things?"

"Over there would be fine," she instructed, as she pointed to an empty corner by the door.

Glen returned with two additional boxes of plenty. "I'll be back tomorrow," he promised, as he made his way to the door.

"Thank you, Glen," the friendly receptionist called out as the phone began to ring again.

Glen left the shelter and returned to the farm. Now that he had Megan's consent to be there, he was going to get things back the way they were before the terrible misunderstanding began.

Megan was still working at the produce stand as he pulled into the farm lane. She had two customers that were keeping her busy. The garden, much to Glen's surprise, was really not in as bad of shape as he had imagined. Megan had done a pretty good job of picking the ripe crop. Some weeds needed hoeing, the sprinklers were overdue to be turned on, and the cows were definitely being unintentionally neglected. The water trough was dirty, which required cleaning and refilling, and more feed had be added to the troughs; but other than that, things were not out of control, and could be caught up easily.

"Everything is pretty well taken care of, Megan. You did a good job picking the vegetables today."

"Thanks, Glen," she replied, trying to act as non-reactive as possible to his compliment. "I *can see* what needed to be picked. It isn't *that hard* to figure out."

"Yeah, I guess it isn't," he answered in a frustrated tone, tired of Megan's attitude towards him. "I'm leaving for the day. If you have any issues or questions call me. Otherwise, I'll see you tomorrow," he affirmed, while turning and not waiting for her response.

Dealing with her attitude would not be easy, he realized as he drove home, replaying each scene with his encounter with Megan that day. Glen looked forward to seeing Eric that evening. He needed a friendly face and pleasant company. *At least he is there for me*, he thought, as he pulled into the garage.

Ellen woke in the early afternoon, feeling just as badly as she had felt in the morning. "*What is wrong?*" she moaned, as she made her way back to the toilet, spewing up the brightly colored yellow bile-liquid that came from her stomach. "*Motherr…*" she called weakly, hanging her head over the toilet.

Marie swiftly came to her daughter's aid once again. "What is it dear?" she asked, with a look of worry etched on her face.

Ellen was wet with perspiration, as she turned to look up at her mother. "Maybe we should call the doctor, and make an appointment. I hope I don't have food poisoning."

"*You feel that badly*?" Marie questioned with concern.

"Worse – if that is possible. I don't even have the strength to pull myself off the floor."

Marie helped Ellen up, and then washed her face with the damp washcloth that was still lying in the sink from earlier in the morning. "Let's get you back to bed, and I will call Doctor Fairchild. Hopefully he can see you yet today."

"I hope so, mother. I just want to feel better."

Marie called Dr. Fairchild's office, but the soonest they could see Ellen was the following morning. "I hate to tell you this, but they won't be able to see you until tomorrow at 10:00 a.m."

"I was afraid of that," Ellen moaned softly.

"The nurse did say that crushed ice with a little cola might help to settle your stomach. She also said not to worry about food poisoning. Your symptoms don't sound severe enough to be that, and a stomach flu is going around."

"I can't imagine feeling any worse than this, but I guess I'll find out tomorrow what this could be," she replied weakly. "I'm going to try to rest again, mother. At least I don't have to deal with the nausea when I am asleep."

Marie smoothed and straightened the covers over her daughter. "You sleep as long as you would like, dear. And please call – if you need me," she instructed, as she bent over to give her a kiss on the cheek.

"Thanks, mom…I love you," Ellen sighed, as she rolled over and closed her eyes thinking about Glen and if she made the right decision of blocking his number so he could not call or text her.

Chapter Forty-One

Eric was closing his brief case, just as Melinda entered his office. "Hi, beautiful," he beamed, with a face full of love.

"Hi yourself," she teased, in a seductive tone. "How does dinner tonight at my apartment sound?" she asked with her hand suggestively placed on her hip.

Eric's face turned suddenly reflective lost in thought. "It sounds wonderful, Melinda, but I can't tonight."

"Oh?"

"Glen needs me. This breakup with Ellen is tearing him up. I promised him that I would spend the evening at home. He needs my brotherly input right now, Melinda," he explained in a serious tone that was so unlike him. "Glen deserves all the support he can get."

Melinda took a seat on the couch in front of his desk. "I totally understand, Eric. Although, I must admit that I am a little disappointed, but I know your brother needs you," she answered sympathetically. For the life of me though, this whole thing has me amazed and in total disbelief. How could Ellen and Megan Delaney, for that matter, be so gullible?" Melinda interjected, as she removed her suit jacket and laid it over the back of the sofa. "To go off the handle like that, and not even give Glen the courtesy of an explanation."

"That's exactly how I feel," Eric remarked, as he joined

Melinda on the black leather couch. "Glen would be better off putting this whole thing behind him, and begin dating again. You have a few cute friends that maybe you could fix him up with, don't you?" Eric asked, as he brushed his palm across Melinda's face.

Melinda warmed to his touch. "I do… but maybe they couldn't handle a Cummings' man. I know I have a hard time keeping up with mine."

"Oh *really*," Eric laughed playfully, as he wrapped his arms around Melinda, nibbling on her ear. "You have a *hard time*, do you? Hmm?"

Melinda giggled at his tickling touch.

"I think *hard* is the key word here," he added huskily while grabbing her hand and sliding it down to the bulge between his legs.

Melinda's breathing took on a more hurried pace. "Oh, Eric, you *know* what that does to me."

"I *know*…" he said, as he unbuttoned her blouse, caressing her breast until the nipple hardened with desire. "Glen will just have to wait an hour. Right now I have other things on my mind," he breathed heavily, as he engulfed her in the first of a series of many passionate hot kisses, stopping to nibble briefly on her ear again. "I *do know* what this does to you…"

The smell of garlic filled the air, as Eric entered the kitchen. Glen was removing the hearty Italian casserole from the oven, placing it on a hot plate. He had found the recipe in the never used, one cookbook that Eric owned, and he thought he could try his hand at making it. The ingredients, surprisingly, were all in the pantry and freezer for his use. Once in awhile, he had cooked while he was with Samantha because he wanted to give her kids a home-cooked meal, which she rarely made. To his surprise and those around him, he wasn't bad at doing so.

Glen's voice rose to a falsetto level. *"I slave away all day over a hot stove, and you can't even be home on time for me to serve it to you."*

Eric stopped, laughing and shaking his head in amusement. "Sorry, honey, but I had to work late."

"Yeah, yeah, yeah…excuses, excuses. That's all you do – give me excuses!"

Eric grabbed Glen in the familiar headlock of their youth, giving him a "Dutch Rub*"* to the top of his blonde locks. "I'm sorry. I'll do better the next time, baby."

"*You sure will,*" Glen teased in his best fake-sounding female voice, coming out of the hold and catching Eric in one of his own.

They ate the casserole and salad, still keeping the conversation as upbeat as possible.

"Didn't know you had it in you. You're damn unbelievable, Glen," Eric complimented, as he dished out a second helping. "I don't think I could be maintaining this well."

Glen looked up from his plate, his fork half way to his mouth, stopping in midair to look at his brother. "I'm *not* maintaining, Eric. I'm trying to stay busy to maintain my sanity. It is a problem," he breathed with a slow sigh, putting his fork back down on his plate. "I just didn't want to dump my problems on you as soon as you came through the door."

"You can't let this thing get to you like this, you know."

"It already has, Eric," Glen replied sadly.

"I know…I know," Eric added in a frustrated tone, as he finished off his last bite of salad. "But Ellen wants you out of her life, and after some time you gotta accept that tough reality. Life *does* go on."

"And where do emotions and feelings come in to your cut and dry philosophy?" Glen bit out, offended by his brother's lack of sensitivity.

Eric put down his fork and pushed the plate away from him, while crossing his arms on the table in front of him. He leaned forward towards Glen to make his point. "Survival bro – survival is the name of the game. This chic dumped you on hearsay, and that's bullshit in my book!"

Glen looked squarely into Eric's face, obviously angered by his callous remarks. "She's *not* some random chic, Eric. She's a beautiful woman that I am still very much in love with. I thought I was going to marry her just a couple of days ago, for gosh sakes," Glen responded while running his fingers through his hair.

"I know…" Eric answered sympathetically, just staring at his brother with genuine concern. "But as I said before, life goes on, always changing and with no certainties. Just look at my life, and everything that has happened to me."

"I get it, Eric. I know you are trying to help me, but I think in your case, as much as I hate to say this, you have brought on unnecessary problems with your relationships. I may be feeling sorry for myself, but I don't deserve any of this because I am loyal to one woman at a time!"

“Ok…I guess I deserve that,” Eric conceded knowing his past behavior with women was less than stellar. “But that is the whole point of what I am trying to tell you. Life is uncertain. Just when you think things are perfect, and you got it all figured out, something or someone comes along to take the wind out of your sails. And unfortunately, bro, it happens to assholes like me, along with good guys like you too.”

“So what are you trying to say – that I should never become vulnerable to my feelings? Never fall in love, and keep a wall around myself?”

Eric sighed, seeing the apparent pain in his sibling’s face. “Yeah, that seems to be the logical answer, but we both know it doesn’t work that way. So grieve. Do what you have to do, but get over her and move on. I’ll be here for you. You got my word on that.”

Glen shuttered and shook his head in frustration, turning to stare out the window with a distant look on his face. “Thanks, Eric, but I’m not giving up on her. Not yet, anyways. I still believe in fate, love, and good things happening for me…for us…Ellen and I. I just have a feeling about all this…”

Chapter Forty-Two

Ellen slept peacefully through the night, but unfortunately woke in the morning to the same intense nausea of the day previous. She barely made it to the toilet, with the seat still in the lifted position.

"*What's wrong with me?*" she moaned weakly, as she hung her head over the porcelain bowl, glaring down at the bright yellow bile again.

"*Maybe a shower will help me get my wits*," she breathed, as she pulled herself up to a standing position, feeling suddenly ready to topple over from the light-headedness that was plaguing her. "*Motherrr...*" she called out, half in panic, bracing herself against the sink.

Marie heard her cry, as she set a plate of bacon and eggs in front of her husband, Howard Meadows. "Oh my…it's Ellen again," she said with a look of concern on her face. "She still must be feeling badly."

"Hurry and go see if she is ok," Howard urged as he took a bite of toast.

Marie found Ellen leaning over the bathroom sink, crying a steady stream of tears. "Are you all right, dear?" she asked, as she assisted Ellen back to the bed, gently helping her to sit down.

“No, mother, I’m not feeling well. Actually, I feel terrible. This flu has me so drained and sick.”

Marie sat on the bed next to her daughter, wrapping her arm around Ellen’s waist, pushing the hair off of Ellen’s face. “You will feel better as soon as the doctor can figure out what is wrong with you,” she reassured. “So why don’t you get a shower, and then get dressed. Your appointment is in an hour and a half.”

“I don’t know if I even have the strength to do that,” Ellen answered in a frail voice.

“You poor dear,” Marie consoled, as she hugged her daughter. “I could help, if you would like.”

“Thanks, but I’ll manage,” she smiled weakly, trying hard to conceal how she was feeling.

Marie got up from the bed, giving Ellen a tender and caring look. “Please call if you need me. I’ll be in the kitchen with your father.”

Marie drove Ellen across town to Dr. Fairchild’s office. Just the ride made Ellen nauseous again.

“How long until we are there, mother?” Ellen asked in a frustrated tone, much like a child’s. She braced her head up with a palm on the car door’s window ledge, just looking out as the scenery sped by.

“Five minutes, dear. We will be on Church Street before you know it.”

“I’m sorry, mother. I don’t mean to snap at you, but I’m just feeling so badly.” Ellen looked at her mother, ready to cry again.

"This whole situation with Glen, and now the flu. It's more that I should have to deal with! I can't even grieve properly!"

Marie sighed, not knowing what to say. "We're here," she announced with relief, pulling the car into the medical center's parking garage.

Dr. Fairchild's office was sunny and bright, with skylights overhead and tropical plants grouped strategically around the room. The aqua-swirl wall covering and wall art, hinted of a tropical-ocean paradise somewhere. The cushioned, rattan furniture added to the whole motif, with vivid shades of plum, lime green, fuchsia, teal and yellow. Even with such pleasant surroundings, it did not brighten Ellen's mood.

"May I help you?" the receptionist asked, with a pleasant smile as equally bright as the room's décor.

"This is my daughter, Ellen Harper," Marie informed, still attempting to steady Ellen at the window. "She has an appointment at ten o'clock with Dr. Fairchild."

"Yes, I see her name on the schedule. Here are some forms to be filled out. Have a seat, and we'll be with you shortly," she directed. "You seem ill. Do you need an emesis basin?" the receptionist asked with concern.

"I'll be fine," Ellen answered, barely above a whisper, as she made her way to a seat. The papers were routine in nature – name, address, date of birth, any known diseases or illnesses, and of course insurance information. Ellen hesitated, searching her memory for the date of her last period. *When was it?* She thought, unable to remember. She looked at her cellphone calendar counting back the days.

"Everything ok?" Marie asked, taking note of Ellen's preoccupation with her phone.

Ellen mustered a smile. "Everything is fine, mother. I just need to figure something out for this form."

"I see," Marie answered without question, dismissing what she was doing as insignificant. She returned to her magazine article that she was absorbed in.

Two months ago…has it really been that long? Ellen questioned silently. *It can't be. We used protection*, she pondered. B*ut what if I am? That would explain the nausea.* "Oh my God, no!" Ellen said loudly, with disbelief at the possibility registering all over her face.

"What is it dear? Do you need a nurse?"

"It's nothing mother," Ellen replied softly, turning her head away, trying to regain her composure.

Marie did not press her, especially since they were in a room filled with other people who were becoming curious now to Ellen's outburst.

Ellen sat quietly by her mother's side with tears beginning to spill from her eyes, which she did her best to hide and control. *This should be a happy occasion, and not one of dread*, she thought ruefully.

A missed period had occurred before, but it had been a few years prior. So she still held a ray of hope that it was nothing more than stress, as had been the case when Jack died. After all, she had been overwhelmed with the farm and the farm hands that were never staying for any length of time as of late. Add the traumatic experience with Glen, and that would certainly constitute being stressful enough to change her monthly cycle. The thought of being pregnant and unmarried was making her anxious and her heart was racing.

Dr. Fairchild's nurse finally called Ellen after a thirty-minute wait.

Marie smiled at Ellen, patting her hand as she got up to go with the nurse. "I'll be here waiting, dear," she reassured, as Ellen looked at her mother with concern.

"Not feeling well today, hmmm?" the nurse asked, as she walked Ellen to the examining room.

"No, I'm not," Ellen irritably replied, keenly aware of the woman's lack of sensitivity to her plight.

"Dr. Fairchild will see you shortly. Take off all your clothes and put on this gown," she ordered.

Ellen obeyed, sitting on the edge of the cold examining table, barely able to sit up.

"Hello, Ellen. It's been quite awhile since I have seen you last," Dr. Fairchild greeted, extending a hand in Ellen's direction.

"Yes, it has been awhile," she answered cordially shaking his hand in return. "You do remember I moved away from Denver, I hope. Otherwise, I would still be coming here on a regular basis."

Dr. Fairchild's friendly older face smiled warmly at her. "I remember, Ellen. I may see many patients in a day, but I would never forget you. Your parents keep me updated on the family when we see them for our monthly dinners. You should know that."

"Yes, mother has mentioned that to me, Dr. Fairchild. Forgive me…I'm just feeling rough today, and not thinking straight."

"I can see that," he observed, as he looked over and reviewed the form that Ellen had filled out.

The stern military-like nurse followed into the room right behind Dr. Fairchild. She made her way to the counter, readying the instruments that would examine Ellen. She donned a pair of surgical gloves, and waited impatiently to get the procedure over with.

"How long have you been nauseated?" he asked.

"Since yesterday. Mother thinks it may be the flu."

"Maybe…" Dr. Fairchild responded, continuing to study the information she provided. "Your period, Ellen… two months ago?" he questioned astutely, looking up over his reading glasses waiting for her answer.

"Yes…" she admitted, casting her glance downward, feeling embarrassed.

"Do you think you could be pregnant?" Dr. Fairchild asked.

The words hit Ellen like a ton of bricks. Thinking and considering that, and actually hearing someone else say those words aloud, were two different things.

"I don't know…" she confessed meekly. "I guess it is possible. I have had an on-going relationship with a man, and we did use protection," she interjected in defense, feeling the need to justify her condition especially in front of the nurse who was staring her down.

Dr. Fairchild looked at Ellen in concern. "If you are pregnant, is this a problem?"

Is this a problem? Is this a problem? You better damn well believe this is a problem! Her mind silently screamed out. "No problem…" she conceded. "It's just a shock, since I didn't plan on being pregnant right now in my life."

Dr. Fairchild examined Ellen from head to toe, also giving her a complete internal exam. "I'll be back in a few minutes," he expressed. "The nurse will want a urine sample, and then we will talk."

Ellen re-dressed and waited anxiously for Dr. Fairchild. Her stomach somersaulted between nausea and nervous anticipation. It seemed like hours before he reappeared even though it was only several minutes.

"Have you figured anything out yet? Is it the flu?" Ellen asked with impatience.

Dr. Fairchild looked at his nurse for enlightenment. She confirmed what he already suspected – nodding her head yes, and then looking towards the floor, shuffling her feet awkwardly.

"You're definitely pregnant, Ellen. It's not the flu, just morning sickness; and in your case, as well as many other expectant women, it is lasting all day."

"*I really am pregnant?*" she asked in disbelief, finding it hard to even say the words.

"Yes, you are Ellen."

"I can't go on nine months feeling this way," she moaned. "I can barely get out of bed, and I don't even want to eat."

"More than likely, in a month or two, the nausea will settle down. I could give you something, but it really isn't the best thing for the baby. The less mediation you take when you are pregnant the better."

"Not eating can't be good for the baby either."

"As of now, that's not a problem. Eat when you are least nauseated. Saltines and cola may be the diet of choice for a few days if you cannot keep anything else down. You can add more food when you feel you can handle it. My nurse will go over a few things with you concerning prenatal vitamins and blood work."

"Alright…"she replied hesitantly, feeling totally overwhelmed and not fully grasping the reality of his words. First, the situation with Glen, and now this too! It was more than she could deal with and absorb in such a short period. *The baby…*Ellen thought. *The baby…I am pregnant…Oh my God…. I am pregnant with Glen's baby!"*

"If you have any concerns feel free to call me, and if not, I will see you back at your next scheduled appointment," Dr. Fairchild said matter-of-factly, shaking her back to reality.

Ellen was left alone in the room with her thoughts as she sat on the chair, numb with disbelief at what fate was throwing her way. Her whole life had changed drastically again within a few short months. Now, she was going to be a mother and a single parent. For a fleeting moment, the thought of an abortion or even giving the baby up for adoption crossed her mind. But, that was all it was – a brief fleeting moment of irrational thought. She could not give up the baby that she and Glen had created. A baby conceived in love…well at least on her part. She was already feeling the beginning twangs of attachment to the growing fetus deep inside of her, even in the few minutes that she knew of her baby's existence. It would take conscious effort to accept the newest hand life was dealing her, but she would. She had always wanted a child anyways, but definitely under different circumstances, with a loving relationship and where marriage was involved. Things could not be changed now, so she would try to be the best mother she could be even though it meant doing it alone.

Marie was still in the waiting room, flipping casually through her 3rd magazine when Ellen walked back into the room. She could see worry etched all over her daughter's face and it concerned her. Ellen motioned to Marie that she would be with her in a minute as she tried to get up and join her. She scheduled her next appointment, and requested that all her bills and correspondence be sent to her parents' address. She turned back to join her mother after all the necessary things were done. "I'm ready, mother. We can go now."

"What is it dear? Did Dr. Fairchild figure out what is making you so ill?"

"I think it is better if we discuss this in the car," she whispered.

"Of course. Anything you say," Marie answered in confusion, noticing Ellen's apparent uneasiness. She grabbed her purse and placed her magazine back on the pile, opening the door so that they could exit the office building.

"I didn't mean to put you on the spot in there, dear. I'm just concerned."

"I know you are, mother," Ellen answered, grabbing Marie's arm as they made their way back to the Cadillac. Halfway to the car, Ellen stopped dead in her tracks, and turned to face Marie.

"I'm pregnant, mother. I'm pregnant with Glen's baby!"

Chapter Forty-Three

Everyday Glen drove to the farm and put in several hours of work. He would arrive at six-forty five, coming directly from his other job at the Quik Shopper. Megan kept her distance as much as possible, but Mike would wave if they encountered each other. By noon, he would be completing his work for the day, gathering up all the old produce to take to the homeless shelter, before he departed. He was dependable, always dropping off his bags or boxes of produce on his way back to Eric's. By one o'clock, he made it home to shower and have something to eat. By two-thirty, he would be asleep and then up again at nine-thirty to start his night-shift job. Rarely, would he run into Eric. Most of Eric's after work hours were being spent at Melinda's anymore. It was rare if he even slept at home these days.

Glen had to be at the Quik Shopper by ten in the evening, and he basically ran the operation except for one helper. The shift didn't end until six-thirty the next morning with most evenings dragging on forever. It was a job, nothing more. It paid for his car and was a distraction that kept his mind busy from thinking about Ellen constantly. The arrangement was working, although Megan felt twangs of guilt for not paying him.

For the most part they avoided each other, and Glen did his thing and Mike and Megan did theirs. Only was the unspoken rule broken, when it was time to get the old produce together for the daily run to the homeless shelter. Glen tried his best to be cordial, but it usually had no impact on Megan to do the same. She only endured that time of conversation with him during the day because it was one less job she had to take on. The produce stand and its patrons kept Megan busy enough, not allowing much time for small talk even if she desired it.

"Any word on Ellen?" Glen asked, as he had done everyday since she was gone.

"Not a thing," Megan replied, as she always did.

"It has been a month. Aren't you concerned, because I sure as hell am!" he added as he packed up a box of corn.

Megan stopped packing up a box of tomatoes, placing her hands on her hips. "For your information, of course I'm concerned, but apparently Ellen isn't ready to talk to anyone just yet."

Glen paused, turning to stare at the spunky hot-tempered female. "That's one way to look at it. But maybe a phone call from her *best friend* would be welcome, even though she may not think so until after she actually hears her voice."

"I think that is quite enough, Glen. I *know* my friend, and she will call me when she is good and ready. So stop trying to convince me to do something I know I shouldn't."

"Ok, then let's change the subject. What about work? Are you going to go back to work?" he pressed on, not ready to give up yet as he had done so many times with her before.

"Why all the questions today, Glen? Let's get this stuff loaded before a customer comes," she answered irritably.

"Alright," Glen conceded once again in defeat, knowing it was impossible to break through the rough exterior of the woman, and get the answers he sought.

The Bronco was loaded, and with the job completed Megan walked away as usual. To Glen's surprise, she turned back around and called him by name. "Oh, Glen?"

"Yes, Megan."

"Not that it is any of your business, but I do plan to go back to work as soon as the produce stand closes for the season."

Glen shook his head and smiled. The woman was incorrigible, but for some reason he still liked her. He knew the sacrifices she was making for Ellen. Loyal and strong – a stable friend - even if her intentions were misdirected towards him. She was true to Ellen, as she should be.

Megan closed up the stand for another day, and headed up to the house. She had spare ribs and sauerkraut baking in the oven. All that was necessary for her to do was to peel and mash some potatoes, and make a salad. That would be dinner for the evening. Megan had to admit to herself, as she sliced up a potato and dropped it in the pot of cold water, that staying home and being domesticated was growing on her. Never did she think that this would be something she would actually admit to liking.

Mike arrived at the farm on time, as usual. "Ummm… what is that wonderful smell?" he questioned, grabbing Megan from behind with a kiss to the neck.

"You're favorite, silly," she giggled, turning to greet her husband with a kiss on the lips.

"You're my favorite," he grinned, having more than food on

his mind.

"Me and sauerkraut, right?"

"You know me too well, Megan."

"As long as it is only sauerkraut that I share your love with, I don't mind in the least," she teased.

The phone rang, just as Mike reached down for another kiss. "Who can that be?" he groaned.

"Probably work again. You would think the place could function without everyone having to call me at least once a day, with a brainless question," Megan whined as she picked up the house phone. "Hello…"

"Meg…Hi!"

"Ellen?" she asked in surprise, looking with raised eyebrows at Mike.

"Yes it's me!"

"God, El…I can't believe it is actually you. To tell you the truth, we have been really concerned about you since you haven't called," she informed her.

"I told you I would call when I was ready to do so."

"I know that, but in the state that you had left us, we couldn't help but worry."

Megan sat down at the table, ready for a long conversation.

"So how are things at the farm?" Ellen asked.

"Everything is fine, but what about you? That's the more important question."

"I'm ok. The first month wasn't easy, but I am doing much better now."

"That's good. I guess being with your parents has helped, right?"

"Yeah, it has. They have been great. Meg look, there's no sense in delaying this. I called to tell you something important."

"What's that, El?" she asked with a pleasant smile for Mike's eyes, so happy that she finally was able to speak to her best friend again.

"I'm pregnant."

Megan's mouth dropped open in shock, and Mike looked at her in concern. *"You're what?"*

"I'm pregnant, Megan, with Glen's baby. As far as I know, I am three and a half months along. I was so nauseated for a month that I just wanted to die; but now it has calmed down considerably, and I only have to deal with it a couple of hours in the morning. I lost almost ten pounds from barely eating."

"You poor thing," Megan consoled.

"It's ok now. I'm hungry most of the time except in the mornings, and I am making up for lost time. I've already gained five pounds back. The doctor says the baby is fine."

"Ellen, I can't believe this! But …I guess this is a good thing, right, since you have always wanted children?"

"I wish the circumstances were different - that I was married and pregnant, instead of unmarried and pregnant; but I have accepted it."

Mike continued to stare at Megan in total confusion.

"You are pregnant… who would have thought?"

Mike's mouth dropped open, as Megan shook her head up and down at him in acknowledgement.

"How is the farm?" Ellen asked again.

"It's functioning. The produce stand is open for business everyday, but Sundays. And the garden and livestock are being kept up with."

"How are you doing all that, and working besides?" Ellen inquired considering that possibility to be exceptional, if she were handling such a full load even with Mike's help.

"I'm not working right now at CWS. I decided to take off until the produce stand closes for the season."

"Megan…I am so sorry to put you in this situation. I never thought you would take off from work."

"Don't worry about it. I'm actually enjoying the break. Staying at home isn't half bad," she admitted with a chuckle.

"Did you hire someone to help out?" Ellen continued with concern and yet guilt with leaving her with so much responsibility.

"Yes and no," Megan replied with hesitancy.

"Yes and no? What does that mean?"

"I'm not sure you want to know, El," she said, while looking at Mike for support.

"Meg, I wouldn't have asked if I didn't want to know. Please tell me what's going on," she said in frustration.

"Alright. It's Glen who is helping. He insisted, practically begging me, until I said yes. Don't worry though, he is working for free."

"*He is?*" Ellen questioned in surprise. "But how can he afford that? I know he has to pay Eric back for the Bronco."

"He seems to be doing ok, although he puts in long hours. I know he has another job working at the Quik Shopper. He works the night shift there, and then comes straight here when he gets off at six-thirty. He gets right to his work and continues until noon. Then he leaves here with the old produce, and I know he stops at the shelter everyday before he goes home. He sleeps in the afternoon El, to make this thing work. Weekends, he is here even longer. The guy is determined. I must give him that."

Ellen's heart ached with the thought of Glen trying to hold down two jobs. *And what was his motivation, if not for pay?* She pondered.

"Does he ask about me?" she questioned timidly.

"Does he ask about you? Every day. I tell him the same thing everyday – that I haven't heard from you."

"Do you plan to ever tell him about the pregnancy?"

"No! And neither must you! Promise me that, Megan," Ellen exclaimed with urgency, as she shifted restlessly on the chair beneath her.

"Calm down, Ellen. Of course I won't tell him that! Those words should come from *your* mouth."

"Not now," she said with quiet reserve. "His involvement with someone else would only complicate things too much."

"She's gone, Ellen.... Gone the day after you left. Glen swears none of it is true. He told me to tell you that."

Megan wanted to kick herself for attempting to defend him, but something deep inside of her was beginning to think that maybe Glen was an innocent victim in all this. And she didn't even have to ask – she knew what Mike was feeling. He liked Glen from the beginning, but was growing even closer to him as they worked together on the weekends at the farm.

"Maybe she's gone, but what about their children? And what about his marriage he has with her?"

"And what if that is all a lie, El?" she continued, knowing she was pressing her luck to continue as she was.

"The girl asked for her daddy that day at the farm."

"That *still* doesn't really prove anything. She may have told her to say that, or some kids just grow up close to a live-in; and they just think of them as mom or dad, even if it isn't their real parent."

"They've had a life together. We know that Megan, for a fact."

"And so did you. And now you are carrying Glen's child. I love you Ellen, and I would never intentionally say or do anything to hurt you, but maybe you need to check this out more carefully before you close that chapter of your life."

"I'll think about things," Ellen promised as an excuse, just wanting to end the conversation about Glen.

Opening that wound back up was way too painful to even consider, especially if the conclusion ended up being the same. There was no sense in chasing after a false sense of hope or a dead dream.

“Maybe you should pay Glen. Matter of fact, pay him for all the weeks he has worked up until this point.”

“If that is what he wants, I’ll offer it to him tomorrow.”

“And by the way, keep the rest of the money for yourselves.”

“No, Ellen, we could never do that. Besides, you will need the money for the new baby now.”

“I’m fine. My parents are insisting that they help me out financially. I refused their offer initially, saying it was my responsibility; but my mother convinced me that my dad was very hurt by my decision. I sat down and explained my feelings to him, but he pointed out that he would have made the same offer even if I were married since this was their first grandchild, and they could afford to help me. I finally agreed, knowing it was making my mother and him happy.”

“That’s great, El. So when do you think you will be coming home?”

“I don’t know, Megan,” she said hesitantly. “I’m considering selling the farm. What life do I have there now? At least in Denver, I have my parents here with me.”

Megan looked at Mike and patted the top of his hand, shaking her head in disbelief. “You know we are here for you too, Ellen…and so is Cuddles. He misses you…and so do we.”

“And I miss all of you. Please give Cuddles a big hug for me. I can’t make any decisions about anything else right now. I just need some more time to sort things out.”

“Well please think about Glen, and what I said,” Megan added gently. “We could very easily discover the absolute certainty of the truth with a few phone calls.”

“I *will* think about things. And Megan, I don’t know how to thank you and Mike enough for keeping the farm running. I never expected all this.”

“You have Glen to thank for that. He’s the one that has showed us the ropes. Take care, honey, and we love you.”

“I love you too.”

“Please try to call us soon again. We worry about you.”

“I will. Mother has dinner on the table, so I should go.”

“Alright. Bye for now.”

“Bye.”

Megan put the phone down, and looked at Mike in astonishment. “Wow, can you believe this?”

“No, I can’t - especially the part about Glen. You know, he has a right to know about his kid.”

“Mike,” Megan warned, with a glare in her eyes. *“Don’t you dare tell him anything!* I made Ellen a promise, even though I’m not sure I agree with it; and I won’t go back on my word with her!”

“I wouldn’t say anything to him, you should know me better than that.”

“I do know you, Mike,” she agreed, wrapping her arms around his waist. “You are tempted to tell him though, aren’t you?”

“That’s not the point,” he grinned.

"I think *that* is the point!"

Chapter Forty-Four

Not only did Glen miss Ellen, but he also missed the delicious dinners that they shared together in the evening, after a hard day's work at the farm. All that he had the time or desire to make and eat anymore were things of simple preparation. He consumed a lot of bacon and eggs and microwave dinners.

"Shit, I burned the toast again!" he irritably complained, as he reached for a knife to scrape the charred surface off of the bread into the sink.

"What's up, bro?" Eric called from the front door.

"I can't believe you're home. It's been a week since I've seen you last."

Eric laughed. "I come home. Just usually after you leave for work, that's all."

"So Melinda likes having you around, hmm?" he asked with a wink.

"Yeah, I guess she does," he admitted. "Melinda and I are getting along *very* well."

"How about you? Are you finally over Ellen?" he asked, propping his hip on the edge of the kitchen table.

"Never…Eric…never. I miss her now more than ever."

"Still no word?"

"None. I ask Megan everyday if she's heard from her, but she claims she hasn't. I have to wonder though," he said, giving up on the scraping and throwing the toast in the trashcan instead.

"Where do you think she could have gone?" Eric asked, while grabbing a beer out of the refrigerator and taking a seat at the table.

"Who knows? I guess a friend or relative's house somewhere. I know her parent live in Denver, and her brother and sister are down in Florida and Texas. I just wish I had one damn chance to sit down with her, and explain my side of this. Just one damn chance…" Glen said quietly, as he popped another piece of toast in the toaster. "Then if she still doesn't see reason, I could finally move on with my life."

"Maybe that day will come bro, sooner than you think."

"I hope so. I really do."

Eric didn't like the effect Ellen was having on his brother. If Glen couldn't get answers, he would! One way or another, Glen deserved happiness in life. It was time for Eric to make sure things moved in a positive direction for his brother, and that time was now!

It has been quite a while since Eric had been out to the farm. The timing had to be perfect – after Glen left for the day, but before Mike arrived home.

Everything looks the same, he observed, pulling in several feet in front of the produce stand. He could see Megan from a distance. She tilted her head in curiosity, wondering who was in the car, realizing it was not one of her regular customers that were easily recognizable.

"Oh my God, it's Eric Cummings!" she said aloud, as she watched the handsome, trim-built man that was dressed in a pin-stripped suit approach her with his typical swagger.

"Hi Megan. Miss you at work," he said all too enthusiastically, with a broad grin that he was famous for.

"I'm not sure I can say the same. Life out here is pretty relaxing."

She crossed her arms in a defensive posture looking at Eric in a guarded manner. "What brings you out this way? If you're looking for Glen, he's already gone for the day."

"I'm not here to see Glen," he smiled, trying to lure her in. "I'm here to talk to you."

"Oh…? What about?" Megan asked, while she relaxed her stance, and busied herself with needless straightening of the already straightened vegetable bins. "Is there a problem at work?"

"No, Megan. Everything is fine at work. It's about Glen and Ellen."

She stopped what she was doing to stare at Eric with a dead-faced glare. "I really don't have anything to say to you about that subject. Furthermore, if Glen sent you out here to work me over, save your breath. It won't work," she said dryly resuming her straightening duties.

Eric chuckled, finding her a worthy opponent. "That spunk of yours is why you are at the top at CWS. But, it doesn't always appeal in non-work related situations, you know."

"I really don't give a damn, Eric, what you think of me! I do my job when I'm at the office. Anything outside of CWS is really none of your business. I don't have to answer to you or impress anyone on my own time. And even though I really shouldn't have to defend my honor to you, I think I do all right in the friend department – thank you – with this so-called *spunk.*"

Megan turned to face him with her hands placed again on her hips, taking a defensive stance once more. "So if you are here for no other reason than this, then this conversation is done. I really need to get back to work. Customers will probably be coming at any moment."

Eric chuckled, shaking his head, amazed at her determined spirit to cast him aside. Merriment continued to dance in his eyes as he considered what he should do next. "I understand, and I won't hold you up." Eric turned to walk towards his car, but turned back as an afterthought. "Megan, I hope to see you back at work soon. The place isn't the same without you."

"Well thanks, Eric," she replied, taken back by his compliment, but equally surprised that he gave up so easily.

He walked away, leaving Megan to stare at his back. She grinned to herself in satisfaction, realizing she had dissuaded the great Eric Cummings so easily. His business reputation of being diligent to the end was becoming "*legend-like*" around the office at CWS. He never gave up until he got what he was after. *Maybe that's because he hasn't had to deal with someone like me,* Megan thought smugly, as she watched him put his hand on the car door handle, ready to open the door. And then he changed his mind, turning back around, and walking towards Megan again.

"I hate to ask this of you, but could I possibly use your bathroom? I have a little touch of something and I need to drive all the way to Lincoln on business, and once on the road I hate to stop."

"*Oh*...well sure, Eric..." Megan replied, feeling caught off-guard by his unexpected request.

Megan was ready to walk with him up to the house when a customer arrived. "Can you wait a minute?" she asked anxiously.

"*I really can't*," he replied with as much emphasis as possible, clutching his stomach low as if in pain.

"Alright...alright, go in the house," she consented reluctantly. "Second door on the left, down the hall."

"Yeah, I remember," he answered, still acting as if he was in misery.

Megan felt a wave of uneasiness at her decision, but erased it just as quickly once a customer approached, preoccupying her with the large order that she needed.

"Thanks, Megan," Eric yelled, waving as he jogged up to the farmhouse, still bending low and clutching his stomach for effect.

"You're welcome, but just don't leave the cat out," she barked, as he was almost beyond ear range, still keeping a suspicious eye on him until he went into the house.

The house was just the same as he had remembered it, during happier times when Jack and Ellen had him over to visit.

"Damn, where could it be?" he said in frustration, as he looked through a coffee table drawer in the living room. "Maybe the kitchen," he decided, having no luck in the other room. He sifted through a pile of papers that were lying on the counter, but with no luck.

Eric peaked out the window, eyeing the produce stand. Megan was still busy helping her patron. *Thank God*, he thought, turning and spotting a desk across the silent room. He opened every drawer, still unable to find a clue to Ellen's whereabouts. "*Now what?*" he uttered in defeat, taking a seat at the desk. He breathed a ragged sigh, not wanting to accept the undeniable; that he could not find what he was looking for. "*Oh well, I tried, bro*," he confessed as he stood up to leave.

Eric swatted a fly away that was buzzing around his head, and traced it to a shelf of cookbooks where it had landed. A piece of yellow paper was folded between the pages of a cookbook on barbequing, with an inch of it exposed to his view. He was drawn to the book, not even sure as to why, but he took it down and opened it. Thumbing nonchalantly through the pages, assuming it to be a recipe or page marker, he became pleasantly surprised realizing he found his needle in the haystack. "*Jackpot!*" he yelled with a triumphant grin. "So you are in Denver with mommy and daddy, huh?" he mimicked sarcastically, with smug satisfaction etched all over his handsome face at his findings.

Eric grabbed a piece of paper off of the desk, and scribbled down the address and unlisted phone number of Howard and Marie Meadows. He reinserted the yellow piece of paper carefully back into the cookbook to the exact page, and placed it back on the shelf just as he had found it. "*She'll never know*," he grinned, stuffing the address into his pant's pocket.

He walked back up the lane, whistling a happy tune as he waved, not stopping to wait for a response from Megan. "See ya, Meg," he yelled with an all-too-happy smile, making his way to the Mustang. "Thanks for the use of the bathroom. *I'm feeling much better now.*"

Megan stopped and stared, mid-sentence. "*Eric Cummings is up to something.... I just know it!*"

Chapter Forty-Five

Rain had been falling all day in a steady pace over Denver. A pretty blonde stewardess stopped repeatedly to talk with Eric on the plane. She asked him if he needed anything else, to the point of obviousness that she was infatuated with him. Even a man sitting across the isle from him was ignored when he asked for a refill on coffee. She slipped Eric her phone number as he walked from the plane.

"Call me sometime," she whispered.

"I would love to, doll, if the circumstances were different. But I'm very much involved with someone, and I want it to stay that way," he confessed with a wink and his million-dollar smile.

She blushed, feeling giddy at the charisma he just dripped with. "Can't blame a girl for trying. Call me, if and when your circumstances change."

"You'll be the first person I think of," he promised with another wink, leaving her to stand and stare at his retreating form. He walked into the terminal and threw away the crumbled paper with her number scribbled on it. He had no intention of calling her, or doing anything else to screw things up with Melinda this time. It would only be his luck that Melinda would find something like that in his jacket pocket one day, and that would definitely be the final end to their relationship. She had warned him that she didn't want to share, and he knew she meant it. He did not tell anyone where he was going except for Melinda, and of course she wished him good luck.

A note lay on the kitchen counter for Glen.

Away on business. I'll see you some time tomorrow.

It was six o'clock and all ends were covered, as far as Eric was concerned. He would buy a sandwich at the airport, and grab a cab. He considered a rental car, but decided against it. Once the cabby dropped him off, it would be harder for them to get rid of him.

Marie had just placed a hardy dinner of meatloaf, mashed potatoes, and lima beans on the table. She was happy to see Ellen's appetite back. It had greatly concerned her that the pregnancy could possibly not go to term, if Ellen didn't begin to eat more than when she first arrived. Fortunately though, the last few weeks had brought about a change in her daughter. Ellen's appetite had returned, and was growing right along with her abdomen. The clothes she wore were getting tighter around the waistline. Within a couple more weeks, they would have to go maternity clothes shopping.

"Marie, I hear the doorbell," Howard announced, between bites of food.

"I wonder who that could be? Maybe the paperboy collecting," Marie replied, dabbling the corners of her mouth with a napkin.

She opened the door to the unfamiliar and yet handsome face that was smiling down at her. *A salesman…* she thought.

"Hello, ma'am. Is Ellen here?" Eric asked.

"Do you know Ellen?" she asked protectively, thinking that maybe it was Glen.

"Yes, I do. Could I please talk to her?"

"I'll be back in a moment," she said, closing the door quietly and then locking it behind her, hoping she wasn't jumping to the wrong conclusion.

"Ellen," Marie said with a whisper. "There is a handsome gentleman at the front door, asking for you. He claims he knows you."

"What does he look like?" she asked in an alarmed startled voice, laying her fork down and taking the napkin from her lap.

"He's tall and fit, with dark brown eyes and a nice smile."

"Not Glen…" Ellen replied, breathing a sigh of relief. "Maybe it's an old friend that heard I'm in town. Did you tell anyone I'm here, mother?"

Marie felt suddenly on the spot and guilty as charged. "Just a couple of my friends at bridge club, dear. Who would they tell anyways?"

"Nancy may have told Stephanie, and that's all it takes for my old group from high school to know I'm back in town."

Howard interrupted. "Instead of upsetting your mother with this line of questioning, why don't you just get up and see who is at the door, Ellen."

"I'm sorry, mother. I'm just not ready for company yet."

"Well maybe it time, Ellen. You need to get on with your life. It's been almost two months since you have been here. You can't lock yourself away in that room of yours forever. Now go see who is at the door," her father urged, as he finished his last bit of meatloaf. "And if you need us – call. We'll be right here."

Ellen made her way to the front door, not sure if she had the emotional strength to face the mystery person on the other side of it. Her baggy sweatshirt took care of the problem of concealing her expanding midriff. She smoothed her hair back in place, took a deep breath, and swung the door wide open.

"Hi, Ellen. *Surprise…*" Eric greeted good-naturedly, with his signature grin. I guess I'm the last person you ever thought you would see standing on your parents' doorstep, right?" he beamed.

Ellen's mouth dropped wide open in utter surprise. "*Whhaat…are you doing here?"*

"I'm here to talk with you. Isn't that obvious."

Ellen's face took on a ridged scowl of incredulity, and her eyes were pierced with bitterness and anger as the questions came out in rapid succession. "How did you figure out that I was here anyways? Did Glen put you up to this, or was it Megan?"

"Could I come in please?" he said with a much-too-pleasant smile. "Then I'll answer all of your questions, along with a few more besides."

"*You are kidding, right?"* she said with her eyes wide with disbelief. "You actually think I'm going to invite you into my parents' home, and then the two of us will sit down and have a nice friendly chat?"

"Yes..." he replied with a pausc. "That's exactly what I was hoping for especially since I am tired from the trip."

"That's your problem, Eric. Not mine. No one invited you here."

"Come on, Ellen. What can a few minutes of your time hurt?" he said with as much charisma as he could muster.

Ellen closed her eyes in frustration. The man was incorrigible – always had been, always would be. "Leave, Eric. Nothing you could say or do will change my mind about Glen."

Ellen turned to go back into the house.

"I *can't* leave, Ellen."

"What did you say?" she asked in a stunned voice, turning back around.

"I said, I can't leave. No car. Taxi brought me. Comprendi?"

Ellen crossed her arms, fuming in frustration. "Eric, you did this on purpose. As far as I'm concerned, you can walk back to the airport, and get on a plane to hell knows where. And forget you ever saw me. I don't want my location getting out!"

"Your secret is safe with me, doll face, as long as we can talk," Eric retorted, with all of his conceited self-assuredness showing.

"Goodbye, Eric," Ellen declared, slamming the door loudly in his face, making the foyer pictures rattle.

Eric chuckled, pushing the doorbell several times in

retaliation.

Ellen was steaming as she turned to open the door again. "Didn't you hear me? Go away, Eric!"

"What is going on?" Howard asked his daughter in confusion, with Marie standing right by his side. A look of bewilderment was etched on both of their faces.

"I want this person to leave, Mom and Dad. I don't wish to speak to him."

"But who is he?" Howard insisted in knowing, looking from Ellen and then to Eric.

"Eric Cummings, sir," Eric offered, extending his hand in Mr. Meadows' direction. He reluctantly accepted the handshake.

"What are you doing here, Eric?"

Eric smiled pleasantly at the man, guessing he had to be more reasonable than his daughter was. "I'm here to speak with your daughter. Glen is my brother, and there has been a bad misunderstanding. I'm here on his behalf to try and straighten things out."

"That's honorable, son, but why isn't your brother here taking care of his own business?"

Ellen clenched her teeth, feeling very childlike as she watched her dad handling her problems.

"Maybe because no one will tell him Ellen's whereabouts, even though he does ask Megan Delaney every day if she knows where he can reach her," Eric explained. "I, for one, am sick of seeing him in such a pitiful forlorn state. I decided enough is enough, so I took matters into my own hands and did a little snooping to get some answers. It really wasn't that hard to figure things out," he said with arrogant pride.

"*A pitiful forlorn state.* That's what Glen is in?" Ellen asked, feeling suddenly guilty with concern.

"*Yes, Ellen, he is quite miserable without you,*" Eric confessed sarcastically, turning to give her his full condescending attention. "And to be honest, I am sick of it! I figure that once the both of you lay out all of your cards on the table, and if you still feel the same way towards my brother, then fine. Hopefully at that point, he can resolve all these feelings of conflict and be able to get over you. Then he can get on with his life."

Mr. Cummings, you make my daughter out to be the villain here," Marie said defensively.

"No more than she has made my brother out to be something he is not."

Ellen glared at Eric bitterly. "*Your brother lied to me!*" she hissed. "He never told me about a wife and two children. Do you think it was fair of him to use me like that?" she blurted out in anger.

"Ellen, I think it would be a good idea to take this inside," Marie suggested softly. "We don't need for the neighbors to hear all this. You know how nosey they can be."

Eric's eyes gleamed with triumph, knowing victory was in his reach. "That's all I want," he said with calm self-assuredness. "A chance for Ellen to hear the Cummings' side of things."

Ellen saw the familiar triumphant look in his eyes. It reminded her anew of what poor Jack must have been subjected to every day at work when he was around him. "Eric, you know are problems go beyond this."

"I have no problem with you, Ellen, other than your constant habitual trait of jumping to the wrong conclusions."

"*How dare you!*" Ellen shot out, tears beginning to sting her eyes.

Howard intervened, sensing Ellen was on the brink-of-no-return, if a civilized discussion was going to continue.

"I think we all need to calm down. Ellen, show Eric to the living room," Howard directed. "And *wait* on us there. Your mother and I will be back in a few minutes, after we clear off the kitchen table."

Ellen flashed Eric a look of warning as she ushered him into the living room. She pointed to the most uncomfortable straight-back antique chair that was sitting alone in a distant corner of the room. "Sit there," she instructed, picking for herself an over-stuffed armchair that was in a cozy grouping by the sofa and coffee table.

Eric just shook his head and chuckled at her intentional rude defiance directed towards him. He ignored her totally and chose to sit on the couch instead. He crossed his legs and leaned back, balancing his out-stretched arms over the back of the sofa. She was fuming at their close proximity, as well as losing another battle to him. Eric smiled brazenly as he chided her.

"You never stop, do you? All this bitterness will make you old before your time, Ellen," he added with a mocking laugh.

Ellen gritted her teeth and exhaled loudly, not responding, only waiting for her parents to reappear.

Howard and Marie chose to sit on the couch by Eric, much to Ellen's displeasure. She shot her mother a look of irritation, but Marie just smiled back with a worried frown, trying to console her silently with her eyes.

"So Eric," Howard began. "May we ask what exactly is your present relationship with your brother?"

"We are roommates. He lives at my house with me. We're close, if that's what you are getting at. Usually at dinner, he tells me about his day, and the subject of Ellen always does seem to come up. I can tell you, he misses her a lot, and he is still very much in love with her."

Ellen's head came up in surprise, meeting Eric's eyes with her own, challenging the powerful words he spoke. "*Glen doesn't love me!* Stop telling my parents a bunch of lies!"

"If that is the case, why does he continue to work at your farm without pay, go to the homeless shelter every day, and still maintain the daily hope that you will contact him? *Why is that Ellen?* Can you explain that to me?" he emphasized much too crassly.

"I don't…. know," she answered softly, casting her eyes downward again towards her lap.

"I'll tell you why," he bit out with the anger he had been holding back. "It's because he loves you, and this whole thing is a lie – made up by a sick desperate woman, who thought for some crazy reason, that a stunt like she pulled would bring Glen back in her arms and life. But it didn't. Samantha Wallace is back in Fredericksburg, Virginia. Glen informed her in no uncertain terms, that he never wants to see her again. My mother called weeks ago to tell us the car was back at her house. Glen told her to put it up for sale. So there are no more connections at all between them."

"What about the children?" Ellen asked, in wide-eyed hurt, and yet anxious anticipation to his response.

Eric shook his head, confirming his answer. "Not his, Ellen. I'll get my mother on the phone right now to verify that. She wouldn't lie – I'll guarantee that! She'll tell you that Glen doesn't have any kids. I will say it one more time," he asserted with much emphasis, hitting one fist into the palm of his other hand trying to make his point known clearly, "He has *never* been married, and he *never* has been the father to any children anywhere!"

Ellen began to cry, bringing her hands up to her face. Marie walked over to her chair, bending down to wrap an arm around her daughter and console her. "Could this possibly all be a big mistake, dear?"

"Oh motherrr…. I don't know. What have I done?" she sobbed, looking up into her mother's caring eyes for solace.

"*Thank God*," Eric said aloud with a sigh of relief. "Call Glen up now, and straighten this whole mess out between the two of you."

"I can't…" she moaned. "He would never want me back now."

"Aren't you listening to me? He hopes everyday for you to come back to him," Eric insisted, as he rose from the chair throwing his arms up to the air in frustration.

"I don't know how things could ever be the same between us," she cried, walking across the room for a tissue. "The trust we had, has been brok…" Ellen explained, as she stopped mid-sentence, collapsing to the floor.

Chapter Forty-Six

"Oh my God!" Marie screamed, bringing her hands to her mouth in fright.

Eric and Howard were by Ellen's side, calling her name and patting her face to revive her.

"Call 911, Marie, and get a cool cloth," her husband instructed, as he looked at Eric with loathing. "Eric, you better say your prayers that your little speech didn't bring this about with Ellen. So help me God – if she is hurt in any way – you will pay!" he blurted out.

Ellen came to just as Marie returned. "What happened?" Ellen inquired groggily.

"You passed out, dear," Marie explained, while dabbing Ellen's forehead with the damp rag. "We were worried sick over you. The ambulance is on its way."

"An ambulance…? Oh, mother, I don't need an ambulance," she slurred, still with somewhat slow speech.

Marie looked at her husband and then at Eric, fixing her gaze on him. "You know this is all your fault, don't you? If you wouldn't have come here and upset my daughter this wouldn't have happened."

"I'm sorry, Mrs. Meadows. I truly didn't mean to upset Ellen.

Surely, you can't think I would wish this on her or anyone else for that matter," Eric said sincerely, never ceasing to be amazed that these negative occurrences always seemed to happen between him and Ellen.

"Now, Marie, we shouldn't be jumping to any conclusions until after the doctor examines Ellen. We may be accusing Eric falsely," Howard interjected level-headedly, feeling suddenly guilty for losing his temper.

"You three talk about me as if I were not even in the room," Ellen added wearily. "No one is to blame. It just happened," she resolved, leaving Eric off the hook with her parents.

The blare of the ambulance's siren could be even heard from the living room as the ambulance pulled into the driveway. Marie ran to let the paramedics in. "She's right in here," Marie informed, walking quickly to keep up with their pace. "She just came to a couple of minutes ago."

"What is her name?" the paramedic asked, carrying a medical bag in with him.

"Her name is Ellen, and she is my daughter."

"Hi Ellen, my name is Scott, and this is Kathy. How are you feeling?" he questioned, trying to put her at ease and yet evaluate her at the same time.

"I am feeling a lot better. I really don't need an ambulance, though. I just got a little dizzy," Ellen, replied, feeling embarrassed that everyone was overreacting.

Scott looked at the others in the room. "Did she definitely and completely pass out?"

Howard and Marie looked at each other in a puzzled way,

hesitating before answering. “We can’t say for certain, but we *think* that she passed out,” Marie answered.

Eric shook his head in agreement. “I saw someone pass out before. She definitely was out.”

“For how long?” Scott asked, turning his attention totally to Eric.

Ellen’s parents were surprised by Eric’s willingness to help, and they allowed him to continue without interruption.

“Maybe three minutes,” he answered, as Kathy unpacked the medical bag, ready to listen to Ellen’s heart and get her blood pressure.

“Has this ever happened before?” Scott continued, as Kathy recorded the results on her computer.

“No, it hasn’t, but I really am feeling better now,” she tried to reassure with a weak smile on her lips. Ellen attempted to sit up, but began to feel light-headed again, reaching out for her mother’s arm.

“We want her checked out at the hospital,” Howard insisted with alarm, springing up on his feet once more. “Here is the proof that she still is not well, even if Ellen doesn’t think so,” he said forcibly, while challenging Ellen to deny it.

“I agree, Ellen. You really should be taken to the hospital and thoroughly examined by a doctor,” Scott advised. “Kathy will stay with you while I go out to the ambulance to get a stretcher. The hospital will be better equipped than we are, to check you out completely. They may want to run some tests. If there isn’t a problem, then they will release you.”

Ellen looked at her mother with pleading eyes.

"It's best, dear. Please go," Marie requested in earnest. "We will follow in the car. You don't want *anything* to be wrong."

She hesitated, reading her mother's mind. "You're right. Take me to the hospital," she resigned, suddenly realizing the silent implications behind her mother's words. To be reminded of the unborn baby that was growing inside of her, was reason enough to change her mind.

Ellen was loaded safely into the ambulance and the rear doors were shut, ready to leave, and get on its was to the hospital. Howard and Marie were walking towards their car when Eric stopped them.

"If it is alright with the both of you, I would like to ride along to the hospital with you and make sure Ellen is doing ok before I leave Denver."

"What do you think, Howard?" Marie asked with a look of misgiving, seeking an answer from her husband.

"If I were in Eric's shoes, I would want to be assured myself that Ellen was going to be alright." He looked at Eric, addressing him with a vote of confidence that was unexpected. "After giving it further consideration, I realize, Eric, your intentions are honorable for coming here. Sure, you can ride with us," he added with a warm smile. "Get in."

"Thank you, sir. I was hoping someone would start seeing things my way," he added with a grin.

Eric climbed in the back seat, and rode with the Meadows' to the hospital. The thought would not leave him, as he stared out the window, that he should call Glen. He would wait on her diagnosis, and then decide. "Has Ellen been ill before today?" Eric asked, breaking the quiet tenseness of those in the vehicle.

Marie's eyes shifted quickly towards her husband, waiting for him to respond. "She was sick when she first got here, but she seemed much better these last few weeks."

"What was wrong with her?" Eric asked in concern.

"Nothing of any seriousness," Marie replied with a strained smile that was etched with superficiality, hoping Eric would stop the line of questioning he was so intent on discussing.

"You know Glen would want to be here if he knew Ellen was sick. I hope you aren't keeping something important from me."

Marie was starting to feel very uncomfortable. She was not inclined at stretching the truth to such a large degree; but she was resolved that the news of Ellen's pregnancy wouldn't be coming from them. She knew those words should come form Ellen and no one else.

They pulled into the hospital's emergency parking area, and walked at a hurried pace to the expansive building that loomed in front of them.

"I suggest that you address Ellen with your concerns about her health, if you have any further questions. If she feels free to talk with you, so be it. Otherwise, I have nothing more to say."

Howard raised his eyebrows in alarm flashing Marie a silent warning. Her nervousness and uneasiness were becoming very apparent. If she continued in this fashion, Eric would surely figure out that something was up.

What were Marie and Howard trying to hide? Eric wondered. The anxious glances that they kept slipping the other were quite obvious. Their unspoken words and actions spoke louder than any confession of the truth. Everyday, Eric dealt with different clients and their body language. He had become a master at determining what someone was really all about, just by observation. The words they spoke came second to their stance, arm movements, and facial expressions. Even the tone of their breathing and a perspired forehead, were dead ringers for sizing up an individual. Something was up – he just knew it. Marie was not a good liar, and her husband's fidgety actions confirmed that.

"I'm sorry for prying. I really didn't mean to be rude, but I am just concerned," Eric added, with a warm smile that was as sincere as a saint's. He did not want them on the defensive. What ever it took to convince them of his sincerity he would say or do. If he kept playing it the same way, he would keep them in his good graces until he got the answers he needed.

Marie appeared to relax somewhat and smiled back at Eric. "We do appreciate your concern for our daughter. I apologize for being rude and harsh. It's really not like me to be so assertive, but Ellen just seems so vulnerable right now to everyone and everything around her. This whole thing just has me so distraught."

"I totally understand, Mrs. Meadows. Don't give it another thought," he reassured with a smile, determined to get some information.

The wait in the emergency room was a long one. Dr. Fairchild had been contacted, and was on his way to the hospital. After two hours of watching the clock against the faded floral wallpaper, a nurse arrived with the news that Ellen was being admitted. Marie had a million questions but the nurse relayed that only Dr. Fairchild could answer all her concerns.

"If you will follow me, I will take you to your daughter's room on the third floor now."

"I would also like to see Ellen," Eric hurriedly requested, looking from Marie to Howard as they got up to leave.

"Maybe that's not such a good idea right now, Eric," Howard answered. "You can wait here, and we will update you as soon as we find something out."

Eric glanced at his watch, realizing the wait had taken longer than he had expected. "That would be alright if I didn't have to catch a flight in an hour. I guess I will just have to leave and hope for the best for her."

"You're welcome to call the house and find out how she is doing," Marie offered with relief washing over her in a noticeable fashion, grateful that he was finally leaving. With the promise of his departure, came the return of her sunny disposition.

Howard glanced at Marie again with the same nervous look of earlier, casting her a signal of caution. "Eric, Ellen heard what you had to say. What more can you do? She needs to think about things and make the decision for herself and what she wants for her future. We will take care of our daughter. She will be fine," he promised, as he threw his arm around Marie's shoulder pulling her closely to his side.

"You're right. Wish Ellen the best for me, and tell her to think about everything that I said back at your house concerning Glen. I know I was making some headway with her before she collapsed.

I must get going to make my flight," Eric conceded.

"So do we. Ellen is probably wondering where we are at right now, so we have to say goodbye."

They left Eric standing alone, as he watched them walk away hand in hand, disappearing into the elevator.

Eric reached for his cellphone that was in his jacket pocket. He dialed All-Star Taxi with the intention of having them pick him up and take him to the airport, but he changed his mind on the second ring and hung up.

"Something is going on. I can just feel it!" Eric exclaimed a little too loudly as he made his way back to the elevator.

He would have to be discreet if he wanted to figure things out. Hopefully, he wouldn't run into Marie and Howard. Eric crossed is fingers mentally as he entered the elevator, and pushed the button to the third floor. Frustration crossed his face as the doors opened to the second floor, but suddenly changed to hope as he fixed his gaze on what could be the key to the answers he sought. There in the distant hallway, stood a cart of green scrub gowns. *This may work*, he thought smugly, as he grabbed one quickly while no one was looking, making his way to a bathroom close by. *Now all I need is a mask and cap…nurse's station,* he contemplated to himself. *"No problem…"* he grinned aloud in satisfaction, giving himself the once over in the bathroom mirror, before leaving to find the rest of his disguise.

The Quik Shopper was exceptionally busy that evening. Glen couldn't even take a break because of the constant crowd coming in and out of the store. It was one of those rare days that he just didn't have his usual stamina. As he rang up a gallon of milk, he thought of the lack of sleep that was his constant companion anymore. Ellen endlessly plagued his thoughts, and even more so lately. *Was she ok? Would she ever come home? Would they love again?* He tried to shake the constant thoughts from his mind, but they continued to bother him everyday. It was hard to stay focused on other things, but he was determined to do so.

Glen hoped Eric would be true to his word, and he would be back home the next day. Although, the time they spent together was infrequent, there was a secure feeling in knowing that he could reach out to Eric at CWS when he was in town. Sometimes a one-night trip had ended up being three. His business dealings were so unpredictable, as were the times he would actually answer his phone when he was out of town.

"Mister, the gas pump ain't workin," a lady barked from the half-opened door, shaking Glen from his daydreaming.

"Oh yeah?" he answered with indifference; growing weary of the grumblings he heard every evening. "Be right with you… Joanne take over," Glen called to the back room, as he made his way out the door to solve another irate customer's complaint.

Eric emerged from the bathroom fully garbed in the hospital green. A nurse even found him a cap and mask, after he claimed ignorance to their location since he was new. She seemed to buy into his story without suspicion.

"I must be crazy to be even trying this," he muttered to himself as he pushed button #3 on the elevator.

The doors opened to the nurse's station. Luckily, Ellen's

name had already been posted on the room assignment sheet, hanging on the wall where all could see it. A plump older nurse greeted Eric, as if she knew him. "Hello doctor. Mrs. Monroe was just brought up from recovery. She's in Room 314."

"Thank you," he answered with a nod, making his way quickly down the hall before she got a closer look at him. Ellen was in Room 316, just two doors down. Eric inched his way closer to Ellen's door. He could hear voices, and the voices were clearly that of Howard, Marie and Ellen's; and probably the doctor's he surmised.

"You'll be fine, Ellen - probably just an iron deficiency and a little anemia. The blood work will confirm that shortly. It is not uncommon for pregnant women to pass out from time to time, although we don't like to see this occurring. Continue eating better, and take the prenatal vitamins I prescribed. If you need to increase your iron dosage I will let you know."

Pregnant! Eric's insides screamed the words. His head felt like it was going to explode if he had to keep quiet one more minute with the news. All of the secretiveness on the part of Ellen and her parents was beginning to make sense now. Never would he have guessed pregnancy though. The least likely candidates - a dentist and a housewife – had deceived him. It was a new experience for him, and one he didn't like having to admit to. Something as basic in life as having a child should have been obvious to him. *She doesn't even look pregnant!* Eric thought. *Glen is going to be a father!*

Eric appeared in the doorway, pulling his mask and cap from his head. "I heard the four of you talking and I know the truth now, Ellen. Glen has a right to know about this!" he announced with firm certainty.

Marie looked at Howard in horror with her hand glued to her mouth in disbelief.

"Oh, no..." Ellen moaned, turning her face into her pillow.

"*Who is this?"* Dr. Fairchild demanded.

"Eric Cummings. The brother of my unborn child's, father," Ellen confessed.

"You could be in a lot of trouble young man," Dr. Fairchild sternly advised, directing his comments at Eric. "If the hospital or the Meadows' decide to press charges against you, they would have a definite case. Impersonation of a doctor or hospital staff employee can carry a stiff fine or even jail time"

"I'm sorry, sir, but I was desperate for answers," Eric admitted loosely, knowing he was probably calling his bluff.

"I can see that," Dr. Fairchild replied, studying Eric from head to toe. "I think it's time for you to get out of that outfit. If it happens again, I will report you to security."

He turned his stance towards Ellen, giving her friendly advice. "Young lady, I think you may want to talk to this person."

"I think so too..." she said quietly, knowing she could no longer avoid the inevitable.

"Oh... and one more thing, Ellen," Dr. Fairchild added as he walked towards the door ready to depart from her room. "Every father does have a right to know about a child that they had a part in conceiving."

Ellen hung her head, and the tears began to flow again. "Eric, you can't tell Glen this," she said in desperation.

"And why not?" he asked in total frustration, as he removed the gown from over his suit. "Glen would be ecstatic to know you are carrying his child. Besides, I can't trust you to tell him yourself. Just look at the measures you and your parents have taken since I have been here, to outright *lie* to me and keep this whole thing a secret!"

"I know you don't understand this Eric, but I felt I had very good reasons for not being honest with you. After everything that has happened between Glen and I, I didn't want to force him into anything."

She looked into his face with pleading eyes. "It was enough of a blow concerning Samantha and the children. Hearing about a pregnancy after what he has been through, I doubt would be taken in a good way. I don't think he would be as ecstatic as you think he would be, Eric."

Howard and Marie stood on the other side of Ellen's bed trying to absorb the conversation.

"Dr. Fairchild is right though, dear. Every father does have a right to know about his child," Marie gently added, looking at her daughter with concern. "I could have never kept that from your father when I was pregnant with any of you."

"Please, mother, don't make me feel any worse than I am already feeling about this," she urged. "I need a promise from all three of you, especially you Eric, that you will not tell Glen about this pregnancy."

"I can't promise that!" Eric replied adamantly, crossing his arms in defiance.

"Eric, please…" Ellen begged, as she pushed the button, making her bed rise up to a sitting position. "I need some time.

Just give me until the end of the month, and then call me. We will reevaluate the situation at that point."

"Mom… dad, would you please let Eric and I talk privately?" she requested, looking at each one of her parents for their cooperation.

"Sure, honey," Howard, answered, grabbing Marie's hand and leading her from the room. "We'll be in the lounge if you need us. Whenever you decide to leave, Eric, would you please let us know? And I just thought I'd let you know that I think you missed your flight," he added knowingly with a nod.

"Aah…sure, thanks," Eric replied with a guilty smile, realizing Howard was on to him.

The door closed behind them and Eric remained in the distant corner standing and staring at Ellen, with frustration detailing his every facial feature.

"I want to say something to you," she said with heart-felt emotion in her voice. "This has been a hard day for me. I still can't believe you had the nerve to come to Denver and find me. I was doing just fine… with just my parents. You don't want me in your brother's life, and you know my feelings towards you. So why all the effort?"

Eric sighed, moving from his planted spot by the wall. He grabbed a chair beside of Ellen's bed, taking a seat close to her. "The effort, Ellen, is for Glen's benefit. I thought I made that clear back at your parent's house. It's not the past and our relationship that is the issue here. No matter what love loss you and I have suffered, this should not affect you and Glen. Sometimes you have to grab the bull by the horns, and that's what I felt needed to be done here. It's *not you* having to see Glen in the state that he's in. It's your friends Megan and Mike, and it's me having to deal with it. *He's miserable!"*

"He is *that miserable?"* she asked timidly with surprise.

"Yes, he is, and I'm *sick* of it! And to tell you the truth, Ellen, I'm probably doing this for old times sake. For the friendship Jack, you and I once shared. I feel with a clear conscience, that your accusations towards me are totally false. I can't change your feelings about that situation anymore than I can change your feelings about this pregnancy now. I figure in some twisted way, I owe you."

"How's that, if you truly don't feel responsible?" Ellen asked.

Eric shifted his position, turning to directly face her. "You think I destroyed your happiness with Jack, and now I'm trying to give it back to you with Glen."

Fresh tears began to form and spill from Ellen's eyes anew. "Eric, I can tell you mean…well," she said with sincerity, while trying to dab her eyes with a tissue. She took a deep breath, knowing it was time to purge herself from the bitterness that had been gnawing at her insides for the past two years. "I'm sorry for blaming you for Jack's death," she began, feeling overwhelming remorse for the way she had unfairly treated him. "Deep inside I knew the changes occurring in him over the final months of his life, as well as the accident, had nothing to do with you. I was so angry though, that he was gone. I needed someone to blame. It's taken me awhile, but I am trying to look at this thing more rationally. I guess it is time to bury the past, if you feel the same way," she meekly questioned, knowing Eric could reprimand her harshly if he chose.

Eric looked at her in surprise. "I never thought I would hear those words coming from your lips, but I'm glad they finally did," he said with a heart-felt smile and a pat to her hand. "Now, how about Glen? Can we remedy that situation today also?"

"Eric, please.... just until the end of the month – that is all I'm asking. I need to rest and get my strength back before I deal with something so emotional again."

"All right, he agreed with reluctance, knowing his resolve was weakening because she had made a valid point concerning her health. "My instincts are telling me not to do this, but I will honor your wishes. I hope you don't drag this thing out to the end of the month, though."

Eric got up, and looked down at Ellen. "You could be back at the farm, you know, and in Glen's arms after you get out of her. You realize that, don't you?"

"I guess I do..." she said quietly, not allowing herself even a moment's consideration to ponder that thought, because she knew it wasn't going to happen.

"I hope you make the right decision. After all, this not only affects your life but your baby's also. And, Ellen..."

"Yes?"

"Thanks again for thinking things out about Jack and me. He really was a great guy and my friend. Whether you realize it or not, I suffered too when he died."

"I know that..." Ellen choked out, holding back a sob.

Eric got up from the chair and reached out to pat Ellen's hand again, and said his goodbyes. "Take care of yourself. I hope this doesn't take you more than a couple days before you decide to get in touch with Glen; but if it does, I will maintain my promise and not tell him what is happening for a while. After all, no one likes deception, Ellen – including you! Think about that…" he challenged, as he walked silently from the room not waiting for her response.

Eric found Howard and Marie in the lounge sharing coffee and talking quietly to each other.

"I'm leaving now and going home. Ellen and I have talked, and I'll honor her wishes for the meantime, and not tell Glen. At least that is, until the end of the month. But I still hope that she comes to her senses before then and contacts Glen."

"You may have a hard time believing this, after everything that has happened today, but we're hoping for that also," Howard interjected. "We were just sitting here discussing that very subject, and we both feel it is time for our daughter to get back to her home and the man she loves…"

It was 2:00 a.m. when Eric pulled into the garage of his home. *Glen is still at work*, he realized. The thought of facing him and concealing the truth about Ellen, didn't sit well with him anyways. Keeping up this charade for a few weeks wasn't going to be easy. He didn't even know how he would have a normal conversation with Glen without spilling his guts. *Ellen just had to come to her senses before that time,* he reasoned. *She just had to!*

Eric left a hurriedly scribbled note on the kitchen counter by the coffeemaker, informing Glen that he was home and in bed. At least this bought him a few more hours of not having to encounter Glen face to face with deception.

He fell asleep considering the day's events. His mind also wandered to Melinda – beautiful, understanding Melinda. Their lives seemed to be so uncomplicated now, compared to Glen and Ellen's. How the tables had turned! He only hoped his good fortune would continue. It felt good to finally be in love.

Chapter Forty-Seven

"Good morning, Ellen," came the cheerful voice of the much-too perky nurse, there to take her blood pressure and temperature again, even though it was way too early in the morning for Ellen's liking. "The doctor says you will be going home today. Breakfast will be here in a few minutes, also."

Ellen drowsily sat up, looking slant-eyed at the high-pitched sounding nurse, who was grinning from ear to ear. She longed to be back in her own bed, not being disturbed throughout the night from the constant interruption of the nurses that entered her room

"Are my parents still here?" she asked sleepily with a yawn and a stretch of her arms.

"No, they left around midnight, but they said they will be back sometime this morning to pick you up and take you home," the nurse replied, as she placed the thermometer in Ellen's mouth.

Her mind began to stir again, just as it had throughout the night. *Should I go home to my parents' house, or home to the farm to be with Glen?* She couldn't believe that the second option was even crossing her mind now. Eric's visit had changed everything.

"98.6 – normal," the nurse announced, sounding very pleased, interrupting Ellen's thoughts. "Dr. Fairchild will be in later to sign your release papers. I'll be back after breakfast to check on you," she promised, as she picked up her supplies and charted Ellen's vitals.

Ellen's hands protectively rubbed over her extended abdomen. *"My baby..."* she breathed. *"Glen's baby...would he want it if he knew?"* she questioned aloud in despair, as she rolled her face into her pillow.

Eric showered and dressed; ready to face another workday. He combed his hair and adjusted the look of his meticulously knotted tie, giving himself the once over, taking in his well-groomed appearance.

"What am I to do about this damn situation now?" he said to his handsome reflection. *"I don't want to break my promise to Ellen, but Glen has a right to know!"*

He splashed cologne on each side of his neck, and grabbed his suit jacked, trying to put the dilemma out of his mind for at least a little while.

CWS was busy with the hustle and bustle of an active office. The room was filled with the sound of computer keys clicking in diversified rhythms, while others talked on the phone to clients. Melinda was at her desk talking to one of her female co-workers, confirming an order that was due for shipment the next day, as Eric entered the building. Melinda's breath caught in her throat as she glanced in his direction from across the room. He was checking his inter-office basket, and gave her a warm smile.

"We'll have to finish this later, Diane. I need to go over a few things with Eric."

"I bet you do," Diane said to herself sarcastically, as Melinda rose and went to meet him.

Her eyes spoke louder than any words could have, as she met him where he stood, handing him another paper for the stack already in his hands.

“Missed you,” he whispered, as he looked lovingly at her.

“The same for me,” she echoed softly. “Let’s take this up in your office. I know everyone is staring at us.”

“Let’em stare,” he grinned, patting her backside.

Diane rolled her eyes, shaking her head with a disgusted jealous laugh, wishing he were hers.

Melinda shut the office door behind her and ran into Eric’s waiting arms. “Why does it seem like you have been gone an eternity, when I know it has only been a day?” she asked lovingly between kisses.

“Maybe because you are hopelessly in love with me, and can’t stand to be apart from me anymore?” he playfully grinned.

“And you don’t feel the same way?” she asked, needing the same reassurance from him.

Eric’s lips swooped down to meet hers in a long soul-searing, intense kiss that left both of them weak with desire. “Does that answer your question?” he whispered against her ear. “I could only think of you, and how long it would be until I was back in your arms.” His tongue met hers and the urgency built between them with each continuing kiss.

“We better stop, darling.”

“I know,” Eric sighed, planting kisses down the side of her neck. “But it’s been a couple days.”

“We have tonight – after work,” she promised, pushing him

reluctantly away at arm's length.

"I know. I can't seem to think about anything else but that," he grinned. "Come here, and sit on the couch with me," he requested with a pat to the cushion, as he made his way to the sofa. "I have something I want to talk to you about."

"What is it?" she asked curiously, with sudden concern, as they snuggled closely on the couch. Eric grabbed her hand, placing it in his lap.

"It's about the trip to Denver."

"Did you see Ellen?"

"Yes, I did, and Melinda, I got myself in one heck of a mess!"

Eric looked intensely into her eyes, wanting for her to understand the full impact of his next words. *"Ellen's pregnant with Glen's baby!"*

Melinda's mouth dropped open. *"No…you are kidding, right?"*

"I wish I were, but no such luck. What's even worse, she swore me to secrecy. She made me promise not to say anything to Glen until the end of the month. I am having a hard time with all of this. He's my brother, for Christ's sake! He has a right to know about his own kid!"

Melinda patted the top of Eric's hand, trying to lend her support. "You really do have yourself between a rock and a hard place, don't you? If she doesn't tell him by the end of the month, will you tell Glen about the pregnancy?"

"She made me promise that I would get back to her before I

attempted to tell him the news," he said with an exasperated sigh. But, she claims she will probably tell Glen before that time anyways. Who knows with her? She has been so mixed up until now. I wouldn't put anything past her."

"You sound skeptical that she won't come to her senses and do the right thing."

"You got it. She may choose to continue to keep it a secret. But that's where I draw the line. I will tell him by then, if she doesn't. I guess this whole thing just really bothers me, because if Glen finds out that I have known about the situation for several weeks without telling him, it could cause a real strain on our relationship. So now you know my dilemma, sweet Melinda," Eric explained, while bringing her hand up to his lips for a soft kiss. He looked at her tenderly, brushing her soft hand repeatedly over his sensuous lips. "So what further advice do you have for me?"

Melinda smiled lovingly into the searching brown eyes of the man she loved. "Give things a couple of days. Personally, I can deal with things better in terms of a couple of days instead of trying to think of the overall picture of several weeks. Hopefully, Ellen *will* come to her senses by then. It really isn't fair for your brother to be in the dark. He *does* have a right to know about all this, Eric."

"So you do see things my way?"

"Absolutely," she reassured with a smile, while kissing his lips lightly.

"I love you, Melinda."

"I love you too, Eric," she breathed, still feeling light-headed every time he spoke those words to her. "I have a feeling things will work out just fine for Glen, as long as his wonderful older brother is looking out for him. You'll see."

"I hope you're right," he sighed. "I hope you're right."

Another 15-hour typical workday, Glen had just put in. He surprisingly was wide-awake, as he made the drive home. He habitually checked the mail before pulling into the driveway. This day was not any different.

"A letter from Mom," he exclaimed happily, as he sifted through the other mail, finding everything else to be for Eric. Glen opened the large manila envelope, as he sat idling with his foot on the brake. A check fell to the floorboard in the amount of $5,000. He was pleasantly surprised and yet shocked also by the sum of money. The car that Samantha had intentionally kept from him had finally paid off. There was an unexpected silver lining to the whole mess after all. His mother penned a letter on her best floral scented stationary, in the familiar handwriting he knew and loved so well.

Dear Glen,

I hope this letter finds you well. Not much new is happening here, except for this whole situation with Samantha. Right up until the end, she tried to convince me that she still loves you, and that I should continue to allow her to use the car. I think that she does love you, Glen, or as least she thinks she does. That's the sad part. I know I surprised her when I said I would call the police in thirty minutes if she wasn't out of here. I don't know where I got the nerve to be so forceful with her. You know me, Glen; it's hard for me to stand up to people. I guess I was just so angry for what she had put you through. Anyways, her children were with her, and she tried to play on my sympathy concerning them also. This mother of yours may be getting older, but I am far from stupid. I showed her the phone, and told her to use it, after she claimed that she had forgotten her cellphone. I wished her well, and the taxi was here within minutes to pick the three of them up. I doubt very seriously if any of us will ever hear from her again. I made it quit clear that she needs to move on with her life, and that things were definitely over between you and her.

I turned the car over to a man named Pete Myers, and he sold the car on his used car lot. I was delighted when he handed me a check for the full amount of what he sold it for. After he heard the story of what happened to you, I believe he thought you deserved every last penny. As luck would have it, Pete asked me out on a date that very day. His wife left him 2 years ago for another man. He is wonderful, and we have been seeing each other every day now. Remember John, your dad's old friend I was dating? Well, unfortunately things didn't work out for us. We stopped dating shortly after you moved away, because he wanted to move out to California to be near his daughter and her family. It initially hurt me, but now I'm glad it happened since I met Pete. Sometimes fate has a funny way of working things out, bringing about pleasant results when we least expect them. Just so you know – I couldn't be happier!

Please come to visit me, when you get the chance. I miss you and Eric, and it has been too long since I have seen you both. I hope things are going better, and the mess between you and Ellen has been straightened out. I'm sorry if the car didn't sell for what you had hoped for, but Pete feels it was a good deal.

Take care, and text or call me when you get the chance.

Love,

Mom

Glen read her letter in total fascination, trying to gain control of his emotions. *"Brought me what I hoped for....?"* he said aloud, still in disbelief as he stared at the check. *"Mother, if you only knew it was beyond what I had expected!"* he added with a look of pleased satisfaction.

Chapter Forty-Eight

Ellen was happy to be home – back at her parent's home that was. Dr. Fairchild had given her strict orders to rest in bed for the next two days, to continue taking the stronger vitamins, and to eat five smaller meals instead of three larger ones a day that she had been accustomed to eating. It wouldn't be too hard to obey those requests. Her appetite was growing rapidly every day, and all she wanted to do now was eat every thing in site.

"Soup and sandwich darling? I think that would qualify as a lighter meal," Marie offered pleasantly.

"I think so too," Ellen agreed, as she smiled fondly back at her mother. "It's so good to be home," she beamed, as Marie placed the tray carefully on her lap.

Marie flashed a look of concern at her daughter. "May I sit and talk with you for awhile?"

"Of course, mother," she replied with a warm smile, patting the one side of the mattress for Marie to join her on the bed.

"Your father and I didn't get too much sleep last night, Ellen."

"I'm sorry, mother," she chirped, biting ferociously into the roast beef with Swiss cheese on rye sandwich.

"No need to say your sorry, Ellen. We just had a lot to talk about. Let me begin by saying you gave us quite a scare. Thank God it wasn't anything serious."

"I know, mother. I was worried too," Ellen replied between slurps of chicken soup.

"Ellen, daddy and I have come to a conclusion."

Ellen hadn't heard her mother use that affectionate name for her father in years, even though she called him that from time to time.

"You *need* to contact Glen. He has a right to know about his child."

Ellen held her soupspoon in mid-air, pausing to absorb what Marie had just said.

"Mother…you know my feelings about this."

"Please, Ellen, let me finish. Even if you choose not to have a life with him, that is your decision; but he *does* have a right to know about the pregnancy and the baby."

Ellen completely stopped eating, and turned to stare at Marie in disbelief. "You surprise me, mother. You and dad have always trusted my decision making in the past. I don't remember you ever getting involved like this before – telling me what to do – even when I was a teenager. I'm a grown woman, and I need to work this out in my own way and in my own time."

"Don't be so surprised, Ellen," she answered matter-of-factly. There is always a first time for everything, and your father and I *do* feel very strongly about the subject. Eric seemed to be sincere enough. Your father and I both have a hard time believing that Eric would have gone through all the time, trouble, and expense of traveling here, if he didn't have strong convictions that Glen is telling the truth. We are convinced that he truly holds to the belief that his brother still loves you." Marie hesitated with her next words. "It may not make you very happy, but your father and I are beginning to believe that maybe there has been a terrible misunderstanding here."

Ellen's eyes began flooding with tears. "*I need some more time, mother...*" she whispered, feeling desperately afraid and vulnerable that she was losing the support of her parents being on her side. "It's been so hard, mother. I guess Jack's death has wounded me far deeper than I ever knew it would or could. I'm so scared of anyone leaving me *ever again!* It's better not to love than to be hurt."

Marie reached out to pat her daughter's arm. "Honey you need to move beyond the memory of Jack, in order to love again, as cruel as that may sound."

"I honestly thought I had done that, mother."

"Well, apparently you haven't. How can you love your child if you can't open your heart to Glen, and at least talk to him?"

"That's different, mother. I already love my baby more than anything."

"But you could lose your baby too, just as you lost Jack. This episode in the hospital should be proof of that. And then what…you close your heart to that kind of pain also, and never have another child?"

"Mother, I just feel so confused…" Ellen whispered, closing her eyes in despair.

"Then do something about it. Call Glen and talk to him. Let him know how you are doing…. and for heaven's sakes, tell him…. about his child," Marie implored as she got up from the bed. "And just one more thing, Ellen. Your father and I take issue with this because not only is this your child, but our grandchild too. If someone kept news like this from us, it would hurt tremendously. We are talking about human life – someone's bloodline and family. Those things should never be concealed. It's just not right."

Marie turned and walked from the room, leaving Ellen alone with her thoughts; not waiting for her to respond.

Chapter Forty-Nine

A note lay on the counter from Eric, informing Glen that he was back in town. Glen signed the back of the check that his mother had sent, placing it beside of Eric's note. He laid out his mother's letter, including a note of his own.

> Eric,
>
> Glad you're back. Mom wrote to me. Please feel free to read her letter. She misses us, and hopes we will visit. The car was sold, and I couldn't be happier! Take the $5,000 and apply it to my payments. See you soon.
>
> Glen

Glen lay down the pen, and smiled contentedly to himself. He was feeling happy and full of hope for the first time in weeks. He had grabbed a sandwich from a local sub shop, on the way home from the farm, so that he could sleep an extra hour. As he climbed the stairs to go to his room, the phone began to ring.

"Probably for Eric," he mumbled sleepily, as the persistent ringing echoed in his ears. *Why isn't the answering machine on anyways*, he thought irritably, not wanting to respond to the determined party that was trying to reach him or his brother. "Maybe it's Eric or Mom, or even the Quik Shopper expecting me to come in early for a double shift," he considered, as he resigned himself to pick up the phone on the nightstand by his bed.

"Hello?"

"Hi… it's me…Ellen," came the timid sounding voice at the other end of the line.

Glen was glad the soft mattress was there to catch him. He had prayed for this moment for weeks, and now he thought he was dreaming.

"Ellen….? My God, is that really you?"

"Yes, Glen, it is me," she said with a tear-filled, quivering voice.

"I have been so worried about you. How are you?" he asked in concern.

"I'm fine, Glen. Just fine."

"Where are you?"

Ellen hesitated, feeling her reserve weakening. She breathed deeply, determined to be strong. "I'm in Denver, with my parents. Glen, I need to talk with you… preferably in person."

"Sure…sure. When and where?" he asked anxiously, running his hands through his hair, trying to absorb all that was happening.

"When can you get off work and fly here?"

"Whenever it suits you. I'll make it work."

"Glen, can you even afford the flight? I didn't mean to be presumptuous."

"Ellen, I am fine. Just say the time, and I'll be there."

"How about tomorrow?"

"Tomorrow is fine," Glen answered, still considering the possibility that he was so tired he was dreaming. "Ellen…I've missed you so much, and just to hear your voice means more to me than you could ever know."

Ellen choked back the tears, trying to check her emotions, agreeing with his confession in her mind, but unable to say the words back to him. *I've missed you too! I have been so miserable without you!*

"I will text you my parents' address and phone number. Please call me when you get into town."

"I will, Ellen. I'll see you tomorrow then."

"Yes…tomorrow," she replied softly before hanging up her cellphone.

Glen held the phone in his hands for several minutes just listening to the dial tone, as if it still held the connection to Ellen somewhere on the other end. As he finally resolved himself to lay the receiver back down in its cradle, he couldn't tear his eyes away from it; still wondering if he had imagined what just took place. He was overly tired, but not that tired. He made his way back down the stairs to the kitchen, grabbing up the ink pen again, writing down another message on the same sheet of paper.

Eric,

Good news – Ellen just called. She wants to talk. Leaving for Denver tomorrow. Wish me luck that I don't come back alone.

Glen

Glen prayed a prayer of thanksgiving, as he smiled up to the ceiling. "I guess you really do hear my prayers. Sorry for doubting you."

He grabbed his keys and headed back out the door, driving to the Quik Shopper. The store was full with its mid-day customers who were complaining of the long wait.

"You're back. Covering for someone, Glen?" Mrs. Vincent asked.

She always came on after Glen's shift, and was as tough as nails. A perfect convenience store worker, because she never seemed to allow the customer's rude comments to shake her demeanor.

"Nope, I'm here to see Mrs. Moore," he grinned. "Is she in the back?"

"Always is this time of day. You know that," Mrs. Vincent said with a wink and a smile, as she rang up a couple packs of cigarettes.

"Yeah, I do," Glen chuckled, opening the door to the office.

"Glen, why are you here?" Mrs. Moore asked in surprise. "I know you are loyal, but for heavens sakes go home and get some rest," she advised in a motherly way.

"I need to ask a favor. An emergency has come up, and I need off tomorrow night. Can you find someone to cover for me?"

Mrs. Moore gazed at Glen in an evaluating way. She had heard many excuses before when people didn't want to come to work. "You know we've come to rely on you heavily around here, Glen."

"I know that, and I wouldn't even ask off if it weren't real important to me."

"Nothing serious, I hope?"

"Nothing I can't handle, but it will demand some of my personal time and attention," he answered with a believable sincere smile.

"We'll manage," she replied matter-of-factly. "But you will be back the next day, I hope?"

"Most definitely," Glen promised. "Thanks, Mrs. Moore, I owe you," he added, bending over to give her a hug before he left.

"Go on and get outta here, before I change my mind!" she growled with an awkward blush and a wave of her arm. "And don't be late tonight!"

"Yes, boss!" he replied sarcastically, saluting her before he left.

That was easy, now the hard part would be Megan, he thought, as he pulled in front of the produce stand.

"Forgot something?" she questioned nonchalantly, as she sat on a stool reading a ladies magazine.

"No, just need to cover something with you."

"What's that?" she asked with curious anticipation, as she laid her magazine aside on the counter.

"I'm going to Denver tomorrow to see Ellen…"

"You're what!" Megan abruptly interrupted, almost falling off her stool. "How do you know Ellen is in Denver?"

"She called and told me so. She wants me to come and talk with her. And Megan, it didn't really come as an unexpected revelation. I had a feeling she was there anyways," he said with sudden irritation, feeling as if Megan really thought he didn't have a brain in his head to figure out where Ellen would have gone. "I just wanted to give her some time to sort things out. I had a gut feeling she would call me one day, but she had to come my direction. I couldn't pressure her."

"Oh…*I see*," Megan acknowledged with a newfound understanding into Glen's keen insight. "And she gave you no hint as to what this is all about?"

"No… she didn't. Do you know what this is all about, Megan?" Glen inquired, with the same suspicious prodding manner that she had put him through for weeks.

"I really don't, Glen," she said with half-convincing truth. "But, I guess it's good that she called."

"Yeah…it is good…I hope it is, at least," he said in a half-distracted state of mind. "Anyways, I won't be here tomorrow. I hope you can manage without me. The shelter can wait until the next day when I'm back."

"Of course it can," she agreed. "Come back when you're ready. We'll get along without you."

"It will only be for one day."

"Alright, Glen," Megan said, as she reached for the magazine again, but put it down immediately as she remembered the message she failed to deliver. "Glen, I did hear from Ellen."

"Oh really?" Glen replied with biting sarcasm. "It's *so*

incredible to me, how your memory suddenly came back to you where Ellen is concerned. He leaned against the counter beside of her, scrutinizing her with a penetrating stare.

"You're not fazing me, Glen," she commented placidly as she met his gaze in the same uninhibited manner. "Save it Glen, for someone who cares. Don't lecture me with your cutting remarks. It shouldn't be a new discovery to you that Ellen's well-being has been my number one priority. Not that I need to justify myself to you, but she has only called me one time, and I honestly did forget to tell you something. So if we can get past all the technicalities here, I will give you the message now," she announced brashly with her arms crossed in defiance.

Glen shook his head with a laugh, never ceasing to be amazed by the woman's spirit. "Go on, Megan, I have a lot to do today before I go to Denver."

"She wanted me to tell you that she wants you to receive your $300.00 a week pay again, and also the back pay from all the past weeks that you have worked."

"I don't want her money. You know that," he replied, shifting uncomfortably and pulling away from the stand again to pace in the dirt in front of Megan.

"So what am I to do with the money?"

"Save it for her. She'll need it to purchase more livestock soon. And maybe if I'm lucky it will be *our* livestock once we are married, if she will still have me," he added with a hopeful smile.

"I wouldn't get my hopes up, if I were you, Glen," she replied coldly. "Are you sure you don't want the money?"

Glen shot her a smug grin. "I'm sure, and *I will* keep my hopes up, Megan."

She raised her eyebrows in a questioning manner, feeling torn by his new determination to be back in Ellen's life. If Ellen agreed to reconcile with him and then marry him, the baby would definitely make a break up harder if anything ever came up between them again. However, he had proven himself in the past weeks – to Megan and Mike both – to be loyal and hardworking. As much as she didn't want to admit it, he was a nice guy.

"Alright then. Well good luck, Glen. I hope everything works out the way that you have been wanting it to," she added reluctantly, with an attempt at being positive towards him. If Ellen wanted this, Megan would support her, even if she still had her doubts about Glen.

"Thanks, Megan," he responded kindly, taken back and yet surprised by her caring words. "I'll do everything in my power to see to it that things do work out, now that Ellen has opened the door."

He waved her a fond goodbye, happy that he finally had Megan's vote of confidence, even if it wasn't her all-out support. Just one phone call from Ellen had changed Glen's whole perspective. It was as if someone had given him a shot of adrenaline, restoring him to his former handsome, virile self. His eyes danced with hope as he drove away, thinking only of having and holding Ellen back in his arms again.

The raw force of energy and determination that pushed him beyond any thought of being tired earlier possessed him now. He went back to Eric's to pack an overnight bag, in case it was needed, and then booked his plane ticket. He tried to rest for a couple hours, but all thoughts were on Ellen, which evaded any hope of sleep.

The hours at the convenience store dragged by, as he glanced at the clock every few minutes. Six-thirty finally arrived, and was as celebrated in his mind as the end of a school year for a student. He hurriedly mumbled a few words to Mrs. Vincent, barely having enough time to shower and change his clothes, before catching the 9 a.m. flight to Denver.

Eric had never made it home the night before. *He probably had a lot of catching up to do with Melinda,* he thought with a smile, as his mind tried to sort out the last 24 hours. The anticipation of a good or bad visit with Ellen weighed heavily upon his mind now. *What if this was just another delayed torture?* He questioned as he rested his palm under his chin, leaning on his armrest and staring at the cloud formations that drifted quickly by. *What if she had been polite on the phone, but had no intentions to come back to the farm?*

The thought of seeing her lovely face, being in her presence, and then suffer her rejection again, was more than he thought he could handle. Even without having her by his side all of these weeks, he still held on to hope; but that could all change within a few short hours. He watched the descent of the jet into the Denver airport from his airplane window, with a sense of restlessness that would not be sated until he spoke with Ellen again.

The sky was overcast, but the clouds were attempting to break at the horizon, giving way to the warmth of the sun once more. He prayed for the same emotional breakthrough with Ellen and their relationship, as he exited the airplane.

His phone beeped, and he reacted by quickly grabbing it from his pants pocket looking to see who texted him. Ellen provided the promised address and phone number of her parents'. He knew she had blocked him for weeks from communicating with her, as he tried to do more times than he could count. Obviously, things were different now, and he was relieved he could text and call her again.

"Hello…?"

"Ellen…it's me. I just got into town, and you told me to give you a call."

Her pulse quickened at the sound of his voice. "Yes…I did, Glen," Ellen answered nervously. "I'll see you within the hour. A taxi should be able to find my parents' home easily enough."

"See you soon," he promised.

He purchased a bouquet of daisies and carnations, which blended in perfect hues of sunny colors, from an airport vendor's stand; and then grabbed the first cab available.

"Where to?"

"1252 Mapleleaf Circle."

"I know the neighborhood. We call that area *Pill Hill*."

"Pill Hill?" Glen asked curiously.

"Yeah, *Pill Hill…* you know, where all the doctors live."

"Oh…" Glen said with a laugh. "I'll have to remember that one," he answered, as he rolled his eyes to himself.

"We'll be there in twenty minutes. Ever been to Denver before?" the driver inquired.

"No, I haven't. First time," Glen replied, enjoying the scenery of the beautiful Rocky Mountains in the distance.

The driver looked at Glen in his rearview mirror with an assessing glance. “Here on business or pleasure?”

“Maybe a little of both,” Glen answered with uncertainty, not really wanting to be drilled any further by the prying man.

He shuffled his feet nervously, as the cabby kept the conversation animated, attempting to be a tour guide as they wove their way through the city streets. Glen sighed, closing his eyes, trying to prepare himself for the upcoming confrontation, oblivious to the majority of what the man was saying. He felt his face, checking his shave, and raked his fingers through his blonde locks in an attempt to look his best. He hoped Ellen approved of what he was wearing. He had purposely picked out his tan khakis and his pale blue shirt, knowing those were her favorites.

“Here we are – 1252 Mapleleaf Circle. That’ll be Twenty Five dollars.”

Glen handed him thirty. “Keep the change.”

“Thanks, buddy,” the cabby barked, as he pulled away, leaving Glen alone to stare at the well appointed, brick colonial.

“Ellen, he’s here,” Marie announced, peaking from behind the drapes as she saw the much-too-handsome man standing on the sidewalk in front of the house. First Eric and now Glen. *Good looks definitely run in the family*, she thought.

“Invite him in mother. I’ll be out in a minute.”

Ellen’s hands fumbled clumsily as she finished brushing her auburn locks that pregnancy had given an even healthier glow to. She secured a portion of her hair at the top of her head in a pearl barrette, and sprayed a quick scent of the perfume behind each ear that she remembered Glen especially liked. She wore a loose fitting black dress with cap sleeves, and only a pearl necklace offset the color of the dress. It was her hope that Glen wouldn't notice her extended abdomen at first glance, but she knew that was almost an impossibility as far along as she was.

The doorbell rang, and Ellen's heart skipped a beat. He was here.... and in minutes the truth would be out. She suddenly felt like running and hiding.

"Hello, is Ellen here?" Glen asked apprehensively, seeing a resemblance between Ellen and the woman standing silhouetted in the door in front of him. He knew it had to be her mother.

"Yes, she is," Marie, answered with a pleasant smile.

"Are you, Glen?"

"Yes ma'am, I am."

"Nice to meet you, Glen," she said warmly, extending her hand in his direction. I am Marie Meadows, Ellen's mother. Please come in. Ellen will be down in a moment."

Glen carefully wiped his feet on the mat, a gesture of respect that Marie took note of. She showed him into the living room, to the same location where his brother Eric had been taken. "I'll let Ellen know you are here," she said with another friendly smile.

Glen liked Marie. She put him at ease. He sat on the couch nervously rubbing his clean-shaven face, feeling as if he couldn't breathe until he saw Ellen again, as he laid his duffel bag and the flowers to the side. He knew she was so close, and all these weeks of separation were finally coming to an end. To see her beautiful face again, was all he thought and dreamt about. Glen hoped he could control himself when she walked into the room.

All he desired to do was to run to her and hold her forever in his arms. If her intentions were not for reconciliation, coming here could bring about his final undoing. He imagined the worst, seeing himself in a fit of rage from her rejection; breaking an irreplaceable antique vase on the coffee table in front of him, or shaking some sense into her until she relinquished her will – making it his own. He could never live with himself if he used that kind of force on her. Only if she came to him freely, on her own accord, would things be as they should be. Anything less would be unacceptable.

Marie found Ellen in her bedroom, looking over her appearance one last time. She turned to face Marie. "How do I look, mother?"

"You look beautiful, darling. You have a special glow about you."

"But look at me," she said as she looked at her abdomen, smoothing the dress to display the apparent bulge. I'm so fat, and Glen will be shocked when he sees the change in my appearance," she whined in frustration.

"Nonsense, you can hardly tell that you are even pregnant," Marie insisted. "Glen is in the living room, dear. And I must say he is so *handsome!"* she praised, grabbing Ellen's hand in her own.

"I know, Mother," she smiled, remembering the total picture of sensuality that he created. She followed her mother from the room, releasing her hand on the way. "Is dad coming home from the office?"

"He can't right now. He has a full day of appointments," she whispered. "He said to tell you that he would call you later though, to see how things went." Marie kissed Ellen on the cheek. "I need to run some errands, so I'm leaving for about an hour. I'll be back later."

"Can't you stay…please?" Ellen pleaded. "In case something doesn't go so well, you will be here?"

"It's better if I don't…you'll be fine," she reassured encouragingly, giving her daughter a hug of confidence.

Ellen took two deep breaths, and made her way to the living room. The couch was in the center of the room, facing away from her. All she could see was the beautiful golden silky color of his hair brushed back in perfect tapered layers, and the bronzed skin of his neck.

"Hello, Glen," she said, barely above a whisper, feeling her head whirl from the exhilaration of seeing him.

He turned to see her standing between the doorframe, more beautiful than he had remembered her. "Ellen…" he breathed, feeling weak at the bare site of here. He stood up with the flowers in hand; ready to come around the couch to meet her.

She put her arm straight out in a gesture to bring him to a halt. "Stop Glen, and look at me…really look at me."

"What is it, Ellen?" he asked in confusion. "What's wrong?"

Her hands moved lovingly to her abdomen, cradling it protectively. She felt the overwhelming urge to get this hurdle out of the way first. If she sensed any negativity on his part, there wouldn't be a need to continue with any further conversation.

"I'm pregnant, Glen."

Glen grabbed the side of the sofa in an effort to steady himself from the full impact of the unexpected news. His eyes registered a look of total bafflement and confusion as he captured Ellen's searching eyes that were looking for the answers she needed.

"You're what? Oh my God," he breathed, laying the flowers down again, and taking the same hand nervously through his hair. A gesture that made Ellen's pulse quicken, as it did so many times at the farm. He paused for a moment, reeling with the news. "Is it mine?"

Hurt raged through her at his insensitive words, wanting only to retreat and run away, back to the security of her bedroom. *"Yes it is yours!"* she bit out with tears already stinging her eyes. "Do you think I found someone else here in Denver so soon?"

"Oh Ellen, I'm sorry…" he replied now with regret for even saying the words that were causing her further pain. "I had no idea you have been going through this," he answered with raw emotion, as he walked away from the couch quickly now to meet her. His eyes lowered as he studied her frame, and the soft outward curve of her abdomen. His child grew inside of her, he realized. Glen felt overwhelmed with the miracle of it all.

"Please, Ellen…let me hold you…" he begged, with all the compassion he was feeling.

Tears freely began to flow down Ellen's face. She stood silently, and Glen did not wait for her response. He wrapped her lovingly in his embrace, not wanting ever to let her go. He breathed deeply of the scent of her, kissing her hair repeatedly. Many times, he tried to remember how her perfume smelled and how soft her skin felt against his face, and now it was a reality again. For minutes they stood entwined in the quiet embrace, with Glen rubbing Ellen's back, while she sobbed the tears that would not stop flowing.

"Glen, I'm sorry for not calling you about this, but I didn't want you to feel responsible for my condition," she whispered into his neck.

He pulled away at arm's length to stare at her in disbelief. "Ellen, how could you have ever thought that I wouldn't have wanted our child? I loved you when we conceived it, and I love you still. Nothing has changed in my heart."

"But your heart has nothing to do with reality."

Glen's face registered confusion again. "Let's sit down, Ellen. I think you are referring to Samantha, and it's about time you have heard the truth instead of the pack of lies she presented to you that pitiful day at the farm.

Glen reviewed with her the unfolding of that day and his dealings later on that evening and the next morning with Samantha and her children.

"So you are saying the two of you have never been married, and the children are not yours?" Ellen questioned with a ray of hope.

"Yes, Ellen, and none of this separation between us would have been necessary if we could have just discussed this. I never stopped trying to get in touch with you while you were gone, but Megan said you didn't want any contact from me. *I never stopped believing in us, Ellen,"* he exclaimed in earnest, as he grabbed her hand and massaged tiny circles with his thumb as he held it.

She smiled affectionately at him, recalling just how loving and tender he had always been with her in the past. "I was surprised when Megan said you were still helping out at the farm. It wasn't necessary for you to continue working without pay again, Glen, like when you first began working for me at the farm."

Glen brought her hand to his mouth and softly brushed the tips of her fingers against his lips. "It was very necessary. I love you, Ellen. I always have, and I always will. Helping at the farm isn't work to me. It's something I wanted to do because I haven't allowed myself to lose hope that it was totally over between us. *I never stopped believing in our dreams – that it was our future – our farm and our life together!* The farm means as much to me as it does to you. You are a part of my soul, Ellen, and every aspect of your life has become ingrained in me. I am not a rich man, but if you will have me still, please marry me," he pleaded in earnest.

Ellen drank in the sight of the handsome and tender-spirited man in front of her, his eyes as blue and sincere as any that she had ever seen. She knew he loved her still, and as much as she wanted to deny it, there was no disputing her love for him either.

"So it is really true then…. you are free to marry me?" she asked with hesitant optimism as he continued to hold her hand.

Glen sighed, not wanting to think of the pain again of the past that Samantha had caused. "Ellen, *please*, never doubt me again! Promise me that. I am very free. Do you believe me?" he asked with unequivocal concern, looking deeply into her eyes, wanting only to see the reassurance of her faith in him that he was telling her the truth.

"I believe you, Glen. Please forgive me for not believing you," she said softly with downcast eyes. "I was wrong to have left you like that, and not give you a chance to explain. I know that now, and I am truly sorry."

Glen raised her chin to meet his own as they stared into each other's eyes. "I am sorry too, if I ever made you doubt me. The past is behind us. We only have the future now. Just marry me, Ellen."

"I will," she affirmed lovingly, with tears of joy flooding her eyes anew.

"Oh darling," Glen groaned in sweet relief, bringing his lips down on hers in a mind-drugging kiss that left both of them weak with desire. "Let's get married right away. I don't want to spend another day apart from you and our child. I need to know you are mine totally."

She held his face tenderly between her palms, after the ending of the lengthy overdue kiss. "Glen, it will take some time to plan a wedding, and I want our friends and family to be there to share it with us," Ellen consoled warmly.

"Then come home with me tonight. We'll plan our wedding together. *Please Ellen…say yes*," Glen implored, while holding her possessively in his arms.

"But this suddenness would come as a surprise to mother and father, and there is all of the packing to do."

Glen chuckled, being reminded anew of her apprehensive tendencies. "Always the worry-wart," he teased, grabbing her chin to plant a well-intentioned light kiss on her lips. "Your mother and I can pack your things, and we can catch the last flight out today," he insisted. "We will be home by midnight."

"Meg and Mike are at the house," she answered, still with a look of worry etched on her brow.

"We'll call them," Glen replied between jubilant kisses, trying to ease her mind and anxieties.

Marie came home as promised, an hour later. “I’m home, Ellen,” she called while coming in the back door that led into the kitchen.

“Mother, can you come here, when you get a minute?” she requested, while taking a deep breath and looking at Glen.

“It will be alright,” he reassured lovingly, squeezing her hand gently.

“What is it dear?” Marie asked with a smile, as she walked into the living room. Her smile turned to open-mouth wonder as she gazed at Ellen and Glen snuggling on the sofa.

“Glen and I have some wonderful news. He asked me to marry him today, and I said yes.”

“Oh…that’s marvelous!” Marie exclaimed, but was instantly taken back by an earlier remembrance. “I thought Glen was married?”

“I thought so too, but I was wrong,” she replied, giving Glen a look of deep regret for what she had put him through needlessly. “He isn’t, mother, and he never has been; and, Samantha’s children are not his. So you see, he is very free, and I have agreed to marry him,” Ellen continued with a look of total happiness beaming from her face.

Marie hadn’t seen her look so lovely or content as she did now since she had been back in Denver. She reached out and hugged Ellen and then Glen both soundly as they rose to meet her. “I am so happy for the both of you and that you found each other again.”

She directed her comments to Glen, warmly offering her supportive words. "Glen, I'm glad you came here to Denver and made this misunderstanding work out between you and Ellen."

Glen grinned. "We were made to be together. I just needed to give Ellen some time to realize that," he stated with astute wisdom, while wrapping his arm around Ellen's waist, drawing her closer into his embrace.

"I'm glad you did, darling," Ellen replied with glistening love-filled eyes. "Mother, we plan to leave today. I know this is short notice, but we do want to get back to the farm today if at all possible. I may not be able to get a flight out today, though."

"I understand perfectly. Dad will be home soon and he wants to have dinner together. Can you stay for that, and then we will drive you to the airport if you can make flight connections?"

Ellen looked at Glen for the answer. "What time does hour flight leave, Glen?"

"Not until 9:30 tonight. We have plenty of time for dinner, and we need to make sure there is a seat available on the flight for you anyways."

"I may need to ride home on a separate plane from you."

"No you won't," Glen insisted. "If this doesn't work out for us to fly home together, then I won't be going home tonight without you." He didn't want to be so over-bearing, but he couldn't help being vigilant after allowing the situation to deteriorate the way it had with Samantha. Never again would he allow time and distance to stand between them.

Ellen smiled at him already relishing in his protectiveness. She knew he would be a wonderful husband and father to their child. "Why don't you call the airlines and see if you can get me a flight? And in the meantime, I will pack my things."

"And I will help you," Marie offered sweetly, already assisting Ellen from the couch.

Glen called the airport, while Ellen and Marie laid out all her clothing on the bed, ready to be packed.

"I didn't realize I had brought so much. I need a another suitcase," Ellen said as she folded a skirt, laying it on top of a stack of sweaters.

"It's the maternity clothes," Marie replied, as she folded the last set of the expandable waistline slacks. "I have an old suitcase that I don't use anymore that you can have. I'll be right back with it."

"Alright," Ellen answered, as she sat on the bed recalling an earlier time in her room that she grew up in – slumber parties with her friends and posters of her favorite singers of her youth. She realized that she would never be here again as an unmarried woman without a child. As much as she wanted a new life ahead of her with Glen as a wife and a mother, a part of her was sad to say goodbye to the security of her parent's home and her room, where she truly felt safe.

"A penny for your thoughts?" Glen asked as he peaked around the doorframe.

Ellen snapped to from her daydreaming, smiling at her intended's handsome face. "It's nothing…just a little sad to say goodbye. Mother and father have been so good to me."

Glen joined her on the bed, taking her hand in his own. "I

understand. Sometimes I wish for that same thing – being at home with my mom and dad again. And now that dad is gone, it makes it even harder on me."

Ellen leaned over to kiss Glen on the cheek. "I'm sorry, honey. I wish your dad was still here for you."

Glen turned to kiss Ellen softly on her receptive waiting lips. "I have you now. Somehow, I think he knows that I have found the perfect woman for me. You are all I need, Ellen," he confessed, lightly brushing his lips against hers once more.

"Glen, I don't deserve you. After everything we have been through, you still never stop making me feel special."

Glen grinned a sexy smile that made her heart swoon. "You do things to me that make me feel very special too," he admitted with heat-filled eyes, gazing languidly at her over-endowed bosom that was swelling from pregnancy.

Ellen blushed as she noticed where his eyes wandered.

"Will it take long until you are finished packing?" he questioned anxiously, wanting only for her to be in his arms again in the bed that they shared at the farm.

"Not much longer," she smiled, as she reached out to touch his hair and brush it back off his face. "Mother is getting me another suitcase, and once I pack these clothes, I'll be finished," she said while pointing to the stack that was still on the bed.

"That's great, because you're not going to believe this, but there is a seat available on my flight. We lucked out, because someone canceled out on the flight several hours ago. The flight was sold out, but as fate would have it, we can now fly home together," he announced with a look of satisfaction.

Marie reappeared with the suitcase in hand, and the last of the items were placed in it.

"Now that the packing is done, I need to start dinner. I'll leave you and Glen alone to visit, and I will go now."

"Mrs. Meadows?"

"Yes, Glen?" Marie answered with a turn.

"May I help you cook dinner?"

Marie smile and Ellen looked at him in fascination. "That's not necessary, Glen, but thank you for offering."

"I really would like to. We're running off so quickly tonight that it's not giving you much of a chance to get to know me. This is my only way of proving to you that I'm not such a bad catch for your daughter," he grinned with his boyish charm and good looks.

"I can see that already. Just remember to always make Ellen happy, and we will always see the best in you."

Glen looked from mother to daughter, seeing the similarity in their emerald green eyes and the beauty in their faces. "I will die a happy man just trying!"

Chapter Fifty

The kitchen was a flutter of activity with all three of them working together to prepare the meal just like chefs in a busy restaurant. Glen concentrated on his assigned duty of chopping up the vegetables for the salad in such a sincere way that Ellen and Marie had to grin knowingly at each other while his head was bent. He was so precise and meticulous with his slicing that he looked as if he were performing surgery. Marie worked on stuffing the pork chops, while Ellen scrubbed the sweet potatoes and cleaned and sliced the ends off the broccoli.

"Glen, you have a whole education ahead of you concerning pregnancy. Handling of raw meat can be dangerous for a pregnant woman, and even being around a liter box for that matter. Did you know that?" Marie questioned, like a schoolteacher.

"No, I didn't," he answered with genuine interest, as he threw the sliced carrots into the bowl.

"In some cases, a woman can contact a disease called Toxoplasmosis which can cause the baby to be born with difficulties ranging from blindness to retardation."

"Well, we won't have to worry about that in our household. From here on out, I will be doing the cooking in the evening, until our baby is born, Ellen. And I guess you have to stay away from Cuddles, although I must admit he won't take to that lightly. He has missed you terribly. He meows pitifully whenever I scratch his head and we have *our conversations* about you," Glen confessed with masculine authority and the new possessiveness that he was now displaying.

Ellen smiled at him lovingly, liking the sound of our baby, and feeling safe in his protectiveness once again. She forgot how wonderful that truly felt, until now. "Cuddles misses me *that much*?"

"That much, honey," he said playfully, winking at her as he continued chopping the vegetables.

"Mother, poor Glen will be a nervous wreck, if you continue to bring up all these concerns with him. I read about Toxoplasmosis, and as long as Cuddles isn't eating raw meat, I'm ok. He rarely uses a liter box, so that cuts back on any exposure that I could encounter. Glen will just have to read the same books that I am, and that will teach him everything he needs to know. And Glen," she added, looking in Glen's direction again with concern, "It's wonderful that you would offer to take over the cooking, but I am perfectly capable of doing that. I'm sure the baby will be just fine."

"I know you are very capable, Ellen," Glen reassured with a smile. "I can still remember all those wonderful meals you prepared for me, but I want to help out in any way I can to make things easier for you and the baby. I'm glad your mother wants to fill me in. I have a lot of catching up to do."

Marie smiled. "I just want my grandchild to be healthy."

"She will be, mother."

"Is it a she?" Glen asked anxiously, looking at Ellen.

Marie and Ellen started to giggle. "I don't know yet, but it is better than referring to the baby as *it*."

"Oh, I see.... I do have a lot to learn, *don't I*?" he grinned with awareness dawning on his face.

Howard came home, just as dinner was being taken out of the oven. Ellen ran to her father with a brilliant smile lighting her way, like he had not seen since she arrived.

"You look so happy, sweetie."

"I am, daddy," she beamed, as she swung her arms around her father's neck lovingly. "Come and meet Glen. He is in the kitchen with mother. "Daddy, this is Glen," Ellen announced proudly.

Glen rose to shake Howard's hand. "How do you do, sir?"

"Just fine, son."

"Daddy, Glen and I are getting married, and I am leaving with him tonight to go back home to the farm."

"Wow...Ellen," Howard answered, lifting a brow, trying to catch up mentally with what he had missed since he went to work. "There definitely have been some changes occurring around here," he replied with a good-natured chuckle, taking a seat at the kitchen table. "If that is what you want, I am happy for the both of you."

"That is what we both want," Ellen confirmed, while looking at Glen with love in her eyes. "I told Glen about the baby, so everything is out in the open now."

"Do I take it then, that all your disagreements have been cleared up?"

"After talking with Glen, I realize I overreacted and chose to believe the lies that woman *Samantha* told me. None of it was true. We are free to marry and Glen has no attachments to her or her children."

Howard breathed a sigh of relief. "That makes me very happy, as I'm sure it does everyone else in the room," he replied candidly. "So…I will be gaining a new son-in-law soon. Hope you play golf," he chuckled.

Glen began to laugh in unison with Ellen and her parents. "I'm not bad. I used to play with my dad and my brother Eric, but I'm sure I would be no match for you, sir," Glen added diplomatically, trying to win Howard's approval. He had hit the right chord with him, as his future father-in-law nodded his head in understanding at his friendly words that he had bestowed.

"We will see about that. I think you are just being modest. You probably could beat me hands down," he confessed good-naturedly, giving Glen an affectionate pat on the back. It was a mutual feeling of compatibility right from the start.

"I hate to break up this discussion, but it will need to be resumed over dinner in the dining room," Marie chimed in. "Everything is ready and we have to get Ellen and Glen to the airport by 8 pm, so we need to start eating," she urged.

"I guess that's our cue to move. Let me give you a piece of advice, Glen," Howard replied warmly, as he rose from the table and wrapped an arm around Glen's shoulder. "When Marie speaks, you listen!" Everyone began to laugh, as Ellen shook her head, observing her parents' playfulness with each other.

"I'm glad you know that, Howard," Marie winked.

The laughing, happiness and conversation continued even as they moved to the new location. Everyone took their seat in the formal dining room. The table was set with Howard and Marie's best wedding china and they ate by candlelight.

"We always join hands to pray when we eat, Glen," Marie instructed, as each one clasped the other one's hand in an infinite unbroken circle of love. Howard led the blessing, as Glen bowed his head along with the others, feeling happy at the prospect of soon becoming a permanent part of their family. They were warm and caring people that he already knew he would share many good times with. He could just sense it.

"So when do you think the wedding will be?" Marie asked, as she finished her dinner, wiping the corners of her mouth with a linen napkin.

"As soon as possible, if I have anything to do with it," Glen grinned, reaching out to grab Ellen's hand lovingly.

"In a couple weeks. We need to do some planning," Ellen stated, looking at Glen for his approval on her decision. "Will you be able to come to Fillmore for the wedding on such short notice?"

"Of course, dear," Marie answered, knowing her husband felt the same way. "We wouldn't miss your wedding for anything."

"Glen," Howard began, "Marie and I are both happy that you and Ellen have worked things out between you. Our grandchild deserves a home with both his mother and father present. Besides that, love like the two of you apparently have, is too precious to just let it slip away. Be good to my daughter. Always treat her the way her mother and I would treat her. She is special. Always remember that."

"Aah…Howard," Marie interrupted, feeling somewhat awkward. "Poor Glen probably feels he is being lectured, since I gave him the same speech earlier," Marie informed clearly.

"Well I'm sorry to hear that, Glen, but we do love Ellen and I guess it's only natural to want only the best for our girl. You'll understand one day what I am saying when you have your own children."

"Sir, I think I can understand now how you feel. I only want the best for Ellen, also. I love her with all my heart, and my fondest desire is just to have her as my wife. I will try my best to make her happy for the rest of our days."

Ellen's eyes began to well up with tears again at his admonition of love. She reached out to grab Glen's hand – taking it in her own. "I want to make you happy too, Glen."

"You already have, Ellen," he smiled. "I couldn't be any happier than I feel right now. The only thing that will bring me more joy is to have you as my wife and hold our child in my arms."

Tears began to stream down Ellen's face.

"Are you alright, dear?"

"Yes, mother…these are just happy tears," she explained while wiping the wet away from her face with her hands. "I have such a mixture of feelings right now. Maybe it's the pregnancy. Dr. Fairchild did say that I would be more emotional right now. I feel so excited to be going home with Glen today," she admitted, giving him a contented loving look, "But at the same time, I feel sad to say goodbye to the two of you. I love you so much, mom and dad."

"Don't cry over us," Howard barked. "We'll be coming to visit you so often, once that grandchild of ours is born, you'll be sick of us! Then you'll breathe a sigh of relief when we go back home to Denver."

"I doubt that, daddy," Ellen reassured.

The car was packed, and all four of them made their way to the airport. The flight was on time so there was little time for delayed goodbyes.

"Flight 657, leaves in an hour and a half," Glen announced looking at the flight schedule on his phone.

"I guess it's time to say goodbye," Marie said with tear-filled emotion as she reached out to take Glen's hand, but instead he wrapped her in a big-bear hug. "We are glad you are marrying Ellen, and will be part of our family soon. Remember she needs extra special care right now with her pregnancy," she whispered in Glen's ear.

"I will remember, Mrs. Meadows, and thanks for reminding me," he grinned before releasing her.

"Please call me, Marie. After all, we will be relatives in a few short weeks."

"And call me Howard."

He grabbed for his daughter and pulled her into his strong fatherly embrace. He spoke softly to her as Marie continued to speak with Glen. "Ellen, believe me when I tell you, my heart was hurting sorely when you first came home. To think that you truly thought that you lost the man you loved, and then to find out you were pregnant besides, was more than most people could even handle without falling apart. But you willed yourself to go on, and you did it well. There was never a doubt by either your mother or myself, that every day was still a real effort for you. And now, my dear," he continued with warm smiling eyes that held her captive, "Your life has turned around again for the best, and you can believe in all those dreams that you only considered were intended for other people."

The tears were streaming down Ellen's cheeks with her father's words of love and hope.

"Even though the circumstances were not pleasant, as we look back at it now, we do thank God for having you back with us for a few short months before you marry again. Ellen, *never* compare Glen to Jack. He deserves your love of today, and not your pain of the past."

She looked affectionately at her gray-haired father with his steel-blue eyes, who was always a source of great wisdom and strength to her through her growing up years. "Thank you, daddy. I will try to do my best at remembering that."

"I know you will, honey," he smiled, as he kissed her fondly on the cheek before releasing her.

Ellen reached out to hug Marie. "I'll be fine, mother. Don't worry about me," she breathed against her ear. "I want to say thank you for everything that you have done. Especially for taking such good care of me during the time I was so sick. I love you so much, mom."

"I know…. and I love you too," Marie whispered with a quivering voice, feeling overwhelmed with compassion by their tender last moments together. "Please promise me you will listen to what Dr. Fairchild said. Continue to rest, eat right, and take your vitamins. And let me know when you locate an gynecologist in your area."

"I will, mother," Ellen promised. "Remember, we have a

wedding to plan, and I want you to help me with all the details," she added happily. "I will call you in a few days when Glen and I have decided on a date."

"We will be waiting to hear from you," Marie answered with a warm smile and a kiss to Ellen's cheek.

Howard extended his hand to shake Glen's. "Take good care of my little girl."

"Always," Glen vowed with sincere promise. "She has been, and always will be, my number one priority.

"We'll see you in a few weeks, and I will text you when we get in tonight," Ellen echoed, as she waved her final goodbye to her parents, departing with Glen into the airport.

The takeoff was uneventful, with Ellen cuddled in Glen's arms. "Any regrets?" he asked with a slight concern at her teary mood, as she stared out the plane's window for one last glance at the city of Denver.

Ellen turned to look at Glen. "No darling, of course not. It really is just the pregnancy. I am so emotional all the time now."

"I can handle that," he grinned, giving her a playful kiss. "Just as long as I know we are handling everything here on out *together*."

"I must tell you something that I haven't told you yet," she confessed, taking on a more serious tone.

"What is it, Ellen?" Glen asked somewhat apprehensively.

"I had a visitor a few days ago, and on that very same day, I passed out and was in the hospital overnight."

Glen's face was etched with panic. "Are you alright? Are you sure you should even be traveling?" he asked in a rush of questions, grabbing for her hand. Then he stopped, taking a moment to register the worst. "Oh my God…tell me it wasn't Samantha again!"

Ellen patted Glen's hand. "I'm fine, Glen; and yes, I can travel. And no, it wasn't Samantha."

"Well, who then?"

"It was Eric."

"Eric?" Glen questioned in total surprise, just as stunned with the news of that name.

"Yes, Glen, it was Eric. He was here trying to look out for your best interests."

Glen clutched Ellen's hand securely to his side, thinking for a moment that the nightmare was starting up all over again. "Please believe me, Ellen, I had *nothing* to do with that. This is the first I have heard of any of this."

"It's fine, Glen," she reassured. "I must admit I was stunned when he showed up at my parents' house unannounced, but he made me see the other side of all this. If it weren't for him, and also my parents' influence, I probably wouldn't be here on this airplane with you today. My folks are a pretty good judge of character and they like Eric. They thought he was sincere. Just the fact that he would come all this way to convince me of your innocence, made a real impression on them both. Also, Eric didn't tell you, because I made him promise me that he would keep things a secret for at least a couple weeks until I could sort things out on my own. It really bothered him, keeping the truth from you. I know now I was wrong to put him in that position, and I do owe him an apology."

"I think I can understand your intentions, Ellen. But it still amazes me that Eric would come here on my behalf. I can't believe Eric did that for me…for us," he said compassionately, reaching over to kiss her again.

"The best part, Glen, is that I feel Eric and I have come to a cease-fire concerning the past. It won't be easy, but I have made a commitment to myself to try."

Ellen looked up into Glen's moist eyes that were overwhelmed with emotion and relief at her admission.

"I know he was Jack's friend. It's not fair to continue punishing him anymore for Jack's death. How foolish I have been to think that he was responsible." Ellen hung her head in shame. "I just couldn't accept the fact that Jack could have been so weak. I'm sorry, Glen," Ellen choked out, sniffling back her tears. "I know this hasn't only effected Eric, but you and I too."

Glen wrapped her safely in his arms once more. "Shhh….no more tears," he whispered. "Only happiness from here on out for all of us."

Ellen clung to him, feeling so safe and secure in his loving embrace. "I love you, Glen. I'm sorry for ever doubting you and our love."

"No more apologies, my love," he whispered as he kissed the top of her head. "We are back together, and that's all that matters."

“Forever, Glen. This time it will be forever.

Chapter Fifty-One

He loaded the luggage, and then surprised Ellen by picking her up in his arms, carrying her to the Bronco.

"Your chariot awaits, Madame."

Ellen giggled, loving his playfulness. "Thank you, kind sir," she teased, as Glen placed her gently in the passenger's seat. "You shouldn't spoil me like this, Glen. I may never want you to stop," she said sweetly, as she watched the handsome profile of the man she adored driving her safely home.

He glanced at her, taking in the swell of her abdomen, reminding him anew of their child that was a part of them now. "I never want to stop, Ellen – taking care of you and our child. We'll be home soon," he smiled. "Are you alright, darling, after the flight?" he questioned in concern.

"I'm fine, Glen. Maybe I won't be able to say that when I'm in my ninth month, but everything is ok for now," she reassured with a slight smile, as she rested her hand on her stomach.

Glen continued to stare at her from time to time, deep in thought as they drove. "I've been thinking that maybe we shouldn't be sending Megan home so soon. Your mother says you need to rest in bed a few more days. Maybe you would feel more secure having your friend there to help you out?"

Ellen just shook her head with a sigh. "Megan is no better equipped at helping me out than you are, Glen. Remember, she has never had children. I really will be fine, Glen," Ellen insisted. "You and Cuddles will be here for me. That's all I need."

Glen responded with his own frustrated sigh, not wanting to disappoint her. "Ellen, I hate to tell you this, but I have a job working nights at the Quik Shopper, and they're expecting me to come back to work as soon as I'm back in town. Even if I quit, which I now plan to do, I need to give them some time to hire someone else. It isn't fair to leave you alone during the night. Something could happen."

"I'll be all right. Megan told me about your job. How have you been able to handle working at the farm, and then all through the night, and still manage to get enough sleep?"

"Easy," he admitted lovingly. "I had no one to come home to. I couldn't let the farm suffer. I love that place almost as much as I love you."

"You really don't need to stop your job at the Quik Shopper if you want to continue working there."

"I'll *gladly* give my notice. I'm needed elsewhere, and I take on my new position *most willingly*," he grinned, capturing Ellen's heart anew with his charm and incredible good looks that stirred her every time she looked at him.

Ellen's breath caught out of habit, as they pulled into the lane. "Still no bumps."

Glen laughed, taking the path as slowly as he could. "I told you I could fix it."

"You sure did," she agreed, shaking her head with a smile. "And I believe you reminded me of that fact more than once."

Glen grinned at her, knowing that she was ribbing him. He considered her teasing to be adorable and so welcome after their time apart.

"Everything else is still functioning the same, just as you left it. The produce stand probably should be shut down in a week or so. There's not too much left to sell out of the garden, and the baked goods have stopped. Megan doesn't seem to have the knack for baking like you do," he said with a wink and a smile. "The customers only straggle in from time to time now. The profit isn't there, like back in the summer months."

"That's the way it always is this time of the year, Glen. They don't come around as much, because there isn't as much to offer them. Although, the bread and other baked goods usually keep the stand going until the end of the month. I don't plan to start the baking up again for this season, under the circumstances. Next year will be soon enough," she said with a smile.

"I'm glad you came to that conclusion, Ellen," Glen replied in relief, looking at her with concern as he parked the car. "I don't think you need to be overdoing it with the baby, especially after what you have just been through. Your mother wouldn't be too happy with me if you began having problems again. I promised her that you would take it easy."

Ellen smiled lovingly at Glen. "You are so good to me."

Glen leaned over to kiss her again. "Let's get you in the house. There's a little guy in there who has missed you for weeks now, and he will be very happy to see you."

"Cuddles?"

"None other," he answered with a grin, as he came around to

the passenger's side of the vehicle and lifted Ellen into his arms. He carried her up the porch steps, unlocked the front door, and carried her over the threshold into the house.

"This isn't necessary," she insisted, as she rested her head on his shoulder.

"If it were, then I wouldn't have offered," he grinned playfully as he pecked her cheek with a light kiss.

As Glen put Ellen down, their mouths dropped open in amazement at the cleanliness of everything. Scents of lemon furniture polish and pine floor cleaner still lingered in the air. An arrangement of pale pink miniature roses and baby's breath sat on the table in a crystal vase, with a note lying beside of it.

Dear Ellen and Glen,

To the victor goes the spoil. We are so happy for the both of you. You are getting quite the man, Ellen. I have come to realize that. And Glen, your patience has won you the prize. Always treasure her, or you will have me to answer too!

Love you both,

Megan

P.S. I know you both will be fine – Mike.

"You have great friends, Ellen," Glen chuckled. "And Megan is as loyal as they come."

"Good ole Meg. What would I have done without her and Mike…and without you…?" she added, giving Glen a kiss.

Cuddles timidly peaked around the corner of the kitchen doorway, squinting between half-closed eyes. He gave a sleepy yawn and a chirping meow.

"Can't do any better than that for Mommy?" Ellen beckoned, quickly bending down to pick her sweet and loving pet up off of the floor. "Mommy missed you," she cooed softly, rubbing her cheek against his soft furry face. Cuddles rough tongue brushed across her cheek, giving her a kiss.

"He missed you too, Ellen."

"I can see that," she beamed happily, hugging the feline securely.

"But I must admit, " Glen confessed, "That Megan did try her best to keep him company," he added while stroking the cat's back while Ellen continued to hold him.

"That's saying a lot since Megan really isn't much of a cat person."

Ellen put Cuddles down, just as Glen reached out and wrapped his arms around her. "I can't believe you are home," he breathed. "Here…with me…together. Am I dreaming this?"

"No, darling, it is real. And I couldn't be happier," she echoed, as he kissed her passionately.

Glen could feel the heat rising quickly in his loins. The desires of passion had been extinguished for way too long. As he held Ellen and felt her lips against his own, he began to ache for the closeness that had been so much a part of them before their breakup.

"I want you, Ellen," he groaned, breathing heavily against her throat, as he kissed the column of her neck. It feels like an eternity."

Ellen's pulse quickened by his nearness and by his words. "I feel the same way, and I want you too, Glen," she replied in kind, taking his hand and leading him to the bedroom.

Lying on the bed, they slowly undressed the other, mesmerized as if it were their first time together.

Glen was in awe of the changes pregnancy had done to Ellen. "You are so beautiful," he said with sincerity, as he fondled her over-endowed bosom and caressed the swell of her abdomen with his lips.

"Put your hand here, Glen," she instructed. "The baby is kicking, and I want you to feel it."

Quietly they waited until the movement within her abdomen began again.

"I feel it!" he said with excitement written all over his face, at the newness of something he had never experienced before. He paused and looked at Ellen with wide eyes. *"Oh my God, I feel our child moving!"* Glen looked at Ellen, locking his eyes with hers in concern. "Do you really think we should be doing this? Maybe it will hurt the baby?"

Ellen smiled, gently stroking Glen's face with the back of her hand. "The baby is quite safe, Glen. Although, you may have a hard time recuperating, as long as we have been apart," she teased.

"I'll take my chances," he said in a raspy voice, reclaiming her lips in a passionate long, deep kiss. "I think I'm up for a long recuperation time – right here in our bed."

Chapter Fifty-Two

The day was beautiful. There was crispness in the November air, but the sun still shone warmly. The organ played its melodic tune as Marie adjusted the headpiece on Ellen's perfectly coifed hair.

"Mother, do I look all right?"

"The loveliest of brides on her wedding day," she said sweetly, while lightly kissing her daughter on her cheek. "Your father is waiting, and so is Glen. Are you ready, dear?"

Ellen smiled happily. "More than I thought I could ever be, mother."

"Then go, and make the man that you love your husband," Marie replied with tears of joy in her eyes.

Ellen walked proudly down the isle of the little church on Bradford Street, while she clung to her father's protective arm.

"I love you, Daddy," Ellen breathed with emotion, glancing up into his strong face.

"I love you too," he lovingly answered with a tear in his eye, giving her a kiss on her forehead before releasing her into Glen's care.

The ceremony was beautiful, with not a dry eye in the sanctuary. Ellen's gown was of satin, encrusted with pearl beading covering the bodice in its entirety. Her sleeves were shear, with a long train of toile flowing dreamily behind her. The headpiece she wore was embellished with the same pearl beading of her gown; and a veil covered her face in a traditional style, ready to be lifted by Glen for a kiss after they were pronounced husband and wife. The bouquet she held was simple in style with a bundle of pink stemmed roses tied in the center with a satin white ribbon.

Glen stood at the front of the church with pride radiating from his face as he watched Ellen walking towards him, finding her more beautiful at that moment than any other woman he had seen in his life. Their mutual smiles were intended only for the other, giving the allure that no one was present in the church except for the two of them.

Ellen found Glen equally as handsome and beguiling, outfitted in a soft gray tuxedo with a white, crisp shirt that made a striking contrast to his suntanned face, neck and hands. He was cleanly shaven and had just had a haircut. He wore a white rose that was framed with a fragile fern pinned to his jacket's lapel.

They joined hands ready for their wedding vows as they were surrounded by their wedding party - Melinda and Megan on Ellen's side and Eric and Mike on Glen's. Words were promised, and rings were exchanged. The pastor gave his eternal blessing, as Ellen and Glen kissed, uniting their hearts and lives as one.

"May I present Mr. and Mrs. Glen Cummings," were the minister's final words, before the congregation applauded in celebration of their happiness and union.

Family and friends gathered at the farm for a reception that Marie, Megan and Melinda planned, and had actually taken part in preparing. As much as Ellen protested, they insisted that they wanted to do it all on their own. In the end, Ellen was happy she obliged them.

As she and Glen pulled up to the farm, they marveled over the beauty of what was lovingly done for them. The house was arrayed with garlands of brilliant fall flowers of yellow, orange, burgundy and white cascading the full length of the porch railing. All was quiet and peaceful, with only a whisper of a breeze. The guests were all inside, waiting for Glen and Ellen to arrive. They had taken a short ride out in the country, wanting the solitude of being alone as husband and wife for just a few minutes before they joined their family and friends again in the celebration of their union of long last.

Glen helped his new bride out of the Mustang that Eric had insisted that they use for the day. *The Bronco just wouldn't do for his new sister-in-law on her wedding day*, he had announced the day before.

"Just look at how beautiful the farm looks. I don't think I have ever seen it look any lovelier," Ellen commented with a contented sigh, as she wrapped her arms securely around Glen's waist.

"It's perfect, just like you," he answered, planting a kiss squarely on her mouth. We should go inside, darling. Everyone is waiting on us."

"I know…. but just to be her with you like this, alone, is a moment that I will cherish forever. Even if it is for just a little while."

"We'll make it last, Ellen…. I promise. Today and everyday," he vowed as the sun shone warmly and the birds chirped merrily in the distance.

Megan greeted them at the door, as Glen carried Ellen over the threshold for a second time within a month; but this time with an audience. "It's about time! This party can't start without you, you know," she said good-naturedly, as Mike rolled his eyes and shook his head behind them.

The house was decorated equally as beautiful inside as it was outside. The fall flowers continued to flow throughout each room, along with tea-lights that were placed strategically on tables and shelves.

Hor d'oeuvres that the three ladies lovingly prepared at Megan's house several evenings before the wedding were presented on endless trays for all to sample. A fountain of bubbling champagne punch, as well as a three-tier wedding cake – baked by Mrs. Miller – sat in the corner of the living room on a linen-covered table. Crystal plates, linen matching napkins, and silverware completed the array.

"You outdid yourselves, everyone," Ellen warmly acknowledged, as she gazed in delight at what her friends and mother had done. "Thank you so very much," she warmly added.

"We wanted to make this day special for you and Glen," Melinda replied as spokeswoman for the group. "And besides, you can do the same for me in a few months."

"*What's happening in a few months?*" Ellen asked in surprise.

"Eric asked me to marry him today."

"That's wonderful!" Ellen exclaimed, hugging her warmly.

"Eric couldn't have chosen a better person, and it will be so nice having you as my sister-in-law."

Eric and Glen sampled the punch, finding a spot to be alone after meeting and talking with Ellen's family, who had flown in for the wedding.

"I have to hand it to you, bro. I never imagined that things would end up this way. You got the whole package. And guess what? I'm getting married too, in a few months. I guess you gave me the fever."

Glen looked at Eric in astonishment and then began to laugh. "I *never* thought I would hear those words coming from your lips, but I couldn't be happier for you," he said while grabbing him and giving him a warm hug. His mood turned suddenly serious, wanting to make an impact on his brother. "It wasn't really Ellen and I giving you the fever. It was, and has been, Melinda. You finally met the right woman, and I'm proud of you, Eric, for finally figuring that out. Congratulations on making such a wise decision."

"Thanks, bro," Eric replied sincerely. "I know she's the right one. By the way, Glen, about your wedding present…"

"The reception is a present enough," Glen said firmly, while taking a sip of the spiked punch.

"Nonsense. That was the ladies' gift," Eric replied, reaching into his jacket pocket, pulling out an envelope.

Glen opened it, keenly reading the note in hand. "I can't possibly accept this," he said in open-mouthed wonder.

"*Yes you can. And you will.* As far as I'm concerned, the

Bronco is yours and Ellen's. No more payments."

"And the check? This is way too much," Glen added, shaking his head in disbelief, as he studied the amount of the gift.

"No, it isn't. Melinda and I agree that we want to see you succeed. Buy some more cattle, and use the rest to buy things for the nursery. Melinda added some to the check also. *We can afford it.* Please…Glen," he insisted, "Make us happy, and let us do this for you, Ellen, and the baby."

Glen checked his tears, as his arms went around his brother's shoulders again, patting him on the back. "You are the best, you know that?"

"I've had a good teacher this year."

"What's that I heard about a teacher?"

"Mom, we were just talking about you. Weren't we, Eric?" Glen chuckled, as his mother joined her two handsome sons.

"You got it," Eric grinned. "We both said how lucky we were to have a fine mother, and *teacher*, who made us the men we are today."

"*Sure…Eric*," she said with a shake of her head, tickled by his humor that was always so much a part of him ever since childhood. "Remember that I *am* your mother. You never did lie very well."

Glen laughed, catching a glimpse of Ellen across the room. She was framed amongst her many friends and relatives, who shared in this, their special day. He could see the soft swell of her abdomen through her wedding gown that she still wore. Even within the short time they had been reunited, her figure had continued to change, much to Glen's delight and amazement. Ellen was even more beautiful to him now, with this miracle of life growing inside of her. He blew her a kiss, and she blew one back to him in return; each capturing it and holding it in their heart, from that day forward – never to be apart.

Epilogue

Three-and-a-half years later….

Ellen lay sleeping peacefully in the hammock that Glen had strung in the oak tree out back behind the house. Isabelle snuggled beside of her mother, as the bed swung gently in the warm spring air. The garden was growing again, and baby calves were being born. *Life is good…*Glen thought, as he rested on his rake handle, surveying the scene. Eric was married, and so was his mother again. Both were happy and doing well.

He made his way down the garden path, and sat on the ground staring at his beautiful wife; much in the same way as he had done a few years earlier under the same oak tree.

Isabelle was a rare beauty, a combination of her mother and father both, with blonde locks and dramatic green eyes inherited from her mother and grandmother. Glen bent over the two of them, smiling in fascination at his two girls. He blew lightly across Ellen's face, waking her from her slumber.

"Wake up, sleepy head. I miss you," he beckoned.

"The baby kicks," she said drowsily. His hand went to her abdomen, feeling the movement of life beneath it once again.

"I love you, Ellen."

"I love you too, Glen," she replied with a contented smile. "You truly are all the wonderful wishes of the heart."

ABOUT THE AUTHOR

Roberta lives in Maryland surrounded by family and her beloved cats Nick and Holly. Creating is always second nature to her – as a decorator, cook and book writer.